LAGUERRE

A GASCON OF
THE BLACK BORDER

By

AMBROSE E. GONZALES

Author of

THE BLACK BORDER—Gullah Stories of The Carolina Coast
WITH AESOP ALONG THE BLACK BORDER
THE CAPTAIN—Stories of The Black Border

COLUMBIA, S. C.
THE STATE COMPANY
1924

CONTENTS

FOREWORD

Catherine de Medici and the horror of St. Bartholomew's, with the century of persecution that followed, gave to the English Province of Carolina one of its finest racial strains. ˜‒‒‒˜

Huguenots, driven from the shores of their beloved France, found sanctuary elsewhere, too, in the Western World, but nowhere else did they take root so readily, establish themselves so firmly, or enter more fully into the life of the province than in this South Carolina settlement of Cavalier English. ˜‒‒‒‒‒

Here, in the spirit of understanding that has so long existed between the cultured French and the cultured English, they found among those of their own faith a more congenial atmosphere, even than among those of their own blood, the Catholic French of Louisiana, while those who established themselves at New Rochelle and other Protestant communities farther north came upon a more rigorous climate and a less responsive people. ‒‒‒

As early as 1700, the French had founded, among others, a prosperous colony of seventy families on the Santee. ˜‒‒‒

On 28 December, 1700, John Lawson, the English surveyor-general of the Lords Proprietors, began his "voyage for North Carolina from Charles Town," going by canoe to the Santee river, "on which there is a colony of French Protestants, allowed and encouraged by the Lords Proprietors."

Hospitably and courteously received by "Mons. Eugee" and his wife, whose house he found fifteen miles up the river, Lawson pays high tribute to the industry, thrift, and fine community spirit of the French; "who live decently and happily as any planters in these Southward parts of America. The French being a temperate, industrious people, some of them bringing very little of effects, yet by their endeavors and mutual assistance amongst themselves, have outstript our English who brought with them larger fortunes, tho', as it seems, less endeavor to manage their talent to the best advantage."

Their houses and plantations were "suitable in neatness and contrivances." And, "all of the same opinion with the church of Geneva," they lived in a "happy and delightful concord in all other matters throughout the neighborhood, living amongst themselves as one tribe or kindred, everyone making it his business to be assistant to the want of his country-man, preserving his estate and reputation with the same exactness and concern as he does his own; all seeming to share in the misfortunes, and rejoice at the advance, and rise, of the brethren." —

In time these fine French intermarried with the English families, and, as the generations passed, the blood of France and England, Scotland and Ireland became so intermingled here that many of the oldest Huguenot names in South Carolina are borne by those preponderantly of English blood, while other families, having come by their French blood on the distaff side, though more than half French, bear English names. And English thought and English ideals have controlled the whole for more than two centuries.

Of this blood was Laguerre—behind him generations of wealthy and cultured planters, around him, until the War came, other planters of French or English blood, or a blend of both, but all cavaliers in spirit, with a high sense of their responsibilities as slaveholders. Pleasure-loving, fond of life—too fond, perhaps, of an easy life—they had softened since the early days of the province when, as pioneers clearing and settling a wilderness, they had been energetic enough. And without the incentive to exertion that necessity imposes, they fell naturally into easy-going ways. Caring little for money, they were content with the steady advance of their fortunes through the increase of their slaves and the enhancement in the value of their lands, for as the young Negroes came to manhood, they had only to clear from the forest additional acres upon which to raise their subsistence.

And as the children of the planters came to maturity, there came along with them the children of the slaves, and when the time came to "settle" sons and daughters, there were usually plantations and Negroes available for the invariable settlement.

An easy life, chiefly because the planter was free from the ordinary hazards of business ventures, for the plantations were always self-sustaining, as far as subsistence for master and slaves. If drought or storm or flood cut short the money crop, or markets were low, the planter, forced to forego a trip to Europe, or Newport, or Saratoga, could at least spend a summer at the Virginia Springs, or Flat Rock—at the worst in a Low-country pineland village—and there are worse places.

But in respect to work and responsibility the planter's life was not easy. As any conscientious executive of a business establishment must enter into and interest himself in the lives of those who work with him, so, to a far greater degree, the slaveholder was forced to concern himself with the lives of his dependents, who looked to him for everything. Not only for their benefit but his own, he had to study and know their temperaments, and peculiarities; how to fit each individual to the task for which he was best suited. And in the adjustment of the frequent disputes and differences that arose among the slaves, the master, as the sole arbiter, was forced to cultivate and develop a sense of justice. And these responsibilities rested upon the planter always, not only for self-interest—the conservation of his own property—but the far higher obligation of humanity.

But, with it all, there was time for hunting, fishing, boating and racing—the healthful out-door sports of men, and cavaliers. And with the love of out-door sports went love of nature—of woods and fields and flowing streams, of fountains and of flower gardens; of books, of gracious, cultured women; of music, and of art. A fine civilization while it lasted.

And then the War!

And then the War! When it was all over, the men who came through had been tried as steel in the blast, and the women as gold in the furnace. And in time, men, who in the heat and exaltation of battle had laughed at death, learned at last to laugh at life—a harder thing to do!

The men of Laguerre's day had their faults— the faults of Cavaliers—convivial men, but, hidden by no mantle of pretense, they were known of all men, and those who had, and owned, these faults were free from the meaner vices of colder, less generous natures. Avarice there was none; nor any of the smug hypocrisy of the "unco-guid."

If there was a touch of the Gascon here and there, it was not "such boastings as the Gentiles use," for they prided themselves neither on power nor possessions, past or present, but merely on their personal prowess, or that of their people, in the manly sports of flood and field—a natural pride that perhaps the exuberance of their high spirits somewhat exaggerated.

And, having learned to laugh, they laughed once more at Death, and died—gentlemen to the last, in the truer, finer meaning of the term—gentle, brave, considerate, compassionate!

Laguerre's office and his official title were very dear to him; partly, perhaps, because its administration presented many phases of Negro life, many shades of Negro character the observation of which afforded an always interesting study and delighted his keen sense of humor. Then, the authority he exercised over them—the legal overlordship that none could dispute—meant much to a man so full of himself, while his rough-and-tumble deliverances from the bench—as picturesque in their way as those of the late Judge Thomas Jefferson Mackey of the Reconstruction period—gave an outlet for a verbal effervescence that could not be repressed. The gift of speech

was great, but greater far the privilege of speak
ing with authority!

But whatever merriment it brought into hi
life, however it fattened his already exuberan
self-esteem, Laguerre's official position mean
even more to him for the service he could do th
poor black people around him—so often involve
in difficulties among themselves, so often impose
upon by white men of the baser sort. Thes
troubles "Jedge" adjusted in a spirit of equity
with little regard for the strict letter of the law
Courts of Appeal were far away on the dim hori
zon beyond Caw-Caw swamp, and there were n
irritating lawyers around to threaten reversals in
higher tribunals, so Laguerre's decisions stood a
steadfastly as Toogoodoo bridge—until, or unless
reversed or modified by "Jedge" himself. This
he sometimes did, leaning always to the side o:
mercy, for if today in a fit of temper he imposec
too heavy a fine, or ruled too harshly for contemp
of court, he could always remit the fine or accep
an apology for the offense upon the morrow.

At last, in the late eighties, the General As
sembly reduced the number of magistrates in
Colleton County, and "Jedge," junior to the Tria
Justice at Jacksonboro, had his chair of office
roughly pulled from under him, and was plumpec
down on the soil of Slann's Island, a private citi-
zen. The black folk of Toogoodoo were bereft

and Laguerre was deeply hurt. But, though now "functus officio," he yet laid great store by the official title by which his black friends had once so proudly called him, and to this, with its memories he now clung, as a veteran clasps to his breast the tattered battle-flag under which he had striven on many bloody fields. "Well," he often said, "they can take away my office, but damned if they can take away my title! 'Judge Laguerre' I have lived, and 'Judge Laguerre' I shall die!" His white friends laughed and forgot, but to the poor black folk of Toogoodoo—the poor can always remember—he was "Jedge" to the day of his death.

In the Presbyterian graveyard of the "Old Burnt Church," a mile beyond the village, on the road to Toogoodoo, Laguerre has long slept his last sleep. Within the sound of a hunter's whoop lies the quiet pineland village beside the sluggish streamlet called the "Run". Here, sixty years ago, the camp-fires of five thousand gray-clad soldiers blazed among the pines, and from the sandy roads by day and night, came the tramp of marching men, the thud of horses' hoofs, the low rumble of artillery, the blare of trumpets, and the roll of drums.

The scene shifts; and twenty years later, not far from the old Confederate head-quarters, stood Marshall's store, or tavern, "where Jamshyd gloried and drank deep," while Zouave, hitched to a crepe-myrtle across the way, hung his weary head, and Doctor Barnwell laughed!

Marshall's store is gone, but the live-oak, whose spreading boughs once sheltered it from summer's suns, still stands, and across the road the myrtles bloom from June until the fall.

And Doctor Barnwell laughs no more, nor any now survives of all the gallant company who once made merry with Laguerre!

Stretching south from the Old Burnt Church runs the road to Toogoodoo. In the dark forest along the way, great magnolias still rear their lofty crowns above the trees around them; still lift in May their silver chalices to the sun and freight with fragrance all the aerial tides that touch them as they pass, while far below, in the cool depths of the woods, the sweet-bays strew their lavish spiceries. Huge grapevine pythons still swing across the road; and saw-palmettoes whisper weirdly in the wind. Beyond the sandy stretch where fiddlers swarm in companies, the high bridge spans the winding creek, and in the pineland glade not far away, so silent now, Laguerre once held his joyous woodland court and the woods echoed with laughter.

Across the road the cherry tree still stands, and here in June the jealous mockingbirds warn other birds away.

FOREWORD

Aloft, the crows still circle in the blue, and caw
and caw, as if for some one loved and lost. The
marsh-hens call the tide. Kingfishers, rattling,
stoop, and dip, and loop the loop. Woodpeckers
tap, and tap, and hammer heavily, but only echoes
come, for the red hatchet of Laguerre has long
been rust, and all the old black folk who once
foregathered with him in "God's Green Inn" have
long since mingled with the dust!

The quiet graveyard of the "Old Burnt Church"
three miles away. In the scanty shrubbery of the
old place mockingbirds sometimes come to sing,
and fluting cardinals. In the wintry dusk brown
thrashers chant harsh vespers, and friendly chip-
ping-sparrows chirp their soft goodnights. And
all around—the pines! Singing sentinels, within
whose lofty tops, at dawn or dusk, at midnight, or
at noon, the wind-harps sound the requiem of the
sleeper, whose epitaph, could he have chosen it,
would have been, not "Justice," "Judge," or "Magistrate," but simply, "Jedge!"

The first five Laguerre stories were written and
published in The State in 1918. The remaining
fourteen were written and published in the late
summer and autumn of the present year.

AMBROSE E. GONZALES.

Columbia, S. C.
December, 1924.

LAGUERRE

A gallant soldier of the Confederacy, formerly a wealthy Sea-Island cotton planter, he lived until about twenty years ago in a cottage on a war-ruined but once splendid plantation; planting a little, hunting now and then, fishing frequently and, a first rate raconteur, talking incessantly. Educated in Paris before the war, and of distinguished Huguenot ancestry, he passionately loved France and all things French, and in his sensitive honor and courtly manners, and the great blond moustache and imperial worn a la Napoleon III, brought to Toogoodoo a touch of the Second Empire.

Laguerre rode, and drove, a thin thoroughbred stallion, Zouave, who carried more sheep-burrs in his tail than corn under his ribs; yet, though now reduced to the ignominy of a buckboard, he came honestly by his flat bone, powerful stifles and slim pasterns, and his coat, which shone in the sun like polished rosewood, whenever it was treated to a touch of the curry-comb, for through Lexington, Boston, Timoleon, Sir Henry, and Sir Archy, he traced to imported Diomed, winner of the first English Derby.

Often the wayfarer, passing through the pineland village whose postoffice served the planters living along Toogoodoo Creek, would see Zouave's

1

drooping head hanging down pathetically at a hitching post, and know that his master, with an audience, perhaps too with a glass and a pipe— a triad of blessings—was holding forth in the store with all the zest of an accomplished "rac- coonter," as it was locally pronounced. Some- times he told spicy stories of the Boulevards, and again recounted wartime experiences; but, what- ever the theme, the sound of his own voice gave him unqualified delight, and whether he talked to a buttonholed audience of one, or to a crowd gathered about the big sheet-iron stove in winter, or on the store veranda in summer, the blue eyes glowed as brightly under the shaggy penthouse brows, the quick Gallic gestures were as eloquent, and the ringing tenor voice as vibrant. "Let me but fill the ears of a people," he might have para- phrased, "and I care not who fills their stomachs" —a sentiment, by the way, not without its ap- peal to the politicians of today! Then, as the shadows of the pines lengthened and Zouave's drooping head hung lower and lower, the thought would come to him of the waiting wife and chil- dren, seven or eight miles away, and, still talk- ing as he drank his stirrup cup, he would climb into his buckboard and hurry home to tell them all he had talked about while absent!

Laguerre loved the young (old men were too garrulous) and was never happier than when

joining in their entertainments. With some histrionic ability, he was fond of amateur theatricals, and appreciated to the full the privilege
of talking from a stage to people who were obliged
to listen and who couldn't talk back. When the
Toogoodoodlers organized a dramatic club and
modestly put Richard the Third in rehearsal, Laguerre essayed the title role, and impersonated
the crookback Gloster so successfully as to win,
not only the approval of the local audience, but
that of his critical kindred from Edisto Island
who came over to see the performance. These
young men were particularly impressed by Richard's successful wooing under great difficulties,
and by his ominous dream on the eve of Bosworth
field. "Cousin —— him *done* fuh kin play Dick
T'ree-Time," was the verdict. "W'en one gal
come 'puntop de stage wid da' cawpse en' t'ing,
Buh Dick T'ree-Time tek one hebby soad en'
obuht'row de cawpse, en' graff de gal 'roun' 'e
wais' en' gone! Den 'e gone een one tent en'
leddown fuh sleep. But 'e yent sleep; 'e duh dream.
Den 'e roll obuh en' obuh lukkuh hawss hab colic,
but 'e yent hab no colic. Some dem Adam Run
gal t'ink suh him binnuh eat crab, en' 'e hab
one pain, but wunnuh boy him ent eat no crab
en' 'e yent gots no pain! Duh nutt'n' but de
pyo' ack mek'um stan' so!"

Laguerre once fancied himself slighted or

treated with discourtesy by a person of mean ex-
traction, who, having made money in some ple-
beian calling "up the country," had recently acquired a fine plantation in the neighborhood.
For days he brooded over his grievance. How
could wounded, or slightly bruised, honor be ap-
peased! Even if the duello had not been outlawed, the code would not have approved his
challenge of one whom he could not recognize
as an equal, and he was too chivalrous to attack
him without notice, or on unequal terms. At
last, his memory harked back a generation or so,
and he decided upon posting! The decision was
reached on Saturday evening. Returning from
the village store he had brought a full gallon
of the yellow corn whiskey so highly esteemed
in the malarial regions of the Low-country, so
he was fortified in his resolution.

On Sunday morning he rose, made an unusually
careful toilet, and, after breakfasting, wrote on a
double sheet of foolscap an elaborate arraignment
of the offensive and offending *nouveau-riche;*
advising him that a copy would be nailed on the
offender's plantation gatepost at 10 o'clock, and
Laguerre, armed, would stand guard at the post
until the setting of the sun, to prove the truth of
his proclamation upon the body of whomsoever
should venture to tear it down! A copy made,
a Negro messenger was dispatched to deliver

it. Laguerre loaded both barrels of his Greener with buckshot, filled a quart flask with the yellow corn, which he put with a hammer and nails in his saddlebags, mounted Zouave and fared forth on as errant a quest as ever inspired La Mancha's redoubtable knight! He had ordered his messenger to await him at the place of posting, and the Negro had already arrived at the gate as Laguerre rode up. He first made him nail the denunciation in a conspicuous place on one of the big posts and then questioned him. "Did you deliver the note, Scipio?"

"Yaas, Maussuh, Uh 'libbuhr'um same lukkuh you tell me. Uh pitt'um een de Buckruh' han'."

"Where did you find him?"

" 'E binnuh seddown een 'e pyazzuh duh eat 'e brekwus', en' 'e hab 'nuf fuh eat. 'E hab uh hebby pan full uh mullet, en' 'e hab swimp en' crab alltwo, en' 'e hab hom'ny en' t'ing. 'E hab 'nuf bittle."

"Confound his 'bittle'! What did he do when you gave him the note? Did he read it?"

"Yaas, suh, 'e read'um."

"Well, what did he say when he read it?"

"Maussuh, 'e yent say *nutt'n'*. 'E yent crack 'e teet'. One saabint gal fetch'um one big plate pile' up wid baddle cake. Him pit two-t'ree 'pun 'e plate en' kibbuhr'um wid muhlassis, en' staa't fuh eat. Den 'e look 'puntop'uh me, en' 'e face kind'uh tanglety up, en' 'e biggin fuh choke."

"Ha! Choked, did he? A good thing, too."

"Yaas, suh, w'en 'e choke, I t'aw't 'e mus'be swalluh fishbone, 'tel I look att'um 'gen, good fashi'n, en' den I see 'e duh laugh."

"Laughed! He dared to laugh?"

"Maussuh, 'e laugh 'tel 'e mos' drap out 'e chair, en' den him Nigguh, 'self, biggin fuh laugh. Den, 'e 'cratch one match, en' twis' up de papuh en' nyuze'um fuh light 'e pipe. W'en I shum do dat, I leff'um en' come yuh."

"By the Great Horn Spoon! He'll laugh on the other side of his mouth! Go home, sir, and tell your mistress to expect me one hour after sundown."

"Yaas, Maussuh," and Scipio departed.

The knight errant dismounted, hitched Zouave to a bushy marshmallow nearby, and, as the May sunshine was hot, sought shelter for himself under a young live-oak whose protecting shade spread conveniently in easy gunshot of the gate. Laying his Greener on the ground a yard away, he cushioned a spot under the tree with an armful of Spanish moss that hung from the boughs overhead, and, seating himself, took a liberal pull from the precious flask, removed his hat to catch the vagrant airs that came up from the creek flowing nearby, and leaned back against the trunk

6

with a sigh of satisfaction. How good the world
seemed! The sweet whistle of a cardinal to his
nesting mate, the soft, liquid fluting of the red-
wing blackbirds in the reeds a quarter of a mile
away, the harsh rattle of the kingfisher as he
"looped the loop" in erratic flight over the glistening waters, came to his ears soothingly, while
his nostrils dilated as they sniffed the wholesome smell of the salt-marsh, blended with the
heavy, sensuous odor of the sweet-bay blooming
in a distant swamp. (Another nip from the amber solace of the flask!) Yes, the world was
good. Good old world! Old, too, very old. Wasn't
he, Laguerre, fighting Saracens for the Holy
Sepulcher a thousand years or so ago? A wave
of holy zeal swept over him, and he intensified
the exaltation with another snifter. Good world!
Young world, too! And there was Paris. Ah,
Paris! The flowering chestnuts, the gardens of the
Tuilleries, the Champs-Elysee, Versailles, Ma-
bille's! O la, la! *"La donna e mobile,"* he hummed.
No! Woman fickle? Never! His noble wife at home
only a few miles away! God bless her! So devoted, so uncomplaining, so sympathetic! No
"gathering brows," and no storm at his house,
however late he came home. Drink to her, bless
her! Noble daughter of old Virginia! Good old Virginia!...Mother of presidents...Mother of wives,
too...Mother-in-law   of   husbands...Mother-

7

in-law of Laguerre!...Good old Virginia! Drink
to her!—Sun unusually hot—Stretch out—Little
nap.—Jus' little nap. Moss! Soft—Good pillow
—Nap!

Down the slope of the western sky the sun slid
to his setting. The kingfisher sounded his last
rattle for the day and dipped off to his roost
through the fading light. From the marshes,
by twos and threes, the "Indian Pullets" flew
over to their nightly rendezvous in the swamps.
A "Po'-Joe" flapped slowly over, his long legs at
the trail. The shadows deepened. Zouave
stamped and shuddered his withers as the sand-
flies swarmed over him. The marsh-hens called
the changing tide. Night fell.

Laguerre slept, but not silently. His nose,
as aquiline as Dante's and as big as Cyrano's,
was "nobly planned" for snoring, and as he lay
flat on his back under the oak he used the talent
with which "designing nature" had endowed him.
The stars came out. A questing mink crept from
his lair under the creek bank, sniffed furtively
and slunk away. From a distant bayou the hollow
"chuhboongkuh" of a bittern boomed across the
waste. The air became cooler. A light wind
from the sea sprang up. In a moment there was
a glow in the east and the rim of the rising moon
topped the horizon. Another moment and the
great orange disk appeared, and, slowly changing

8

from golden to silver, flooded the world with light, and dewdrops glistened on a thousand spears of grass.

A mocking-bird came from the myrtles, and alighting on the gatepost where Laguerre's defiance, still unchallenged, gleamed pallid in the moonbeams, filled the night with melody. The moon rode higher and neared the zenith.

"Come'up, mule! Wuh de debble— You t'ink you duh gwine chu'ch, enty?" The crack of a whip, the rattle of wheels over the corduroy of the causeway, and Scipio, driving a mule to the buckboard, appeared with an anxious face. He hurried to Laguerre and gave a grunt of relief as he heard the welcome snore. A ray of light fell upon the flask and, simultaneously, upon the understanding of Scipio. Holding it up toward the moon he discerned a dram, which he quickly swallowed with a "t'engk-gawd 'e lef' uh leetle tetch," and proceeded to shake his master vigorously. Laguerre awoke a very Gascon. "Ha! Scipio! I bettered my word! I held the gate against all comers, all day and half the night. Laughed, did he! I've taught him how to laugh. Shut him up all day within his own gates! By the splendor of the constellations! Eh, Scipio?"

"Yaas, Maussuh," said the wise old darky, as he cut his eye at the roadway and saw, from the fresh hoofprints and wheel tracks, that a double

9

team had recently passed through the gate, outward bound, "Yaas, Maussuh. Git een de buggy now en' leh we go home. Missis duh wait fuh we."

"Scipio," asked Laguerre as he climbed into the comfortable buckboard, while Scipio tied poor Zouave's bridle to the rear axle, "Scipio, how did your mistress happen to send you in the buckboard instead of on horseback?"

"Maussuh, w'en daa'k come en' *you* ent come, Missis gone en' shake de jug wuh you fetch frum billage las' night, en' de jug shake so light, Missis tell me fuh hitch'up."

"Bless her!" said Laguerre reverently, as Scipio took up the lines and drove off. "Bless her!"

ON THE JUDGMENT SEAT

When Laguerre was appointed Trial Justice, his estimate of his own importance, in the community and in the world, increased enormously. Always dignified with strangers and with those whom he held as his social inferiors, his haughtiness under the magisterial mantle that now hung upon his shoulders, would have become a grandee of Spain. His whole bearing changed. When he rode his old thoroughbred, Zouave, he straightened in his stirrups and carried himself more jauntily; when he drove in his buckboard, and the springy slats bounced him over the roots of the pineland road, each jolt and joggle seemed to send him higher and higher up in the world, for was he not now a Trial Justice!—the sole representative of the law in forty to fifty square miles of lower Colleton County, with the power to commit his fellow-citizens to jail, there to languish among the Walterboroughians until the convening of the circuit court should give them freedom or prolong their exile? Could he not try causes involving the ownership of property not exceeding one hundred dollars in value? Didn't every cow, calf, or ox that fed in forest or field, every acorn-hunting pig that rooted the woods, every cock that crowed and every hen that cackled from Adams Run to Toogoodoo, do so within his jurisdiction? Hadn't he the legal power to hitch up man and woman in the holy bonds of wedlock, irrevocably to be bound together, each unto the other, with all the appurtenances thereunto appertaining, until unhitched by the State of Georgia, if white, or by the State of Mind of either or both, if colored?) Was one in such authority to hold himself lightly? He would say not.

Nineteen-twentieths of those who came before him were Negroes, the occasional malefactor among the sparse white population of the locality regarding it as contemptible to commit any offense small enough to subject him to magisterial jurisdiction, when, by going into the matter more deeply, he could command the presence of the sheriff! Although fierce to truculence toward the insolent or surly, Laguerre's tender heart made him compassionate to those who threw themselves on his mercy, and as his sympathies were always with the weak or distressed, his decisions were usually on all fours with those of the Sherwood Forest courts under the late Robin Hood. But he invariably ruled for contempt of court, and punished with a severe lecture, any Negro who failed to "pull wool," or scrape his foot when approaching the Presence.

When the weather was fine Laguerre held an open air "Court" in a little glade in the woods, just beyond the high bridge that spanned the turbid waters of Toogoodoo. Here, a few feet distant from the highway, with an empty packing case in front of him for a table, he sat in awful majesty on a comfortably cushioned box. Spread open before him was a copy of the huge Revised Statutes, 1882—a formidable looking doomsday book to the poor darkies, while the big red hatchet he used as a gavel, added to the impressiveness of the legal "layout." Woe to the witless wight who should ride hard-mouthed mule or wilful ox past this dread tribunal without making suitable obeisance or acknowledgment!

One warm June day, the Court was sitting on the chintz-cushioned box, and the Negroes in attendance squatted on the ground roundabout, some of them moody over their impending fate, but most of them laughing and talking in subdued tones, or lazily picking the berries that grew within reach. Just across the road stood a big wild-cherry tree and, balancing upon its top with uplifted wings, a mocking-bird, in harsh tones, warned other feathered depredators away from the ripening fruit. Cudjo Hawlback, the tall, grim Ashanti-looking constable who stood at His Honor's right, leaning upon a long hickory staff, kept order and combined the duties of tipstaff and crier. "Oh, yaas! Oh, yaas! All yunnuh Nigguh en' t'ing wuh duh seddown 'puntop de groun' duh 'cratch flea en' pick huckleberry, 'tan'up en' come'yuh close to de Co't weh de Jedge kin look 'puntop'uh yunnuh. De Co't done op'n. Silunt een Co't!"

The first case was that of the Slann's Island Fold of the "Sons and Daughters of I Will Arise" vs. Sister Judy Chizzum, Treasurer-Lady of the lodge. The charge preferred by Bina Fields, Secretary-Lady, was that the Treasurer-Lady, notwithstanding the robust health with which she had been blessed during all the preceding year, had disbursed to herself at Christmas two weeks' sick benefit—to wit, Seven Dollars. Upon the physical and verbal protest of the Secretary-Lady, the case, accompanied by the cash-box, had been referred for arbitration to the masculine president of the society, and the Old-He having reserved both decision and cash-box, the tangled skein was now, after nearly six months of heart-burning, wool-pulling, and recrimination, submitted to Judge Laguerre "fuh ontwis'um."

The heavy hatchet fell upon the box with a thwack that silenced the scolding mocking-bird and sent a shiver through the guilty and near-guilty among the Negroes. "Bina Fields, stan'-up!" roared Cudjo. Bina, a tall angular person, was already almost on tiptoe, but at the harsh summons she grew as stiff as a ramrod.

"Tek de book!" and as a small greasy looking Bible was handed her, she dropped a curtsy and

14

clasped it tightly in both hands while the entirely superfluous oath was administered.

"Kiss'um, 'ooman! *Kiss de book!"* Which she did with a resounding smack as she dropped another curtsy.

"Bina," said Laguerre impressively, "tell your story."

"Well, Maussuh—"

"Maussuh!" thundered Laguerre, *"Maussuh!* with ninety thousan' dollars' worth of Niggers loafing around this court and no power to make one of you strike a lick of work save on the chain-gang! *Maussuh!* No—Judge!"

"Yaas, suh, Maussuh Jedge."

"Tell your story."

"Well, suh, me is de Seckryterry-Lady, en' Sistuh Chizzum him is de Tredjuruh-Lady, en' us alltwo dey onduhneet' de Prezzy*dent* en' him dey 'puntop'uh we, 'cause him duh we pastuh en' t'ing, en' him duh de Lawd' renointed, dat w'y-mekso us mek'um de S'preme een de 'Syety. Now, w'enebbuh de membuh sick, de 'Syety pay'um t'ree dolluh en' fifty cent uh week; but alldo' Sistuh Chizzum hab uh hebby he'lt' eenjurin' de Gawd-blessed yeah, w'en C'rismus come 'e pit 'e han' een de Tredjuh box en' tek'out seb'n dolluh fuh 'eself; so den I 'taguhnize'um tuh de Prezzy*dent* fuh git de t'ing resplain, but him tek him recision en' de box, alltwo, en' de t'ing tanglety up so, 'tel

15

us fetch'um yuh fuh you fuh onrabble'um, suh."

"Judy Chizzum!" called Cudjo, and the plump, self-satisfied "Tredjuruh-Lady" of the I Will Arise kissed the book and smiled at the Court, while she fanned herself with a green frond of the saw-palmetto.

"What's your story? Tell all you know."

"Jedge, suh, ef Uh tell all wuh Uh know 'bout deseyuh Nigguh, trouble fuh pile'up een dishyuh pinelan' high mo'nuh Toogoodoo Bridge!"

"Perjure yourself and you go to jail."

"Puhjuh! wuh him, suh?"

"If you don't tell the truth you perjure yourself."

"Oh, Gawd, Uh yent fuh puhjuh! Maussuh Jedge done tu'n me loose! Yunnuh Nigguh haffuh tek yunnuh chance! Well, suh, we 'Syety hab t'irty-one membuh, en' all duh freemale 'scusin' Pa Tumbo Middletun. Him duh we pastuh en' him duh de Prezzy*dent*. Him duh fuh lead we; we duh fuh folluh she, en' Pa Tumbo ent 'low none dem t'odduh man fuh jine, 'cause him say suh dat will mek uh cunfusion een de fol'. Now, een de fus' biggin uh de yeah, Sistuh Limehouse him sen' 'e two leetle gal fuh tell me suh him sick, en' 'e claim de sick benefit. One de gal name Bullfrog, t'odduh one name Cootuh. Bullfrog black sukkuh chimbly back, but Cootuh yalluh ez uh punkin. I ax'um, 'Cootuh, hukkuh

16

you stan' sukkuh yalluhhammuh, en' Bullfrog
black lukkuh crow?' Den de gal mek ansuh en' say
him bin hab de yalluh janduss, mek'um stan' so,
en' 'e say Bullfrog nebbuh bin hab no yalluh janduss. I tell'um *'Yaas*, umhm, jaybu'd' fedduh
green, en' blackbu'd' fedduh yalluh, rabbit heng
by 'e tail frum de 'simmon tree, en' 'possum jump
duh briah-patch, cow suck aig, en' mule seddown
'puntop de chimbly, sukkuh hawn-owl.' Den Uh
ax'um 'smattuh 'long 'e ma, en' 'e say suh 'e ma
hab one—"

"Talk'um 'traight, 'e hab *two!*" interrupted a
voice.

"Silunt een Co't!" roared Cudjo.

" 'E say suh 'e ma hab *two twin*," continued the
witness, "so I pay'um *him* benefit. Den Sistuh
Poachus, him en' him juntlemun fight en' 'e juntlemun cripple'um, en' *him* git 'e benefit. Now,
Sistuh Gibbs come fuh *him* chance, en' 'e leddown
duh bed en' mek uh great cumplain, en' alldo' Uh
s'pishun suh 'e tie one 'tring 'roun' 'e knee fuh
mek 'e foot fuh swell, Uh nebbuh quizzit'um, en'
Uh pay'um, 'cause him hab uh berry ondeestunt
mout' w'en 'e bex, en' Uh yent wantuh agguhnize
'long'um. Den Sistuh Grant en' Sistuh Flood en'
Sistuh Fields, dishyuh same Seckryterry-Lady
wuh 'taguhnize me to de Reb'ren', ebb'ry Gawd
one uh deseyuh 'ooman wuh duh 'cuze me fuh tek
my benefit, ebb'ry Cryce *one*, down to Pa Tumbo'

17

lawfully-lady, *'self,* hab one pain, eeduhso baby, uh one sump'n'nurruh, en' git dem benefit, 'tel to de las', none lef' een de 'Syety fuh git benefit 'cep' Sistuh Sukey Hawlback—"

"Talk'um, tittuh, talk'um!"

"Talk'um, ti' Judy! Talk'um!" interrupted women's voices.

"Silunt een Co't!" called Cudjo, while Laguerre brought down his hatchet furiously.

"Yaas, Uh haffuh talk'um, 'cause Jedge mek me fuh tell de trute, 'cause Uh yent fuh puhjuh! Maussuh Jedus, Uh *yent* fuh puhjuh! Well, suh, 'long 'bout de fus' uh de fall—'cause Uh 'membuh Uh binnuh dig 'tettuh attuh de fus' fros' done come—Uh yeddy one tarrify kind'uh soun' sukkuh hog ketch een baa'b' wire fench, en' Uh call to Bredduh Paul Mannigo—him duh my class lead-uh—en' Uh ax'um fuh tek my niece Joe, wuh bin-nuh dig 'tettuh 'long we, en' ontwis' de hog out de fench. Alltwo de man run, en', bumbye, Uh yed-dy'um call fuh me fuh come. W'en Uh git dey, Jedge, Uh fin' da' same black Aff'ikin Nigguh wuh yunnuh hab fuh counstubble, da' same longmout' oagly Cudjo wuh stan' sukkuh 'ranguhtang—"

"Talk'um, tittuh Judy! Talk'um!"

"Yaas, Uh fuh talk'um. Cudjo duh swell'up sukkuh town pidgin duh sashay 'puntop'uh roof, but Uh yent got no kibbuh 'puntop me mout' 'cause Jedge done tek'um off, en' Uh yent fuh

18

puhjuh! Well, suh, da' same 'ranguhtang Nigguh
hab 'e lady tie wid one plow line, hog fashi'n, duh
beat'um wid hoe handle! W'en us tu'n de po'
'ooman loose, 'e yent able fuh walk, en' 'e fambly
haffuh 'n'int'um wid hawss lini*ment*, en' rub'um
wid axil-greese en' kyarrysene. Now, w'en I see
how him juntlemun bruk'um'up, I pay'um *him*
benefit, en' him duh de las' one in de 'Syety. So,
Jedge, w'en C'rismus come, en' Uh 'membuh suh
Uh binnuh agguhnize summuch wid all deseyuh
t'odduh sistuh en' t'ing de whole yeah, Uh fuhgit
fuh git sick fuh git my benefit, so den I tek'um
same lukkuh de odduhres'." —————— .

"Right," said Laguerre. "Judy, you are dismissed. Cudjo," as he turned to his court official,
"you black rascal, what have you to say for yourself? Don't say it, sir! How dare you attempt
to justify yourself before this court? You are
sentenced to buy your wife a new frock and a pair
of shoes, and if I ever hear of this sort of thing
again I'll commit you to jail! The cause of the
State of South Carolina versus Tumbo Middleton
for misappropriation of trust funds is continued
until next Saturday at 12 o'clock noon. Dismiss
the court."

"Oh, Jedus, dishyuh duh one *Jedge!*"

"Yaas, tittuh, 'e mek de 'ranguhtang fuh buy
frock!"

"En' 'e pit shoe 'puntop de 'ooman' foot!"

As the chorus of feminine approval of his sentence swelled about him, Cudjo shouted truculently, "Oh, yaas! oh, yaas! All wunnuh Nigguh come'yuh nex' Sattyday middleday fuh sprosecute de Reb'ren' Middletun fuh tek dem 'ooman' tredjuh-box en' t'ing!" Then, as the Negroes broke up into laughing and talking groups, he turned wrathfully to Judy who, delighted with her part in the day's doings, was smiling broadly, "*Yaas*, you good-fuh-nutt'n', 'ceitful, debble'ub'uh 'ooman, duh *yo'* mout' mek me fuh git een trouble."

"Yaas, fuh true, bubbuh, enty de Jedge done onkibbuhr'um?"

"*Onkibbuhr'um!* 'E nebbuh *yiz* bin hab kibbuh 'puntop'uhr'um! 'E fuhrebbuh stan' sukkuh fishpon' full'up wid fry-bakin frog!"

PA TUMBO AT THE BAR

Since early morning the Negroes, always ahead of time, had been foregathering at the Crossroads, near which Laguerre had pitched his judicial tent, and by the time the court convened at noon a hundred or more expectant members of Pa Tumbo's flock were eagerly awaiting the inauguration of the proceedings against him. The defendant was late in arriving, and drove up only a short time before the coming of Laguerre, accompanied by his "lawfully-lady," as the Negroes call the wife to whom a man is married. The "lawfully-lady" was a small, meek creature of the type usually affected by large, important men. The women paid her scant attention, but greeted Tumbo effusively, while the men, especially the younger ones, looked askance at the monopolist, whom they regarded much as the small butcher does the Meat Trust.

When Laguerre had taken his seat, Cudjo opened court and the defendant was called.

"Tumbo Middletun!" A huge middle-aged black Negro waddled pompously to the "witness stand," a spot of ground upon which the weeds and grass had been worn away by the shod and unshod feet of the Negroes, and took the oath. His long, black coat was thrown open and his fingers fumbled clumsily at a heavy gilt

21

watch chain that looped about the rotundity of his well filled paunch. Laguerre bent his brows fiercely upon this putative and potential father of flocks as he appraised the fat that covered the bull neck and broad jowls whose enlargement had pinched so many poor households, for no monk-ridden people in the early centuries of Christianity were assessed more heavily by the priesthood than these wretched but devoted Negroes for the support in idleness, too often corrupt and vicious idleness, of their spiritual shepherds! Laguerre, who had dealt so leniently with the women at the last trial, was in no such disposition toward Tumbo. As a planter he resented the habitual idleness of a "fifteen hundred dollar Nigger," while as a man and a humanitarian he despised him for battening upon the pittances of the poor.

"Tumbo Middleton, you are upon the historic soil of Adams Run Township, Colleton County, South Carolina! Upon the soil aforesaid you stand before this court charged with breach of trust, to wit: the abstraction, retention and appropriation of a cigar box of the length of eight inches, of the width of five inches, and of the depth of three inches, the same being the Treasure-Box and financial depository of the Slann's Island Fold of the Sons and Daughters of I Will Arise, all of which is against the peace and dignity of the State, county and township aforesaid

22

and in contravention of the statutes thereby made and provided; also, by alienating the contents of the box, if any, you have committed mayhem upon the financial resources of the Society to which you stand *in loco parentis—spiritualis et naturalibis,* and the devil knows what besides! Now, you —justification of the Darwinian theory—what have you got to say for yourself, and be confoundedly careful how you say it, or I'll pop you into jail for perjury!"

"Oh, Jedus! Pa Tumbo fuh puhjuh!" shrieked the Secretary-Lady. "Him fuh sen' Walterburruh!"

Tumbo talked slowly and unctuously, almost smacking his lips over his words as if he enjoyed their savor, as his sonorous tones fell upon the ears of his audience. Most of them were members of his congregation and, used as they were to his pompous pulpit platitudes, which delivered *ex cathedra,* were accepted without question, they were yet human enough to enjoy the grilling of even their beloved pastor, the Negro nature at all times being able to extract considerable pleasure out of the mental anguish of their friends and themselves, so, though paradoxical, his more devoted women members were miserably happy over his plight, while the men, who had long questioned the equity, if not the propriety, of the sequestration of so many desirable females within the fold of the I Will Arise, were frankly delighted.

"Well, Jedge," he began, almost condescendingly, "you see, I is de pastuh ub de Slann' I'lun' Met'dis' Chu'ch, en' I hab de 'sponsibility fuh t'ree hund'ud sinful soul, en' I done chaa'ge by de 'Zyd'n Elder fuh shep'u'd dem lukkuh de shep'u'd gyaa'd 'e sheep, en', so dis 'sponsibility kin filfil, I done orguhnize de Slann' I'lun' Fol' ub de Son en' Daughtuh ub de I Will Arise—"

"How many sons and how many daughters?" interrupted Laguerre.

"I duh de only son, Jedge, en' dem farruh!"

"You are not the first who has aspired to the paternity of his country, in the fullest meaning of the term! How many daughters?"

"T'irty, Jedge, ub de nyung sistuh dat 'quire puhteckshun een de fol' frum de wolf dat roam bidout, seekin' whom dey may devour, en' t'ief do not break t'ru nor steal."

"Haa'kee att'um! Him duh elly*funt,* en' him duh call we wolf!"

"Elly*funt!* him duh *bull alligettuh!*"

"Yaas, bubbuh, him fuh puhteck'um sukkuh suck-aig-dawg puhteck hen nes'!" the men shouted with derisive laughter which the court did not check.

"Now, Jedge," the witness resumed, "it 'quire uh berry pashunt man fuh agguhnize en' nullify

24

wid all deseyuh nyung sistuh en' lead dem fuh sanctify onduh de Lawd' renointed. 'Ooman iz shishuh onreasunubble t'ing w'en dem git tanglety up, dishyuh one en' t'arruh one, wid summuch'uh she-she talk—"

"She-she talk!"

"Yaas, Jedge, 'ooman talk. W'en dem git twis'up een dem quarrel*ment,* en' all deseyuh gwinin' en' gwinin', dem pastuh haffuh pashunt 'long dem sukkuh hen duh seddown 'puntop'uh duck' aig, befo' him kin onrabble'um. Now, Jedge, all eenjurin'uh de yeah deseyuh sistuh binnuh 'spute en' agguhnize 'long demself 'bout dishyuh sick benefit. Seem lukkuh ef Sistuh Washin'ton hab ub teet'ache dishyuh week, Sistuh Rab'nel him haffuh hab baby, eeduhso snake bite'um, nex' week. Dem all try fuh sick 'nuf fuh git dem benefit befo' de yeah done out, en' dem all hab uh good luck en' git dem chance, 'scusin' Sistuh Chizzum, him iz de Tredjuruh-Lady, en' w'en 'e seem lukkuh nutt'n' ain' gwine happ'n to *him,* den 'e tek out *him* benefit fuh shayre'um eeb'n. W'en de Seckryterry-Lady shum do dat, 'e 'taguhnize'um to de Prezzy*dent,* dat w'ymekso me tek'um fuh onrabble'um."

"Well, what did you 'onrabble'? How much money was in the box?"

"*Money,* suh! Ef yo' b'leebe me, Jedge, de box

25

bin full'uh de pyo' *nutt'n'!* 'E ain' hab uh fi'-
cent, needuhso uh t'ree-cent, een'um—"

Tumbo's testimony was suddenly cut short and
never concluded.

A concert of yells from the women, some of
whom jumped up from the ground and ran in
several directions, while others rolled over and
over like armadilloes until they got behind the
trunks of protecting pines, put a sudden stop to
the proceedings. The Court plied his hatchet
while he glared about him seeking some one whom
he might hold responsible for thus rudely inter-
rupting the dignified and orderly processes of the
law. His fierce regard fell upon Cudjo, who,
staff in hand, had seized and was holding by the
grapevine bridle a plunging ox, whose sudden
burst into the crowd in a clumsy bovine imitation
of a bucking bronco, had caused general con-
sternation. The wild-eyed rider had rolled off the
moss-stuffed crocus bag that served for a saddle
and stood trembling before the Presence into
which his steed had projected him so unceremo-
niously. The ox, rolling his eyes as is the way
with panicky creatures of his species, seemed as
apprehensive as his master of the fate in store
for him.

"What do you mean, sir, by disturbing this
Court? Pull your wool, you black rascal! What
brought you here?"

PA TUMBO AT THE BAR

"Oxin, suh," stammered the unhappy wretch, as he pulled his forelock and scraped his foot in humble obeisance.

"Don't trifle with me, sir! Why did the ox bring you here?"

"Haa'd mout', suh, en' cowfly."

"Hard mouth and cowflies, eh? I fine you one dollar for contempt and one dollar for your flippancy!"

"My *Gawd*, Maussuh! Me yent fuh do nutt'n', en' da' las' t'ing wuh you call'um, me nebbuh yeddy 'bout'um sence Uh bawn, much less fuh *shum*, suh. Maussuh, me dey een uh hebby trouble. Please, suh, fuh tu'n me loose so uh kin go Adam Run fuh baig Mas' Henry fuh credik me fuh git some med'sin fuh da' po' leetle gal, Uh leff'um so sick, en' 'e ma duh cry 'cause 'e yent got nutt'n' fuh g'em, 'cause you see, suh, me en' 'e ma alltwo duh wu'k out obuh to Dr. Paul' place, en' Nigguh don' git pay'off 'tel Sattyday night, en' us lib to Mas' Jawge Jinkin' place, close dishyuh same Toogoodoo, en' Uh got one deseyuh coonoo duh crik, 'e mek out'uh cypruss log, dem call'um *trus'-me-gawd*, 'cause w'en man gone een'um him haffuh hab fait' fuh cya'um t'ru, but chillun en' t'ing ain' know nutt'n' 'bout'um, en' las' night Uh gone duh crik fuh cyas' fuh try fuh ketch some deseyuh finguh-mullet fuh kind'uh tas'e we mout', 'cause cawn-hom'ny shishuh dry

27

bittle, en' bakin so skaceful Uh yent kin git none
fuh pit 'puntop'uhr'um, en' Uh yent ketch mo'nuh
han'ful uh mullet 'cause pawpuss come een de
crick en' 'e run'um all up een dem leetle lead duh
maa'sh, en' w'en Uh git sho', Uh lef' de trus'-me-
gawd haul' up, 'cause tide binnuh rise en' Uh didn'
want'um fuh too fudduh frum sho' w'en tide high,
en' one fool Nigguh name Mingo Puhlite, wuh lib
to Mas' Jawge', him hab uh ole mule, Uh dunno
w'ymekso 'e hab'um 'cause 'e nebbuh hab no
bittle fuh g'em fuh eat en' de mule fuhrebbuh
hongry, en' dem Nigguh call'um 'tumpsuckuh,
'cause w'en him hongry him tek one tree 'tump
een 'e teet' en' ketch 'e bre't' en' try fuh swalluhr'um, en' las' night Mingo hab t'ree-fo' ear
cawn—no, suh, Uh yent know weh 'e gitt'um,
but Uh know berry well 'e yent duh him'own,
'cause Mingo stan' sukkuh Buh Rabbit, him ent
fuh plant no crap 'cause ebb'rybody' crap duh
him'own w'en de man wuh 'e blonx to tu'n'way
'e yeye, so Mingo fin' 'e mule duh bite maa'sh 'long
de crik aige, en' 'e ketch'um by 'e yez en' lead'um
dey to de coonoo, weh Uh leff'um, en' 'e pit de cawn
een'um en' gone Nigguh-house-yaa'd, en' w'en
de good-fuh-nutt'n' mule done nyam 'e bittle, him
t'ink suh de trus'-me-gawd duh 'tump, en' 'e graff
de aige wid 'e teet' en' ketch 'e bre't' en' bite hole
out de gonnil, en' teday w'en my leetle seb'n yeah
old gal gone duh crik en' git een de coonoo en'

paddle'um 'bout fuh play, him nebbuh study 'bout
de aige done bite out, en' 'e yent know nutt'n'
'tel de watuh come een en' tu'n'um obuh, en' w'en
da' chillun gal try fuh git sho', 'e 'tep 'puntop'uh
oshtuh bank, en' de shaa'p rokkoon-oshtuh shell
cut 'e foot mos' een half, en' dem 'ooman tek'um
up en' cya'um to 'e ma, en' 'e ma tayre'up uh
w'ite shu't yo' lady gimme C'rismus, suh, en' 'e
tie'up de po' leely gal' foot, en' 'e tell me fuh gone
billage fuh baig fuh de lini*ment* fuh pit on'um,
en' Uh ketch dis 'ceitful haa'd-head oxin, en' Uh
binnuh ride'um fas' duh paat', en' cowfly bite'um
onduhneet' 'e hanch, en' 'e twitch 'e tail but 'e
cyan' reach'um, en' de t'ing 'ting'um so keen
'e run'way, en' 'e mout' haa'd sukkuh 'e head, en'
Uh yent hab nutt'n' but grapewine fuh bridle
en'—"

"*Stop!*" cried Laguerre as the tomahawk descended. "Ride like the devil to the village and
get your medicine, and if you loaf by the way
I'll punish you on sight! Here," he continued,
handing the astonished Negro a silver dollar,
"If 'speech is silvern,' you've earned it."

A FEUD IN FEATHERS

It was high noon at the Toogoodoo trysting place of "Jedge" Laguerre's woodland Temple of Justice.

The brilliant July sunshine filtered through the glistening needles of the pines and fell upon a wealth of forest flowers; the pink-tipped spires of the deer-grass, the glaucous foliage of the partridge-peas, thickset with blossoming clusters of old-rose and salmon, and the beautiful white and yellow orchis; whose tall stems, branching at the top into fairy candelabra of feathery blooms, flecked the dark scrub of the undergrowth with points of gold and silver light. Here and there in the damp open glades were upstanding ranks— platoons and companies—of the sinister sarracenia, their painted throats luring myriads of buzzing insects to destruction.

In the moister spots along the roadside the fragrance of the blossoming wild-grape and the ruddy pendants of the trumpet vine delighted the senses. Down toward the sea, on a soft wind from the west, light clouds, singly and in fleets, floated in stately procession across the blue, each ship and shallop under full sail for the far horizon.

Three neighborhood roads converged near the court, and one by one, and in chattering groups

31

the Negroes came, a few in response to legal summons, but most of them impelled by curiosity to witness the discomfiture of their friends and neighbors. The proceedings were charged with unusual interest, for news had gone about the countryside of a fierce feud between Sister Daphne Poinsett, resident on the Whaley plantation, and her neighbor, Sister Phoebe Polite. Now, Daphne had planted a garden and tilled the soil, but Phoebe, like the mythical Leda, leaned toward feathers, and while loving nor swan nor goose, she fervently affected the frizzled hen that cackled and the cock that crowed nocturnally, matutinally, and upon such other occasions as the challenging of a rival in the neighborhood, gallantry toward the ladies of his court, or the vanity and boastfulness which we are told inheres in all males of whatsoever species, prompted.

Now, the cock that was charged with the paternity of Phoebe's feathered flock, the warning away of hawks and other chanticlerical duties, was a "forward-looking" fellow—he was ashamed to look behind, for he had no more tail than a penguin! Lacking the long, drooping plumes that constitute the crowning glory of a rooster's hinterland, he sported only short, incurving feathers, forming a sort of bustle, and, like Richard, somewhat curtailed of his "fair proportion," also like Richard, his courage was fierce, and

32

though cutting no more figure among his long-tailed rivals than a Tuxedo at a St. Cecilia ball, he was always ready to fight, and, lacking the tail to turn, of course he never turned tail!

So Daphne tilled the soil, while Phoebe engaged in animal-husbandry, in the Creation-old competition between these two branches of outdoor industry, and the advantage was with the latter, for while Daphne delved, Phoebe watchfully waited, knowing that in the fullness of time when the garden should bourgeon forth with "the kindly fruits of the earth," her feathered "Tumbo" and his feminine following would find the way over the wattled clapboard fence that enclosed the garden, while the downy little biddies, summoned by the maternal cluck, would creep through the cracks to join in the revelry of destruction.

Daphne had protested against the several invasions with whatever odds and ends of sticks and brickbats she could command. These, hurled with the curving trajectory for which the female of the species is famous, flew wide of the mark, but, whatever the propulsive limitations of the feminine scapula, nature has imposed none on the esteemed larynx, and she supplemented her battery of hand-thrown missiles with a rapid fire of Gullah imprecations, projected with a directness of aim that tingled the ears and excited the ire of her neighbor.

LAGUERRE

"Me fuh bruk my back fuh 'toop down en' pull up not-grass en' t'istle en' t'ing, fuh mek gyaa'd'n fuh 'cratch'up 'long frizzle hen en' rumpletail roostuh, enty? De *debble!* Ef oonuh ain' cut dem wing fuh keep'um frum fly obuh my fench, Uh gwine tek'um'up onduhneet' de stock law, en' mek oonuh fuh pay dammidge."

"Mek me fuh pay *dammidge!* You mus'be fool! You t'ink bu'd duh anni*mel,* enty? *Tek'um up! Tek'um up!* Uh'll tek you spang Toogoodoo Bridge to Trial Jestuss!"

"Tek me Trial Jestuss fuh refen' de gyaa'd'n wuh Uh mek wid my own lavuh! 'Ooman, don' mek me bex! Oonuh t'ink 'cause yo' juntlemun bin een Walterburruh jail fuh t'ief hog, suh ebb'rybody haffuh tek Trial Jestuss? Don' mek me fuh bex, 'cause ef Uh haffuh knock you teday, Uh fuh knock you hebby 'tel Uh fuh hab sin!"

"You fuh hab sin dis minnit," and then they hitched. Two quarreling African males will often bristle up and exchange epithets and challenges for hours without locking horns, but the women come to grips on slight provocation, especially if a masculine name is brought into the controversy, and by the time these ladies were dissevered, each had acquired somewhat of the wool and the raiment of the other. Diplomatic relations were suspended, and their cabins and the ears of their lords were filled with mutterings for several days. A climax was reached when Daphne, baiting a coop with corn, within the privacy of her palings, captured Rumplestiltskin and half a dozen of his affiliated females, and, impounding them under the stock law, held the flock in ransom for three dollars damages. Phoebe swelled with rage, but the memory, fortified by the marks, of her neighbor's finger nails, made her contain herself, and, hurrying to Laguerre, she lodged complaint, upon which Cudjo, the constable, was despatched with a summons to Sister Poinsett to appear as defendant and Sister Polite as prosecuting witness.

And now the belligerents, surrounded by their friends, came in sight and neared the Cross-roads. In the centre of Daphne's group moved a small oxdrawn cart, the defendant on the driver's seat, and behind her a coop containing the impounded poultry. Most of the men walked, while the women rode in carts. The headstalls of oxen and mules were stuck full of sweetgum boughs to keep off the tormenting flies, the mass of foliage suggesting from a distance the coming of Birnam Wood to Dunsinane! At last plaintiff, defendant, witnesses, and spectators met the appointed hour at the appointed place, but he who had bidden them to the legal feast was absent. There were anxious looks for Laguerre. What could have detained one who always disciplined

so severely those who were tardy in attendance
upon his Court? The Negroes exchanged opin-
ions.

"Eh, eh, Uh wunduh 'smattuh 'long de Buckruh!
Him tell we *'sponsubble* fuh git yuh befo' middleday."

"Uh 'speck' 'e meet somebody duh paat' en'
stop fuh talk."

Him ain' lub fuh talk," (derisively).

"Fuh true, bubbuh, Jedge him ain' lub fuh talk,
en' deer him ain' lub fuh eat peawine, en' rokkoon
him ain' lub oshtuh, en' 'ooman him ain' lub—"

"*Yuh 'e come! Yuh 'e come!*" and from the
Slann's Island road Laguerre drove up with his
body servant, Scipio; but, instead of Zouave, the
animal between the shafts of the buckboard was
a sullen looking beast whose large ears flopped
dejectedly. His master seemed in a thundering
temper, and, seating himself without a word, commenced turning over the pages of his book, looking up the stock law applicable to the pending
case. Meanwhile, Scipio enlightened the Negroes
as to the cause of their delay. "Ole Zooab him bin
lame dis mawnin' w'en Maussuh ready fuh staa't,
en' him tell me fuh hitch up dis t'odduh hawss,
name Dead Lock. Now, one time Maussuh bin
een Maa'shull' sto' to Adam Run billage, duh talk,
en' dishyuh same hawss bin hitch to de fench
wid 'e head heng down, duh study. Dr. Baa'nwell

36

binnuh walk pas' de sto', en' him berry lub fuh
yeddy Maussuh cuss, en' him sick 'e bull tarrier
'puntop Dead Lock, en' de tarrier bite'um on
'e yez, en' de hawss bruk loose en' run'way.
Maussuh sho' hab uh gifted mout' fuh cuss. *'E
cuss, 'e cuss, 'e cuss, en' 'e cuss,* en' Dr. Baa'n-
well git 'e pledjuh, 'cause 'e stan'up on 'e po'ch
'cross de road, duh buss' 'eself wid laugh. Attuh-
w'ile, yuh come Dead Lock back down de Bu'n
Chu'ch road, duh drag 'e bridle, en' Maussuh
b'leebe 'tel now, suh 'e *cuss'um* back. Ebbuh
sence da' tarrier bite'um, Dead Lock him lub fuh
balk. Teday we binnuh dribe 'long 'bout two
mile frum yuh, en' puhzac'ly to de cross-road,
we see weh somebody kill one t'unduh snake en'
leff'um middle'uh de road. 'E yent bin dead,
'cause t'unduh snake, Uh dunkyuh hummuch
oonuh kill'um, 'e ain' gwine dead 'tel t'unduh roll.
W'en Dead Lock look 'puntop de snake 'e jump
mos' out de road, en' w'en 'e light back een de
road 'e yent fuh moobe. Maussuh *coax'um, 'e cuss-
'um! 'e coax'um, 'e cuss'um!* 'E tie up one 'e befo'
foot, 'e onloose'um, 'e nebbuh moobe; 'e twis' 'e
tail, 'e cuss'um, 'gen. 'E cuss'um all 'e weeky-day
cuss en' 'e cuss'um all 'e *Sunday* cuss. Dead
Lock' foot *tie een de du't;* 'e nebbuh moobe. Den
Maussuh biggin fuh bex fuh true! Maussuh
hab two bex, 'e bex 'long 'e mout' en' 'e bex 'long
'e yeye. W'en 'e bex 'long 'e mout', 'e kin cuss'um

37

off, but w'en 'e shet 'e mout' en' 'e yeye biggin fuh
tu'n red, da' duh him *dainjus* bex. All ub uh
sudd'nt Uh shum shet 'e mout' tight, sukkuh box-
cootuh, en' 'e yeye tu'n red ez game roostuh' eye.
Den Uh *know* trouble fuh come! 'E study two-
t'ree minnit, 'tel 'e 'membuh 'bout Dr. Baa'nwell'
bull tarrier, den 'e jump out de buggy en' run
to Dead Lock' head en' pull'um down en' ketch
one de hawss' yez een 'e teet' en' mek uh growl
sukkuh tarrier, en' bite'um haa'd ez 'e kin. Dead
Lock *rayre* en' 'e *pitch*. 'E *rayre* en' 'e *pitch*.
Maussuh hab 'e two han' 'roun' 'e neck en' 'e
teet' een 'e yez. W'en de hawss come down to de
groun' Maussuh tu'n'um loose en' climb een de
buggy en' tek'up de reinge en' dribe off bidout
no trouble."

The court convened. Daphne Poinsett was
called.

"Well, suh, Mis' Puhlite him en' me duh navuh.
Us alltwo lib W'aley. Him lub lazy tummuch
fuh mek gyaa'd'n, but 'e berry lub tu'nup en'
t'ing w'enebbuh Uh g'em some. Him hab him
yaa'd full uh fowl. 'E hab 'nuf kind'uh fowl,
some raise duh yaa'd, en' some raise off'uh roos',
'cause him juntlemun berry schemy, en' 'e done
bin Walterburruh two time fuh t'ief hog; one
time de Buckruh ketch'um duh 'ood wid de hog
on 'e back, t'odduh time de Buckruh binnuh ride
pas' 'e house; en' dishyuh same Mis' Puhlite

come to de do' fuh look, en' 'e mout' shine, 'cause Nigguh' mout' w'en 'e greesy shine same lukkuh town Buckruh' shoe, en' w'en de Buckruh look 'puntop de 'ooman' mout' 'e s'pishun hogmeat mek'um stan' so, en' 'e gone een de house en' 'e fin' half de hog heng up, en' one fry'-pan full, duh fiah. Dat mek two time dis 'ooman' husbun' git ketch, but 'e mo' smaa't fuh fowl den 'e yiz fuh hog, en' nobody nebbuh ketch'um 'long fowl, 'cause 'e hab sense 'nuf fuh nebbuh t'ief no roostuh, 'cause w'en roostuh crow, 'fo' dayclean, you kin yeddy'um fudduh, en' ebb'rybody ruckuhnize him own roostuh' crow, en' w'en dem loss roostuh, dey berry aps fuh git up soon duh mawnin' en' liss'n, en' dem kin ruckuhnize puhzac'ly who got dem fowl, ef dem ain' done eat'um, but Mis' Puhlite hab frizzle hen en' Dammynickuh hen en' t'ing, but 'e only hab dishyuh one debble'ub'uh rumpletail roostuh; 'e tail stan' sukkuh rabbit' tail, but 'e fly lukkuh bu'd, en' w'enebbuh 'e fly obuh my fench, you kin yeddy'um, *'cuk, cuk, cuk,'* en' ebb'ry Cryce hen de 'ooman got, hice dem wing en' folluhr'um een my gyaa'd'n en' biggin fuh 'cratch fuh who las' de longes'. Las' week, Jedge, w'en Uh quizzit dis 'ooman 'bout 'e fowl, 'e bex 'cause Uh tell'um him juntlemun bin Walterburruh, en' me nuh him hitch. Den Uh ketch 'e fowl en' pen'um up, en' hol'um fuh t'ree dolluh dammidge, en' dat all wuh Uh got fuh say."

"And very well said," commented the Court.

"Now, Phoebe, for your story."

"Jedge, suh, nutt'n' but de pyo' mean mek dis 'ooman stan' so. 'E bex 'cause I hab fowl en' him ent hab none. 'E yent got nutt'n' een 'e drat gyaa'd'n but two-t'ree tu'nup en' cabbidge, en' 'nuf Jimsin weed en' t'istle. 'E go een 'e gyaa'd'n fuh mek b'leebe suh him duh wu'k, en' all de time 'e duh hide behine de fench fuh yeddy w'at dem t'odduh 'ooman duh talk 'bout him juntlemun. Pinesett, him iz uh berry spo'ty leetle Nigguh, en', 'cause him own lawfully-lady so oagly, him lub fuh talk sweetmout' talk to dem t'odduh 'ooman, en' w'enebbuh 'e go Adam Run, 'e does fetch gunjuh en' nickynack en' t'ing fuh g'em, en' sometime w'en 'e gone duh crik wid 'e cyas'-net fuh ketch mullet en' swimp, him does lef' some uh what 'e ketch to dem t'odduh 'ooman do', en' dat kind'uh mek Mis' Pinesett jallus, 'cause, alldo' him so oagly, seem lukkuh him ent sattify fuh hab him juntlemun fetch bittle fuh none dem t'odduh 'ooman! En', Jedge, Uh yent sattify fuh pay no t'ree dolluh dammidge, 'cause de 'ooman' gyaa'd'n ent wu't', en' 'e git t'ree-fo' aig ebb'ry day 'e hab my fowl een 'e pen, en' 'e got my roostuh shet'up en' lef' my yaa'd full'uh lonesome hen, en' all day dem duh cyackly, en' no roostuh dey dey fuh ansuhr'um, en' please, suh, fuh mek de 'ooman tu'n'um loose."

A FEUD IN FEATHERS

Laguerre looked puzzled. How could "the likeness of any winged fowl that flieth in the air" be brought on all fours with the quadrupedal contemplation of the South Carolina Legislature? It couldn't be done. He must release the darkies and the poultry and have done with both Tar and Feathers! Meanwhile, he was curious to see the rooster which had so rumpled the roseleaves under Daphne, and the constable was commanded to open the coop. A few blows of the hatchet loosened the top, which Cudjo wrenched from the box with a force that sent him backward, as "rumpletail" and his flock, terrified at the abundant local color about them, leaped squawking from their quondam prison and, under leg and wing power, scattered among the undergrowth in every direction. The instinct of the Negroes for their unlawful prey was too strong to be resisted, and nine-tenths of them started in pursuit, forgetting for the moment their fear of Laguerre, whose sense of humor overcame his dignity as he ordered the dismissal of court and case. "Oh, yaas! Oh, yaas!" cried Cudjo, "All yunnuh Nigguh frum W'aley, you done tu'n loose. Ketch yunnuh fowl, eeduhso yunnuh anni*mel*, en' gone home!"

"MORE DEADLY THAN THE MALE"

It was noon on a hot Sunday at the end of August. Laguerre, in shirt sleeves and slippered feet, sat in a big armchair on the wide front piazza of his plantation home. A setter dozed at his feet, rousing himself now and then to snap at the flies that disturbed his rest. On a table at his master's side were papers and magazines and, best of all, a tall tumbler filled with an amber julep. There was no frost upon the glass, because there was no ice in August within a day's journey of Slann's Island, but cool spring water sufficed for the very little dilution that Laguerre tolerated in his favorite drink. The sun was warm, but the breeze was cool and his house, high from the ground, with tall steps running up to the first story, gave full sweep to the winds from the sea. Laguerre mused, and drank—and drowsed, and drank again. Fond as he was of the society of others, he always found himself good company, and when alone was constantly communing with himself in the spoken as well as the unspoken word. How many happy conceits he had with himself, how many droll jokes, as he reviewed in his mind the clever things he had said to others or thought to himself! What a blessing from Heaven is the sense of humor which permits one to laugh at himself, as with himself! Laguerre had the "merry heart" that "goes all the way" and his spirits—save those he drank—were never down very long.

It was harvest season. The Sea-Island cotton fields were just beginning to show the first open bolls, and on the rice plantations a few miles away they had commenced cutting the early rice. The harvest season is a joyful one everywhere, but particularly so to the gregarious Negroes, who love to work in gangs and usually flock from the small farms to the big plantations where they may exchange quip and jest with their fellows. All the morning, groups of happy Negroes, the women decked out in bright calicoes, ginghams and head-kerchiefs, had been passing along the road a few yards in front of the door, on their way to church, shouting and laughing and exchanging pleasantries, as only these childlike, irresponsible people can. However empty the larder, however bare the backs or limbs of their little children, however tortured with pain and trouble their kindred, the merry laugh or the joyous shout is always near the surface.

As one of these groups passed his house, Laguerre, through half-closed eyes, noticed one member of the party, a young man, leave the crowd and walk slowly toward the gate. Lifting the latch he entered and, hat in hand, ascended the tall steps. The dog sprang up and growled, but

at a word from his master turned around a time
or two, lay down, and settled back to his nap.

Laguerre's visitor, who pulled his wool and
scraped his foot on the top step, was in a pitiable
plight; his nose was swollen, his half-closed eyes
were bunged and bloodshot, and a blood-stained
cloth was tied around his head over the left ear.

"Well, Christopher," said Laguerre, "what's
your trouble?"

" *'Ooman,* suh," he replied.

"You seem to be badly hurt."

"Yaas, suh, me nose, one yez, en' alltwo me
yeye, suh. De nose butt, de yez bite, en' alltwo
de yeye 'cratch, suh."

"Who did it?"

" *'Ooman,* suh; da' same Mimer, my lady, wuh
you hitch me to las' C'rismus; en', Jedge, please
suh fuh tu'n we loose, 'cause me nuh him alltwo
onsattify. Ebb'ry time de 'ooman look 'puntop
me 'e yeye red, en', 'ez fuh me, Uh yent wantuh
shum, *'tall.* W'en Uh co't dishyuh 'ooman las'
yeah, Uh bin 'tenshun fuh tek'um to Pa Tumbo
fuh hitch we, but de 'ooman git een 'e head suh
him wan' fuh tie'up *tight,* sukkuh Buckruh, en'
'e coax me fuh fetch'um yuh to you, suh, en' you
done tie we two dolluh wu't'. Now, alldo' Uh
wu'k so haa'd en' g'em mos' ebb'ryt'ing wuh Uh
mek, seem lukkuh ebb'ryt'ing wuh Uh do mek'um
bex, en' him eat 'e bittle w'enebbuh 'e hongry,

45

en' lef' col' hom'ny fuh me fuh eat w'en Uh git home, en', Jedge, uh col'-hom'ny 'ooman ent *wu't'*.

"Las' week Uh binnuh wu'k to Doctuh Grimbull' place duh cut rice, en' Uh nebbuh come home 'tel Sattyday night. W'en Uh git pay'off, Uh buy de 'ooman uh callicro frock en' uh shoesh, en' one Buckruh hat mek out'uh straw, wid two roostuh' fedduh on'um. Attuh Uh walk seb'n mile, en' git home 'bout fus' daa'k, de 'ooman duh seddown een 'e rockin' chair een de yaa'd, en' 'e hab one fiah fuh smoke san'fly. Uh ax'um wuh 'e got fuh eat. 'E say de bittle dey to de fiah. Uh t'row de t'ing wuh Uh fetch een 'e lap, en' w'ile 'e duh ontie'um, Uh gone een de house fuh eat. De fiah done out een de chimbly, en' Uh tek de kibbuh off de pot, en' nutt'n' bin een'um but de staa't *col' hom'ny!* Uh gone out de do'. Uh ax'um, ' 'Ooman, oonuh t'ink man fuh wu'k haa'd to Grimbull' fuh buy callicro frock, en' shoesh, en' Buckruh hat wid two roostuh' fedduh on'um, fuh uh *good-fuh-nutt'n', debble'ub'uh col'-hom'ny 'ooman* wuh binnuh seddown 'puntop 'e rockin' chair eenjurin' de whole week duh do nutt'n'?' De 'ooman suck 'e teet' at me.

"Uh ax'um 'smattuh 'long'um, mekso him ent t'engkful fuh de callicro frock en' de shoe en' de Buckruh hat wid de two roostuh' fedduh on'um. Him say suh 'e bex 'cause Uh nebbuh fetch'um no cawsett, en' 'e say him bin see uh punkin-skin

46

"MORE DEADLY THAN THE MALE"

gal to Adam Run deepo, hab one cawsett fuh mek
'e wais' stan' leetle same lukkuh rice pestle, en'
'e say suh him want cawsett fuh mek him'own
stan' same fashi'n. I tell'um, 'Yaas, ef da' yalluh
gal' wais' stan lukkuh *pestle*, you'own stan' sukkuh
rice *mortar!* You fat wid de pyo' lazy, 'tel you
greesy! Oonuh t'ink fat 'ooman kin 'queeze demself lukkuh t'in 'ooman! Cawsett fuh Buckruh,
en' town Nigguh. Wuh de debble ricefiel' Nigguh
know 'bout cawsett? Dem oughtuh t'engkful
fuh grapewine fuh wrop 'roun' dem wais' fuh hice
dem 'coat up out de jew en' t'ing w'en dem walk
duh paat'! Oonuh wais' stan' sukkuh yo' maamy'
own, en' him'own stan' sukkuh gunjuh barril!'
"W'en Uh tell'um dat, Jedge, de 'ooman bex
'tel 'e fool, en' uh bex 'ooman iz uh *debble'ub'uh
t'ing!* 'E yeye red. Him buzzum duh rise en'
fall sukkuh grummole swell up de du't w'en him
duh bowre t'ru'um. 'E ketch 'e bre't' 'tel 'e stan'
sukkuh watuh-mokkasin duh swalluh frog. 'E
dat bex 'e choke! *'E cyan' talk, t'engk-gawd!*
"W'en Uh shum stan' so, Uh know suh dat
'ooman haffuh lick dat night, 'cause nutt'n' else
gwine sattify'um. One chinkypen t'icket grow
close me house, en' Uh tek me knife out me pocket
en' Uh gone een de t'icket, en' Uh cut two sooply
switch, en' Uh name one 'hom'ny-pot,' en' Uh
name t'odduh one 'fry'-pan,' en, Uh mek up me
min' suh Uh gwine lick dem two t'ing onduhneet'

47

da' 'ooman' skin befo' Uh tu'n'um loose, 'tel him will 'membuh hot bittle long ez 'e lib! Uh feel so sattify een me min', dat Uh didn' bex no mo', 'cause Uh know suh Uh gwine lick dat 'ooman 'tel Uh sattify'um, en' Uh know Uh gwine bring'um to me han'. Uh know suh de cawsett gwine lick *out*, en' de t'odduh t'ing gwine lick *een*."

"Well, did you bring her to your hand?"

"Jedge, suh, lemme tell you. Uh only bin hab da' 'ooman sence las' yeah, en' alldo' 'e mek me bex two-t'ree time, Uh nebbuh hab 'cajun fuh lick'um befo', 'tel now. W'en Uh gone back duh yaa'd wid de two switch een me han', de 'ooman duh seddown een 'e chair, duh *rock*, 'e duh *rock*. Uh tell'um, *''Tan'up, gal.'* 'E 'tan'up, *'traight*. Uh tell'um, 'Drap yo' 'coat.' 'E hab on one deseyuh Balmuhral sku't, dem call'um, mek out'uh one grey clawt' wid some red stripe run 'roun' de bottom. 'E drap him, en' 'e step out, en' 'e yent hab on nutt'n' but 'e shimmy. 'E ax me ef 'e mus' tek him off. Uh tell'um 'No 'cajun fuh do dat, 'cause deseyuh chinkypen kin cut t'ru'um,' but Uh glad fuh yeddy'um talk saaf'ly, 'cause den Uh know Uh gwine bring'um to me han'."

"Well, did you bring her to your hand?"

"Jedge, suh, Uh yent done tell you. Uh tell'um, 'Dishyuh chinkypen name "hom'ny-pot," en' t'arruh one name "fry'-pan." Uh gwine lick dese two t'ing een yo' 'membunce 'tel you nebbuh lef' me

48

fuh eat col' hom'ny 'gen, no mo'.' Den Uh tek
hom'ny-pot en' Uh come down on 'e hanch,
'*chaow!*' De t'ing sweet'n'um so, 'tel 'e jump
off de groun' same lukkuh 'e duh jump rope; but,
Jedge, w'en 'e light, 'e nebbuh light 'puntop no
groun'! '*E light 'puntop'uh me,* en' 'e light sukkuh
wil'cat, wid 'e claw en' 'e teet', alltwo!

"Jedge, de 'ooman so 'ceitful! All de time Uh
t'aw't 'e bin tek off 'e 'coat fuh 'blige me, so Uh kin
lick'um cunweenyunt, but, Jedge, 'e strip 'eself
out'uh de pyo' *schemy,* so 'e kin fight wid nutt'n'
fuh hampuhr'um. Da' 'ooman light 'puntop me so
swif', en' 'e 'taguhnize me so rappit, Uh yent hab
time fuh ketch me bre't'. Fus' t'ing, 'e graff hom-
'ny-pot en' fry'-pan een 'e han' en' bruk alltwo   de
switch. Den 'e ketch alltwo me yez een 'e two han',
en' 'e butt me duh nose, en' mek'um bleed same
lukkuh hog kill! 'E wrop 'e two foot 'roun' my'own
en' 'e t'row me duh groun', '*bim!*' W'en da' fat
'ooman wuh try fuh mek 'e wais' stan' lukkuh rice
pestle fall 'puntop me, Jedge, '*e hebby sukkuh
harricane tree!* 'E t'row me same lukkuh oonuh
t'row cow fuh bran'um en' maa'k 'e yez; en'
him maa'k my'own, too, 'cause 'e mos' bite off
de lef' han' yez, 'tel 'e pit swalluh-fawk een'um.
Den 'e biggin fuh 'cratch out me two eye. Uh
shet'um tight, fuh sabe'um, en' Uh try fuh tu'n
obuh fuh git me yeye close de du't, but da'
debble'ub'uh col'-hom'ny 'ooman seddown 'pun-

top me same lukkuh dem chillun deadfall drap
'puntop'uh sparruh duh stackyaa'd, en' all de
time 'e duh fight 'e nebbuh crack 'e teet', en' da'
duh de t'ing mek me 'f'aid'um so! W'en dem
t'odduh Nigguh een Nigguh-house-yaa'd pull'um
off me, Uh mos' ready fuh dead. Me yeye en'
me nose en' me yez, stan' same lukkuh you shum,
en' Uh kacely able fuh walk. Uh gone to me
bredduh' house fuh sleep las' night, 'cause Uh
yent gwine sleep een no house 'long no shishuh
'ooman 'gen, long ez Uh lib, Jedge, en' please,
suh, fuh suffuhrate we en' ontwis' we, so me nuh
him kin paa't. De Scriptuh say suh man ent
fuh dead mo'nuh one time, but, Jedge, w'en da'
'ooman bin 'puntop me, Uh dead *fo' time*, one de
time w'en 'e butt me nose, 'nodduh time w'en 'e
bite me yez, en' de two t'odduh time w'en 'e binnuh 'cratch out me two eye."

"Don't you know that the Scriptures also say
'whom God hath joined together let no man put
asunder'?" asked Laguerre, quizzically.

"Jedge, suh, Gawd nebbuh jine me en' da'
'ooman! Duh *you* jine we fuh two dolluh, en' 'e
mus' be de debble pit de t'unduh een'um. Jedge,
ef oonuh cyan' ontie me frum da' 'ooman en'
tu'n me loose, Uh gwine fudduh ez Uh kin! Uh
gwine New Yawk! Ef dem Nyankee sell me,
Uh dunkyuh! Ef Uh kin git me bredduh fuh go

een me house en' git me clo'es, Uh nebbuh stop
'tel Uh done cross Stono ribbuh!'"

"Wait," and Laguerre rose and went within,
returning in a few minutes with writing materials
and a replenished glass. Filling out a sheet of
foolscap with a strongly worded admonition to
Mimer enjoining good behavior, he pasted upon
it an impressive red seal and, handing it to Christopher, said: "This will protect you. Hold it
in your hand when you enter your house, and she
will not dare to interfere with you."

"T'engky, Jedge. Uh berry glad fuh tote dis
t'ing fuh mek dem t'odduh Nigguh t'ink suh me
duh counstubble, but Uh nebbuh gwine een me
house no mo' bidout Uh got axe een me han'.
Well, good ebenin', suh. Uh gone now, but, Jedge,
Uh keep on study 'pun how da' 'ooman fool me!
'E so schemy. W'en 'e drap 'e 'coat en' stan' dey
een 'e shimmy, 'e mek me b'leebe suh 'e gwine tek
e' lick so peaceubble, en' all de time him dat 'ceitful, him jis' bin strip fuh fight!'"

"According to the sonnets, Christopher," observed Laguerre, as he buried his nose in the
mint, 'the wiles that in the women are,' their
most intimate acquaintance of the masculine
gender 'shall not know.' "

"Yaas, suh, *da' duh him!*"

"CLEVER ALICE"

Out of a book of German fairy-tales comes the story of. "Clever Alice," a bumptious maiden of the Fatherland, standing, with none too "reluctant feet, where the brook and river meet."

Clever Alice, one supposes, was of an embonpoint not unusual in the land of malt and hops, wherein the brook and river of budding womanhood meet with rather more facility than the buckle and tongue about the belted waistline of the bud!

One evening, as the story goes, Clever Alice was bidden by her parents to go the cellar in, and draw some ale to allay the parental thirst. A dutiful daughter, with doubtless a thirst of her own, she took, the kitchen shelf from, a great pewter tankard, and went below stairs, set her candlestick on the stone floor, drew a low stool before the huge cask, sat down in the cushioned luxury possible only to German maedchen of an embonpoint, placed the flagon the spigot under and turned the tap.

The cask was full and the ale was new, so, until the bubbles should have spent themselves, somewhat, the maiden permitted but a tiny stream to issue from the tap, and while she waited for the slow filling of the tankard, she looked about her. Glancing upward, Clever Alice saw just above her head, a heavy hammer suspended by a thong from a nail driven into a beam in the ceiling. With her mother instinct, her soul was straightway filled with apprehension. "Ach, Gott," she cried: "Suppose, some day, I have a little son, and send him in der cellar down to draw ale, and suppose my little son should sit where I now sit, and suppose by then, the nail should become rusted and fall out, or suppose the thong, become old, should break, and the hammer should drop on my little son's head and kill him! Ach, mein Gott, mein Gott! What shall I do, what shall I do?" And, putting her apron to her eyes, Clever Alice wept!

But a quick thought dried her tears. A husband! A father for her little son! She had not thought of that! And now her thoughts moved in the orderly precession of the equinoxes, canvassing, with the slow precision of the German mind, her marital aspirations in the order of their desirability. Not the individual men! No primitive idea of natural selection found lodgment in the sophisticated mind of a well-ordered young German person. Ach, no! Clever Alice thought in terms of position! As first choice for husband, and father of her little son, her mind soared to the dizzy height of a Sub-lieutenant! Ach, if the so good God would bless her marriage bed with an officer of the Kaiser! Then, as Frau

Sub-lieutenant, she would take precedence over Frau Tax-collector, Frau Professor, Frau Merchant, and on down the line to Frau Undertaker, at the very bottom of the sofa! What a happiness, at all the social gatherings in the village to sit at the upper end of the sofa and queen it over all the other Fraus in the community! But if the God so good denied her the Sub-lieutenant so exalted, perhaps He would graciously send a town clerk, or even a Herr Professor, her way. As Frau Professor she could do very well. Very well indeed, and be sure at least of a position on the upper half of the sofa! But, if it pleased the good God, who always knew best, to commit her to the arms of a husband of lowly station, according to the social standards of the Fatherland, then, His will be done! And, at the worst, a husband was a husband, and a potential father for her little son. Her little son! Ach, Gott! she had forgotten her little Nordic son, who might some day be sitting—just where she now sat so capably—a heavy hammer, hanging by a rotting thong from a rusty nail right over his poor little dolicho cephalic skull! In her agony the sluices were again opened and her tears fell to the floor. And as they fell, they mingled with the ale that, having overflowed the flagon, now flooded the floor of the cellar.

Meanwhile as the tides of malt and brine rose

55

higher and higher over the flags of the cellar, the thirsty parents whom Clever Alice had left upstairs, becoming troubled at the long absence of their cup-bearer, descended into the cool depths to investigate. Here they found Niobe, with her apron to her eyes, sobbing passionately! "Oh," she said, when her anxious mother demanded the cause of her grief, "Suppose some day I have a little son and send him down in the cellar to draw ale, and he should sit just where I am now sitting to draw the ale, and that hammer hanging up there should fall on my little son's head and kill him! Oh, what shall I do? What shall I do?" And her sympathetic parents wailed and blubbered with her, while the ale gurgled rhythmically from the tap and ran away into the distant ratholes of the cellar, arousing their occupants to squeaking protest.

Not until the guttural "glug-glug" of the liquid changed suddenly to a hollow gasp, like the choking sob of a dying man, did the parents of Clever Alice realize that another and more imminent tragedy was before them, for the great cask was empty, while their little grandson, for whose safety they had trembled; their little grandson—the dreamship of their daughter's hopes—was not yet in the offing!

The cask was empty, but the flagon, at least, was full, so a drop of comfort remained! The

Frau took it tenderly in her arms and, followed by her husband and daughter, slowly went the stairs up—and of this story out.

———

A far cry from Thuringia to Toogoodoo; but when, on a sultry September morning, Laguerre drove up to his woodland temple of justice, alighted from the buckboard and threw the lines to old Scipio, he found awaiting him an ebony counterpart of the heroine of the German fairy tale!

Alice Middleton, daughter by an early marriage of the Reverend Tumbo Middleton, of Slann's Island, was born to trouble as the sparks fly upward, and if trouble, abashed, but peeped hesitantly over the rim of the horizon and showed a disposition to come her way, Alice, good hospitable soul, always set out exultantly to meet the visitor and offer the freedom of her house and of her heart.

Alice Middleton was black; not the rusty black of old iron, nor yet the lifeless black of charcoal, but the glossy shade of deep-sea waters under stormy clouds—known on Slann's Island as black-snake-black, in Laguerre's day, but chromatically softened in fashionable circles a generation later into "midnight-blue!"

And out of the midnight that whelmed Alice, the china-whites of her round, unwinking eyes

57

shone forth as the lamps of Charon's craft might have pierced the awful shadows of the Styx!

Laguerre seated himself behind the great box, opened the huge Revised Statutes, thumped heavily with his red hatchet, and with "Oh, yaas! Oh, yaas! Oh, yaas!" Cudjo, the tipstaff, called the court to order.

Other dusky folk clustered about the court awaiting the untangling of the several snarled skeins they had brought to the Law; but Alice would not be denied, and, shouldering her way through the crowd, she stopped in front of Laguerre and fixed him with her eye. Indicating with a contemptuous elbow a stolid young Negro who had followed in her wake, she dropped a low and deferential curtsy and commenced to unwind her ball of yarn.

"Jedge, dishyuh Nigguh, name' Cephas, mek baa'gin fuh hab me fuh wife. W'en him ax me Uh tell'um yaas, 'cause Uh ready fuh hab husbun' en' t'ing, en' da' 'ooman Pa hab fuh wife me en' him cyan' git 'long none'tall, en' Uh glad fuh git'way frum de 'ooman, 'cause you know, Jedge, ef yo' Pa hab 'ooman fuh wife en' de 'ooman—"

"Shut up! Go on with your story."

"Yaas, suh. So w'en de Nigguh ax me Uh tell'um yaas, 'cause Uh ready fuh hab husbun' en' t'ing, en' da' 'ooman Pa hab fuh wife me en' him cyan' git 'long none'tall, en' Uh glad fuh git'way frum de 'ooman 'cause you know, Jedge, ef—"

"Confound your Pa and his ' 'ooman'!"

"Yaas, suh, Jedge; dishyuh Nigguh, name' Cephas, mek baa'gin fuh hab me fuh wife. W'en him ax me Uh tell'um yaas, 'cause Uh ready fuh hab husbun' en' t'ing, en' da' 'ooman Pa hab fuh wife me en' him cyan' git 'long none'tall, en' Uh glad fuh git'way frum de 'ooman, 'cause you know, suh—"

"Stop!" cried Laguerre, as a violent thwack of his red hatchet added emphasis to the order. "Muzzle her," he commanded Cudjo, the tipstaff. "If she says ' 'ooman' again tie a grapevine over her mouth, and *muzzle* her! Now, go on," he said to Alice, "and be devilish careful how you go!"

"Yaas, suh, Jedge; dishyuh Nigguh, name' Cephas, mek baa'gin fuh hab me fuh wife. W'en him ax me Uh tell'um yaas, 'cause Uh ready fuh hab husbun' en t'ing, en' da' lady Pa hab—"

"Lady!" stormed Laguerre, "lady! How dare you use such language to my face?"

"Jedge, him iz Pa *lawfully* lady wuh him hab fuh 'e reg'luh wife."

"Regular or irregular, lawfully or unlawfully, what the devil do I care about your Pa's confounded marital relations! But whatever they

59

are, tho' they be as unnumbered as a flock of blackbirds, never dare to speak of a Toogoodoo pluff-mud Gullah as 'lady' to my face again! Now, go on."

"Yaas, suh, Jedge; dishyuh Nigguh, name' Cephas, mek baa'gin fuh hab me fuh wife. W'en him ax me, Uh tell'um yaas, 'cause Uh ready fuh hab husbun' en' t'ing, en' da' somebody Pa hab fuh wife me en' him cyan' git 'long none'tall, en' Uh glad fuh git'way frum de somebody Pa hab fuh wife, so Uh tell de Nigguh yaas, en' den de Nigguh mek baa'gin fuh hab me fuh wife, but befo' de baa'gin filfil me en' him fall out, en' we nebbuh git hitch, en' me en' him git een shishuh hebby 'tanglem*ent* 'tel Uh fetch'um yuh so you kin tell'um him iz fool, Jedge, 'cause Uh done tell'um 'tel Uh w'ary, en' de Nigguh so haa'dhead 'e yent b'leebe me w'en Uh tell'um!"

"An inexcusably unreceptive individual."

"Yaas, suh. Da' w'at Uh tell'um. Uh 'cuze-'um en' 'buze'um alltwo, but 'e dat stubbunt, 'e shet 'e yez en' 'e nebbuh yeddy me."

"Well, why didn't Cephas 'filfil' his contract? What did you fall out about?"

"Chillun, suh."

" 'Chillun'! Whose 'chillun'?"

"We'own, suh."

" 'We'own'!"

"Yaas, suh. Him'own en' my'own."

"CLEVER ALICE"

"What!" thundered Laguerre. "Have you had the audacity to increase the black population of Adams Run township, St. Paul's Parish, without having previously invoked the sanction of your church—such as it is—or of the magisterial authority invested in me under the statutes made and provided?"

"Suh!"

"What the devil do you mean by having children within my jurisdiction without having either divine or temporal authority?"

"Jedge, suh, me en' da' Nigguh nebbuh bin hab no chillun, neeeduhso no 't'oruhty. We jis' bin mek plan fuh hab'um—de chillun en' de 't'oruhty, alltwo. En', Jedge, da' duh wuh me nuh him binnuh 'spute 'bout, 'cause *me* haffuh *hab* de chillun, enty, suh? En' ef me haffuh hab'um, enty de 't'oruhty fuh tie 'puntop de chillun? Man ent *wu't'* fuh hab no chillun. Gawd nebbuh mek'um fuh hab none. All him fuh do iz fuh be dem farruh. En' farruh ent *nutt'n'!* Enty 'e stan' so, Jedge?"

Laguerre, holding rather strongly to the popular masculine conception of fatherhood, would not commit himself, and commanded Alice to proceed.

Alice proceeded. "You see, Jedge, dishyuh Nigguh, name' Cephas, mek baa'gin fuh hab me fuh wife, en' las' T'ursday ebenin' me en' him

61

staa't fuh gone to Pa' house, so him kin tie we. Uh yent lib to Pa' house 'cause da' somebody him hab fuh wife me nuh him cyan' git 'long none-'tall. Uh lib to me Aunty' house, da' wuh mekso me en' da' Nigguh haffuh gone to Pa' house, fuh git tie."

"Well, did you get tied?"

"No, Jedge, we nebbuh git tie, we nebbuh git to Pa' house, we nebbuh git nutt'n'!—'cep' bex."

" 'Bex!' " mimicked Laguerre, " 'Bex!' What the devil did you 'bex' about?"

"Jedge, me en' da' Nigguh Cephas, wuh mek baa'gin fuh hab me fuh wife, me en' him binnuh gwine 'long de road fuh go Slann' I'lun', en' jis' ez we git to da' low place een de road weh yo' hawss bin balk da' day munt' befo' las' w'en you binnuh comin' yuh fuh sprosecute dem 'ooman wuh lib to W'aley place, 'cause de 'ooman' fowl en' t'ing fly obuh de t'odduh 'ooman' fench en' 'cratch'up 'e gyaa'd'n; da' same low place een de road weh yo' hawss bin balk 'tel 'e foot tie een de du't, 'cause 'e see weh somebody bin kill t'unduh snake en' leff'um een de road, only de snake ent bin dead, 'cause, alldo' de somebody kill-'um, Uh yeddy suh t'unduh snake him nebbuh dead fuh true-true 'tel t'unduh roll; en' w'en yo' hawss look 'puntop de snake, 'e 'f'aid de snake, da' de reaz'n w'ymekso 'e balk, en' same time 'e

62

balk, you jump out de buggy, en' ketch de hawss'
yez een yo' teet', en' mos' bite'um off en'—"

"Stop!" shouted Laguerre. "Confound the
woman! If I had a calaboose I'd fine you for
contempt and lock you up! How dare you say
'yez' to me?"

"Yaas, suh. W'en me en' da' Nigguh, name'
Cephas, wuh mek baa'gin fuh hab me fuh wife;
w'en me en' de Nigguh git to da' low place een
de Slann' I'lun' road weh yo' hawss bin balk munt'
befo' las' w'en you binnuh comin' yuh fuh sprosecute dem 'ooman wuh lib to W'aley place, 'cause
de 'ooman' fowl en' t'ing fly obuh de t'odduh
'ooman' fench en' 'cratch'up 'e gyaa'd'n—da'
same low place een de road weh yo' hawss bin
balk 'tel 'e foot tie een de du't, 'cause 'e see weh
somebody bin kill t'unduh snake en' leff'um een
de road, only de snake ent bin dead, 'cause, alldo'
de somebody kill'um, Uh yeddy suh t'unduh
snake him nebbuh dead fuh true-true 'tel t'unduh
roll, en' w'en yo' hawss look 'puntop de snake,
'e 'f'aid de snake, da' de reaz'n w'ymekso 'e balk
en' same time 'e balk, you jump out de buggy en'
ketch one dem t'ing de hawss hab fuh yeddy wid,
een you teet', en' mos' bite'um—"

Laguerre shot up from his seat as suddenly as
if impelled by the spring of a jumping-jack!
Too full for sound, but not for foam, he sputtered
wrathfully, while through his red hatchet he ut-

tered the thoughts that arose in him: Whack!
Whack! Whack! Whack!—each blow as full of
doom as a clod upon a coffin lid: Whack!
Whack! Whack! Whack!—each stroke a mechan-
ical imprecation! At last he found his voice and
spoke.

"Shut—up! Shut—up! *Shut—up!*" he commanded as he saw clever Alice catch her breath
as if to make a fresh start. "If you dare to say
'yez' or 'yeddy' again, I'll make Cudjo *bite* you!
Now, go on!"

Alice, thrice stung, gave one look at the blue
gums of the grinning tipstaff and began all over
again, with the intentness of an old hound that,
going back to the starting point, essays the trail
once more, while taking thought how to avoid
the nests of yellow-jackets along the way.

"Yaas, suh, Jedge, me en' da' Nigguh Cephas,
wuh mek baa'gin fuh hab me fuh wife, binnuh
gwine 'long de Slann' I'lun' road, en' w'en we git
to da' place weh yo' hawss bin balk da' day munt'
befo' las' w'en you binnuh comin' yuh fuh sprosecute dem 'ooman wuh lib to W'aley place, 'cause
de 'ooman' fowl en' t'ing fly obuh de t'odduh
'ooman' fench en' 'cratch'up 'e gyaa'd'n; da' same
low place een de road weh yo' hawss bin balk 'tel
'e foot tie een de du't, 'cause 'e see weh somebody
bin kill t'unduh snake en' leff'um een de road,
only de snake ent bin dead, 'cause, alldo' de some-

body kill'um, Uh yeddy suh t'unduh snake him
nebbuh dead fuh true-true 'tel t'unduh roll; en'
w'en de hawss look 'puntop de snake 'e 'f'aid de
snake, en' da' de reaz'n w'ymekso 'e balk, en'
same time 'e balk you jump out de buggy, en'
cuss'um 'tel de hawss' foot loose out de du't en' 'e
staa't 'gen.

"Well, suh, Jedge, w'en me en' da' Nigguh
Cephas, wuh mek baa'gin fuh hab me fuh wife,
w'en me en' him git to da' low place een de road,
Uh look onduh me foot een de du't, en' de groun'
kibbuh wid dem big black bull grape. W'en Uh
shum, Uh hongry fuh de t'ing 'tel me jaw leak,
but de grape ripe 'tel, w'en 'e drap, 'e buss' op'n
en' mash'up een de du't, en' dem ent fitt'n' fuh
eat. Den Uh rise me yeye en' look obuh me head,
en', Jedge, w'en Uh look 'puntop de grapewine
wuh dem t'ing bin drap off, 'e full wid grape 'tel
'e black!

"W'en Uh shum stan' so, Uh call da' Nigguh,
name' Cephas, wuh mek baa'gin fuh hab me fuh
wife, en' Uh tell'um Uh hongry fuh dem grape,
en' Uh ax'um fuh climb de tree en' t'row'um
down fuh me so Uh kin gitt'um fuh eat, but de
Nigguh treat me berry no-mannusubble. 'E
suck 'e teet' at me en' 'e say him ent mongkey,
needuhso 'possum, fuh climb tree fuh shake down
grape fuh 'ooman. De Nigguh say him too hebby
fuh climb tree en' swing frum no grapewine,

65

'cause ef 'e han' en' 'e foot slip, him ent got no tail fuh wrop 'roun' de limb fuh sabe 'eself.

"Uh tell'um yaas, Uh know berry well de tail wuh 'e got cyan' specify, 'cause 'e yent w'ut'. Uh tell'um Uh wish 'e *yiz* bin mongkey, den Uh wouldn' haffuh hongry fuh grape, 'cause uh mannusubble mongkey woulduh climb' tree fuh git grape fuh 'e wife en' t'ing, en' dem wouldn' haffuh baig'um so haa'd.

"Den 'e say, ef dat de way how me min' stan', ef Uh t'ink mongkey stan' high mo'nuh man, mekso Uh yent hab mongkey fuh husbun' 'stead-'uh Nigguh? Uh tell'um 'e stan' so fuh true. De only reaz'n Uh yent hab'um iz 'cause none ent fuh dey 'puntop Slann' I'lun.' 'Cause mongkey wuh hab tail, en' willin' fuh climb, iz mo' saa'bis to 'ooman den Nigguh wuh yent got no tail mo'-nuh rabbit, en' too lazy fuh climb!

"Jedge, w'en Uh tell'um dat, de Nigguh swell'-up wid bex 'tel 'e b'ile obuh. Uh nebbuh say nutt'n' mo' to de Nigguh, Jedge, 'cause Uh done say me say, enty, suh?"

"If you have left anything unsaid," observed Laguerre, quizzically, "the court has not charged the omission against you!"

"Yaas, suh. Attuhw'ile de Nigguh biggin fuh cool off, en' de bex leff'um, en' 'e staa't fuh talk peaceubble, same ez ef him nebbuh bin bex, but stillyet 'e stubbunt ez cow, en' e' nebbuh climb no tree. Bumbye, 'e cut 'e yeye 'puntop de grape wuh duh heng obuh we head, en' 'e ax me ef Uh hasty fuh nyam dem grape. Uh tell'um Uh hasty fuh true, 'cause Uh done fuh hongry fuh dem grape. Den de Nigguh say suh nyung Nigguh kin climb tree mos' ez good ez mongkey, 'cause 'e light, en' 'e nebbuh 'quire no tail fuh wrop 'roun' de limb, so 'e say ef Uh kin wait fuh nyam dem grape 'tel some uh we chillun git big 'nuf fuh climb tree, him kin sen' 'e oldes' son fuh swawm up da' grapewine en' shake down de grape, den Uh kin eat 'tel Uh full.

"Jedge, w'en da' Nigguh Cephas done talk, en' Uh look obuh me head en' see how high da' wine swing, en' how dainjus 'e stan', me h'aa't rise een me t'roat, en' w'en Uh try fuh swalluhr'um 'gen, 'e choke me 'tel Uh mos' strangle! Uh say, 'Nigguh, who' chile dat you gwine sen' een da' high place weh nutt'n' 'cep' squerril hab bidness fuh go? Duh my'own, enty?'

"De Nigguh say de chillum fuh be my'own en' him'own, alltwo, 'cause me en' him, alltwo, fuh hab'um. En' 'e say me kin tek 't'oruhty obuh de gal chillun, but him fuh tek 't'oruhty obuh de boy chillun en' rule'um, cause him iz man, en' me duh nutt'n' but 'ooman, en' 'e say man haffuh dictate obuh boy chillun, en' 'ooman ent fuh hab nutt'n' fuh do wid'um. 'E say him kin sen' him son fuh jump off de tree top, en' eb'nso ef 'e dead, 'e maamy ent got nutt'n' fuh do wid'um, 'cause de boy blonx to 'e farruh.

"Jedge, w'en de Nigguh talk 'bout dead, me h'aa't en' me mout' alltwo full'up 'tel dem alltwo run obuh one time! Me ap'un haffuh ketch de watuh wuh run out me yeye, but da' Nigguh yez haffuh ketch wuh come out me mout', enty, suh? Uh tell de Nigguh: 'Wuh you got fuh do wid dem chillun me fuh hab? *Nutt'n'!* Enty me fuh hab de boy en' de gal alltwo? Ef 'e *yiz* hab, enty me fuh hab'um? En' ef me haffuh hab'um, enty me fuh tek 't'oruhty obuhr'um? Ef you wan' boy fuh climb tree lukkuh squerril, hab'um fuh you'-self. Don' bodduh no 'ooman fuh hab'um fuh you! Ef you so smaa't, budduh, *hab'um, hab'um!*'

"Jedge, w'en Uh gitt'ru empty me mout', me yeye staa't fuh leak, 'cause Uh look 'puntop dem obuhripe grape mash'up een de du't, en' Uh study 'bout da' po' leely Nigguh wuh me fuh hab, en' Uh shum een me sperrit weh him drap out de tree en' mash'up een de du't same lukkuh dem grape, en' Uh see de grape' skin duh bleed, en' Uh see de leely Nigguh duh bleed, en' me h'aa't so hebby Uh roll obuh een de road fuh leh de watuh run out me two eye! Uh tell de Nigguh Uh yent wan' no chillun! Ef me po' leely chillun haffuh dead en' bleed lukkuh dat, Uh nebbuh *yiz* fuh hab none!—En' Uh yent fuh hab nutt'n' fuh do wid no man, needuh!"

68

"A very proper afterthought, a very wise precaution," remarked the Court quizzically. "And now, what do you want me to do?"

"Please, suh, Jedge, tell dishyuh Nigguh Cephas him iz fool."

"Take 'dishyuh Nigguh Cephas' and go to the devil," shouted Laguerre. "Stop! Fetch him here to me next Saturday."

"THE MAN IN THE CASE"

Mid-September with its burning suns and heavy dews. Late corn in wide fields and narrow patches had been stripped of its blades, and the bundles of greenish-gold fodder, slowly curing on the "topped" cornstalks upon which they were impaled, filled the heavy air with the fragrance of new-mown hay, but, withal, an added acrid tang that brought to sensitive nostrils a sneezy suggestion of hayfever.

Crows flapped slowly over the ripening fields, flying straight, though turning inquisitive heads from side to side to spy out the land and appraise the promise of the harvest. And as they flew they uttered the contented "all's-well-with-the-world" note with which they always welcome the autumn. Circling over the marshes, their congeners the fish-crows, intent upon fiddler-crabs, drawled their double notes raucously: "caw-aw, caw-aw," with a flat Low-country—almost a Gullah—intonation. In the live-oaks, bluejays, yet other feathered kindred, scolded and chattered in the sharper, livelier tones their voices take in the fall, as if they were counting over the acorns they would presently cache for the winter's store.

In the wide angles of the fence corners tall stalks of goldenrod supported lovely drooping heads, among whose heavy, honey-laden blooms bees swarmed and droned. In other crooked corners, clumps of sumac slowly changed from green to bronze and red; leaves and berries, nearing life's winter together, as a loving couple, growing old, walk hand in hand toward the sunset.

The open broomgrass fields, changing to darker shades of green as the summer passed, now faintly blushed in sea-shell tints of pink that would deepen as the season advanced, until the coming of ice would chill the ruddy sap of life, and its beauty would vanish in a night, leaving the tawny straw to a slow and wasting death— bundled into primitive brooms to sweep the rough floors of lowly cabins, or to go up in smoke, swiftly and gloriously, in the fires that sometimes sweep in rolling billows of flame, across fields of tinder. But winter with its brooms and fires was yet far away, and now, at the threshold of autumn, the wine of life still throbbed in every blade of grass.

And the edges of myrtle thickets and briarpatches, the paths and roads that traversed fields and open spaces were broidered with the soft purple "petticoat-grass" so called because of its affinity for ladies' petticoats in the mid-Victorian days when ladies wore them. In the icy grasp of winter these, too, would presently be as grass cut

ADAMS RUN VILLAGE SCENE.

down and withered, and the winds of March would send them whirling down the open roads, or dancing across the plowed fields as lightly as dandelion seeds on silken wings. But fairy flights were for their wild and reckless age. Deep-rooted, now they clung to the soil with the passionate ardor of youth all through the burning days from sunrise, when, drenched with dew, the purple clusters glistened like amethysts strewn along the way, to nightfall, when, through the veil of the dusk, dim violet eyes, like those of cloistered houris, peered out of the shadows!

The pinelands, too, were full of loveliness. The forest floor was flower-flecked with the opulent yellow and purple blooms of autumn, as if Nature, about to die, lavishly set forth her bier! The pygmy oak scrub that clustered thick among the pines, showed here and there a ruddy leaf—a wound, a clot of blood, where soon, under the sharp knife of the frost to come, the woods would bleed as in a shambles!

The glossy blue-black pods of partridge-peas were ripened now, and rattled at the touch; and those who walked the pinelands were often halted, as their feet set off the alarm for which all who traverse Low-country forests must ever listen apprehensively. The faint rattle of the partridge-peas at his feet has brought many a bare-foot boy "up standing," poised for a spring, while he listened for the further warning of the diamond-back, always so hard to locate.

In the swamps, the feathery foliage of the cypress slowly changed to the yellow tints of autumn, and the leaves of the tupelos reddened, while their berries deepened from green to purple, with the rich bloom of ripe damson plums. Here in December, the robins, wintering in Low-country forests, would feast, "far from the madding crowd's ignoble strife," far, too, from the deadly guns of the thoughtless and the ignorant, whites and blacks, that would offer them "Southern hospitality" when, in the late winter, they would cluster thick among the shrubbery around the settlements, their ruddy breasts glowing like the dimmed lamps of Christmas-trees as they flecked the dark foliage of cedar and wild-orange. Here, too, they would feast, but, like Belshazzar's, a feast of death!

But in Laguerre's day robins were still thick in the swamps, and often they came down as early as October, upon which the local weather-prophets invariably predicted an early and a severe winter. When their prophecies were verified, the prophets hugged themselves, preened their prophetic feathers, and shivered happily all through the winter, until spring warmed the world again. If, despite the prophecies, Nature had her way, and the winters were mild, the prophets went into winter quarters, dumb. For that man is rare indeed who loves truth enough to confess a fault, or admit an error of judgment!

Under the ardent sun, the gray-green marshes became more gray than green, with here and there a touch of yellow light like that which rests upon wide fields of ripening grain. But only a touch, for the marshes, whatever the season, always show, however dull, the green of life, of hope!

The early rice on the great plantations had all been cut and stacked, and the rice-birds, first fattening themselves on the milky, unripe grain, had tithed their flocks to fatten the planters and their epicurean friends in "the City", and now moved on in leisurely flight to their winter quarters in the far South.

Laguerre inclined to materialism. The blue September haze meant less to him than the fragrant incense that rose from his richly colored meerschaum. The faint "tweet, tweet" of rice-birds, passing over in the night, brought not poetic thoughts of the pathetic little migrants, guided through the pathless dark to distant unknown lands under the magic and the mystery of an unseen hand—but regrets that for nearly a twelvemonth his table would lack the rice-bird-rice pilaus his palate so approved.

The broad marshes, sweeping to meet the sky;

the rimpling river winding through them to the sea, told him nothing of the flowing tides that rise and fall as the heart of Nature throbs in all the oceans, near and far. He only hoped the plantation boys would not forget to catch the crabs, and that at low water in the evening old Scipio would remember to "cast" in the creek for mullet and shrimp. And if the beauty of the purple petticoat-grass fed for a moment the roving lust of the eye, the ear of his mind quickly caught the whisper of starched cambric, for petticoats were petticoats, while grass was only grass!

So Laguerre fared forth to his outdoor Court-room, a little glade in the pine forest not far from Toogoodoo bridge, whither he had commanded Alice Middleton to appear in her own proper person, fetching with her "dishyuh Nigguh Cephas," a dusky swain who had bargained to take her to wife. Before the promise had ripened into fulfilment, however, the minds of Alice and Cephas had clashed in respect to the authority each of them should exercise over the children they purposed having, according to the laws of Nature made and provided. Cephas, yielding the prospective girl children to Alice, staked out in advance his claim to all the boys that should come their way; but Alice, having strong matriarchal convictions, insisted that she who bore the children should have dominion over them, and held

that man's part in the scheme of life was but a
minor and perfunctory one, at best. Having
called Cephas a fool, Alice, complaining that the
stubborn creature wouldn't take her word for it,
had brought him to Laguerre on the preceding
Saturday for a ruling, but the Court, not caring
to give a "horseback" opinion on so momentous
a matter, had bidden the disputants hold their
peace for seven days and attend him here.

The twain were waiting when Laguerre drove
up, and with them many neighbors, men and
women, who had come to see the fun, for laughter was always on tap at these weekly sessions
of the Sylvan Court.

Cudjo Hawlback, Laguerre's constable and tipstaff, raised his raucous voice; his flat Gullah
"Oh, yaas, oh, yaas, oh, yaas!" echoed through the
pineland and convened the Court.

Laguerre was in a rollicking humor, and, loving the sound of his own voice, prepared to enjoy himself as only a lone and loquacious Aryan
can among half a hundred blacks, all of them
hanging upon his words, and none of them daring
to dispute him.

Whacking his red hatchet vigorously to command order where all was already as orderly as a
Quaker meeting, he looked fiercely at Clever
Alice, who stood in the front row, poised for
speech, with Cephas in a telepathic leash, at heel.

"Well," the Court demanded: "Have you and 'dishyuh Nigguh Cephas' reached an amicable adjustment of your differences?"

"Suh?"

"During your seven days of mutual meditation, have your minds met in respect to bull-grapes, children and monkeys? In short, is his mind now 'on all fours' with yours?"

"Jedge, da' Nigguh Cephas' min' dey pun all fo' 'e foot fuh true, 'cause 'e stubbunt ez mule en' cow, alltwo one time, en' 'e nebbuh climb no tree. Uh talk to de Nigguh 'tel me jaw w'ary, en' stillyet 'e min' jam all fo' uh 'e foot een de du't en' back 'e yez en' heng back. Me mout' cyan' moobe'um out 'e track, 'cause 'e min' balk sukkuh yo' hawss bin balk da' time munt' befo' las' w'en you binnuh comin' yuh fuh sprosecute dem 'ooman wuh lib to W'aley 'cause de 'ooman' fowl fly obuh de t'odduh 'ooman' fench en' 'cratch'-up 'e gyaa'd'n; en' de hawss balk 'cause w'en 'e get to da' low place een de Slann' I'lun' road weh somebody bin kill t'unduh-snake, only de snake ent bin dead fuh true-true, 'cause Uh yeddy suh, Uh dunkyuh how dead you kill'um, t'unduh-snake—"

"Go to thunder with your 't'unduh-snake'— dead or alive!" shouted Laguerre. "And the next time you say a word about my horse balking; the next time I hear 'sprosecute dem 'ooman

wuh lib W'aley', I'll make Cudjo build a pen and
lock you up! Stop! You've talked enough.
Let's see what this downtrodden masculine worm
has to say for himself. Stand forth, Cephas!"

Cephas stood forth, hesitantly, while Alice put
her arms akimbo and regarded him contemptuously, as one who would presently, under the
mandate of the Court, usurp her precious privilege of speech!

"Well, what have you to say for yourself?
Why the devil don't you say it?" Laguerre demanded, while Cephas twisted his battered wool
hat in nervous hands and licked his dry and reluctant lips. "Are you dumb?"

"Jedge, suh, me mout' dead, fuh true, 'cause
Uh nebbuh git chance fuh nyuze'um none'tall,
eb'nso fuh crack me teet', sence you tu'n we loose
yuh las' Sattyday. En' me mout' done dry'up!
See how 'e stan', suh? Uh yent got nutt'n' but
yez!

"Jedge, sence you tu'n da' gal loose 'puntop me,
en' tell'um fuh 'suade me fuh gone him way, Uh
nebbuh bin hab no peace! Me yez bin full'up
wid chillun en' grape en' mongkey, 'tel Uh dream
'bout'um! Ebb'ry night w'ile Uh duh sleep dem
t'ree t'ing tangle'up een me dream, 'tel Uh cyan'
suffuhrate'um! Fus', Uh see de grape 'pun de
wine, en' de mongkey een de tree, en' de chillun
'pun de groun'. Den, attuhw'ile, de chillun dey

79

'puntop de wine, de grape dey een de tree, en' de mongkey dey 'pun de groun'. Bumbye, grape dey 'pun de groun', mongkey 'pun de wine, en' chillun een de tree! Fus' t'ing you know, w'en 'e change, 'gen, de wine duh choke de chillun, de tree duh try fuh root 'eself up out de du't, en' de grape duh bite de mongkey een 'e yez! Jedge, suh, dat how da' gal' mout' mek shishuh cunfushun een me min'! 'E twis' me up *tummuch!*

"En' ebb'ry time 'e stop fuh ketch 'e bre't', ef 'e see me staa't fuh crack me teet' fuh 'spute'um, him bruk een 'gen, en' tell me you say him fuh talk'um out, en' 'e nebbuh 'low me fuh say nutt'n!"

"You seem to be doing pretty well now," said the Court.

"Yaas, suh, Jedge, dis bin de fus' chance Uh bin hab, en' me jaw jis' biggin fuh git limbuh good. Las' night, suh, da' gal staa't fuh talk soon ez sundown come. Me en' him binnuh seddown 'pun de step to 'e Aunty' house. De gal nebbuh eeb'n ax me fuh eat! Uh hongry 'tel me belly nyaw me sukkuh squerril nyaw hick'rynot! De gal him full'up wid wu'd 'tel him nebbuh seem fuh hongry none'tall! Him hab wu'd een 'e mout' same lukkuh him bin hab watuh een piggin, en' same fashi'n him por'um een alltwo me yez, one time! Me yez full 'tel dem run obuh, but de gal nebbuh stop! Soon ez 'e empty 'e mout', de wu'd

80

full'um up 'gen, en' soon ez 'e full'up, him t'row'um 'puntop me!

"Jedge, w'en da' gal fus' biggin fuh talk las' night, de sun yent bin down good. Bumbye, w'en de sun gone 'e lef' de gal duh talk behine'um, en' same time 'e lef' 'bout half de moon duh ride high een de element. Attuhw'ile, de gal' Aunty, him yez git w'ary, en' 'e gone een 'e house fuh sleep. Attuh him gone nutt'n' dey dey fuh yeddy'um 'cep' me en' da' moon', en' Uh glad fuh shum een de sky, 'cause, alldo' 'e stan' fudduh, him is sawt'uh cump'ny fuh me, 'cause him haffuh yeddy de gal too, enty, suh? Berry well.

"Jedge, Uh dunno wuh kind'uh yez da' moon got, but attuhw'ile seem lukkuh him yez fuh full'-up sukkuh my'own. Him do berry well at de fus', but attuh two hour done pass, Uh shum stoop 'e head, en' 'e seem ez ef him duh mek plan fuh sneak down da' sky easy ez 'e kin, en' creep off to 'e res' en' lef' me fuh yeddy da' t'ing by meself wid nobody fuh keep me cump'ny. Me h'aa't hebby, but Uh cyan' do nutt'n', so Uh haffuh tek'um ez 'e come—en' 'e come fas'! Jedge, suh, Uh nebbuh know summuch bull-grape, en' mongkey, en' Nigguh chillun bin een de New-nited State lukkuh Uh bin yeddy 'bout las' night!

"De moon creep down de sky. 'E creep, creep, berry slow, but 'e duh gwine, enty, suh? W'en 'e come to de tree top, seem ez ef him pick 'e

chance fuh dodge, en' 'e drap behine de tree,
quick, en' 'e git'way frum de 'ooman en' gone!
Ebb'ry now en' den Uh shum peep t'ru de tree
fuh watch, but 'e nebbuh shine fuh true-true no
mo'. Jis' befo' 'e gone 'e peep out at me one mo'
time, lukkuh him duh say, 'So long, Budduh. Uh
sorry fuh lef' you, but man haffuh 'fen' fuh 'eself,
you know. Uh gwine now, en' you haffuh yeddy'-
um fuh you'self, you, one—en' you Gawd.' En'
de night swalluhr'um up!

"Jedge, you t'ink de daa'k mek da' 'ooman slow
'e mout'? 'E nebbuh do'um! 'E onrabble'um
mo' fas'! 'E roll'um, en' 'e roll'um. 'E nebbuh
stop! De mo' 'e daa'k, de mo' 'e roll'um, 'tel
bumbye, middlenight come—"

"And dark as winter was the flow of Iser,
rolling rapidly," quoted Laguerre, delightedly.

"Dat duh de Gawd' trute, Jedge! De mo'
daa'k de middlenight stan', de mo' rappit de gal
roll'um! Uh nebbuh say nutt'n'! Uh nebbuh
hab chance. Uh stan' sukkuh hog wuh git pen'up
een fench. Ebb'ry time de hog t'ink 'e see gyap
een de fench weh him kin git out, en' mek fuh de
hole, befo' him kin reach'um, somebody dey dey
wid stick fuh jook'um back! W'enebbuh Uh
nigh de hole, da' gal' mout' dey dey fuh jook me
back! So, Uh le'm'lone, en' de gal' mout' stop
by 'eself, 'cause man ent fuh stop'um. Den,
Jedge, Uh t'engk Gawd, en' same lukkuh da'

82

moon bin do, Uh creep off easy fuh sleep. En' dat duh all wuh Uh know."

"You have imparted your knowledge graphically and have illuminated a dark subject."

"Suh?"

"You have shown the prospective wife of your bosom to be quite as black as she had been painted."

"Yaas, suh, Jedge, de gal black, fuh true, but Uh yent bodduh 'bout dat, 'cause Uh black meself, en jackdaw ent hab no bidness fuh fau't crow 'cause 'e fedduh stan' leetle kind'uh daa'k. Uh yent min' 'bout de black, lukkuh Uh min' 'bout de bex. De bex een da' gal duh de t'ing wuh bodduh me; en', ef Uh fuh hab'um fuh wife, do, Jedge, ef you please, suh, git de gal straight een 'e min', en' tell'um wuh him fuh do befo' me nuh him git tie, 'cause ef you wait fuh 'splain'um 'tel attuh we done hitch, me en' de gal fuh 'taguh-nize one'nurruh sukkuh jackass en' cow haa'-ness'up togedduh een de same oxin-cyaa't—needuh one fuh pull nutt'n'!

"En', Jedge, ef me en' him fuh hab chillun, please, suh, tell'um w'ich one him fuh hab, en' w'ich one me fuh hab—attuh de chillun done bawn! Da' gal' mout' binnuh gwine sence T'ursday befo' las', jis' 'cause Uh tell'um w'en we chillun git big 'nuf fuh climb tree Uh gwine mek one de boy climb da' grapewine en' shake down de grape fuhr'um, en' de gal 'f'aid 'e chile gwine drap out de tree en' dead, en 'e staa't fuh cry 'bout 'e dead chile, alldo' 'e yent staa't fuh mek plan fuh hab de chile, en w'en 'e gitt'ru cry, 'e biggin fuh quawl, en' 'e nebbuh stop quawl frum dat to dis! Eb'nso, Jedge, de gal 'buze me so sabbidge, 'e say ef mongkey bin 'puntop Slann' I'lun', him woulduh hab'um fuh husbun' 'stead'uh me, 'cause mongkey kin climb tree!"

"You are at least second choice. Lacking the monkey, Alice has set her cap for you!"

"Yaas, suh, Jedge, da' wuh de gal say. Dat how 'e bex me summuch. Him bin pit de mongkey fus'!"

"According to the anthropologists, Cephas, the monkey, as the ancestor of the African, has always been 'fus'!' Now," said Laguerre, turning to Alice, who tense with excitement awaited her turn, "the ground, including trees and grapevines, has been pretty fully covered by the two of you, who have cut such verbal antics before high heaven as would have made your arboreal and anthropoidal ancestors weep for very envy!

"Now," he demanded, "lacking the monkey, do I understand that you have picked out Cephas for your husband?"

"Jedge, suh, me nebbuh pick'um, suh, him pick me!"

"A euphemism! A fable! Pick you! How

84

the devil did that myth of natural selection get loose on Toogoodoo?"

"Yaas, suh, Jedge, dishyuh Nigguh Cephas mek baa'gin fuh hab me fuh wife. W'en de Nigguh ax me, Uh tell'um yaas, 'cause Uh ready fuh hab husbun' en' t'ing, en' da' somebody Pa hab fuh wife me en' him cyan' git'long none'tall en'—"

"I'm not at all surprised, if the 'somebody' has ears to hear! Well, having intimated, as is the way of your sex, that you were ripe and hanging on the tree ready to be picked, I suppose 'dishyuh Nigguh Cephas' summoned up the courage to pick you."

"No, suh, Jedge, de Nigguh nebbuh pick me off no tree. Him ax me to me Aunty' house."

"And you, as there were no monkeys on Slann's Island, were graciously moved to accept him."

Alice covered her face with her apron. When she withdrew it, her eyes glistened with unshed tears. "Jedge," she whimpered, "Uh sorry Uh ebbuh bin call da' mongkey name. Uh nebbuh study 'bout hab no mongkey fuh husbun'. Uh yent fuh hab none! Uh yent wan' nutt'n' fuh do wid no mongkey, Jedge. Uh jis' call de mong-key' name fuh bex de Nigguh, en' Uh bex'um 'cause Uh lub'um."

Weeping freely now, her grief touched some human chord in the hearts of the humble black folk about her, and they were silent.

"Jedge," she sobbed. "Nemmin', suh, 'bout tell dishyuh Nigguh nutt'n' 'bout dem chillun me nuh him fuh hab, needuhso' bout no 't'oruhty, 'cause me en' him kin 'gree 'bout dat. Soon ez sundown come, Uh gwine tek dishyuh Nigguh Cephas to Pa' house, so him kin tie we. En', Jedge, las' Sattyday Uh bin ax you fuh tell Cephas him iz fool, but nemmin' 'bout dat, suh. No 'cajun fuh tell'um now, 'cause me kin tell'um, en', attuh Uh lub'um summuch, enty Uh kin 'buze'um fuh meself? You know how 'e stan', enty, suh?"

"Yes," said Laguerre, "I know."

THE TRIALS OF TUMBO

Among those who had attended the last session of the Sylvan Court, Laguerre's roving eye had fastened upon the burly form of the Reverend Tumbo Middleton, father of "Clever Alice", as meat for investigation.

Tumbo, not content with the privileges inhering in the pastorate of the Slann's Island Methodist Church—privileges regarded by the masculine members of the congregation as being above computation—had organized a local chapter of the "Sons and Daughters of I Will Arise," the entire membership, excepting only himself, as President, composed of the younger women of his flock, married and single.

The Society, a benevolent organization, had chosen from among the thirty sisters, a Secretary-lady and a Treasurer-lady, whose duties included the investigation of claims for sick benefits, and payments for those found to be just.

With only one man to quarrel over, and he an experienced male, wise enough to distribute his attentions impartially, the Slann's Island lodge functioned smoothly enough. There had been no friction to speak of until the close of the preceding year, when it was discovered that at Christmas, Sister Judy Chizzum, Treasurer-lady, finding that she, alone, among the entire membership, had drawn no sick benefit during the year, because she had not been sick, paid herself seven dollars, the sum each of the others had claimed and received for alleged distempers, which Judy suspected were rather more of the pocket than of the body. This, she conceived to be equity, if not law, but her position was challenged by Sister Bina Fields, Secretary-lady, who complained to "Pa Tumbo," president of the society, that his Treasurer-lady had exceeded her authority. The president took the treasure-box into his keeping and, like a wise man, reserved his decision in respect to the dispute between the warring sisters. But he also reserved the old cigar box which contained the treasure—held on to it so long that the sisters haled him before Laguerre for an accounting.

At the hearing, during one of the midsummer sessions of Laguerre's Court, Tumbo insisted that the treasure-box when opened contained nothing— " 'e bin full'up wid de pyo' nutt'n'!" as he expressed it. Before the court could go further into the case, the proceedings were interrupted by the breaking into the circle of a stampeding ox, whose rider, with only a grapevine bridle, could not control him. When the ox had passed, the laughter that followed the incident so convulsed Laguerre that he suspended for the time further consideration of the proceedings against

Tumbo, and, as the Society sisters thereunto appertaining had said no more about the matter, he dismissed it from his mind, assuming that the Negroes had adjusted their differences among themselves.

When in mid-September, however, Laguerre saw Tumbo, flanked by Sisters Judy Chizzum and Bina Fields, among those present at the rapprochement between Clever Alice and "dish-yuh Nigguh Cephas," who in the home-stretch of the matrimonial sweepstakes had come in first, with the monkey nowhere, his mind harked back to the former trial so suddenly suspended and, at the thought that they might have come together of their own accord without the exercise of his good offices or the authority of his honorable court, his anger began to rise, and before the rising of his court, he ordered Cudjo to command Tumbo's presence on the following Saturday, accompanied by the feminine officials of the "I Will Arise."

A threatening day, cool and overcast. An easterly wind that, with the harvest moon, now at the full, brought brimming tides that topped the causeways and spread far over the marshes. Gulls and other sea-birds followed the flowing tides, to feed at their recession in the shallows.

Modern weather-sharps hold the equinoxes lightly, but in Laguerre's day, when daily news-

papers and Government weather reports seldom
came into the hinterlands remote from the rail-
ways, local prophets, white and black, with long
memories of September gales, watched the approach of the autumnal equinox with apprehension, and if a full moon brought spring tides, and
a flying scud suggested a tropical disturbance in
the Yucatan channel, apprehension ripened into
anxiety, if rice was yet in the fields.

Local weather observers, always out of doors
and close to Nature, are not to be held lightly.
As the Minnesota Swede, smelling a coming snow
storm hours before it arrives, will sniff the air
and say to a compatriot:

"Ay tank he bane going shnow. Ay shmall
him."

"Ay tank he come in apoudt two yoomps. Ay
shmall him too." So if the dusky Low-country
prognosticator cuts his eye at the clouds and the
wind and, sniffing the moisture, grunts: " 'e gwine
we'dduh," it usually does.

The easterly winds that sweep the Low-country, always biting and penetrating in winter,
charged with the rawness of the sea, become in
summer the softest, sweetest winds that blow,
for the chill of winter is but the tonic freshness
of summer, tempering the torrid heat as winds
from no other quarter do.

And the first cool September days, like twilight

in the desert, bring solace and relief to those who
have borne the burden of the day through the
long hot summer. But with the energizing hint
of bracing winter weather to come, there's always a pang at the passing of summer—in the
hearts, at least, of those who are near to Nature.

Laguerre fared forth to his trysting place in
the woodland glade. Old Scipio drove the
springy buckboard with Zouave between the
shafts. Scipio was a good listener—not the least
of the qualifications that commended him to Laguerre—for Laguerre talked incessantly. Had
he been without human companionship, he would
have talked just the same, to Zouave—or the
buckboard—but 'twas a great comfort to have an
intelligent and sympathetic listener just at one's
elbow; a trained servant who knew exactly when
to chuckle, when to say "dat's so, suh," or "Gawd's
trute, Maussuh!" and, when a laugh was expected
but not warranted, knew just how to jerk the
lines and whip up the horse to hide the hollow-
ness of the cachinnation!

Such a servant was beyond price, and Laguerre
held him highly; but, more than servant, the old
Negro was guide, philosopher and friend, helping his volatile master out of many small difficulties, and knowing just how long to let him blow
off steam and when adroitly to shut him off.
And Scipio's knowledge of Negro nature was far

deeper than his master's, for Laguerre talked too much to be observant—his ears were too busy listening to the sound of his voice, his eyes were too intent upon watching the effect his voice was having upon the ears of others, for him to see or hear less important things—and, as a rule, he didn't!

But Scipio, old and shrewd and wise, could thread the tangled thickets of the Negro mind as easily as a raccoon climbs a tree. "Maussuh, Nigguh ent nutt'n' fuh know! Uh kin see t'ru-'um too easy. 'E min' twis'up en' tanglety, suk-kuh briah-patch, fuh true, but 'e hab paat' t'ru-'um, en 'alldo' de paat' stan' crookety ez Toogoodoo Crik, Uh know how fuh trabble'um, enty, suh? Berrywell."

And he did. Often when Laguerre stubbed his psychological toe while trying to lay hands on the truth, flitting like a will o' the wisp through a witness's wilderness of words—a quiet hint from Scipio would show him how to head off the elusive stranger, and gain him credit within his jurisdiction for a knowledge of Negro character that, save through old Scipio, he did not possess.

And now that Tumbo lay heavily upon the magisterial mind, Laguerre questioned Scipio as to the sturdy black oak and the many clinging vines that hung upon him.

THE TRIALS OF TUMBO

"Scipio, what do you know about that bull-alligator, Tumbo?"

"Maussuh, you name'um right, 'cause dat puhzac'ly wuh 'e yiz. No, suh! W'en you call da' Nigguh bull-alligettuh you nebbuh call'um out 'e name! En', Maussuh, you ax me wuh Uh know 'bout'um. Uh know'um t'ru en' t'ru same lukkuh Uh know all deseyuh Nigguh preachuh. Dem all stan' same fashi'n. Dem hab only two t'ing fuh study 'bout—bittle en' 'ooman! Some de preachuh study mo' 'bout de bittle, en' some de t'odduh one study mo' 'bout de 'ooman, but all deseyuh hebby bull, lukkuh Buh Tumbo, dem fuh study 'bout alltwo! En' de bittle en' de 'ooman stan' close togedduh, 'cause ebb'ry time de preachuh wisit de 'ooman, de 'ooman haffuh cook fuhr'um, enty, suh? Berrywell. En' de preachuh keep de 'ooman po', 'cause w'en de preachuh eat to de 'ooman' house, him fuh nyam de bes'! Nutt'n' 'cep' de bes' fuh suit. En' ef de 'ooman got uh ten cent tie een 'e ap'un, da' preachuh fuh ontie de knot en' grabble'um out. Him fuh grabble attuh da' ten cent sukkuh tarrier grabble attuh grummole, en' 'e nebbuh stop 'tel 'e gitt'um. W'en de po' 'ooman look 'puntop 'e ten cent een de preachuh' han', 'e berry mo'nful but 'e drap uh cutchy en' 'e say 'me money gone, but, tengk-gawd, Uh g'em to de Lawd'; en' de preachuh gone!

93

"Maussuh, Uh tell you de trute, ef Gawd bin pit hoe een dem Nigguh han' en' tell'um fuh knock grass all t'ru de week en' preach w'en Sunday come, da' pulpit nebbuh woulduh shum. W'en Sunday come dem woulduh 'tretch'out een de sunhot duh sleep! Dem ent lub da' pulpit 'cause 'e dey een de Lawd' house fuh Him saa'-bunt fuh stan' een fuh resplain Him wu'd. No, suh! Dem lub'um 'cause de Nigguh kin hab chance fuh talk out'um fuh tickle de 'ooman' yez, so dem kin gone to de 'ooman' house en' seddown close to de 'ooman en' 'e skillet, en' watch'um all-two one time.

"En' ez fuh Buh Tumbo! Him ent sattify wid de 't'oruhty wuh 'e done got obuh all de female een de chu'ch, so him haffuh pen'up dem t'irty nyung sistuh een da' 'Syety, en' mek sanctify fench 'roun'um, sukkuh dem bin pullet lock'up een coob! En' him duh de only roostuh! Him duh de only roostuh! En' w'en 'e crow, en' de t'odduh roostuh outside de fench yeddy'um, dem done fuh bex. Dat de reaz'n all dem t'odduh man 'taguhnize'um so hebby, en' dat w'ymekso de man so glad fuh shum een shishuh hebby trouble, 'cause 'e dey een trouble now, Maussuh, sho's you bawn! Da' bull Nigguh tanglety up een dem 'ooman' sku't en' t'ing sukkuh wawss git ketch een spiduh web! En' nobody sorry fuhr'um, 'cause 'e too greedy! De man ent gwine stan'

94

by'um 'cause 'e tek'way all de 'ooman, en de'
'ooman stan' by'um so close 'tel dem tromple'um!
So, Buh Tumbo dey een trouble fuh true!"

Laguerre imposed great restraint upon himself in keeping quiet during the five minutes it
took Scipio to give the once-over to the ewe lambs
huddled within the fold of the dusky King Solomon of Slann's Island. As nestlings flutter
tremulously when the motherbird with a worm in
her beak alights on the edge of the nest, so, always, when someone else was speaking, Laguerre's ear-drums hungered quiveringly for the
sound of Laguerre's voice. Only the importance
of Scipio's information justified the exercise of
the Spartan discipline of silence!

While Scipio talked he had punctuated his sen-
tences with gentle flicks of his whip on Zouave's
ribs, and the slim stallion moved along so briskly
that by the time he wound up his story with the
prediction that trouble was brewing for Tumbo,
Scipio and his master came in sight of the glade
in the pineland, where, on fine days, Laguerre
held his court.

"Maussuh," commented Scipio, as they drew
near and saw the black faces of those that clustered about the big pine box, "seem ez ef blackbu'd duh swawm, en' crow duh mustuh!" and Laguerre chuckled as one who, whetting the knife
of his wit for the dissection of character, sees the

95

groaning board set forth with dark meat ready for the carving!

Laguerre took his seat and the court was called to order by Cudjo. Tumbo stood out in front of his society sisters, who squatted on the ground in a semicircle behind him, as the cows and calves of a buffalo herd range themselves behind the old bull when danger threatens. But with a difference, for within the deep bosoms of the dusky sisterhood of the Slann's Island fold of the "I Will Arise," there lurked more than a suspicion that the Reverend President had not played fair with them in respect to money matters, and that the cigar-box treasury of the fold had contained far more than "de pyo' nutt'n'" when committed into Tumbo's keeping. So, unlike the buffalo herd, they hoped that the great bull before them would be slashed and harried by the verbal fangs of the grim white wolf who had brought him to bay. Harried, but not hamstrung, for the burly black priest, altho' he bore heavily upon their lean larders and the small store of silver knotted in the corners of their aprons, meant much to them in many ways. His unctuous appreciation of the food they prepared for him, the gracious condescension with which he accepted "the pennies of the poor" they so humbly bestowed, and the spiritual consolation, that, when full-fed and fee'd, leaked out of him, exalted their souls.

THE TRIALS OF TUMBO

About the time of Laguerre, a little St. Nicholas jingle told the story of a canny and forward-looking Japanese maiden, who, sought in marriage by the wealthy husband of seventy-nine wives, besought the Emperor to tell her, before giving her hand, what "an eightieth widow's third would be."

"The Mikado was wondrous wise,
He opened his mouth, and he shut his eyes.
'An eightieth widow's third will be—
Whatever the Law will give to thee!'"

Tumbo was not at all concerned with eightieth-widow's thirds. His problem was the difficult one of distributing his pastoral and personal attentions equitably among the feminine members of the fold, so that each of the thirty would be sure she had received at least the thirtieth to which she was entitled, and, in addition, whatever her spiritual needs demanded or her personality warranted! Tumbo's skill in sailing his bark, or paddling his "trus'-me-gawd" through the tortuous channels that separated the thick-clustered islets of his human archipelago, and touching upon each siren shore just long enough, but not too long, had earned him the envious admiration of all the other men in the community. "Pa Tumbo, him *done* fuh know 'ooman!"

"Yaas, man! Him haffuh know'um! 'Ooman

duh weh him lib! Him know'um sukkuh dog know 'e flea! Him kibbuhr'up wid 'ooman!"

And now, as Tumbo stood forth, "upstage," with his mute petticoated chorus spread out fan-like behind him, Laguerre's wrath kindled, and flared up!

"Well, you black Bull-of-the-Woods, what have you got to say for yourself? Have you brought all the young heifers with you?"

"Jedge, de t'irty nyung sistuh, dey iz all prezunt, I beleebe, suh."

"And the bell-cow! What have you done with the bell-cow?"

"Suh!"

"The bell-cow. Your 'lawfully-lady,' as you call her."

Tumbo's gravity was unshaken by Laguerre's pleasantry, and he replied with great dignity:

"Yaas, suh, she also is prezunt."

"Is she the one with whom your daughter Alice couldn't 'git'long none'tall'?"

"Yaas, suh, Jedge, de berry same."

"Why the devil don't you make them 'git'long'? You have all the petticoats on Slann's Island stuck to you like sheep-burrs to a mule's tail, and you don't know how to manage women?"

"Jedge, suh—"

The master-mariner knows his ship, from stem to stern—to him she is a sentient thing, responsive to every mood of the mighty deep upon whose bosom she is alternately cradled and tempest-tossed. The eagle knows the air, and all the shifting winds that sweep the blue empyrean— afloat, broad planes outstretched, on soft aerial tides, or, with pinions sharp as a felucca's prow, buffeting the storm! And there are men, made in God's image, but wise in their own conceit, who know women—"know them through and through." Tumbo was not one of them!

"Jedge, suh, Uh tangle'up en' ractify wid heap-'uh 'ooman, fuh true, but de mo' I iz know 'bout de 'ooman, de mo' I iz know dat Uh yent know nutt'n'tall 'bout de 'ooman."

"A Daniel come to judgment," said the court.

"Oh, me Jedus! Yeddy'um," shouted the squatting sisters.

"Yaas, suh, Jedge," continued Tumbo, " 'ooman iz shishuh cuntrady t'ing, you dunno how fuh tek'um! Ef you tek'um ez 'e come, fus' t'ing you know, him duh gwine! Ef de 'ooman staa't fuh we'dduh, en' de win' out de 'ooman' mout' blow frum de Sout', en' you hice you ambrelluh fuh puhtec' you'self, fus' t'ing you know, da' win' shif' 'roun' en' blow out de Nawt', 'e wranch de ambrelluh out you han', en' t'row rain 'puntop you! En' ef man hab two 'ooman een 'e house, 'speshly ef one duh 'e lawfully-lady, en' t'odduh one duh 'e daa'tuh wuh 'e bin hab by one de t'odduh 'ooman

99

'e bin hab at de fus', befo' 'e hab 'e lawfully-lady
—befo' dem two 'ooman gitt'ru 'taguhnize one-
'nurruh, de man fuh stan' lukkuh de 'Gypshun
wuh folluh dem Jew en' t'ing een de Red Sea.
Him gwine bog'up! Jedge, suh, man ent fuh
rule two 'ooman een one house. De debble haffuh do'um! 'Cause 'ooman iz uh *sometime t'ing,*
sho' ez Gawd duh ride 'puntop'uh Him cloud!
Sho' ez Gawd!"

Under the stress of excitement Tumbo, ordi-
narily more careful of his speech than the other
Toogoodoo Negroes, had lapsed into the broadest
Gullah, and his vehemence provoked his auditors
to laughter.

"Ki!" shouted a critical sister, "Pa Tumbo bex!
W'en you shum stan' so, him fuh t'row'way 'e
Sunday talk, en' full 'e mout' wid pluff-mud suk-
kuh dem Nigguh 'puntop Wadmuhlaw!"

"Yaas," said an envious male, ' 'e talk pluff-
mud talk, fuh true, en' w'en 'e *yiz* talk'um, dat
duh de sign him duh talk trute, 'cause, sometime,
w'en man dey een uh hebby trouble, de trute
jump out 'e mout' en' gone befo' him kin ketch-
'um! En' 'e bruk'out da' ole ram' mout' en' git-
'way cause dem 'ooman kibbuhr'um so hebby.
De 'ooman kibbuhr'um 'tel dem smudduhr'um!"

Truth, emerging from the smother, showed Laguerre a changed attitude of the sisters toward
the dusky guardian of the fold, for now they

frankly laughed at one they sometime held as sacrosanct within "the awful circle of the church!"

"Well," said Laguerre, "you have expressed the opinion that only the devil is competent to rule the two women within your own household. How are you going to rule the thirty lambs you have out in the pasture? Is the devil going to take those off your hands, too?"

"Jedge, *you* fuh do'um, suh."

"Me!" screamed Laguerre, "me! What the thunder do you mean?"

"Jedge, you fuh tell'um how fuh do, please, suh, 'cause my 't'oruhty obuhr'um git kind'uh loose, ebbuh sence da' time de sistuh git tangle'up 'bout de sick benefit een de 'Syety. De sistuh fetch de 'spute to me fuh onrabble'um, en' same time dem bin fetch de 'spute, dem fetch de tredjuh-box, en' ax me fuh hol' de tredjuh-box 'tel de 'spute done 'spute; but Jedge, da' 'spute nebbuh *yiz* done 'spute, 'cause dem t'irty sistuh iz 'ooman, enty, Jedge? Uh nebbuh bodduh 'bout de 'spute w'en de 'ooman 'spute 'mong demself, 'cause 'ooman haffuh do dat, but dem fetch me een'um en' ax me wuh'smattuh wid all de money wuh bin een de tredjuh-box, en' alldo' Uh tell'um 'sponsubble suh de tredjuh-box bin full'up wid *nutt'n'*, w'en Uh pry'um op'n, dem ent b'leebe me, Jedge, en' de 'ooman keep on onrabble dem debble'ub'uh mout'

101

at me 'tel me yez duh sing sukkuh bee binnuh swawm een'um!"

"Oh, Gawd! Yeddy Pa Tumbo cuss! Him duh de Lawd' renointed, en' him call de debble' name!"

"Yaas, tittuh, him bex, now. W'en you shum bow 'e neck lukkuh bull, Pa Tumbo *done* fuh bex! En' 'e yent bex wid man! 'E bex wid nutt'n' but we po' 'ooman wuh ent got nutt'n' but we mout' fuh puhtec' weself!"

"Mout'!" bellowed Tumbo, "Mout'! Jedge, dem mout' wuss' mo'nuh alligettuh' jaw! 'E heap wuss'! Alligettuh leddown een de sunhot fuh sleep. 'E crack 'e jaw 'tel 'e mout' full'up wid fly en' bug en' t'ing. 'E shet 'e mout' fuh swalluhr'um, den 'e crack 'e jaw, 'gen. But 'e shet 'e mout' *sometime*, enty, Jedge? De 'ooman nebbuh do'um! De only t'ing him hab fuh swalluh iz 'e bex, en' fas' ez him swalluhr'um, da' bex b'ile up 'gen. So de 'ooman fuhrebbuh gott'um een 'e mout'!"

"Jedge, ef you hab 'tettuh een de pot, ef watuh dey een you kittle 'pun de fiah, ef you want'um fuh b'ile fas', you haffuh pit kibbuh 'puntop'um, enty, suh? 'Cause ef you tek off da' kibbuh him tek mo' longuh fuh b'ile. Jedge you t'ink 'ooman mout' stan' so?"

Laguerre slowly shook his head.

"Berrywell, suh," said Tumbo, triumphantly,

"you know'um, Jedge, 'cause de mo' de 'ooman
onkibbuhr'um, de mo' swif' 'e b'ile! En' Jedge,
all dem t'irty mout' binnuh b'ile obuh en' scal'
me, 'tel Uh sorry Uh ebbuh bin orguhnize de
'Syety en' tangle'up wid de drat 'ooman!"

"Oh, Jedus! Him duh drat we!"

"Yaas, tittuh! Pa Tumbo drat we good!"

"Jedge, suh, ef de 'ooman *iz* bin hab money een
dem tredjuh-box, me yent hab no 'cajun fuh
s'aa'ch'um! Wuffuh de Lawd' renointed haffuh
run 'e han' een de 'ooman' tredjuh-box en' t'ing
fuh git money, w'en de knot een de 'ooman ap'un
stan' so cunweenyunt? Enty de 'ooman haffuh
feed de preachuh? Enty de 'ooman haffuh pit
money een 'e han'? De man wu'k fuh de bittle
en' de money, fuh true, but de 'ooman tek'um'way
frum de man en' g'em to de preachuh. Da' duh
him bidness. Ef de 'ooman' sinful soul en' t'ing
iz fuh sabe, de preachuh haffuh sabe'um, en' ez
de 'ooman gwine 'long, him haffuh sabe de man,
'cause de man ent gwine bodduh fuh sabe 'eself
en' 'e yent gwine pay no preachuh fuh sabe'um,
needuh! W'ichebbuh way de 'ooman go, de man
gwine folluhr'um—ef 'e kin. Ef de 'ooman
gwine to 'e Jedus, en' 'e try fuh lif' de man off
de du't fuh cya'um wid'um, de 'ooman haffuh
fluttuh fedduh fuh hice da' man sukkuh hawk
beat 'e wing w'en 'e ketch uh hebby fowl een 'e
claw en' try fuh rise'um off de groun' fuh fly'way.

"But ef de debble ketch de 'ooman en' cya'um down dey to da' place weh him lib! Jedge, de man fuh folluhr'um swif' sukkuh ottuh slip down da' slide 'pun de backwatuh dam! But w'en de ottuh done slide 'e slide, him fuh drap een de watuh, but w'en de man git da' place weh 'e duh gwine, 'e foot nebbuh wet, 'cause no watuh dey dey. De debble cyan' b'ile'um, so him haffuh swinge'um!

"So, Jedge, de 'ooman haffuh pay de preachuh fuh resplain de Lawd' wu'd en' tell'um 'bout Pharaoh en' Buhrabbus, en' all dem t'odduh 'postle en' t'ing een de Scriptuh, 'cause de lab'ruh wu't' 'e hire, en' long ez de preachuh hab prib'lidge fuh ontie de knot een de 'ooman' ap'un, 'e yent haffuh run 'e han' een 'e tredjuh-box, en' Jedge, suh, deseyuh t'irty sistuh kin tek de 'Syety en' run'um fuh demself. Ef man cyan' do'um fuh suit, leh de 'ooman do'um, enty, Jedge? Some deseyuh new 'ooman wuh grow'up sence Freedom nebbuh count man nohow, 'tel Sattyday night come—den, dem count all wuh 'e got, en' tie'um up een dem ap'un! De 'ooman ent count de man, but 'e nebbuh try fuh raise no fowl 'cep' 'e got roostuh een 'e yaa'd!

"Jedge, suh, deseyuh nyung sistuh done 'taguhnize de fait'ful roostuh wuh bin min' de hawk off'um; en' now, ef dem iz so smaa't, le'm do bedout no roostuh! Befo' t'ree week done pass, da' same oagly Cudjo fuh fetch dem t'irty sistuh yuh, 'cause ebb'ry one fuh tayre t'odduh one' shimmy off'um! En' Jedge, yuh dem drat tredjuh-box!" and Tumbo, pathetic in his renunciation, laid the empty cigar box before the court.

"Place aux dames!" said Laguerre—but he pronounced it "damn!"

"PLACE AUX DAMES!"

A sunless solar system!

A fold of Sons and Daughters whose only Son, having placed himself "under some prodigious ban of excommunication," was now a Son no more!

A rudderless ship adrift on the heaving tides of an ocean, whose bosom, unruffled now, would presently seethe with the passion of angry waters!

Only close observers of human nature realize the importance to many families of having a poor relation about the house—a "fifth-wheel" as he is sometimes called. This odd and unattached member of the household may do chores enough to more than pay his way, but he is a fifth-wheel, nevertheless, and the fifth-wheel may, for want of oil, creak and groan as it moves, but it is always there to turn or be turned upon!

And what a comfort to have it to turn upon! Jarring members of the regular family are often held together by the cement of a common criticism—a blessed goat! A gift from heaven, like Abraham's sacrificial ram!

So, sometimes, for half a generation, the fifth-wheel serves his turn, and then—for God is good —he dies and is laid away. Then the members

107

of the household, having acquired the habit of criticism, look around for a common subject and finding none, turn upon one another, and, if he could, the fifth-wheel would turn over in his quiet grave, and smile!

———

Tumbo, having rid himself of the petticoat-grass that not long since clung to his knees so ardently, by simply divesting himself of his presidential pantaloons, was now, by his own act, an outcast from the "I Will Arise," and, like a "rogue" elephant outlawed from the herd, kept surlily to himself, for he was contemned by the men, first for greed in having gathered so many women into his own hands, and then for folly in having turned them all loose again, while the women were angered because he had scorned and flouted them in public.

For a week the old bull moped around, giving scant attention to his pastoral duties, but when Sunday came, he stamped the floor of his Slann's Island pulpit 'til the loose boards rattled, and bellowed like a "bloodynoun." And he bellowed at the women. The thirty young sisters of the "I Will Arise" sat near the front, and at these he hurled denunciations of vanity, untruthfulness, tattling, and other faults to which women are said to be addicted, but which men will by no means relinquish exclusively to the gentler sex.

"PLACE AUX DAMES"

With many a florid gesture and whole-arm swing, Tumbo thundered, and the sisters, knowing he was preaching at them, and why, smiled tolerantly, and responded frequently and fervently.

"De debble done git een dese nyung 'ooman!"

"Amen!" groaned a deep-voiced man.

"You cyan' shum, but de debble dey dey!"

"Yaas, me Jedus! him dey dey," conceded a shrill sister.

"Ef you don't t'row'um out, 'e gwine rabbidge you h'aa't."

"Oh! me Kingdom come! We h'aa't fuh rabbidge!"

"En' w'en de debble done rabbidge'um, him fuh cya' you down to da' place weh him lib, en' w'en you shum, en' see how de fiah stan', you gwine t'u'sty 'nuf fuh swalluh Toogoodoo Crik, salt ez 'e yiz, ef you kin gitt'um, 'cause no watuh dey dey!"

"No, me Jedus! no watuh dey dey!"

"En' de t'ing wuh mek de mores' trouble fuh wunnuh 'ooman, iz wunnuh mout'! Wunnuh sinful mout'! En' de trouble 'e mek fuh wunnuh ent nutt'n' to de trouble 'e mek fuh ebb'rybody else. W'en woodpeckuh mek 'e nes' een de holluh tree, him sattify wid one hole. Da' hole him hab fuh gone een 'e nes', him nyuze da' same hole fuh come out'um. But wunnuh 'ooman ent

109

stan' so. 'Ooman fuh hab t'ree hole een 'e head
—'e two yez en' 'e mout'! En' dem all t'ree fuhrebbuh open. Dem nebbuh shet."

"Oh, Jedus! Him duh call we name!"

"En' ebb'ryt'ing wuh gone een de yez fuh come
out de mout'!"

"Amen! Amen!" grunted the double-bass.

"But 'e yent fuh come out lukkuh 'e gone een!
De t'ing wuh gone een 'e yez, ent stan' same
fashi'n w'en 'e come out 'e mout', 'cause da'
'ooman' sinful h'aa't fuh change'um 'tel de wu'd
ent fuh ruckuhnize 'eself."

"Maussuh, Jedus! De debble gwine git we!"
shouted a sister, mockingly.

"Him dey 'pun you track, my sistuh! En' w'en
you see da' fiah come out 'e mout' en' yeddy'um
pop 'e tail, '*paow!*' lukkuh dem boy pop lash fuh
min' bu'd out de rice-fiel', you foot gwine trabble
so swif' you mout' ent gwine hab chance fuh
laugh!

"So, ez Uh tell wunnuh, 'ooman' yez en' 'e
mout' stan' lukkuh cawn furruh. Ef somebody
drap grain uh cawn een de 'ooman' yez, you t'ink
da' leely grain fuh come out 'e mout' lukkuh dat?
No, beliebuh! 'E nebbuh do'um. 'E nebbuh
do'um! 'Cause da' cawn haffuh sprout fus'!
En' w'en you look 'puntop'um, da' seed fuh hab
long shoot 'pun 'e top en' long root 'puntop 'e
bottom."

110

"We mout' duh sprout, me Jedus! We mout' duh sprout!"

"En' dat de reaz'n w'ymekso wunnuh 'ooman iz shishuh hebby sinnuh, 'cause ef de trute gone een you yez lukkuh da' leely grain, da' cawn fuh come out you mout' 'cawd'n' to you h'aa't, 'cause you h'aa't fuh sprout'um. Ef you h'aa't mek plan fuh tell leely lie, de cawn fuh hab leely root 'puntop'um; ef de lie fuh be middle-size lie, de cawn fuh be 'bout knee high; but ef you h'aa't wickety fuh true-true, w'en da' cawnstalk come out you mout' him fuh stan' high mo'nuh man' head, en' fuh hab tossle 'puntop'um!"

"Now, him duh tell we!"

"Yaas, my bredduh," bellowed Tumbo with rising voice, "en' dem sistuh een de 'Syety wuh bin 'taguhnize dem pastuh to de Jedge, en' 'cuze-'um 'bout run 'e han' een dem tredjuh-box, stan' sukkuh dem 'ooman wuh sprout de cawn. Dem cawnstalk got tossle 'puntop'um!"

"Oh, Gawd! We cawn duh tossle! We cawn duh tossle!"

But, after Tumbo had eased his spirit by the Sunday outburst, he softened toward the sisters, old and young. He knew that, as the river flows to the sea, so in time would the petticoated membership of the "I Will Arise" run again to the Man of God—or he to them. Meanwhile, he was content to wait, and watch with interest their

111

efforts to reorganize the headless society along feminine lines, with entire independence of the, for the moment, obnoxious sex.

Tumbo resumed cautiously and furtively his pastoral visits, but, keeping clear of the young sisterhood, addressed himself to the middle-aged, or "settled" members of his congregation, and from these he began to extract bits of gossip about the feminists.

"Yaas, suh," said a wise and settled sister. "Uh bin to Sistuh Judy Chizzum' house night befo' las', en' him en' Sistuh Fields binnuh 'taguhnize one'nurruh 'bout w'ich one fuh be de Prezzy*dent* attuh you done t'row'um 'way. Dem alltwo want'um, but only one kin hab'um, so attuh dem 'spute en' aa'gyfy 'bout'um 'tel dem mos' bex 'nuf fuh fight, dem 'gree fuh tek de 'spute to Jedge en' ax'um ef dem alltwo kin be Prezzy*dent* one time, 'cause needuh one de 'ooman willin' fuh leh de t'odduh one hab'um. So las' night de two 'ooman en' two-tree de t'odduh sistuh gone to Jedge' house fuh ax'um."

"Wuh Jedge tell'um?"

"Jedge tell'um 'sponsubble suh only one man kin be de Prezzy*dent*. Alltwo de 'ooman cyan' hab'um one time. Jedge tell'um fuh 'membuh now, dem iz man. Dem gone en' tek man 't'oruhty 'puntop demself en' dem haffuh behabe lukkuh man. Jedge ax'um ef dem t'ink dem

112

iz hen, 'cause ef two hen duh lay een one en' de
de same nes', soon ez one de hen done lay en' git
off de nes' fuh cackly so him kin tell de roostuh
'bout da' aig, de t'odduh hen tek him chance fuh
gone een de nes' fuh lay him'own, en' Jedge tell-
'um shishuh gwinin' en' gwinin' lukkuh dat do
berrywell fuh hen en' 'ooman, but attuh dem done
tek de 't'oruhty 'puntop demself wuh nyuse to
blonx to Pa Tumbo, dem haffuh be sukkuh man;
same ez ef dem bin hab on britchiz; dem ent fuh
swap 'roun' lukkuh dem bin 'pun hen' nes'! Alltwo cyan' be Prezzy*dent*. Only one fuh hab'um.
En' Jedge exwise'um fuh leh one de 'ooman be de
Prezzy*dent*, en' t'odduh one fuh be Wice-Prezzy-
dent, den alltwo de 'ooman fuh sattify, 'cause
Prezzy*dent* dey een alltwo dem name."

"Wuh de 'ooman do, w'en Jedge exwise'um?"

"Dem 'gree fuh tek Jedge' exwice. Alltwo de
'ooman hice dem 'coat up high fuh keep'um out
de hebby jew, en' dem en' dem cump'ny tek de
paat' fuh home. En' ez dem duh gwine 'long de
narruh paat' t'ru de bush, da' name duh sing een
alltwo de 'ooman' yez, 'cause dem nebbuh yeddy
nobody call shishuh name lukkuh dat befo'.
Chinkypen duh grow 'longside de paat'. De
shaa'p buhr jam een de 'ooman' knee en' sting'um.
De 'ooman nebbuh feel'um. Briah wrop 'roun'
de t'odduh 'ooman' shin ez 'e gwine, en' 'e bite de
'ooman' meat. Him nebbuh bodduh 'bout'um

113

'cause da' name duh sing, en' de mo' 'e sing, de mo' rich 'e soun'. Wice-Prezzy*dent!* Wice-Prezzy*dent!*

"En' ez dem foot duh trabble 'long de paat' en' da' name duh trabble t'ru dem head, each one de 'ooman duh mek plan fuh git da' title fuh 'eself 'cause 'e t'ink Wice-Prezzy*dent* stan' rich mo'nuh Prezzy*dent*."

" 'Ooman iz uh foolish t'ing."

"So, bumbye, Sistuh Fields him staa't fus'. 'E h'aa't schemy, but him duh hide 'e h'aa't wid 'e mout', en' 'e mout' berry saaf'.

" 'Sistuh Chizzum,' 'e say, 'Uh so glad Jedge tell we 'bout da' Wice-Prezzy*dent*, 'cause me kin tek him, en' den you fuh be de Prezzy*dent*, wid nobody fuh 'spute you 'bout'um, en' Uh sorry Uh bin 'taguhnize you so hebby 'bout da' Prezzy*dent*, 'cause da' place blonx to you, yaas, ma'am, en' so, w'en Uh yeddy Jedge tell you fuh tek'um, Uh bin glad we yent fuh 'spute obuhr'um no mo', 'cause Uh sattify now fuh tek de Wice-Prezzy*dent*, wuh you ent want, en' do de bes' wid'um wuh Uh kin.'

"Reb'ren', w'en Sistuh Chizzum yeddy dat, 'e h'aa't drap, 'cause Sistuh Fields tek de wu'd out 'e mout'! Him bin jis' gwine fuh say da' same berry t'ing, but befo' 'e kin crack 'e teet' fuh gitt'um out, Sistuh Fields tek'um'way en' gone! Wuh him fuh do, now? Him wan' da' Wice-

114

"PLACE AUX DAMES"

Prezzy*dent*' name mo'nuh him bin wan' de Prezzy*dent*' name, at de fus', 'cause de name soun'
so rich, en' nobody een we neighbuhhood, needuhso 'puntop Toogoodoo, nebbuh bin yeddy'um
befo'.

"So, Sistuh Chizzum' min' staa't fuh twis'.
'E twis' en 'e twis', 'e scheme en' 'e scheme, en'
'e study 'bout how him kin twis' da' Wice-Prezzy-
dent out da' t'odduh 'ooman' head. 'E know 'e
gwine be haa'd fuh do, 'cause da' t'ing done tek
root een de 'ooman' head, en' 'e root gone deep,
sukkuh bamboo-wine en' cane root, en' dem t'ing
haffuh chop'up wid hoe! En' Reb'ren', de 'ooman
do'um! Befo' 'e gitt'ru, 'e 'queeze da' t'ing out
de t'odduh 'ooman' head. Him tell me so dis
mawnin', 'eself."

"How 'e do'um?"

" 'E nice'um up wid 'e 'ceitful mout'. 'E tell-
'um suh w'en him 'membuh how dig*nify* you
stan' w'en you binnuh seddown een da' Prezzy-
dent' seat de time you binnuh dictate obuh de
'Syety, him shame fuh seddown een da' chair, en'
'e say him cyan' cross 'e foot stylish obuh 'e knee
lukkuh you bin do'um, 'cause 'e yent got on no
britchiz, en' ef 'e yiz bin hab britchiz, 'e shame
fuh do'um, 'cause him iz 'ooman, en' 'ooman ent
fuh do shishuh t'ing lukkuh dat, nohow, en' 'e
tell'um 'e know berrywell suh ef you yeddy suh
de 'ooman wuh bin 'taguhnize you so hebby duh

115

seddown een da' digni*fy* place you bin hab one time, 'e gwine mek you bex, wehreas, ef Sistuh Fields tek'um, you ent gwine bex, 'cause Sistuh Fields nebbuh bin 'taguhnize you. En', fudduhmo', 'e say 'e sorry him ebbuh bex you, 'cause you iz we pastuh, en' de only somebody we hab fuh 'pen' 'pun fuh be we shep'u'd, en' sabe we sinful soul en' t'ing."

" 'E say dat, enty? De 'ceitful t'ing."

"Yaas, Reb'ren', dat wuh 'e say. En', mo'obuh, 'e tell Sistuh Fields, suh him en' de 'Syety lub you, en' 'e say befo' him will ho't you feelin's, him mo' redduh fun t'row'way alltwo de place, 'cause him lub you tummuch!"

"Yeddy de 'ceitful Satan! Yeddy'um!"

" 'E 'ceitful, fuh true, 'cause befo' dem git home, Sistuh Chizzum' hoe done root da' Wice-Prezzy*dent* out Sistuh Fields' head, en' 'e jam da' Prezzy*dent* een'um, en' him tek de Wice fuh 'eself. Da' 'ooman *done* fuh schemy! Sistuh Fields bin hab da' t'ing een 'e mout' sukkuh king-fishuh hab fish, en' befo' him kin hice 'e head fuh swalluhr'um, Sistuh Chizzum snatch'um out 'e mout' en' gone!"

"Yaas, en' ef 'e yent min', da' same Wice gwine choke'um befo' 'e git t'ru. You watch'um!"

Tumbo's sinister prediction was speedily verified, for, before the week was over, if not a meeting of "the best minds," there was certainly a

116

meeting of the kinkiest feminine heads on Slann's Island, at the house of Sister Judy Chizzum, where the sonless daughters of the "I Will Arise" assembled to reorganize by the elevation of Sisters Bina Fields and Judy Chizzum, sometime Secretary-lady and Treasurer-lady of the Society, to the exalted positions of President and Vice-president, respectively; the first to fill the vacancy created by the explosive and tempestuous abdication of Pa Tumbo, the second to clothe fittingly in feminine flesh the titular apple of discord, thrown among them—innocently or malevolently—by "Jedge" Laguerre.

The night was close. The room was close, for Sister Chizzum's living-room was none too large for the thirty seething sisters, who milled around like range cattle on the verge of a stampede, while their tongues clacked like the busy shuttles of a loom!

Two kerosene lamps in diagonally opposite corners of the room, flared fitfully, for, however wise, otherwise, the virgins of the black sisterhood, when they trim their lamps, trim them smokily, and the yellow light that flickered over the dark faces was as dull as that of a murky winter's sunset swiftly merging into dusk.

And out of the dusk their round eyes shone like marbles—round with expectancy—they knew not what, for, novitiates in feminism, without a man, they were without a rudder.

When Tumbo had originally organized the Society, he had masterfully taken short cuts, with entire independence of Cushing's Manual, Hardee's Tactics, or any other formulas whatsoever, civil or military, by simply naming himself President, and Sisters Chizzum and Fields, Treasurer-lady and Secretary-lady, respectively, and then permitting the petticoated membership to elect them by acclamation. But now there was a difference, for while they bowed their necks willingly enough to the masculine yoke they would in no wise be borne upon by members of their own sex, and that is the way with women, on Toogoodoo as elsewhere, for breeks are breeks for a' that—whether they be the doeskin trousers of Regent Street, the grass-cloth breech-clout of the Gaboon, or the nearer and dearer jeans "britchiz" of Slann's Island!

Sister Wineglass, a lady with a presence—cornfed women didn't "bant" on Toogoodoo in those days—wriggled her way through the steaming sisters, and, by dint of many jabs of vigorous elbows in ribs that once were Adam's, emerged from the ruck and took the floor. The floor shook!

Sister Wineglass, arrayed not as Solomon, was, nathless, becomingly attired in a sprigged

calico. The sprigs were small and brown and
thickly sown over the white ground of the fab-
ric, and the broad expanse of the lady's ample
bosom, and more than ample hips, looked like the
breast and quarters of an iron-gray, flea-bitten
horse!

When Mis' Wineglass removed the masculine
wool hat, whose wearing indicated the possession
of a husband, more or less her own, she revealed
a coiffure that aroused at once the envy and the
chagrin of her fellows—envy of its stunning ap-
pearance, and disappointment that none among
them had thought of it first.

In Laguerre's day Yankee Negroes had not
learned how to coin the kinkiness of Afro-Ameri-
can heads into dollars, and no hair-straightening
devices had ever been heard of in St. Paul's
Parish; but the heads of all self-respecting Negroes were frequently combed, and those of
women and girl children were laboriously plaited
into "pigtails" and tightly tied with strong white
thread or small cotton cord. Strange that white
should have been used, for coarse black spool
cotton was sold everywhere. Perhaps 'twas for
the sharp contrast while the thread was clean and
white. It soon got black enough!

The children's pigtails were left in the plait
until it pleased their elders to untwist, comb out,
and do them up again, for the pigtails didn't ac-

cumulate dry leaves, feathers and sheepburrs; but
those of the women were frequently unplaited and
combed out into a greasy glory of kinkiness—a
"permanent wave"—that would have whelmed
with envy a fifty-dollar New York Coiffeur!

Mis' Wineglass had arranged "woman's crowning glory" according to a plan of her own—entirely new to Toogoodoo. Some cell of African
thought must have harked back two or three hundred years to the jungles of the Limpopo, for,
parted in the middle, she had coiled her thick
locks on either side in perfect imitation of the
massive frontlet of a Cape Buffalo bull! And as
the great horns went twisting backward they
narrowed over the ears, ending at last in two
tightly plaited points, wrapped and bound at the
tails with coarse white thread.

Easily the most physically impressive among
the sisters, Mis' Wineglass was mentally the most
aggressive, and now as she thrust forward her
horned frontlet as if about to charge, the gabble
suddenly ceased, twenty-nine pairs of ears opened
expectantly, and twenty-nine martyred mouths
shut tight! She opened hers!

"Wunnuh sistuh," she began, "two week done
pass sence Pa Tumbo t'row'way dishyuh 'Syety,
en' de 'Syety ent do nutt'n' yit. Pa Tumbo en'
Jedge alltwo tell we fuh orguhnize'um fuh we-
'self, but, 'stead'uh orguhnize, all we bin do iz

fuh agguhnize en' 'spute 'bout'um, en' all de odduh Nigguh 'pun Toogoodoo, man en' 'ooman, alltwo, duh laugh at we en' say suh 'ooman ent wu't' fuh hab no 'Syety, 'cep' dem got man obuhr-'um fuh tell'um wuh fuh do en' mek'um do'um! 'E stan' so, too, 'cause yuh we binnuh shif' 'roun', shif' 'roun', sukkuh fox-squerril sukkle 'roun' pine tree w'en man duh folluhr'um! En' weh we git? Weh we git? We yent git no place, 'cause we git 'roun' da' tree to de same place weh we bin staa't at de fus'! En' we dey dey now!"

"Weh da' Prezzy*dent* we bin fuh hab? Weh 'e dey? Uh yeddy 'bout'um but Uh yent shum yit! En' ef Uh *yiz* shum, him fuh hab on frock! Prezzy*dent* fuh hab on *frock!* En' ef 'e yiz hab on frock, da' frock gwine tayre off'um befo' 'e gitt-'ru, 'cause w'en two 'ooman quawl obuh one man, dem two 'ooman gwine hitch, sho' ez Gawd, en' dishyuh place dem duh 'spute 'bout got on man' britchiz, enty? Berrywell."

Mis' Wineglass paused for breath, but before she could take it, Sister Fields, upon whose loins the Presidential "britchiz" had been wished by Sister Chizzum, rose to remark:

"Sistuh, wunnuh all, me nuh Sistuh Chizzum binnuh 'spute 'bout w'ich one fuh be Prezzy*dent,* en' we didn' able fuh 'gree, so we gone fuh see Jedge, en' him tell we suh one kin be de Prezzy-*dent,* en' de t'odduh one kin be de Wice-Prezzy-

121

dent—him iz de man wuh come een place w'en de Prezzy*dent* sick, eeduhso gone Town, en', attuh Jedge tell we dat, me nuh Sistuh Chizzum 'spute 'gen, 'bout de two place, same lukkuh we binnuh 'spute at de fus' 'bout de one place, 'tel, finully at las', him 'suade me fuh be de Prezzy*dent* 'cause 'e say him shame fuh seddown een Pa Tumbo' place, so den Uh tek'um, en' now me duh de head, en' me hab de 't'oruhty fuh dictate obuh all wunnuh sistuh same ez ef Uh bin man."

"Man, de debble! Us fuh hab 'ooman obuh we; en' him fuh call 'eself *man!* Who gi' you shishuh prib'lidge lukkuh dat? Jedge tell you, enty? Ef him gi' you man' 't'oruhty, him mus'-be gi' you de britchiz fuh cya'um 'long, enty? Weh de britchiz? Leh we shum! Leh we shum!"

But Mis' Wineglass called in vain for the bifurcated symbol of the lordly male, and Sister Fields resumed.

"Wunnuh kin fuss 'bout hab 'ooman 'puntop wunnuh fuh dictate obuh de 'Syety, but ef you ent hab him, you ent fuh hab nobody, 'cause no man iz fuh git. En' now we done orguhnize, so all us hab fuh do iz fuh git de tredjuh-box en' staa't fuh pit money een'um. W'en Pa Tumbo bin de Prezzy*dent* en' Sistuh Chizzum bin de Tredjuruh lady him en' Pa Tumbo 'taguhnize one'nurruh 'bout da' tredjuh-box 'tel de 'Syety bruk'up, en'

"PLACE AUX DAMES"

Pa Tumbo lef' we bedout no man to we name. So now, me, one, fuh be de Prezzy*dent* en' de Tredjuruh-lady alltwo. Uh know berrywell Uh yent fuh 'spute wid meself 'bout no money, so de 'Syety ent fuh ractify no mo'!"

But this short-cut to concord was promptly challenged by the now treasureless Tredjuruhlady, who had hoped to combine the offices of Vice-President and financial agent to her prestige and profit. Sister Chizzum rose wrathfully.

"Who tell you dat? Drat de 'ooman! Attuh Uh done mek'um Prezzy*dent*, now him fuh tek *me* tredjuh-box 'way frum me! Drat de 'ooman! 'E yent wu't'!"

"Shet you mout', 'ooman, shet you mout'! You hab de no'mannus fuh eentuhrup' you Prezzy*dent* en' drat'um, alltwo! Who gi' you prib'lidge fuh crack you teet' w'en him duh talk?"

"Crack me teet'! Crack me teet'! Gawd gimme prib'lidge fuh crack me teet'! Him mek me mout', enty? Him gwine be op'n 'tel Uh dead, en' no 'ooman, needuhso no man, ent fuh shet'um. 'E yent fuh shet!" The sisters promptly agreed.

"En' who *you* iz fuh tell de Wice-Prezzy*dent* fuh shet 'e mout'? Enty you know Uh stan' high mo'nuh you? De Wice-Prezzy*dent* rise high mo'-nuh de Prezzy*dent*. Him iz *two* man, en' de Prezzy*dent* ent but one, so de Wice hab prib'lidge

123

fuh talk fus'. En' now 'ooman you shet *yo'*
mout', 'cause me iz fuh talk fus'!"

The suspicion that Judy had wheedled her out
of the Vice-Presidency, intending to claim for
this title, unknown on Toogoodoo, some super-
Presidential prerogative, was too much for Bina,
and she flew at the presumptuous one like a barnyard rooster at a feathered rival!

The ladies came together grimly but silently.
There was a rending of raiment, a quick clawing
of faces, and a spiteful pulling of wool, but the
other sisters clustered so closely around the com-
batants as to restrict their sea-room, and they
were quickly torn asunder.

Then, out of the troubled waters—an Aphro-
dite in a sprigged calico—uprose once more,
Mis' Wineglass, who voiced the thought that
lurked in all their hearts!

"Wunnuh sistuh," she said, "we iz 'ooman,
enty? How we fuh git 'long bedout man? We
cyan' do'um. Ebbuh sence Pa Tumbo lef' we
de po' 'ooman een dishyuh 'Syety bin tanglety
up wid one'nurruh same lukkuh snake twis'up
w'en dem duh fight! De snake' head en' 'e tail
stan' so close togedduh, you cyan' tell w'ich one
duh swalluh t'odduh one! En' all dese drat
'ooman stan' same fashi'n!

"Wunnuh gal, us haffuh hab man! Drat de
man! Drat all de man! You lub'um en' you

124

"PLACE AUX DAMES"

'spize'um alltwo onetime. 'E yent wu't', but you haffuh hab'um! So now, leh we ax Pa Tumbo fuh come back en' dictate fuh we lukkuh him bin do at de fus', en' us nebbuh fuh bex'um no mo'!"

The motion was carried by acclamation, and ended abruptly the first Slann's Island move toward feminism!

THE CRUSADER AND THE COW

At the very threshold of October the rains, that for a week had followed the autumnal equinox, suddenly ceased and the sun shouldered his way through the broken clouds and poured his splendor upon field and forest, wide marshes, and the winding river. And his warmth brought comfort to the sodden earth and to the heavy hearts of men—the scattered planters and the swarming black folk of the sea-islands and the coastal plantations of the mainland, for, lacking the serene faith of modern meteorologists, they had not then—nor have they yet—learned to look for halcyon days around the 23rd of September! They did not know anything about the swing of the great pendulum with the changing seasons, but they did know winds when they blew, and whelming waters when they rose and swept away their crops, so when at last the flying cloud-wrack that had blown so steadily out of the east had passed on, with its spiteful, spitting rain, their fears passed with it, and with light hearts they looked upon a smiling world.

In a few hours the thirsty sun drank up the moisture that weighted down each drooping leaf, each bending spear of grass, each heavy-petaled flower. Then glossy leaf and pointed spear and

heavy-petaled flower looked up again and said,
" 'tis day! 'tis day!"

And the glistening needles that topped the
towering pines shone more brilliantly, and the
rain-washed boles of the great trees were purple
in the sunlight, and as far as the pineland
stretched the forest floor was covered for miles
with a carpet fresh from the looms of God, the
rich and exquisite colorings of which would have
shamed Sheherezade and all the magic rugs woven
by her marvelous imagination. Into the dominant
red of the low oak scrub were interwoven sprays
and leaves of bronze and green and brown, and
flower patterns of splendid purples, and blues
and yellows.

With the passing of the clouds, the birds,
native and migrant, dried their rain-drenched
feathers, and burst into song—each after his
kind. In the evenings, warblers, brief sojourn-
ers, on their way to winter quarters in the far
south, whistled sweet farewells; flycatchers,
from high perches atop dead limbs and snags,
pitched and vaulted at the insect life that
swarmed about them, while, also taking toll from
the gauze-winged legions of the air, purple mar-
tins wheeled and curvetted and charged, by companies and squadrons.

Here and there along the creeks and rivers,
blasted trunks stood sentinel, and from their

jagged tops crested kingfishers scanned the flowing tides for the swirl of rising fish, one stooping to the surface from time to time as the water
broke, rising to his perch again to swallow his
prey, or, if the quarry that had tempted him sub-
merged again, or looked too formidable for his
strength, flying along the stream to another post,
rattling his disappointment.

In leafy copses, ruddy now with the fires of
autumn, the liquid songs of catbirds mingled
with their querulous scoldings, while from tree-
top, shrub and fence stake, mocking-birds—
spendthrift ministers of song—poured out their
golden notes.

From open pineland and deep forest the tap-
ping and hammering of woodpeckers, great and
small—the swift roll of musketry, the slow and
measured pounding of heavy guns—came as
from a distant battlefield. Partridges whistled
from briar-thickets and tangled fence corners,
and swift doves passed from field to field, hurtling, as evening fell, to their roosts in the myrtles
and thick saplings.

The clean freshness of the rain-washed world;
the genial sunshine, the bracing autumn air,
seemed to bring new life to every living thing—
tree and shrub and flower, man and bird and
beast: save only Laguerre, who, slouched down
in the comfortable seat of the buckboard, mut-

tered deep imprecations upon an innocent creature grazing in a distant pasture, while his faithful servitor, Scipio, flicked his whiplash lightly over Zouave's flanks, as, at a walk, the lean stallion pulled the buggy through the deep sand of a heavy stretch of road, while, as he pulled, the narrow steel tires and the sand through which they tracked sang in low whisperings, as if there came from far away the crash of billows on the shore. How many solitary travelers on lonely Low-country roads, have been soothed as they drove slowly through the sand by whisperings that fell upon the spirit as softly as the wind among the pines!

"Damn the cow! Damn the cow!" growled the lord of Slann's Island, gritting his teeth and frowning savagely.

"Dat's so, Maussuh," agreed his henchman.

"Damn the cow! Damn the bull! Damn the calf!"

"Yaas, Maussuh," said the comforter. "Cuss-'um, Maussuh! Cuss de whole fambly. Cuss 'e hawn, en' 'e foot, en' 'e tail, all-t'ree. 'E do you good fuh cuss'um!"

He did, and it did, for when Laguerre had unloaded from his spleen and loaded upon his soul an outfit of expletives that would have ripped the rind from a scaly-bark hickory, he was once more at peace with the world and came again into the fellowship of man! His screwed-up face relaxed, the tawny thatch of his penthouse brows; the hairs of his sweeping mustache, that but now had bristled "like quills upon the fretful porpentine" resumed their normal curves, and a smile as soft as a little child's crept furtively over his hawk-like visage. Gradually it spread and broadened into a sudden laugh, as Scipio paid his tribute—received as gratefully as a kneeling knight his accolade!

"Maussuh," said he, "you do'um fine! W'en you call da' cow en' 'e fambly out 'e name, you nebbuh fuhgit nutt'n'! You 'membuhr'um all! Ef da' cow coulduh yeddy'um jis' ez 'e come out you mout', da' cow nebbuh fuh hab no peace no mo'! Ebb'ry time 'e 'toop 'e head down fuh bite grass, him fuh t'ink cucklebuhr en' briah dey een 'e mout', 'cause, w'en man' yez duh bu'n, him mout' gwine bittuh, Uh dunkyuh ef 'e got muhlassis een'um; en' ef him bin hab chance fuh yeddy dem wu'd en' t'ing wuh you t'row 'puntop-'um, Maussuh, da' cow' yez fuh bu'n sukkuh rozzum tree bu'n een de dry-drought w'en fiah git-'way een de pinelan'! 'Cause w'en you cuss da' cow you nebbuh shayre'um out. You g'em all wuh blonx to'um, en' den you heap'up de medjuh 'tel 'e run obuh! Maussuh, Uh tell you de trute, w'en 'e come to cuss, Uh nebbuh see nobody free-han' wid 'e mout' lukkuh you!"

131

Laguerre smiled reminiscently as he thought upon the events of the morning that had touched a match to the tinder of his irascible temper and, feeling that he had done all a biped with only whiskers could do against a quadruped with horns and a tail, he was not displeased with himself.

After breakfast on the eventful morning, "Jedge" sat on his front piazza enjoying the sunshine and the landscape, and listening to the voices of the wild creatures that came to him from forest and field and marsh—mingled with them the occasional bleating of sheep and the lowing of cattle from a distant pasture. "Jedge," drowsing the hours away until the time should come for hitching up and starting for his pineland assizes, suddenly bethought him that a milk punch would be just the thing to tune up the judicial mind to meet the legal problems that were probably awaiting solution. If there were none, so much the better, but there might be, and Laguerre took no chances. *"Animis opibusque parati;"* and—after all, a punch was a punch.

With characteristic impulsiveness "Jedge" jumped up, almost upsetting the rustic rocking chair in his haste to be at his pleasant task. There was no ice on the plantation, but there was a big shaker with which to bring the punch to the creamy foaminess of new ale (ah,

132

the good old days!) sugar and nutmeg were in the storeroom, and a nutmeg-grater, while in a stone jug in the dark closet—a darkness through which Laguerre's feet led him unerringly to his goal—there was still a shake left of the old yellow corn whiskey. With loving care, with infinite tenderness; reverentially, as one approaches a sacrament, Laguerre brought these things to the dining room and assembled them upon the table. Into a tall cut-glass tumbler he poured the gentlemanly "three fingers" of the Low-country planter, and then, as he really had four fingers, which he loved equally well, he poured another, which, remembering his occasional relation to the law, he conceived to be both equity and justice. And then, as the palm of the hand was, after all, a fairer and—for a man whose fingers tapered—a more liberal measure, he poured a little more!

Sure then that he had done himself no injustice in respect to whiskey, Laguerre took thought for milk, the next essential ingredient, but a brief search assured him there was none in the house. What could he do? He heard a cow lowing in a small pasture near by, but how could he get the milk? All the other members of his family were abroad for the morning and there was no servant within call. Even old Scipio, faithful man of all work, was away, search-

133

ing for Zouave at the far end of the big pasture. Laguerre knew how to milk, but milking was no work for a man! Certainly not for a Huguenot and a gentleman! Should he, the descendant of Crusaders, squat on an empty soap-box or a three-legged stool like any plump and stodgy dairy-maid, stick his aristocratic head against the flank of a confounded cow, and squeeze her unresponsive udder for a cupful of reluctant milk? Certainly not—not by a jugful! Yet, there was the jug, nearly empty, and there was the tall tumbler whose amber spirit beckoned, and called coaxingly for nutmeg, sugar and milk!

Laguerre heard the call, and, as there was nobody about to witness his compromise with dignity, he took a cedar "piggin" from the pantry shelf, and went forth in a spirit of exaltation, sure that He who sat in majesty beyond the stars would not judge too harshly a lordly male who descended from the high Olympus of his amour propre to milk a cow!

On his way through the yard to the pasture Laguerre picked up an old soap-box to serve as a milking stool, and, coming to the bars, he let them down and turned the cow into the lot where the waiting calf greeted her with the disinterested affection customarily shown by those who receive, to those who yield, the milk!

The cow, already milked in the morning, had

very little milk to yield, and for that the lusty calf made play after the manner of his kind, with many bumpings and buffetings of the maternal fount. Meanwhile, "man, proud man," seeing how the wind lay, and realizing that the calf, on all fours with the cow, was in the position of a country with a "favored nation" clause in its treaty, quickly placed his soap-box in strategic position on the starboard side of the cow, sat down, clamped the piggin tightly between his knees, and began to dispute with the calf for posession of the slippery teats.

The calf was a sturdy disputant. A cross of Ayrshire blood had bred into his marrow a touch of Scottish stubbornness, and he fought for his teats as tenaciously as a Covenanter for the tenets of his faith. But Laguerre was game, and in spite of bruised and slobbered knuckles that brought muttered imprecations from his wrathful lips, two tiny streams trickled intermittently into the yawning piggin from the lacteal fount, covering the bottom and giving promise of coming in time to a tumblerful—when, out of a clear sky, tragedy stalked upon the stage!

Youth—God bless it!—is exuberant, and as lads in Boy-Scout sizes chatter assiduously around a flapper's skirts, so the young lords of the barnyard, just learning to crow, try the charms of their uncertain pipes upon all wear-

ers of feminine feathers that flutter in the vicin-
age. True, their reedy efforts are usually off
key, and sharp at that, for, whatever the scope of
the feminine larynx, neither man nor cockerel
can hold the key with a frog in his throat; but
pullets are patient—they have to be—and in time
the fowl swallows the frog and comes into his
own. And what is true of these two vain strut-
ting bipeds applies with equal force to the un-
bashful bull!

In the home pasture of Laguerre, at the moment the Crusader was consigning the cow's for-
bears and her present and future progeny to
everlasting torment, and including in the sweeping condemnation the entire Bos family, a member of the clan, an adolescent male, was parading
about, trying his voice on the cow, the calf, and
anything else that might be within the magic of
its sound. 'Twas not very much of a voice, for
a bull, for it lay well within the treble clef, and
could approach no nearer masculinity than a
tenor, at best a light baritone, and its quavering
plaintive break was very pathetic.

Not much of a voice, but not much of a bull,
for, just crossing the borderland that lay between veal and beef, he was the nondescript the
Low-country calls "Harrydick." But even if
Harry had known what they called him, he
wouldn't have cared, for he knew that if the black

THE CRUSADER AND THE COW

rievers didn't slaughter him in the swamp to
make a Christmas holiday, he would be a bull bye
and bye; meanwhile he was having the time of
his life, pawing dirt and shrieking in a falsetto
that, all right as to tempo, was as unmelodious
as a cracked B-flat clarinet in a Tannhaeuser or-
chestra!

At last, as the milk in Laguerre's piggin rose
almost to the mark he had set as his goal, the
high pitched complainings of the little bull got
on his nerves. Himself a tenor, perhaps he resented the competition, but, whatever impulse
moved him, he turned his head toward the bars
to tell the creature what he thought of him. The
cow's tail was toward the bars, and at the moment the milker turned, a sudden impulse moved
her to switch the tail, whose tuft, stuck full of
early sheep-burrs, whisked across his face.

Exploding like a pack of firecrackers, Laguerre sprang to his feet with a sudden movement that upset the piggin between his knees and
spilled the precious milk. The astonished cow
was off and away, but not until her wrathful
master had smitten her with the empty piggin
and had thrown the soap-box after her for good
measure. Then, his anger yet unappeased, he
rushed into the house, to emerge a moment later,
gun in hand, for the discipline of both cow and
bull. He wouldn't go so far as to kill them.

LAGUERRE

His anger was not deep enough for that, but he
felt that a peppering in the hindquarters with
bird shot, would satisfy wounded honor and
soothe the Gallic spirit.

Beyond the pasture bars the little bull still
moaned, and thither the outraged cow, her ribs
yet tingling from the impact of the piggin,
turned for sympathy and companionship. The
calf, having taken all she had to give, showed no
further interest in the giver—as is the way with
calves—sometimes with men—and turned away
to nibble grass.

As the Crusader—now would-be matador—got
within easy range of his intended victims, they
moved so close together as to offer hope of sprinkling them both with a single fire, but his passion
called for more, and as their quarters presented
a tempting target, he cocked and leveled his
Greener and pulled both tender triggers simultaneously, bracing himself for the double kick,
whose recalcitrance he felt would do him good!
But there was no more kick in the Greener that
day than in a mug of "½ of one per cent." that
had been personally inspected and smelled-over
by a committee of the "unco' guid!" Not a cap
popped to cheer his spirit. Even such mimic
explosions would have helped, for, to men of Laguerre's temperament, wrath that cannot be ex-

pressed in sound, is no wrath at all to speak of—certainly none to boast about!

Laguerre's percussion caps were none of the best, and the long wet spell had so dampened the ardor of the fulminating powder that 'twas as free from latent fire, as incapable of sparking, as a hen-pecked and uxorious husband! So, when the graceful hammers fell, there was only the dull sound of tempered steel upon crimped copper, and a thoroughly disgusted Crusader, restraining an impulse to throw the gun at the cow, returned dejectedly to the house, where the sugar, the nutmeg, and the tall tumbler with its four fingers of liquid comfort (why do men speak of "solid comfort?") awaited him.

Why should man need milk—tipple for babes and women? He didn't, and as "Jedge" mixed his stiff grog and drank it, he felt himself more of a man for his independence of the pallid fluid, and by the time old Scipio had brought in and hitched up Zouave, the master of Slann's Island was on as good terms with himself as mellow men usually are.

But his mellowness did not, like a merry heart, go all the way, for, by the time the buckboard tires sang to the deep sands of the heavy stretch nearing Toogoodoo bridge, the cider of his spirit had turned to vinegar, until, encouraged by Scipio, he "cussed" himself out and came again to peace.

LAGUERRE

The second case called by Cudjo Hawlback, court crier, a short time after the opening of Court at high noon, was a dispute between Caesar Wineglass and the buxom wife of his bosom, the masterful Mis' Wineglass whose impressive personality had influenced the sisters of the temporarily expurgated Society of the "I Will Arise" to turn again to man, and recall Pa Tumbo to rule over them. The dispute involved, not only the Wineglasses—now almost brittle enough to break—but a Jewish merchant on Wadmalaw island, a chattel mortgage, and—an ox!

The ox, patient, useful, unassertive creature, whom no calf calls father, is well enough, and, beyond the Black Border, none calls him "out of his name"; but on Toogoodoo the ox, like the bull, is "cow"—a term including horned and hornless cattle of all ages, sexes, and modifications! So, when old Scipio, knowing the present tenseness of his master's nerves in respect to the Bos family, heard what the dispute was about, he scented trouble, and advised the disputants to postpone the case until a more propitious occasion when, perchance, the magisterial mind might "set fair."

"Budduh," the old man advised, "you bettuh tek care how you call cow' name een dishyuh co't yuh teday, 'cause Maussuh ent got no appetite fuh yeddy nutt'n' 'bout cow. Ef you call 'e name you

140

gwine git een trouble, sho' ez crab hab claw!
Cow duh him pizen, dis day!"

"Hukkuh dat?" he was asked.

"Comeyuh, lemme tell you;" and drawing the
persons interested to the edge of the crowd, out
of earshot of the court, he began.

"Dis mawnin', attuh Maussuh gitt'ru 'e brekwus', him binnuh seddown 'pun 'e pyazzuh duh
study. Nobody dey home 'cep' him, one, 'cause
Missis, dem, gone out fuh wisit, en' me bin gone
to de pastuh fuh ketch Zooab fuh pit een de
buggy fuh come yuh. Berry well.

"Bumbye, Maussuh biggin fuh t'u'sty. Him
ent t'us'ty fuh watuh. No, man! Maussuh' well
deep, but him nebbuh bodduh da' t'ing 'cep' 'e
t'row uh leetle tetch een'um out da' jug een de
sto'room. En' de mo' Maussuh t'u'sty de mo'
'e h'aa't hankuh attuh da' t'ing Buckruh mek out-
uh milk en' sugar en' brandy en' t'ing. Maussuh
nebbuh lub fuh milk no cow, but he h'aa't so
strong fuh da' t'ing, en' nobody dey dey fuh git
de milk, 'cep' 'e gitt'um fuh 'eself, 'tel Maussuh
tek de piggin off de shelf en' 'e gone een de yaa'd
fuh milk."

"Ki!" said Mis' Wineglass, "Uh wish Uh coulduh shum! Jedge too dig*nify* fuh milk cow."

" 'E dig*nify*, fuh true, but sometime w'en man
t'u'sty, 'e t'row'way da' dig*nify*, enty?

"So Jedge him squat down 'pun de box, 'e

141

butt 'e head een de cow' flank, en' him en' da' calf fight fuh de leely bit uh milk wuh de cow got. Him en' de calf! Jedge 'pun de one side, calf 'pun de t'odduh! But Jedge binnuh do berry well 'tel da' leetle yellin' bull een de pastuh biggin fuh holluh. 'E woice ent wu't', fuh no bull, but him lub fuh yeddy'um, en' 'e belluh so swif', 'tel, bumbye, Maussuh bex, 'cause him nebbuh lub fuh yeddy nobody talk 'cep him, one!"

"Bull kin talk?"

"Yaas, 'e talk. Bull iz man, enty? En' Maussuh t'ink none de man' woice ent wu't' 'cep' him- own; so, jis' ez Maussuh tu'n 'e head fuh cuss de bull, de cow tek notion fuh twitch 'e tail, en' 'e ketch Maussuh 'cross 'e face. Ki! Maussuh jump up lukkuh him binnuh seddown een wawss nes'! De pyo' bex rise'um! De milk t'row- 'way, 'e knock de cow wid 'e piggin, en' 'e run een 'e house fuh git gun fuh shoot de cow en' de bull alltwo."

"Ki! Shoot 'e own cow! Buckruh iz uh dain- jus t'ing!"

"But, t'engk-gawd, de gun nebbuh bin gone off, 'cause de we'dduh bin wet de cap en' dem couldn' speci*fy*, so him nebbuh shoot no cow, needuhso no bull; en' attuhw'ile Jedge gone een 'e house, 'e drink 'e dram en' 'e git peaceubble 'gen, but, ef you tek my exwice, you nebbuh call no cow name yuh teday!"

THE CRUSADER AND THE COW

But masterful woman, however willing to give, was not willing to take "sage advices," and when her case was called Mis' Wineglass started—but only started: "Jedge, Uh come fuh see you 'bout dishyuh cow—"

"Cow!" stormed the court, "Cow! Damn the cow!" and he postponed the hearing and proceeded with other cases involving no mention of the forbidden name.

THE CRITIC ON THE HEARTH

"Thank God for friends and kindred—they keep us humble!"

The cynic was a philosopher and realized that through criticism comes sometimes self-examination; self-analysis. If the criticism be just and the spirit be strong enough to see the truth, it comes out fine and clean; if unjust, the spirit is stronger in the knowledge, for in the final analysis man deals with himself alone, and, sure of himself, he can laugh the world to scorn—as he sometimes does!

But criticism, to be helpful, must be just and kindly and the critic must have the unquestioned right to criticise—a right by no means inhering in all men—or in all women!

So it was that Caesar Wineglass, husband of Mis' Wineglass, whose dominant personality had thrust Pa Tumbo back into the tumultuous bosoms of the thirty sisters of the "I Will Arise," was abroad on a bright October day, trying to find in the painted forests, the flowered fields, the wind-swept open pastures, surcease from the clatter of his own hearthstone, whereon, with legs out-spread in manly fashion, arms akimbo, and back to the fire, the wife of his bosom had stood, off and on, during the waking hours of three successive days, telling Caesar what she thought of him, and then, lest he forget, telling him all over again, as is sometimes the way with those whom God hath appointed to admonish man!

Over the marshes, up in the hazy blue, fish-crows "mustered," alternately sailing and flapping, wheeling and crossing, in the fantastic evolutions of an aerial Virginia reel, drawling their disagreeable notes. Lower down, flapping questioningly over field and forest, taking note, and taking toll of ripened corn and ripening acorns, their congeners the common crows cawed cheerfully.

As to the merits and demerits of this sable fellow, ornithologists and agriculturists are in hopeless disagreement, the scientist holding his destruction of noxious insects to be worth far more to the farmer than the little corn he destroys, but the farmer, a practical man, doesn't see the bugs, real or theoretical, in the crow's crop, while he does see the uprooted corn; so he shoots the protegee of the ornithologist—when he can—and ties him to a tall stake in his corn field as a terrible example.

But, whether helpful or harmful, the Negro, bothered with no scientific theories, judges for himself. He knows that crows often harry destructive hawks and drive them away from his chickens, and that's in his favor; on the other hand he knows that the crow pulls corn, pulls it

146

destructively, so unless he can get coal-tar with which to coat the seed corn and make it crow-proof, he, also, tries to get the crow, and hang him up.

But whatever the crow's economic relation to the Gullah, socially he is a boon companion, a fellow-black whom he often denounces jocularly, as "Nigguh!" while at other times he borrows his name, without a by-your-leave, to indicate a brother of particularly dark pigmentation.

And now the alert, cheery and impersonal chatter of the crows fell soothingly upon Caesar's ear, and calmed his tortured spirit. He knew they were scolding, but not at him, thank God, and for that he was grateful—grateful as only he can be, who, lonely among men, finds solace and companionship in solitude, with his own thoughts among the wild creatures whom God hath not made in His image!

A crow flew slowly over, circled and lit on the top of a pine nearby.

"Caw! Caw!"

"Mawnin', budduh! Uh yeddy you."

"Caw! Caw! Caw!"

"Yaas! Yaas! Yaas!"

"Caw! Caw! Caw! Caw!"

"Now you duh talk! Tell we 'bout'um budduh, tell we 'bout'um. De 'ooman bin onrabble 'e mout' at you, enty?"

"Caw! Caw!"

"Uh t'aw't so! Yaas, da' jis' de way 'e stan',
en' me yez stan' same fashi'n lukkuh you'own.
'E full'up wid 'ooman' mout'!"

"Caw! Caw! Caw!"

"You ax me wuh de 'ooman bex 'bout, enty?
'E bex 'bout nutt'n'! 'E bex 'cause him is
'ooman en' Gawd mek 'ooman fuh bex, so man
kin cruci*fy!* Da' w'ymekso de 'ooman bex!"

"Caw! Caw! Caw! Caw!"

"Aye! Aye! You ax me w'ymekso Uh yent
knock'um, ef de 'ooman so mischeebus, enty?
Budduh! Lemme tell you. Da' 'ooman ent fuh
knock. 'E too hebby! You nebbuh shum, enty?"

"Caw! Caw!"

"Uh t'aw't so, 'cause da' 'ooman strong tummuch! 'E strong ez cow! Ef Uh hadduh bin
know een exwance how strong da' 'ooman stan',
Uh nebbuh woulduh hab'um fuh wife. 'E too
dainjus! Now, 'e too late. Uh git ketch een de
trap, en' Uh cyan' git'way. De 'ooman ent got
no use fuh me, needuhso me ent got no use fuh
him, en' stillyet de debble'ub'uh 'ooman wunt tu'n
me loose! Him cuntrady to dat!"

"Caw! Caw! Caw!"

"Yaas, 'e yiz. You talk trute. Dat puhzac'ly
how 'e yiz. En', budduh, now you know how de
t'ing stan', tell me wuh fuh do. Wuhebbuh you
exwise me fuh do wid de 'ooman, Uh gwine do'um,

ef Uh kin, 'cause Uh know crow hab sense mo'nuh Nigguh."

"Caw! Caw! Caw! Caw!"

"Budduh, stop tell me fuh lick da' 'oman! Enty Uh tell you 'e yent fuh lick? You wan' me fuh dead, enty? Uh t'aw't you bin me frien'!"

"Caw! Caw!"

"Now you duh talk! You gimme good exwice *dis* time, en' Uh gwine fuh see Jedge same lukkuh you tell me fuh do. Well, so long, budduh. You iz crow fuh true, but you woice sweet'n me yez, attuh all da' pizen de 'oman pit een'um. You wash'um out clean! You do me heap'uh good, tengk-gawd!"

"Caw! Caw! Caw!" And the crow was gone.

On the preceding Saturday Caesar's wife, not above suspicion of a Jewish merchant on Wadmalaw from whom she had bought an ox, giving a chattel mortgage for part of the purchase price, had brought the ox, the merchant, and Caesar, as a witness, before Laguerre's court for an adjustment of the warring interests, but Laguerre, having had a misunderstanding with the family milch cow during the morning, was indisposed to hear any causes involving the ownership of horned cattle, and dismissed the case forthwith. The merchant returned to the island whose comprehensive name suggested at once shotguns, maternity and litigation, the ox was turned out to grass, and Mis' Wineglass returned to her hearth, whereon she chirped so blithely, that on this Tuesday morning, Caesar broke bounds, followed the ox and turned himself out to grass, and came in time to the friendly companionship of crows!

Taking his foot in his hand, Caesar took the road and came to Laguerre's house at noon—a most propitious time, for "Jedge" had just poured out a generous four fingers from the jug and, adding water, sugar and nutmeg, had mixed a tall tumblerful of the old-fashioned toddy that always brought a reminiscent smile to his face, as if his mind harked back to pleasant dreams of the long ago. These were the kindly moods of a volatile and irascible man, well known to those who came in contact with him, and to the entire Negro community, as well, for from these black folk little is hidden of the lives and characteristics of the few whites who live among them.

So, knowing that the safest time to approach "Jedge" was when, with half closed eyes he leaned back in his rocking chair on the piazza and slowly sipped his fragrant tipple, Caesar doffed his hat, pulled his wool, and deferentially approached the Presence.

"Jedge, suh, da' 'ooman wuh Uh got fuh wife— you know'um, suh, 'cause ef you nebbuh bin shum, you mus'be bin yeddy'um! Ebb'rybody haffuh yeddy'um, 'cause mout' duh him name! Well, suh, da' 'ooman tangle 'eself up wid da' Jew sto'keepuh 'puntop Wadmuhlaw 'bout uh leetle oxin wuh 'e buy. De 'ooman mek baa'gin fuh pay'um t'irteen dolluh fuh de creetuh, puhwid'n' him kin speci*fy*, but de Jew say ef de oxin too light fuh pull de plow, him willin' fuh tek off t'ree dolluh frum de ten, en' him will sattify fuh tek seb'n dolluh fuh de odduhres' wuh jue on de oxin.

"Jedge, da' duh de wu'd wuh come out de Jew' mout', but de papuh wuh 'e tie 'puntop de oxin ent stan' so. 'E nebbuh call no seb'n dolluh name. Ten dolluh duh all da' papuh duh talk 'bout."

"How do you know what the paper said?" Laguerre asked. "Can you read?"

"No, suh, Jedge, Uh cyan' read, but las' Sattyday w'en you bin bex 'cause de 'ooman call cow' name, de Jew fetch de papuh to we house, en' him read'um out loud, en', Jedge, w'en Uh yeddy'um Uh bin tarrify, 'cause Uh nebbuh yeddy no wu'd lukkuh dat befo'! De papuh say de Jew fuh hab'um, en' hol'um alltwo, en' all shishuh t'ing lukkuh dat, den 'e say de Jew fuh hol' de 'ooman' hair fuhrebbuh. How him fuh do'um? Great Gawd! Jedge, Nigguh ent got no hair! Weh 'e dey? De 'ooman comb'um out en' quile'um up 'puntop dem head en' call'um hair, but w'en you quizzit'um close, 'e stan' sukkuh black moss, enty, suh? Jedge, w'en you look 'puntop black sheep'

back, you look 'puntop Nigguh' head! Ef da'
Jew fuh hol' Nigguh' hair fuhrebbuh, lukkuh da'
papuh say, him haffuh hab claw! 'E nebbuh
ketch'um wid 'e han'!"

"What the devil is that paper you are talking
about?" asked Laguerre.

"Da' mawgidge de Jew pit 'puntop de cow,
Jedge."

Laguerre chuckled, understandingly. "Her
heirs and assigns forever," he quoted.

"Yaas, suh, Jedge," Caesar shouted, delighted
that his recollection of the letter of the law had
been confirmed, "da' duh him, da' duh him! Dat
puhzac'ly wuh de papuh say."

"Well, did you sign the paper?"

"Jedge, suh, ebb'rybody sign'um! At de fus'
gwinin' off de Jew fetch de papuh en' tell de
'ooman fuh sign 'e name 'puntop de papuh. Ef
'e hadduh bin man, 'stead'uh 'ooman, him woulduh
sign de papuh bedout ax no squeschun 'bout'um,
but 'ooman ent fuh do no shishuh t'ing lukkuh
dat, 'cause him too s'pishus 'bout man. Soon ez
him see britchiz, him biggin fuh s'pishun'um. No
use fuh tell you how 'e stan', Jedge, 'cause you
know 'ooman tummuch!

"So de 'ooman biggin fuh quizzit de Jew, en'
ax'um wuh de papuh yiz, en' wuffuh him haffuh
sign'um. De Jew tell'um de papuh iz de 'ooman'
wu'd fuh pay de Jew de t'odduh ten dolluh wuh jue

on de oxin. En' 'e say w'en man pit 'e wu'd 'puntop de papuh, 'e mek'um stan' mo' 'sponsubble. Da' de reaz'n him wan' de 'ooman' wu'd fuh write down.

"Ki! Jedge, w'en de Jew talk 'bout wu'd to da' 'ooman wuh Uh got fuh wife, Uh haffuh laugh een de man' face, 'cause wu'd duh weh da' 'ooman lib! Him full'up wid wu'd, en' Uh know suh ef da' Jew nebbuh yeddy no wu'd befo' sence him lef' Juhruz'lum, him fuh yeddy'um now!

"De 'ooman gyap 'e mout', 'e ketch 'e bre't' one time, en' 'e gone! Da' one time duh all de chance de 'ooman gwine hab fuh ketch 'e bre't' t'ru 'e mout' 'tel 'e done talk, 'cause attuh 'e yiz staa't, da' bre't' haffuh ketch t'ru 'e yez, 'cause 'e mout' ent hab no time fuh stop! Berry well.

"Jedge, ef you coulduh yeddy da' 'ooman aa'gyfy 'long de Jew, you woulduh t'ink him bin een Walterburruh co'thouse duh 'spute wid dem lawyuh en' t'ing!

"De 'ooman ax'um ef 'e yent sell 'e oxin fuh t'ree dolluh een 'e han' en' ten dolluh on credik? De Jew say yaas, 'e stan' so fuh true. De 'ooman ax'um wuh 'e got fuh de ten dolluh wuh lef', attuh 'e done pit de t'ree dolluh een 'e han'? De Jew say 'e yent got nutt'in' fuhr'um, 'cep' de prommus fuh pay'um wuh de 'ooman done mek. De 'ooman ax'um wuh de prommus bin mek wid —w'edduh 'e mek wid wu'd, eeduhso papuh? De Jew say 'e mek wid wu'd out de 'ooman' mout'. De

153

'ooman say berrywellden, dem same wu'd out 'e
mout' haffuh sattify'um 'tel 'e cotton done pick,
'cause wu'd duh all wuh him got. De Jew say de
'ooman gott'um fuh true, but him mo' redduh hab
dem wu'd 'puntop de papuh, den fuh leff'um een
'e mout', 'cause sometime de wu'd wuh lef' een'um,
ef you tu'n yo' back, fus' t'ing you know de wu'd
git'way en' gone!

"Jedge, da' Jew know 'ooman berry well,
'cause de 'ooman' mout' stan' so fuh true. Him
mout' stan' sukkuh pot duh bile! Ef you stop
watch'um, ef you tek you eye off'um two-t'ree
minnit, him fuh bile obuh, en' eb'nso ef you yiz
watch'um, him fuh bile obuh same fashi'n! 'E
yent wu't'!

"So de Jew tell de 'ooman ef de wu'd come out 'e
mout' so fas'; ef 'e hab wu'd fuh t'row'way, him
kin t'row'um 'puntop da' papuh, den 'e yent fuh
loss. De 'ooman talk all de talk wuh 'e got, fuh
try fuh 'suade de Jew fuh tek wu'd out 'e mout'
'stead'uh write'um 'pun de papuh, but 'e yent
no use, de 'ooman cyan' shake'um en' de Jew
hol' to da' papuh sukkuh briah hol' 'ooman' sku't!

"Attuhw'ile de Jew say him woulduh tek de
'ooman' mout' 'stead'uh de papuh, ef de 'ooman
hadduh bin lib 'puntop Wadmuhlaw, eeduhso ef
de Jew bin lib Slann' I'lun', 'cause, w'en two man
lib to de same place, mout' do berry well, but
w'en one de man lib to Wadmuhlaw, en' t'odduh

one lib to Slann' I'lun', dem stan' too fudduh fuh yeddy, so, bumbye, w'en de Jew done flattuhr'um en' nice'um up wid gunjuh en' t'ing, de 'ooman tell'um berry well, him willin' fuh sign de papuh.

"Yuh de debble now! How him fuh do'um, w'en de 'ooman cyan' write 'e name? De Jew tell'um dat ent mek no diff'unce, 'cause him kin write de 'ooman' name, en' den de 'ooman kin tetch de pen een de Jew' han' w'ile de Jew duh mek cross maa'k 'puntop'um, en' de name kin specify jis' ez good ez ef de 'ooman bin write 'puntop de papuh wid 'e own han'.

"Jedge, w'en de 'ooman yeddy dat, 'e done fuh glad. Da' Jew sweetmout'um out'uh all dem s'pishun him bin hab 'bout man! Him so hasty fuh help da' Jew mek 'e cross maa'k, 'e nebbuh ax'um fuh read de mawgidge, nuh nutt'n'. Dat how come 'e nebbuh yeddy 'bout da' 'gree*ment* 'pun de papuh, wuh gi' de Jew prib'lidge fuh hol' de 'ooman' hair en' t'ing fuhrebbuh, 'cep' 'e pay da' t'odduh ten dolluh 'pun de oxin. So de 'ooman tetch de pen, en' de Jew mek one hebby cross maa'k 'pun de papuh, en' de 'ooman t'ink 'e *done* fuh stylish.

"Den de Jew say him haffuh hab witness to de 'ooman' name, en' 'e tek me fuh witness, en' 'e write my name 'pun de papuh, en' w'en 'e done write'um 'e tell me fuh tetch de pen, en' 'e mek cross maa'k fuh my'own same lukkuh 'e do'um fuh de 'ooman, 'cep' my'own stan' leetle mo'nuh him'own, 'cause da' Jew know 'ooman is uh jallus t'ing, en' w'en 'e see de 'ooman' eye 'puntop-'um, him 'f'aid fuh mek my cross maa'k big ez de one wuh 'e mek fuh de 'ooman.

"Den, attuh my cross maa'k done mek, one Nigguh, name Quakoo Frajuh, come een de sto', en' de Jew mek'um witness my maa'k, 'cause 'e say Jew ent fuh tek no chance, en' 'e say me en' de 'ooman iz one en' de same somebody, lukkuh de Scriptuh tell we fuh jine togedduh, en' 'e say dem wuh Gawd done jine togedduh, man ent fuh pit no t'unduh een'um! En' de Jew say ef me en' da' 'ooman iz one, den him haffuh hab 'nodduh witness 'puntop'uh me. But, Jedge, da' Jew ent know! Me en' da' 'ooman ent lib togedduh lukkuh one! Me nuh him lib togedduh lukkuh t'irteen! Him iz de twelbe, en' me, po' creetuh, duh de one! Jedge, da' 'ooman change 'e min' so swif'; 'e cyan' keep count 'pun 'e ten finguh, so, attuh 'e finguh done run out, him haffuh tek off 'e shoesh en' count 'pun 'e toe! Berrywell.

"So de Jew mek Quakoo tetch de pen, en' him mek cross maa'k fuh witness me, same lukkuh me bin mek'um fuh witness de 'ooman, en—"

"Lo! what a cloud of witnesses—" quoted Laguerre, reverently.

"Yaas, suh, Jedge, en' dat ent all, 'cause attuh Quakoo' cross maa'k done mek, de Jew tu'n 'roun'

en' sign de papuh 'eself, 'puntop all dem t'orruh
one, fuh witness Quakoo' maa'k, 'cause 'e say me
en' de 'ooman alltwo lib to Slann' I'lun', en' 'e say
Slann' I'lun' Nigguh ent fuh trus' tummuch, so
him haffuh hab two Wadmuhlaw man fuh stan'up
fuhr'um puhwid'n' me en' de 'ooman try fuh
obuht'row'um. So, me witness de 'ooman, Quakoo witness me, en' de Jew witness Quakoo. De
Jew do all de han'write, but him nebbuh mek no
cross fuh 'eself."

"Ha!" cried Laguerre. "Witnessed an instrument pledging property to himself, did he? We'll
see about this Wadmalaw law! Caesar," he demanded, "an hour ago you started to tell me what
your wife did to you, and you ended up by telling
what Wadmalaw did to your wife! Now, what
the devil did your wife do to you, and why the
devil did she do it?"

Caesar shook with laughter. "Jedge, suh, you
tek de wu'd out me mout'. You ansuhr'um fuh
you'self. Da' same man wuh you call 'e name,
him dey een de 'ooman, en' him mek de 'ooman
do'um! Satan duh 'e name, en' Satan duh 'e mannus! Lemme tell you, suh.

"We'n de 'ooman done buy 'e leetle cow frum de
Jew 'e fetch'um home. De t'ing leetle but 'e
willin'. Uh hitch'um up een de plow, but 'e too
light fuh pull de plow deestunt, lukkuh plow iz
fuh pull, 'cause, 'stead'uh bruk de groun', 'e jis'

'cratch'um, en shishuh plowin' ent wu't'. So, Uh
nyuze de oxin fuh 'cratch 'bout leetle bit, en'
w'en 'e yent duh wu'k, Uh tu'n'um out fuh grow.
'E grow, too, 'e grow berry well, but 'e nebbuh
staa't fuh grow soon 'nuf fuh mek de crap, so
t'odduh day w'en de Jew come fuh 'e money,
de 'ooman tell'um de oxin bin too light fuh pull
plow, en' 'e 'membuhr'um 'bout 'e prommus fuh
tek seb'n dolluh fuh de t'ing, 'stead'uh ten, ef de
cow could'n' specify, but de 'ceitful Jew tell'um no,
him nebbuh prommus'um no shishuh t'ing, en' 'e
say ef 'e yiz bin do'um, wu'd wuh come out 'e mout'
ent wu't' 'cep' de papuh ketch'um, en' den 'e pull
de mawgidge out 'e pocket, en' de mawgidge call
ten dolluh name, en' 'e fawtify wid all dem witness en' t'ing, en' w'en de Jew read'um obuh
two-t'ree time, 'bout how him fuh hol' de 'ooman'
hair en' t'ing fuhrebbuh, 'cep' de ten dolluh iz pay,
de 'ooman git mos' 'stractid, 'cause 'e only got
seb'n dolluh to 'e name. Dat bin las' Sattyday,
en' w'en me en' de 'ooman fetch de Jew en' de
oxin to you fuh ontwis'um fuh we, Buh Scipio
tell we you ent bin hab no appetite fuh yeddy
nutt'n' 'bout no cow, 'cause you en' cow bin hab uh
hebby 'spute befo' you lef' you house, en' den
soon ez de 'ooman call de cow' name, you bex, en'
cuss de cow, en' de Jew gone Wadmuhlaw, en' 'e
say him gwine come back dis Sattyday fuh 'e
money, eeduhso de cow; en', Jedge, Uh dunno

158

wuh fuh do, 'cause Uh cyan' go back een me house long ez da' 'ooman dey dey, en' him dey dey, Jedge, him dey dey, sho' ez ribbuh got mout'! En' him duh wait fuh me. Him dey t'ree mile off, but me sperrit yeddy'um now—en' me yez duh bu'n!"

"But, Caesar," said Laguerre, teasingly, "Your wife is a just woman, isn't she? Why should she blame you for the bad trade she made with the Wadmalaw man for the ox?"

"Yaas, suh, Jedge, him iz jes' 'ooman, fuh true! Jes' *'ooman!* 'E yent nutt'n' else. Da' de reaz'n no jestuss dey een'um! W'en him binnuh mek da' baa'gin wid de Jew, 'e so sattify wid 'eself 'e nebbuh ax me fuh no exwice, en' Uh nebbuh g'em none. Uh nebbuh crack me teet'. Uh le'm'lone 'tel him en' de Jew done tangle'up togedduh fuh suit demself. Now, attuh 'e fin' out las' Sattyday 'bout how de Jew obuhreach'um, en' 'e bex wid 'eself 'cause de Jew smaa't mo'nuh him, de bex tek'um so hebby him jump 'puntop-'uh me, same lukkuh me bin de Jew!"

"A long jump from Jerusalem to Slann's Island."

"Yaas, Jedge, but him iz 'ooman, enty? W'en 'ooman' min' git ready fuh jump, nutt'n' nebbuh bodduhr'um. Uh dunkyuh how fudduh 'e stan'. Him kin jump obuh de Red Sea en' nebbuh wet 'e foot!

LAGUERRE

"So w'en 'e git back een we house Sattyday ebenin', en' de 'ooman see suh no Jew dey dey, him tek me fuh mek Jew."

"Hail to the High Priestess!" laughed Laguerre.

"Jedge, soon ez de 'ooman git een de house, 'e shet de do', 'e mek fiah, en' 'e staa't fuh cook. Befo' de pot hab time fuh bile, de 'ooman' mout' biggin fuh bile, 'cause him staa't fus', en' da' pot nebbuh ketch'um!

"All de time de bittle binnuh cook, de 'ooman onrabble 'e mout' at me jis' 'cause me duh man! De Jew hab on britchiz, en' me hab on britchiz, en' de 'ooman jump 'puntop'um en' 'buze'um 'cause britchiz duh him pizen! Jedge, de cuntrady creetuh fau't me jis' 'cause me bin one de witness 'pun de debble'ub'uh mawgidge him gi' de Jew. Uh ax'um mekso 'e yent 'buze Quakoo en' de Jew 'stead'uh onload 'e mout' 'puntop'uh me, en' 'e mek ansuh en' say ef him bin hab'um yuh him woulduh 'buze'um fuh who las' de longes', but me duh de only man wuh stan' cunweenyunt, so 'e say me haffuh tek'um fuh all t'ree, 'cause me iz man, en' Uh yent wu't' no how. Uh tell'um Uh haffuh do de bes' Uh kin, but Uh only got two yez to me name, en' ef dem bin long, sukkuh rabbit' yez, eeduhso jackass' yez, dem wouldn' long 'nuf fuh hol' all him duh try fuh t'row een'um.

"Jedge da' de las' wu'd Uh git chance fuh say fuh t'ree day! W'en de 'ooman done eat, 'e stan'

160

wid 'e back to de fiah, en' spraddle 'e foot lukkuh him bin man, 'e 'kimbo 'e two aa'm 'pun 'e two hip, en' 'e t'un loose! Da' 'ooman tell me all de mean t'ing Uh ebbuh do een me life frum de time Uh binnuh creep, befo' me maamy done wean me. Den, w'en 'e done, 'e tell me all de mean t'ing Uh bin study 'bout, en plan fuh do, but nebbuh git chance fuh do'um! Uh dunno how de drat 'ooman happ'n fuh know summuch!

"En', Jedge, den him pit 'e han' behine 'e back en' cross'um obuh 'e debble'ub'uh hanch en' wawm'um befo' de fiah, en' 'e tell me all de mean t'ing me fambly bin do ebbuh sence me gran'-daddy binnuh climb cokynot tree een Aff'iky, en' hab tail en' t'ing! Him do dat off en' on, ebb'ry chance 'e git fuh t'ree day, so dis mawnin' Uh watch me chance en' Uh git'way, en' Uh gone duh 'ood fuh talk wid crow, 'cause him iz me bredduh, en' 'e woice sweet'n me yez tummuch."

"Bring the wife of your bosom before me next Saturday."

"Suh?"

"Bring your wife, then, and I'll see if I can't stop her mouth for you."

"T'engky, Jedge, but Toogoodoo crik ent fuh stop! Gawd mek'um fuh run!"

161

THE ROAD CALLED STRAIGHT

October forests were ablaze with the funeral pyres of the summer, long fading, now at rest, awaiting the promised resurrection, when, in God's great cycle, as long as time shall last, the seasons come into their own.

Redoaks and the lowly scrub, their kindred, burned dully now, as they slowly changed to russet, to wear at last until they fell and turned to mold, the somber garb of monks. Sassafras and sourwood shot the woods with brighter reds, and flaming hickories splashed them far and wide with gold. Blackgums glowed redly, and harlequin sweetgums along the bays showed every shade of green and red and purple and yellow.

All nature was changing, save the pines—stalwart pillars of the forest—upon whose rugged characters the passing seasons wrought as vainly as ocean waves upon a rock-bound shore. A little purple flowering in spring, a soft sprinkling of pollen like golden dust, the faltering fall of brown needles slowly carpeting the forest floor, and that is all. The winds that sweep their lofty tops, chant solemnly in organ tones, or croon low lullabies; while emerald needles, shining in the sunlight or glistening in the rain, hold high, under bright or lowering skies the symbol of hope! So, steadfast men keep their way unswervingly

through a restless world, holding to their tra-
ditions, their standards and their faiths, unmoved
by the turmoil that beats about them—the changing liveries of custom and of thought!

During the autumn and winter months other
voices were added to the music of the wind-harps
in the tops of the great pines, for here, to feed
upon the sweet mast of the *palustris,* came
swarming flocks of black-birds, singing all at
once in a liquid tumult of sound, and here came,
singly and in squads, noisy crows "telling the
world," as crows and men so often do, all about
themselves and their achievements and inciden-
tally disclosing the shortcomings of their neighbors.

But, with a finer tribal spirit than men, crows
and their kindred, bluejays, are ever on the watch
for enemies, not only of their clan, but of all the
furred and feathered creatures of the wild. A
black snake draped gracefully among the leafy
boughs of a low bush, wherein a songbird is build-
ing her nest, a diamond-back rattler slowly drag-
ging his dreadful length across the fallen leaves
under a spreading beech, a hunter at a stand listening for the cry of the distant pack and waiting
for the oncoming deer, are no sooner spotted
by these blue or sable watchmen of the woods,
than far-flung warnings issue forth, and songbird flutters questioningly around the bush, the

164

wild four-footed things give the Upas-beech a
wide berth, and the on-coming deer pricks his
apprehensive ears, and swerves swiftly away to
another pass, leaving a chagrined stander to
curse the crow!

Thus, as in the affairs of men, the service of
those who serve, is taken as a matter of course,
often accepted with condescension, while to him
who serves—the guardian—comes always the
enmity of the sinister influence he has thwarted.
So often, among the unthinking, the unseeing,
must virtue be its own reward!

On Thursday morning, bright and beautiful,
Laguerre rose early and paced the long piazza
impatiently, as is the way with masterful men
who wait for breakfast—men who, demanding
waffles, dismiss the idiosyncracies of waffle-irons
as unworthy of consideration.

Almost sharp enough for frost, the first rays
of the sun set the myriad dewdrops sparkling on
yellow, green and purple grass, and the white
lace-like spreads of the great spiders. As old
Scipio came to announce breakfast a little cloud
of vapor rose from his mouth.

"Looks like frost, Scipio," said his master, with
a sweep of his arm toward the glistening fields.

"Yaas, maussuh, 'e yiz look lukkuh de fus'
w'ite fros', but 'e nutt'n' but de hebby jew. You
shum stan' so, 'e look dainjus, but soon ez sun

165

git leetle mo' stronguh, him will drink'um up so swif' 'e nebbuh wet 'e mout'! Attuh da' jew done gone, ef you look 'puntop de 'tettuh wine en' t'ing you will shum stan' jis' ez green ez dat. Uh dunkyuh how hebby de jew stan', him ent man 'nuf fuh bite'um. No, suh. 'E mos' time fuh fros', but 'e yent come yit!"

Thus ended a discussion that came up with each recurrent October, Laguerre, like many men, and all boys, hoping for early frosts, and feverishly anxious to be the first to see it, though he knew it would bite the sweet potato vines and stain the late-opening bolls of Sea-Island cotton. How many early-rising white boys on Southern plantations, in the old days and the new, have had the ardor of discovery chilled by the authoritative dictum of some wise old darky: "Dat ain't fros', my chile. 'E nutt'n' but de hebby jew!"

Before the sun had drunk up the dew, Laguerre and Scipio, with Zouave in the buckboard, drove off. Laguerre was making an early start to meet a call at a distant plantation, whither he had been summoned by messenger the night before to sit in a "crowner's 'quest" upon the body of an unfortunate Negro upon whom a tree had fallen. This business he hoped to finish in time to meet another engagement, so Scipio touched up Zouave with the whip and he started at a smart trot.

The road was unfamiliar, for they had never

been to the place before, and, following the rather vague directions of the messenger, they had turned off from the main road after two or three miles to enter another that showed little evidence of travel, threading a forest area that, starting with open pineland of virgin growth, soon thickened, as the land lay lower, to shortleaf and swamp hardwoods. They drove two miles through this wilderness without meeting any one. Nor were there any settlements along the way; the lonely forest—nothing more.

At last, when Laguerre, fuming with impatience, was about ready to express himself vigorously as to the quick and the dead of the African race—the one, whose poor stark body had called him, and the other who had misdirected him to where it lay—an old Negro came in sight in the road ahead, and neared them rapidly. Though gnarled and bent, the old fellow moved briskly, carrying in his hand as he swung along a heavy hickory stick. He stepped to the side of the road and bowed low as the buggy halted and then, as Laguerre gave his name and title, he bowed again, for "Jedge" was known by reputation throughout the countryside and, as "Jedge" didn't hold with Pope that "honor and shame from no condition rise" and was ever astride upon his title, as upon a hobby-horse, the Negroes knew that title had to be saluted!

167

"Daddy," said Laguerre, "do you know the way to Blake's?"

The old man smiled as if pitying the simplicity of his questioner. "Oh, yaas, suh, obco'se Uh know'um. Dat jis' t'odduh side de place weh Uh lib. Da' place jis' 'bout uh mile t'odduh side uh me, en' me place stan' jis' 'bout uh mile dis side uh him."

"Very enlightening," said Laguerre.

The old man brightened at the supposed compliment. "Yaas, suh, dat jis' de way 'e stan'."

"Well, then," he was asked, "how far is Blake's?"

"Puhzac'ly fo' mile, suh."

"Can you show me the road?"

"Uh kin dat, suh, Uh kin dat! Uh trabble da' road all de time."

"Well, tell me how to find it."

The old man stepped to the middle of the road, raked away the pinestraw with his stick, and with its pointed end began to mark roads and crossroads in the firm sand, while Scipio turned the horse's head so as to afford Laguerre an uninterrupted view of the draughtsman.

"Shum yuh, suh, shum yuh! Now, dishyuh road yuh—de one wuh Uh got me stick een'um—dishyuh duh de road, de one wuh we dey een now, en' you haffuh hol' him fuh 'bout uh mile, 'tel you git to de fus' cross-road."

168

THE ROAD CALLED STRAIGHT

"The devil!" cried Laguerre, petulantly. "Are there two cross-roads?"

"Yaas, suh, two dey dey, but you ent fuh bodduh 'bout de fus' one, you ent fuh folluh him to de right han', neeeduhso to de lef' han', you fuh keep straight on 'tel you cross obuhr'um. Now, Uh done wid de fus' cross-road en' Uh rub'um out," and with a scrape of his foot, the first cross was obliterated and the surface smoothed for the second drawing.

"Now, suh, dishyuh one mek de two cross-road wuh dey dey, en' dishyuh one duh de one you haffuh bodduh 'bout. Attuh you done pass de fus' cross-road 'bout uh mile, you come to dis one. Uh call'um cross-road, but 'e yent cross-road, fuh true, 'cause no road nebbuh cross'um. Nutt'n' dey dey 'cep' dishyuh same road we dey een now, but w'en 'e git dey de road split, sukkuh fawk, en' one side de fawk lean to de right han' en' t'odduh one lean to de lef' han'. 'E yent lean berry hebby, 'cause alltwo de road run close togedduh 'longside one'nurruh fuh 'bout uh mile, but ef you chance fuh git een de wrong one at de fus', you ent gwine folluhr'um too fudduh 'cause attuh you trabble'um 'bout uh mile, ef no log dey cross'um, you fuh know you dey een de wrong road, en' you haffuh tu'n back to de fawk, en' tek t'odduh one, but ef da' log dey dey, den you fuh know you got de right road; you dribe 'roun' de

169

log t'ru de bush, you come back een de road, en' you tek'um, en' gone!"

"Well, how far do I go after leaving the log before I get to Blake's?"

"Jedge, you ent staa't fuh git to Blake! Attuh you pass da' log 'bout uh mile, you see anodduh road mek uh shaa'p slant 'cross da' road wuh got de log cross'um—da' duh you road now—shum yuh! En' you ent fuh leff'um 'tel Uh show you, suh."

"The devil! Hold on! When you started you said it was four miles from here to Blake's."

"Yaas, suh, dat puhzac'ly wuh 'e yiz, fo' mile."

"Well, you said it was one mile to the first cross-roads, another mile to the second, a third mile to the log across the road, and a fourth to the slanting road you're just talking about—that makes four already and you say I haven't started yet."

The old darky scratched his head. "Well, suh, ef 'e yent fo' mile, Uh know berry well 'e yent mo'nuh seb'n!"

"Well, then, what road am I supposed to be in, now that I have gone four miles from here?"

"Shum yuh!" the topographer said, drawing another mark with the point of his stick, "shum yuh, suh! You dey right yuh. You ent git dey yit, fuh true, 'cause you ent staa't, but you dey

dey, 'cause dat weh you duh gwine, enty? Berrywell.

"Now, yuh you iz, en' yuh da' slantin' road Uh
bin tell you 'bout, but you ent fuh tek him. No,
suh, you ent fuh bodduh wid him none'tall, 'cause
da' place him duh gwine stan' fudduh frum de
place you duh gwine, da' w'ymekso Uh tell you
fuh le'm'lone en' le'm gone weh 'e duh gwine,
'cause da' road ent wu't' fuh git to Blake, en'—"

"How the devil will I get to Blake's or anywhere else if you don't get to the point?"

"Yaas, suh, Uh gwine git to da' p'int now.
Uh bin 'splain'um 'sponsubble, so you ent fuh
git tanglety up. So, attuh you done pass da'
slantin' road 'bout half uh mile, you see 'pun you
lef' han', close to de aige uh de road, weh somebody bin t'row down uh harricane tree. Uh
call'um harricane, 'cause 'e top stan' sukkuh harricane, but 'e yent harricane fuh true 'cause
win' nebbuh blow'um down, en' true-true harricane de win' haffuh blow'um down, en' 'e root
stick'up high, but dishyuh harricane Uh duh
talk 'bout, Nigguh bin cut down wid axe fuh ketch
rokkoon, en' de Nigguh cut de 'tump off clean, da'
mekso 'e nebbuh hab no root fuh stick'up lukkuh
him woulduh hab ef 'e hadduh bin true-true harricane, en'—"

"'Harricane! Harricane,'!" mimicked Laguerre, "Damn your 'harricane'! Get to the point."

"Yaas, suh, Uh gwine git dey now. Well, suh, w'en you git to da' harricane you nebbuh stop, you jis' dribe right on 'tel you done pass'um, en' attuh dat you jis' hol' de road 'tel, bumbye, you come to anodduh road wuh run 'cross de road wuh you dey een. Dishyuh road nebbuh slant lukkuh da' t'odduh one you bin come 'cross befo' you git to de harricane tree. 'E run smack cross'um, 'cause dishyuh duh cross-road, fuh true. Berrywell.

"Now, suh, w'en you git to da' place uh duh tell you 'bout, you ent fuh hol' da' road you dey een now, no mo'. You fuh t'row'um'way attuh you git to de cross-road, 'cause 'e cyan' speci*fy* no mo'. Ef you folluhr'um attuh you cross de cross-road, 'e yent wu't' fuh tek you to da' place you duh gwine 'cause him fuh gone fudduh frum da' place, so jis' tell'um t'engky fuh dem t'ree-fo' mile you bin trabble'um, en' le'm gone 'bout 'e bidness.

"Attuh dat, you tu'n you hawss' head smack to you right han' en' you tek de right han' road wuh run 'cross de road you done t'row'way. W'en you trabble dishyuh new road 'bout half uh mile, you fuh see some house to de lef' han' side de road, en' w'en you git dey de road kind'uh split-'up—two-t'ree road dey dey en' 'e haa'd fuh tell you w'ich one fuh tek, but w'ichebbuh one you hawss tek, jis' folluhr'um 'tel you come to uh

deep watuh slash wuh run 'cross de road. You
dribe t'ru'um, en' ef de watuh come up to you
hawss' knee, you kin gone; 'cause you dey een
de right road, but ef da' watuh splash stan'
shalluh 'tel 'e yent rise mo'nuh halfway to de
hawss' knee, you fuh know you dey een de wrong
road, en' you haffuh tu'n back to da' place weh
de road split, 'cause t'ree road dey dey en' you
haffuh try one de t'odduh one.

"Now, attuh you trabble de t'odduh one leetle
w'ile, ef no watuh slash dey dey, you haffuh t'row-
'way da' road lukkuh you bin do de fus' one, en'
tu'n back, 'gen, 'cause two de road got watuh
een'um, en' t'orruh one dry ez Nigguh' t'roat
w'en 'e see Buckruh tu'n de jug obuh 'e elbow
fuh po'r out 'e dram! So you haffuh keep on
try 'tel you fin' da' deep watuh slash, en' you
hawss' knee wet fuh true-true, den you kin gone,
'cause you trouble done obuh, en' da' road blonx
to you 'tel you git to Blake."

"How shall I know when I get there?"

"Jedge, you fuh know'um by de Nigguh. De
pyo' Nigguh dey dey sukkuh buzzut duh roos'!
'Bout t'ree hund'ud Nigguh dey dey. One de
Nigguh dead, 'cause tree drap 'puntop'um, en'
all de t'odduh Nigguh iz libe, en' all dem mout'
duh gwine one time! De dead Nigguh duh de
only one wuh nebbuh crack 'e teet'! Uh know de
cawpse woulduh bex ef 'e coulduh bin yeddy all

dem t'orruh Nigguh' mout' duh gwine obuhr'um —he-Nigguh en' she-Nigguh, alltwo—but de po' creetuh cyan' he'p 'eself none'tall! Him dey dey, en' de tree wuh drap 'puntop'um, him dey dey, en' needuh one fuh say nutt'n'!"

"Stop!" shouted Laguerre. "Stop! When did you see your black brethren at Blake's?"

"Uh shum dis mawnin', suh. Enty Uh jis' come frum Blake? Dat how Uh know suh summuch Nigguh dey dey. Uh bin yeddy de news las' night 'bout how da' man wuh dead bin hab acksi*dent* 'long pine-tree, en' now de man dead en' de tree dead, 'eself. Dem alltwo dead, de man en' de tree, only de tree dead fus', 'cause him bin light'ood tree, dat how de man happ'n fuh cut-'um down. Ef 'e did'n' bin light'ood tree de man nebbuh woulduh bodduh wid'um, en' Gawd might'uh spayre de Nigguh' life, but dishyuh light'ood tree bin een de new groun' close by de aige uh de swamp, en' w'en de man shum, en' see how fat de tree stan', 'e git 'e axe en' staa't fuh chop'um down. Attuhw'ile, de tree mos' cut t'ru en' git ready fuh drap, en' jis' ez 'e biggin fuh crack, de man yeddy sump'n'nurruh close'um een de swamp duh mek shishuh hebby racket, him haffuh stop fuh look, en' w'en 'e look 'e see uh hebby fox squerril duh climb one dem big loblolly-pine-tree, en' 'e claw duh 'crape de baa'k ez 'e gwine 'tel 'e soun' sukkuh you duh saw log wid cross-cut saw.

174

De man tek 'e yeye off de light'ood tree fuh look,
en' 'e shum, but dat squerril duh de las' t'ing him
fuh see wid 'e yeye, en' de racket da' squerril'
claw mek, duh de las' t'ing him fuh yeddy wid 'e
yez, 'cause da' same time him loose 'e yeye off de
light'ood tree, 'e seem lukkuh de tree mus'be bex
'cause de Nigguh nebbuh count'um, en' jis' den
de tree crack, en' 'e drap 'puntop de man, en' de
Nigguh' sperrit gone to 'e Jedus, en' de 'ooman en'
t'ing staa't fuh holluh, en' dem binnuh holluh all
night, en' bumbye de man jine'um, 'cause w'enebbuh 'ooman bunch'up en' biggin fuh shout, ef man
yeddy'um, dem haffuh dey dey too. En' all night
dem Nigguh' mout' binnuh gwine, man en' 'ooman,
man en' 'ooman, man en' 'ooman, sukkuh dem big
bloodynoun frog w'en dem duh hol' praise-meet'n'!
En'—''

Laguerre, too fond of talk to be a good listener,
was so amused by the old Negro's flow of speech
that for a time he let him run on without interruption to see if his ball of yarn would run out,
but as it now seemed interminable, he broke in
suddenly and wrathfully: "Damn your bloody-
nouns! If you have been to Blake's, tell me what
they have done with the dead man."

"Jedge, suh, dem ent do nutt'n'tall wid'um. Da'
pine-tree dey 'puntop'um now, en' Uh yeddy suh
attuh you git dey, you'self haffuh seddown 'puntop'um fuh see wuh kill'um, en' ef 'e dead fuh

175

true-true. But, Jedge, ef you iz fuh seddown 'pun da' Nigguh lukkuh de law say, da' pine-tree haffuh roll off fus', 'cause de way 'e stan' now da' log gott'um pin to de du't. En', 'cep' da' log roll'off, eeduhso chop'off, de law haffuh stan' up, 'cause him ent fuh hab no place fuh seddown 'puntop no Nigguh.

"But dem duh wait fuh you, Jedge, en' w'en Uh bin dey dis' mawnin', dem tell me dem 'f'aid de Nigguh wuh gone to you house las' night nebbuh 'splain'um 'sponsubble 'bout de road, so dem ax me fuh come fuh meet you, so ef you ent know weh you duh gwine Uh kin pit you een de right road. Da' mekso Uh bin tell you so straight, so you ent fuh loss you way."

"Straight!" cried Laguerre, "Straight! If Dawhoo were a demijohn and Slann's Island a cork, I could take that road for a corkscrew, and pull out the whole plantation! Straight! Jump up behind this buggy and show me the road, and don't say a word 'til you get to the first crossroads, and then just say 'right hand' or 'left hand' and shut right up! Why the devil didn't you tell me when you first came up that you had come to show me the road? We could have been half way there by now, instead of listening for half an hour to your 'harricane, harricane!' Damn the 'harricane!' Jump up, and shut up!"

The old Negro swung up behind the buckboard,

176

Scipio touched up Zouave, and they drove off briskly, Laguerre thoroughly outraged at having been forced to listen for so long.

They trotted past the slanting road, the fallen log, the cross-roads, the water slashes, and all the other landmarks described so meticulously by their guide, who indicated each as he came to it by a grunt, Laguerre permitting him no more liberal form of expression.

At last they came to Blake's, an old plantation showing by the unkempt condition of buildings and fences, and by the weeds that choked the gardens that the place had been abandoned by the whites and given up to Negro occupancy.

The entire population of the place and a hundred or more from nearby settlements were now gathered in a little clearing—a new ground—whose pines, several years earlier, had been girdled with the axe and left to die, the freedmen meanwhile grubbing up the roots and tilling the land that lay between. The pines, long dead, had been seared by the fires with which Negroes clear their land, and had turned to lightwood, and one of these, standing at the edge of the forest, the poor Negro had cut down for fuel, and, looking away for a moment just as the tree had begun to fall, was caught in the deadly trap.

Fearful of the white man's laws, these black folk clustered around the fallen pine and their dead comrade, awaiting through the long night and half the morning, the coming of "Jedge," whose sanction would permit them to cut away the log and prepare the poor stark body that lay beneath for the "sett'n'up" or wake. This—an overture to the regular performance—had been going on all through the night by the watchfires built around the log.

As "Jedge" got out of the buggy, a group of the elders, the wise men of the plantation, met him with low obeisance, and escorted him to the scene of the tragedy, where they repeated with great elaboration the details of the story already told by the guide who had gone forth in the morning to meet him.

The acting coroner took charge of the proceedings. Two powerful axemen were set to work cutting away a six foot section of the dead pine that lay upon the poor bit of clay that only yesterday had been a sentient thing, filling his appointed place in the world. Now that his spirit had left the flesh, the lifeless flesh, like all black flesh, would move the world far more without, than with, the spirit, for only a funeral or a wake could stir the hearts of this primitive people to the depths. Now, the suddenness of the tragedy, and the long wait for the inquest had added richly to their emotional ecstasy, for they were assured of another night of exaltation!

THE ROAD CALLED STRAIGHT

The log was pried off and rolled away, and Laguerre summoned six of the older men to determine first, if the man were dead, and if dead, what killed him. These indisputable facts were arrived at and announced with the impressiveness with which so many men proclaim the obvious, with a solemn reiteration that bears so heavily upon those whom God has given keen perceptions.

"Jedge, suh," said the foreman, looking about him for the acquiescent nods of his fellows, "dishyuh man dead, enty? Dishyuh hebby tree binnuh leddown 'puntop'um ebbuh sence yistiddy ebenin', en' 'e nebbuh crack 'e jaw frum dat to dis!"

"You talk trute, my bredduh, de Nigguh dead!" confirmed the other jurors, in chorus.

"En', fudduhmo', Jedge," continued the foreman, "anodduh reaz'n Uh know 'sponsubble suh de Nigguh dead iz 'cause, las' night, all night long, him wife binnuh seddown 'pun da' tree wid 'e ap'un to 'e yeye duh praise de man en' groan 'cause 'e done loss'um, w'en all uh we know berry well suh w'en da' man bin hab bre't' een 'e body, de 'ooman tell'um ebb'ry day suh 'e yent wu't'—'e bre't' en' 'e body alltwo, 'cause 'e hab rum 'puntop 'e bre't', en' lazy 'puntop 'e bone!

"En' ef da' Nigguh bin hab life een'um las' night w'en da' 'ooman roll 'e praise so high, him

179

woulduh ansuhr'um en' 'spute'um, en' 'e woulduh ax'um hukkuh no'count Nigguh kin tu'n eento ainjul so swif', en' hukkuh crow kin change to w'ite crane jis' 'cause 'e dead! But de Nigguh nebbuh crack 'e jaw fuh 'tarrygate de 'ooman nuh nutt'n', so attuh dat Uh know de Nigguh done fuh dead!"

"Well," said Laguerre, "you find that the man is dead; now, what killed him?"

"Tree, suh. Pine-tree. 'E drap 'puntop de Nigguh en' kill'um. En', Jedge, de po' man bin kill 'eself, but him nebbuh bin know. Shum yuh, suh, shum yuh," and the old Negro showed Laguerre where, several years earlier, lightning had riven the great pine, probably during the summer it had been girdled. Among the other dead trees of the new-ground, the Negro had not noticed that upon this, God had put His mark and set it apart as sacrosanct. Only after the fall of the pine had loosened the bark, was the long wound revealed—the wreak, long years ago, of a mighty kris flashing out of the infinite!

With bared head the old Negro looked up reverently, as if in prayer, while with awed voice he said: "Attuh Gawd pit Him han' 'pun da' tree, man ent fuh tetch'um! De po' creetuh nebbuh know. 'E nebbuh bin know!"

And Laguerre drove slowly away, subdued by the wailing of the mourners behind him.

TO HAVE AND TO SCOLD

All through Friday, the memory of the tragedy at Blake's, and the poignant wailing of those who mourned the victim of the avenging lightning-tree, had somewhat repressed the usually high spirits of "Jedge" Laguerre, who went about his plantation tasks more quietly than was customary with one usually so full of himself, but no cork of compassion could restrain for long so volatile a spirit, and by Saturday morning he was again full of himself and running over, and he set forth for his court as jauntily as a knight to a tourney, bubbling over with the thought of how he would bait the spiritually fragile Wineglasses and the Jewish merchant from Wadmalaw, an island which—lying within the limits of Berkeley County and subject to the jurisdiction of its magistrates—he regarded almost as enemy country, peopled by "lesser breeds without the law," and any of these who set foot in the Toogoodoo country he conceived it his duty to discipline, not only for the good of their souls, but for the exaltation of his own official position as a Trial Justice for Adams Run township, St. Paul's Parish, Colleton County, a jurisdiction wherein he was sure the law was administered more picturesquely, if not more justly, than anywhere else in South Carolina. And "Jedge's" attitude toward

LAGUERRE

Wadmalaw was well known to the Negroes, who, since the summoning of the merchant and his black witness, Quakoo, to attend Laguerre's pineland court presently to be held, had discussed the weight of the hand Toogoodoo law would lay upon them.

"Jedge, him sho' lub fuh bu'n dem Wadmuhlaw Nigguh! Ef any dem man frum Wadmuhlaw come 'puntop Toogoodoo fuh ramify 'roun' 'mong we 'ooman en' t'ing, ef Jedge ketch'um, eb'nso ef him yeddy 'bout'um, da' Nigguh fuh bu'n'up! Fus', Jedge fine'um, en' den 'e cuss'um! Him bu'n de Nigguh' pocket en' 'e yez, alltwo!

"At de fus' gwinin' off, him fuh ax'um: 'Nigguh, wuh you duh do yuh 'puntop Toogoodoo? You mus'be t'ink you iz range bull, enty? If you iz, you bettuh keep 'puntop da' Wadmuhlaw range, 'cause dishyuh Toogoodoo range blonx to ole Tumbo, en' no Wadmuhlaw man hab prib'lidge fuh ramify obuhr'um, 'cause Tumbo hol' 'eself 'sponsubble fuh sabe dese 'ooman' sinful soul en' t'ing, en' you en' de debble ent got nutt'n'tall fuh do wid'um. Uh dunkyuh w'edduh you call you'-self class-leaduh, eeduhso preachuh, ef you ebbuh mek track 'roun' dis place 'gen, Uh fuh call you waggybone, en' t'row you een Walterburruh jail fuh t'ree week! En' now, fuh mek you 'membuhr-'um, Uh gwine pinch you pocket, en' Uh fine you dolluh en' uh half, 'cause w'en you bin climb obuh

182

da' fench wuh run 'roun' Nigguh-house-yaa'd t'odduh night bedout ax no 't'oruhty fuh do'um, you iz bin trespass. En' now you kin gone!'

"Budduh! W'en Jedge tel de Nigguh fuh gone, him nebbuh wait fuh yeddy'um two time. 'E gone! De Nigguh tu'n 'e pocket eenside out, en' w'en 'e see how 'e stan', 'e foot hasty fuh reach de crik; 'e jump een 'e trus'-me-gawd, 'e ketch 'e paddle een 'e han', en' him en' da' coonoo gone t'ru da' ribbuh sukkuh pawpuss! 'E nebbuh stop 'tel 'e git Wadmuhlaw!"

" 'E ebbuh come back?"

"Yaas, 'e come back. Him iz Nigguh, enty? Him stay off fuh 'bout t'ree week, en' den, w'en de daa'k uh de moon come 'roun' 'gen, da' same Nigguh climb da' same fench en' peruse 'roun' 'mong dem Slann' I'lun' 'ooman, lukkuh him bin do befo', en' nobody nebbuh tell on'um, 'cause 'nuf sto' dey to Wadmuhlaw, en' de man full 'e pocket wid gunjuh en' tubackuh fuh de 'ooman en' de man, alltwo, en' Jedge nebbuh yeddy nutt'n' 'bout'um, 'cause Nigguh nebbuh fuh tell Buckruh no news 'bout no odduh Nigguh, 'cep' him en' de Nigguh fall out, en' 'long ez da' Wadmuhlaw man got gunjuh en tubackuh een 'e pocket, none uh we Nigguh gwine g'em'way, Uh dunkyuh hummuch 'e ramify!"

"Yaas, man, Nigguh haffuh stan' by 'e own colluh, enty? Nigguh haffuh stan' sukkuh night,

183

'cause we alltwo iz black, en' same lukkuh night
hide de Nigguh w'en 'e mischeebus, da' same way
Nigguh iz fuh hide one'nurruh fuh sabe'um frum
de Buckruh w'en 'e git een trouble. Wuhebbuh one
Nigguh do, all we t'odduh Nigguh haffuh kibbuhr'um up. Da' duh we *prinsubble,* enty?
Berrywell."

"Uh know Jedge fuh haa'd 'pun dem Wadmuhlaw Nigguh. Uh wunduh ef him fuh be haa'd 'pun
da' Wadmuhlaw Buckruh—da' sto'keepuh wuh
sell sistuh Wineglass da' leely cow?"

"Yaas, man! Jedge berry tetchy, you know, en'
berry shawt-pashunt, en' Buckruh kin bex'um jis'
ez quick ez Nigguh. 'E bex'um mo' quickuh, 'cause
Jedge know suh Nigguh iz nutt'n' but Nigguh
en' 'e nebbuh bodduh 'bout'um 'cause de Nigguh
so eegnunt, but ef him ebbuh bex wid Buckruh
'e bex fuh true-true! Ki! Him fuh moobe 'e yeyebrow up en' down sukkuh mongkey, en' da' hebby
hair 'pun 'e mout' fuh rise 'tel 'e 'tan'up sukkuh
dem wil' bo'hog een de swamp rise de bristle 'puntop dem back, w'en dog git 'roun'um! W'en Jedge
stan' so, 'e look mischeebus ez de berry Satan, but
'e mout' dainjus mo'nuh 'e h'aa't. W'en 'e bex 'e
bex, but attuh him cuss'um off, 'e yeyebrow git
smood 'gen, en' da' hair 'puntop 'e mout' drap
down lukkuh 'e bin at de fus' befo' de bex tek'um.
But Uh know him fuh ride dem Wadmuhlaw man
teday, teday—de Buckruh en' de Nigguh alltwo!"

THE OLD "PINK HOUSE" IN THE VILLAGE.

TO HAVE AND TO SCOLD

On this Saturday morning, bright and cool, with a sharp wind out of the East, Laguerre and old Scipio, having made an early start, jogged along easily to meet the noon engagement at the pineland court. Zouave, given a day of rest, had been turned in the pasture, and Scipio held the lines over Deadlock, a stubborn brute, whose balking propensities had prompted his master several years earlier to bestow upon him a name at the moment before the public in newspaper headlines through the deadlock in a great National convention.

A few months earlier, Laguerre, on his way to court had been forced to bite Deadlock's ear to move him out of a stubborn balk, and between man and horse there was little love lost.

Deadlock had once sported a long tail, but of this his master had despoiled him long since to make a histrionic holiday. Stagestruck, and devoted to amateur theatricals, Laguerre was sure to be prominent in any cast that tramped the boards of Toogoodoo. Like Edwin Forrest and Salvini, he was partial to heavy, tragic roles, and when he was cast for an Indian chief—an heroic part—he knew that only Deadlock's luxuriant tail could supply a fitting scalp-lock. So with ruthless shears his master snipped it off close to the bone. The scalp-lock was worn with great distinction and added tremendously to the big chief's

185

opinion of himself, but poor Deadlock's hindquarters never looked the same again, and all
through the summer heyday of flies and mosqui-
toes, he paid dearly for his master's vanity.

"Deadlock, him tail look stylish 'nuf, da' way
Maussuh saw'um off, en' 'e do berry well fuh
wintuhtime tail, but 'e yent wu't' fuh summuh-
time, 'cause fly en' muskittuh needuh one nebbuh count'um, Uh dunkyuh how haa'd 'e switch-
'um."

Scipio was right, and Deadlock, while his tail
was slowly lengthening, was seldom driven in
summer, and only now, when cool weather had
put an end to the flies, was he again between the
shafts of the buckboard.

As they neared the court, about which half a
hundred Negroes had gathered, Laguerre noticed
the smoke from the fires they had built of lightwood knots, after first raking away the pinestraw
with forked sticks to prevent the flames from getting away. All Negroes love fire, but none so
well as the black folk of the Low-country. If
the weather be cold, or even cool, timber-cutters,
field hands, ditchers—however warming the
nature of their work—must stop from time to
time to huddle over a pitiful handful of coals
to warm themselves. It seems almost a rite, as
with the ancient fire-worshipers, and they never
realize, as does the white man, that warmth which

comes from physical exertion is far more lasting than that which comes from fire.

"Scipio," said Laguerre, "why are you darkies so fond of fire?"

"Maussuh, Nigguh haffuh hab fiah, 'cause Gawd mek'um dat way. Uh dunkyuh weh 'e yiz, da' fiah haffuh git, en' de Nigguh haffuh mek'um fuh 'eself. Maussuh, Uh tell you de trute, ef you tek Nigguh en' pitt'um een da' place weh de debble lib, him wouldn' dey dey fibe minnit befo' him fuh quizzit de debble en' ax'um, 'Budduh, wuh kind'uh fiah you call dis? Ef you gimme some match, Uh fuh mek fiah fuh meself, 'cause we man wuh come frum Slann' I'lun' nebbuh gwine sattify wid no shishuh fiah lukkuh dis! 'E yent wu't' fuh roas' 'tettuh; hukkuh him kin speci*fy* fuh roas' Nigguh?' Duh so 'e stan'. Nigguh! Fiah duh him Jedus!"

When Cudjo had called the court to order, Laguerre looked the crowd over and took stock of its possibilities for entertainment. The Jewish merchant was there, flanked by his black witness Quakoo, and both, having heard of Laguerre's testy temper, and not having heard that his bark was worse than his bite, wore anxious faces.

Of the Wineglasses, Daphne looked the more apprehensive, for though she was unaware that Caesar had reported her tantrums to Laguerre, she was afraid it might come out at the hearing, and having heard "Jedge's" rasping of Tumbo, she had a very wholesome respect for the punitive power of "Jedge's" tongue.

Caesar, although always subdued in the presence of his wife, believed she had done her worst, for after the dreadful cannonading she had poured upon him during the week, he thought her verbal caissons must, by now, be empty. Then, too, he hoped that Laguerre, knowing how matters stood between them, would presently haul her over the coals and abate somewhat her shrewishness; so, with nothing to lose and something to gain, he awaited with composure the fortunes of the day.

Laguerre, though knowing the Jewish merchant for a usurer and a cheat, was unwilling to submit him to the indignity of having his name called familiarly by a Negro court crier, so he summoned him to the bar and demanded a statement in detail as to the sale of the ox to "Mis' Wineglass." This information, or Caesar's version of it, he already had, and knowing that Caesar had nothing to gain by lying, he believed Caesar had spoken the truth.

"Vell, Chudge," the merchant began, "it vos dis vay. Dis Vineglass voman, she come to me to buy my ox. I sell de voman my ox. De voman, she pay to me t'ree tollar kash, ant de voman, she owe to me ten tollar. Now, ven I come for mine ten tollar, dis Vineglass voman, she haf only sefen tollar ant—"

"Stop! What evidence have you that this woman owes you ten dollars, or anything? Did she give you a note, or promise with her mouth?"

"Chudge, de vorts of dis voman's mouth iss not vorth to me anything vhatefer on Vadmalaw. I haf de voman's bont for mine ten tollar."

"Produce the bond!" Laguerre demanded, and when it was handed over, he studied the instrument amusedly for several minutes. The merchant's cross marks were plain enough, but the poor foreigner had found Daphne, Caesar and Quakoo too much for him orthographically—however easily he overreached them in money matters—and his phonetic conceptions of these popular Toogoodoo names would have been weird even in Warsaw.

Laguerre would not shame him before the Negroes, however, but turned instead upon "Mis' Wineglass" and made scornful play upon her name. "Daphne," said he with a smile, "Daphne! A sweet and gentle name to bestow upon a tempestuous termagant! When they named you, Daphne, no balmy breezes blew over your cradle. Boreas himself must have been abroad! Daphne! Daphne! Damn!—Tell your story!"

She told it. Going over, foot by foot, the ground so fully covered by Caesar on his surreptitious

189

visit to "Jedge" earlier in the week, she came at
last to the merchant's visit to her domicile, when,
as he read from the mortgage form, she realized
the dreadful bondage in which she had placed her
"heirs and assigns forever."

"Jedge, suh, w'en da' Buckruh—Uh dunno wuh
'e yiz, but dem call'um Jew 'puntop Wadmuhlaw
—w'en him 'suade me fuh le'm pit me name 'puntop da' papuh, en' mek cross maa'k en' t'ing 'pun-
'um, him nebbuh read de papuh, nuh nutt'n'! Da'
Jew say da' papuh tek 't'oruhty obuh de oxin, 'e
nebbuh crack 'e bre't' 'bout no hair. Ef Uh hadduh bin know suh him plan fuh tek 't'oruhty
obuh my hair en' t'ing fuhrebbuh, Uh woulduh
bog een da' maa'sh up to me crotch, eeduhso jump
een Wadmuhlaw ribbuh, fuh git'way frum'um!
No, suh! all de hair da' Jew fuh git dey 'pun da'
oxin' tail. Him haffuh sattify wid dat. 'E yent fuh
hab my'own!

"So, attuh him done mek all da' baa'gin wid
'eself, en' pit all 'e han'write en' cross maa'k
'puntop de papuh en' call'um my'own, him tek da'
Caesar, wuh Uh hab fuh husbun', en' 'e han'write
him name 'pun de papuh en' likewise, also, him
mek cross maa'k fuh Caesar, en'—"

"Pelion upon Ossa! I thought Caesar's marital
cross was heavy enough!"

"Suh!"

TO HAVE AND TO SCOLD

"I thought poor Caesar's cross was heavy enough at home."

"Dat's de Gawd' trute, Jedge! Uh see you know Caesar, 'cause da' Nigguh cross fuh sowl! En' 'e so stubbunt! Uh haffuh scol'um all de time fuh keep'um straight!

"So attuh de Jew done pit 'e cross 'puntop dishyuh Caesar wuh blonx to me, him t'row uh hebby eensult 'puntop all we Toogoodoo people, en' 'e say suh none de Slann' I'lun' Nigguh ent wu't', so him haffuh hab 'norruh man frum Wadmuhlaw fuh witness dem cross en' t'ing, so de papuh kin speci*fy*, 'cause 'e say him 'f'aid ef Uh ebbuh git ready fuh 'spute de papuh, Uh gwine mek Caesar fuh lie 'bout'um, en' say suh de baa'gin nebbuh bin mek. So, jis' ez de Jew gitt'ru talk, en' look 'roun' fuh hunt witness fuh t'row 'puntop'uh we name en' t'ing, please me Jedus, de sto' do' bin open, en' dishyuh Nigguh, Quakoo, come een!

"Jedge, you shum dey, en' you see how 'e stan'. W'en da' Nigguh come een de do' en' Uh look 'puntop'um, Uh haffuh buss'out laugh een de Nigguh' face, en' Uh hice me ap'un obuh me yeye fuh kibbuhr'um! Soon ez 'e come een de do', de Jew call'um fuh witness. De Nigguh bin een de crik duh ketch crab, en' 'e basket full'up wid crab. W'en de Jew call'um, him pit 'e basket 'pun de flo' 'tel him kin tetch de pen een de Jew' han', en'

191

same time de Nigguh tu'n 'e back 'pun de crab, de crab biggin fuh climb out de basket en' sashay 'roun' 'pun de flo'! De Nigguh ketch'um'up een 'e han' en' t'row'um back een de basket, but befo' 'e do'um some dem ole rusty crab clabbuhclaw'um good.

"Jedge, w'en Uh yeddy de Jew call de Nigguh 'Quakoo,' Uh haffuh laugh 'gen. De name suit'um so good! Uh tell de Nigguh, 'Budduh! Uh dunno w'ich way de win' duh blow, but 'e mus'be duh blow frum Aff'iky, enty? 'E mus'be ketch you up en' fetch you yuh frum da' place weh we gran'-daddy en' t'ing come frum een dem cokynot tree, 'cause you hab uh cu'yus face en' you hab uh cu'-yus name. Quakoo, Quakoo! 'E fuh tek Po'-Joe en' pidgin alltwo fuh talk one time fuh call da' name lukkuh 'e yiz fuh call!

" 'En', budduh,' Uh tell'um, 'you iz black! Ef Jedus yeddy me, you black! Uh bin look 'puntop buzzut en' crow een me time, en' Uh bin look 'pun-top chimbly back w'en nutt'n' but de pyo' sut dey dey, but Uh nebbuh look 'puntop'uh no shishuh black lukkuh you iz! Da' mekso w'en dem crab bin look 'puntop you en' see how you stan', you t'row'um een uh hebby strance, en' dem nebbuh cheep, but soon ez you tu'n'way you eye off'um, de crab haffuh jump out de basket en' shake dem foot fuh dance! Budduh! You done fuh oagly!'

"Jedge, w'en Uh tell'um dat, de Guinea Nigguh swell'up sukkuh toad-fish! 'E oagly mo'nuh 'e bin at de fus'! Uh tell'um, 'Budduh, lemme tell you! Dishyuh Buckruh pick you out fuh witness 'puntop'uh we, enty? 'Cause 'e say him s'pishun we Slann' I'lun' Nigguh gwine try fuh cheat'um. Ef you ebbuh come Slann' I'lun', black ez you iz, you fuh cheat we fowl, 'cause ebb'ry Gawd fowl wuh we got fuh t'ink fus' daa'k come, soon ez dem look 'puntop da' face wuh you got, en' dem fuh fly up 'pun de roos' fuh gone sleep, Uh dunk-yuh ef 'e duh middleday! En', Uh tell'um, 'fudduh-mo', you bettuh min' how you blin'-gawd fool you fuh mek track 'puntop Slann' I'lun' wid dem splay foot wuh you got, 'cause Jedge ent got no use fuh Wadmuhlaw Nigguh, nohow, en' ef 'e ebbuh ketch you duh 'dultri*fy* 'roun' him Nigguh-house-yaa'd, Jedge fuh t'row you 'pun da' chain-gang, en' fus' t'ing you know you hab ball en' chain 'pun you foot, en' shubble een you han', duh wu'k road een da' stiff blue clay to Little Pokytaligo, t'odduh side Jacksinburruh!'"

"You seem to have left nothing unsaid."

"Suh!"

"You seem to have told Quakoo everything you had on your mind," said Laguerre.

"Yaas, suh, Uh tell'um fuh true, 'cause you know, Jedge, how 'ooman stan'! Ef 'e got sump'n-'nurruh 'pun 'e min', da' t'ing haffuh come out 'e mout', en' ef any man dey dey w'en 'e come out, de 'ooman haffuh t'row dem wu'd en' t'ing 'pun-top'um, 'cause man iz man en' 'ooman iz 'ooman, en' duh so Gawd mek'um. One haffuh talk, en' t'odduh haffuh yeddy."

"An equitable give and take!"

"Yaas, suh, me fuh gib, en' him fuh tek. En' man iz shishuh stubbunt t'ing 'ooman haffuh po'r 'e mout' 'puntop'um fas', ef him fuh bowre t'ru 'e yez. Man kin bex you tummuch! Ef 'e ansuh you back, him fuh bex you, en' ef 'e yent ansuh you, him fuh bex you mo'nuh ef him bin crack 'e teet' fuh jaw at you! W'en man quawl deestunt, en' 'spute wid you, en' ansuh you back, you kin do berry well, 'cause 'ooman mout' fuh trabble fas' mo'nuh him'own, en' Uh dunkyuh how swif' de man staa't, 'ooman mout' gwine obuhtek'um! But ef man shet 'e jaw sukkuh osh-tuh, en' nebbuh crack'um open, nuh nutt'n', wuh de po' 'ooman fuh do? Ef de man nebbuh gi' you no aa'gyment fuh 'taguhnize'um 'bout, you stan' sukkuh man duh run race wid 'e own shadduh. You nebbuh fuh obuhtek'um! En' da' de t'ing mek me so bex wid de man, 'cause w'en 'e nebbuh an-suh you back you dunno wuh him duh t'ink 'bout! Ef 'e hab pizen een 'e min', you ent fuh know 'e dey dey, 'cep' de man spit'um out, en' ef him neb-buh spit, da' pizen fuh lock'up een de man en' spile'um!"

194

TO HAVE AND TO SCOLD

"Well, did Quakoo take all you told him without answering?"

"Jedge, lemme tell you, suh, how da' Aff'ikin fool me—him en' de Jew, alltwo. W'en de Jew call'um fuh tetch de pen, Uh shum duh mek sign at de Nigguh, but Uh nebbuh s'pishun nutt'n' 'bout'um, 'cause Uh binnuh look 'puntop de Nigguh. De t'ing stan' so black, Uh cyan' tek me yeye off'um! Den, w'en Uh biggin fuh 'buze de Nigguh, de Jew staa't fuh grin, but Uh t'aw't 'e bin do'um 'cause him iz Buckruh en' 'e glad fuh yeddy me call Nigguh out 'e name, but all de time him bin fool me.

"Jedge, suh, Uh nebbuh bin hab nutt'n' fuh shame me so sence Uh bawn! All de time Uh binnuh talk at de Nigguh, en' tell'um how 'e stan', Uh notice de Nigguh' face nebbuh moobe, 'e nebbuh laugh, nuh grin, nuh nutt'n', en' 'e nebbuh gyap 'e jaw fuh 'spute me, but Uh t'aw't de Nigguh chupit to dat! 'E face smood en' black en' shiny ez fry'-pan w'en you pit'um 'puntop de fire en' greese'um fuh fry flapjack! Uh bin s'pishun 'e yent got good sense, mek 'e stan' so, en' Uh nebbuh know, 'tel anodduh Nigguh come een de sto' jis' ez Uh staa't fuh gitt'ru, en' 'e say: 'Tittuh, Uh sorry fuh ho't you feelin's, but all dem wu'd done t'row'way, enty? 'Cause dishyuh Nigguh deef!'

"Jedge, 'e stan' so! Ef you shoot gun close 'e

195

yez, en' 'e see de smoke, him fuh t'ink you 'cratch
match fuh light you pipe! Him kin look 'puntop'uh
lightnin', but 'e nebbuh yeddy t'unduh roll! Quakoo deef, 'e *deef!* 'E bin bex me tummuch fuh
haffuh t'row'way all dem w'ud—but, Jedge, 'e
yent t'row'way fuh true-true, 'cause dishyuh
Caesar bin yeddy'um, enty, suh? Berrywell."

The assembled Negroes, knowing Daphne's
gift of speech—many of them, indeed, having felt
the sharp edge of her tongue—were highly elated
at the story of her waste of words upon the unreceptive Quakoo, who, poor fellow—without hearing—had been dragged into the case by the ears!
When the laughter had subsided, Laguerre addressed himself to the ox and its vendor, from
whom he extracted the admission of an oral
amendment to the contract, promising an abate-
ment of three dollars if the ox should prove too
light to plow the stubborn glebe of Slann's Island.
There followed a lengthy argument as to the cul-
tural qualities of the soils of Wadmalaw and of
Toogoodoo, respectively; the merchant holding
that as the ox was entirely competent on Wadmalaw, his guarantee contemplated the tillage of
lands of the Wadmalaw type, but the Negroes insisted that as the "creetuh" had been sold to
Slann's Island service, it must be able to "specify"
in the tough "j'intgrass" with which the Negroes'
lands were infested.

"Jedge" held with his people, and Daphne paid the seven dollars, which the merchant accepted. The bond and mortgage, with its dreadful reference to "heirs and assigns," was put into Daphne's hands and promptly committed to the flames.

As the paper crackled in the blaze, Cudjo said to the now radiant "Mis' Wineglass:" "Tittuh, you hair en' t'ing duh swinge, enty? Uh smell'um duh bu'n!"

"No, budduh! Da' hair you smell duh bu'n een da' papuh duh de switch 'pun da' oxin tail. 'E yent my'own! Attuh dis, Uh gwine hol' me own hair en' t'ing fuhrebbuh. Jew ent fuh hol'um!"

And now, Caesar, looking at Laguerre with the wistful eyes of a setter on a frosty winter's morning, reminded "Jedge" that he had promised the poor Negro to rake over the ashes of his marital relations, and see what embers of authority he could blow into life to restore the self-respect of the master of the house— a designation that had long been a mockery. So, rapping savagely with his red hatchet, he called "Mis' Wineglass," and, seizing the nettle danger, proceeded to rough-ride her.

"Daphne! What's this I hear of your jawing at Caesar, half the day and all the night?"

"Jedge, suh—"

"Shut up! How dare you answer me?"

"Jedge, suh, how you—?"

"Stop! Never mind how I heard it, I know it, and it has got to stop! Every week I hear of some confounded frizzle-headed woman running over a man! It's getting so none of you have any respect for a pair of breeches!"

"Jedge, suh, britchiz haffuh be 'ooman' Gawd? Man fuh heng up 'e britchiz en' 'ooman fuh bow down befor'um en' praise'um? Uh dunno how Buckruh' britchiz stan', but Uh know none uh we Slann' I'lun' 'ooman fuh tek no Nigguh' britchiz fuh mek Gawd! No, suh! W'en de man tek off de britchiz en' heng'um up 'pun de nail een de do' jamb, wuh 'e yiz? Nutt'n'! W'en 'e yent got man een'um 'e yent wu't', en' w'en 'e *yiz* got man een-'um, ef de man no'count, dem alltwo ent wu't'! En' duh so all deseyuh man stan' een dishyuh neighbuhhood. 'Ooman hab'um een dem house, 'cause 'ooman haffuh hab man; we haffuh hab-'um en' we haffuh scol'um, but none de drat man ent wu't'!"

"To have and to scold, eh?"

"Yaas, suh, da' duh him!"

"Well, Daphne, as far as Caesar is concerned, I'm going to make him take a hoe handle in his house, and the next time you straddle your legs before the fire and lay down the law man-fashion, I'm going to make him dress you down. You ought to have a deaf husband like Quakoo to make 'the punishment fit the crime.'"

TO HAVE AND TO SCOLD

"No, me Jedus! Da' fine too hebby! Uh redduh hab da' hoe handle 'cross me hanch!"

"CAESAR....TURNED TO CLAY"

On a mild November morning Laguerre sat in the sunshine on his front piazza while Caesar, on the top step at his feet, told the sad story of his failure to master the masterful "Mis' Wineglass."

"Well, did you manhandle her as I told you to?"

"Suh?"

"Did you manhandle your wife as I told you to?"

"Great Gawd! Jedge, man ent fuh handle da' t'ing. Him fuh handle man! Nobody wuh got on britchiz kin handle da' 'ooman! De debble kin do'um ef 'e tek notion, 'cause him ent got uh britchiz to 'e name, but him ent gwine do'um, 'cause him en' de 'ooman iz two twin. W'en you look 'puntop one, you look 'puntop'uh alltwo! Dem meat stan' diff'unt, 'cause de debble got hawn 'pun 'e head, en' 'e hoof split lukkuh cow' hoof, en' 'e tail hab fawk een'um, en' him kin quile'um suk-kuh snake quile, wehreas de 'ooman ent got no shishuh fixin' lukkuh dat; but, Jedge, w'en you quizzit dem h'aa't, de debble' h'aa't en' de 'ooman' own, you fuh shum stan' sukkuh two aig wuh come out de same nes'! Ebbuh sence you bin tell de 'ooman t'odduh day, suh him haffuh treat de britchiz digni*fy*, de 'ooman nebbuh count de britchiz! Jis' 'cause 'e blonx to man, britchiz duh da' 'ooman' pizen!"

"Didn't I tell you to stand up to her? Didn't I promise to back you up?"

"Yaas, suh, Jedge, duh so, fuh true, but w'en you stan' to me back, you dey fudduh, en' w'en de 'ooman stan' to me face, him dey close, enty, en' him duh look een me yeye, en' da' 'ooman got blacksnake' skin, but 'e hab rattlesnake' eye! Jedge, suh, w'en you tell me fuh knock da' 'ooman fuh mek'um mannussubble, you bin tell me fuh do uh dainjus t'ing! You t'row me een de lion' den sukkuh dem Jew en' t'ing bin do Dannil een de Scriptuh!"

"Well, Daniel came through, didn't he?"

"Yaas, suh, 'e come t'ru, but 'e do'um 'cause Gawd' sperrit bin gone een de lion' h'aa't en' tell-'um fuh peaceubble, en' de lion haa'kee to Him wu'd, en' do lukkuh de Lawd tell'um; but Jedge, Gawd' sperrit nebbuh git chance fuh gone een no bex 'ooman' h'aa't—not long ez 'e bex!—'cause de debble dey dey, en' him iz uh jallus creetuh, en' 'e shet de do' uh de 'ooman' h'aa't 'pun de Lawd' sperrit, en' 'e watch ebb'ry crack, en' soon ez 'e see Gawd' sperrit duh try fuh creep t'ru fuh saaf'n de 'ooman' h'aa't leely bit befo' 'e done spit out all 'e pizen, Ki! de debble jump to da' crack en' stop'um up tight! De debble stan' to de 'ooman' back, 'tel 'e done gitt'ru say 'e say, en' sometime de t'ing wuh 'e *yiz* say fuh bodduhr'um long ez 'e lib—him en' de man, alltwo!"

202

"A philosopher in black! How do you know woman so well?"

"Jedge, ef you lib wid 'ooman enty you fuh know'um? Obsco'se you nebbuh yiz fuh know-'um *puhzac'ly;* you nebbuh yiz know'um fuh true-true! You know de t'ing him duh do, but you nebbuh know w'ymekso 'e do'um. Him stan' sukkuh dem t'unduh cloud een de ele*ment.* You see de lightnin' crack de cloud op'n, you yeddy de t'unduh roll, en' you feel de rain duh drap 'puntop you. You shum, you yeddy'um, en' you feel'um, but you nebbuh know hukkuh 'e come fuh do'um. Gawd, Him know, en' some de Buck-ruh know, but Nigguh en' po'-buckruh, dem ent fuh know. But, w'edduh we know, uh w'edduh we yent know, w'en da' we'dduh come out de 'ooman' mout' all uh we po' creetuh wuh hab on britchiz haffuh tek'um ez 'e come, enty, suh?"

"Yes, I suppose so," said Laguerre, reflectively, "but, Caesar," he added, "I told you that the man, as the head of the household, must be the master in his house. That is the law. I told you to keep a hoe handle in your house and gave you authority to use it on Daphne if you couldn't rule her in any other way. Now, when you had the authority, why the devil didn't you use it?"

"Jedge, you bin t'row de 't'oruhty 'puntop me, fuh true, but wuh use fuh hab'um 'cep' you han' strong? 'E cyan' speci*fy,* en' 'e yent wu't'! W'en

203

Uh git ready fuh knock de 'ooman 'cross 'e hanch, lukkuh you tell me fuh do, Uh bin fool 'nuf fuh tell de 'ooman 'bout'um fus'. Uh tell'um, 'Enty Jedge tell me fuh knock you ef you sassy? Uh gwine tek da' hoe handle en' dress you down 'tel you fuh jump Jim Crow.'

"Jedge, suh, dat weh Uh bin t'row 'way me sense! Uh had bidness fuh knock'um fus', en' den, attuh Uh done dress'um down good, Uh coulduh tell'um wuh Uh lick'um fuh. You know, Jedge, w'en you got meat fuh pit een you smoke-house duh wintuhtime, you nebbuh rub da' salt-peter en' salt en' t'ing een'um 'tel de meat done cool off, den de salt en' t'ing fuh soak een'um good, en' de meat ent fuh spile, but 'ooman en' chillun ent stan' so. Ef you ketch'um col', Uh dunkyuh how strong you mout' stan', de exwice you g'em ent wu't'—long ez de 'ooman' meat col'; but ef you wawm'um up wid lick 'tel de meat duh bu'n! Ki! da' exwice gwine soak een'um 'tel 'e git spang to 'e h'aa't! Den de lickin' fuh do'um good, en' 'e sweet'n 'e sperrit! En' dat duh de Gawd' trute!"

"Well, did you sweeten her spirit?"

"Jedge, enty Uh tell you suh Uh bin staa't fuh lick de 'ooman too late? W'en Uh tell de 'ooman een exwance wuh Uh bin mek'up me min' fuh do, Uh done t'row'way me chance fuh do'um, en' de 'ooman buss'up me plan, en' 'e nebbuh *yiz* git de lick Uh bin prommus'um, en' de 'ooman' hanch ent bu'n yit."

"I'm afraid it never will be burned if you are afraid to use the authority I gave you in the name of the law—and you a man!"

"Jedge, Uh iz man, fuh true. Da' w'ymekso Uh 'f'aid de 'ooman! En' da' 't'oruhty you bin pit 'puntop me—da' law you tell me fuh nyuze—weh him dey? 'E dey to *you* house; 'e yent dey to *me* house! Nutt'n' dey dey 'cep' da' 'ooman. *Him* dey dey, Jedge, him *dey dey!*

"You 'membuh, suh, how da' 'ooman do wid da' papuh you pit een 'e han' t'odduh day, attuh him done pay de Jew? Berrywell. Da' papuh, da' mawgidge, bin de law, enty, suh? En' 'e gi' de Jew prib'lidge obuh de 'ooman hair en' t'ing. Wuh de 'ooman do wid'um? Him pitt'um een de fiah, enty, suh?

"Now, las' night, w'en da' fiah fus' staa't fuh bu'n een de 'ooman, Uh mek'up me min' fuh do wuh you bin tell me fuh do, soon ez 'e git hot good, but de Satan bin git hot so fas', Uh loss me chance! Uh bin lef' da' skillet 'pun de fiah too long; w'en Uh staa't fuh tek'um off, 'e too hot fuh hol'um! Uh bin fool!

"Jedge, soon ez de debble biggin fuh swell een de 'ooman en' Uh shum duh peep out 'e yeye, Uh tell'um, ' 'Ooman, Jedge tell me fuh be man een me own house, en' de law fuh stan' to me back, en'

Jedge, him iz de Law. Now, shet you mout', en'
shet'um fas'! Ef you leff'um open, Uh gwine flam
you.'"

"Well, did you shut her mouth, or did you have
to flam her?"

"Jedge, Uh nebbuh do needuh one, 'cause da'
'ooman mout' ent fuh shet, en' man ent fuh flam-
'um! Soon ez de wu'd git out me mout', de 'ooman
jump fuh de hoe-handle behine de do', 'e graff-
'um een alltwo 'e han', en' 'e holluh at me lukkuh
him bin lion!

"'Come on,' 'e say, 'yuh me! Knock me wid da'
law you got een you han', da' 't'oruhty wuh Jedge
tie 'puntop you! Lemme see ef da' law kin knock
haa'd mo'nuh dishyuh hoe-handle wuh Uh got een
me han'! Lemme see ef you man 'nuf fuh do'um!
Jedge tell you you iz de law, enty? Berry well!
Wuh de Law iz? De Buckruh write'um 'pun de
papuh, enty? You see wuh fiah do wid da' papuh
t'odduh day? Now, fetch'um on, fetch'um on! Me
duh de fiah fuh bu'n'um! Come on!'"

"Well, did you 'come on'?"

"Jedge, Uh binnuh wait 'tel de 'ooman gitt'ru
talk, en' w'en Uh lef' me house twix' middlenight
en fus' fowl-crow las' night, 'e yent bin gitt'ru,
en' Uh dunno ef 'e gitt'ru yit, 'cause Uh lef' me
Sunday britchiz duh heng up behine de room do',
en' attuh me yent dey dey, him kin 'buze dem
britchiz, en' quawl wid'um, same lukkuh him bin

do wid me. Needuh me nuh de britchiz fuh ansuhr'um back, en dat mek'um mo' bex.

"Jedge, Uh bin obuhrun meself een me talk.
Uh gone too fas'. Uh haffuh gone back to de fus'
gwinin' off. W'en Uh bin tell de 'ooman suh you
bin tell me fuh be man een me own house, 'stead-
'uh 'e skayre'um lukkuh Uh bin 'speck'um fuh do,
please me Gawd, Jedge, de 'ooman laugh, en' 'e
hab uh wickit laugh—'e soun' sukkuh goose duh
hiss. Da' t'ing jis' suit'um! 'Jedge tell you fuh be
man, enty?' 'e say, 'Berrywell, Jedge tell you right.
Da' wuh Uh binnuh tell you all de time, en' Jedge
hab good sense fuh tell you de same t'ing. You iz
man, fuh true, da' mekso you ent nutt'n' een dishyuh house! Man! Man! Come on, man! Jedge
tell you fuh manhandle me, en hoe-handle me, alltwo, enty? Berrywell. Do'um, ef you man 'nuf,
do'um, do'um! Him tell you fuh t'row hoe-handle
'cross me hanch, enty? Berrywell, shum yuh!
Yuh de hoe-handle, yuh de hanch; wrassle'um out
me han' en' knock'um—You en' de Law!' "

"Well, did you accept her challenge?"

"Suh?"

"Did you knock her?"

"Jedge, man ent fuh knock da' 'ooman! Man
duh him meat! De 'ooman' mout' so scawnful, en'
'e hol' man so cheap, Uh shame fuh ansuhr'um,
so him gone 'pun de back trail 'gen, 'cause da'
t'ing you bin tell'um 'bout hoe-handle, duh nyaw

207

een' e min' sukkuh wurrum duh nyaw een dem chinkypen! So 'e say, 'Budduh, lemme tell you one time! Long ez man dey een dis house me duh de hoe-handle en' de hoe, alltwo, en' him iz nutt'n' but de grass duh grow een de du't. W'en Uh git ready, Uh fuh chop'um up, enty? En' w'en 'e git een me way en' tangle up me foot, Uh fuh chop-'um up befo' Uh git ready! Now,' de 'ooman say, 'You know how you stan', en' wuh you yiz. You iz nutt'n' but de du't, en you ent wu't'! Now, git out me way, git out me way!'"

"Did you oblige her? Did you get out of her way?"

"Jedge, Uh 'blige'um. Uh git out 'e way. W'en Uh look 'puntop de 'ooman en' see how sabbidge 'e stan', me Jedus tell me fuh le'm'lone, so Uh nebbuh ansuhr'um, nuh nutt'n'. Uh g'em de flo'!—ef Uh didn' bin g'em, him woulduh tek'um jis' de same, but Uh g'em. Jedge, Uh *g'em!* Uh git out de 'ooman' way lukkuh him bin tell me fuh do. Uh watch me chance w'en 'e tu'n 'e back, Uh ketch me hat off de nail, en' drap'um 'pun de flo', en' nex' time de 'ooman tu'n 'e yeye off me Uh grab me hat, Uh crack de do' easy, en' Uh gone!— Uh haffuh sneak off out me own house, Jedge, same lukkuh me bin ketch een Buckruh' smokehouse! En' w'en Uh git outside de yaa'd, en' Uh feel me two foot loose onduh me, en' nebbuh yeddy nutt'n' een me yez 'cep' dog duh baa'k to de Buckruh'

208

house, en' owl duh hoot een de swamp, en' alltwo stan' fudduh, en' Uh know suh needuh one duh 'buze me, Jedge, me h'aa't git so saaf' en' peaceubble, Uh haffuh drap 'pun me two knee een de du't, en' tell me Jedus 't'enkgawd.' W'en Uh done pray, Uh gone een de pinelan', Uh rake'up some pine-trash onduh one de big tree, Uh mek me bed, en' Uh gone sleep. Dis mawnin' Uh gone to me cousin' house fuh eat, en' attuh Uh done eat, Uh cut some wood fuhr'um, en' help'um fix 'e fench, 'tel time fuh come yuh to you, suh."

"What do you want me to do? I told you what Daphne needed, and told you what medicine to give her. Two or three good trouncings is what she needs, and nothing else will cure her."

"Jedge, you bin gimme good exwice, en' da' physic you bin tell me fuh t'row 'puntop de 'ooman woulduh cyor'um ef Uh coulduh do'um, 'cause da' physic strong. But 'e tek two man fuh do da' t'ing, 'cause ef one man try'um, him fuh dead! Dat wuh Uh bin know all de time."

"Then, what the deuce are you going to do about it? Are you going back into the house of bondage?"

"No, me Sabeyuh! Nebbuh, no mo'! Him fuh tek him road, en me fuh tek my'own! Him kin tek him road fus', en' soon ez Uh see w'ich way him toe duh p'int, me foot fuh lean de t'odduh way, en' ebb'ry step wuh Uh step gwine tek me

209

mo' fudduh frum de 'ooman, en' me foot fuh hol'
da' road, Uh dunkyuh ef 'e lead me een de sea,
'cause Uh know him ent fuh dey dey. En' now,
Jedge, ef you please, suh, tell me how de law stan',
en' 'splain'um fuh me so Nigguh kin onduhstan',
'cause Uh nebbuh gwine back to me house no mo'.
Uh done!"

"Are you going to give up the house and all you
have been working for all these years?"

"Yaas, suh, Jedge, ef him haffuh go 'long wid de
house, 'e kin hab'um. De 'ooman kin tek me bed,
me jacket, me shu't, me britchiz—ebb'ryt'ing wuh
Uh got, 'cep' me skin! Ef him lef' dat 'pun me
bone, Uh will sattify, 'cause, ef Uh nakity—if
nutt'n' dey 'puntop de skin—Uh know da' skin
fuh kibbuh peaceubble h'aa't, en' ef man got dat,
him oughtuh sattify, enty, suh?"

"Yes, Caesar, your philosophy is sound for a
kinky head."

"Jedge, 'e tek kinky head fuh match kinky head!
Buckruh ent fuh know'um too good. Same way
Nigguh' head stan', him h'aa't fuh twis'up en'
tanglety same fashi'n. 'E nebbuh fuh comb out
straight, lukkuh Buckruh' own. Nigguh' head,
en' Nigguh' h'aa't fuh kinky 'tel de Nigguh dead!
Duh so 'e yiz."

"Caesar," asked Laguerre, "are you regularly
married to Daphne? Is she your lawful wife?"

"Yaas, Jedge, him iz me reg'luh wife, same

210

lukkuh mos' all dese Slann' I'lun' man hab wife.
Nigguh ent got time fuh bodduh tummuch wid
preachuh en' t'ing w'en him git ready fuh hab
wife. Sometime Nigguh frum town come yuh
een we country fuh wisit, eeduhso fuh stay, en'
you kin yeddy de 'ooman wuh de man fetch wid-
'um tell de t'odduh 'ooman 'roun' Nigguh-house-
yaa'd, 'bout how dem bin hab preachuh fuh hitch-
'um to de man, but da' preachuh de 'ooman talk
'bout dey een town, enty, suh? Nobody 'puntop
Toogoodoo nebbuh shum, en' de 'ooman jis' ez well
fuh say him bin hab preachuh fuh hitch'um een
New Yawk! Nobody cyan' 'spute'um, en' nobody
nebbuh b'leebe'um, en' nobody nebbuh bodduh
'bout'um. Dem jis' tek'um fuh she-she talk, en'
le'm'lone.

"Den, now en' den, some dem Nigguh frum
Adam Run en' Jacksinburruh come yuh down on
de salt fuh git wife en' t'ing 'mong we 'ooman,
'cause deseyuh gal wuh lib 'pun oshtuh, en' mullet, en' all da' ralishin' bittle dem ketch out de
crik, stan' fat mo'nuh dem Pon-Pon gal, en' dem
skin mo' shiny, en' de Pon-Pon man lub fuh hab-
'um een dem house; so w'en de Nigguh quizzit de
gal, en' ax'um fuh come een 'e house fuh wife, ef
de gal smaa't, him fuh tell de Nigguh yaas, him
lub'um strong, but him iz uh deestunt gal, en'
Pon-Pon stan' fudduh, en' him 'f'aid fuh gone so
fudduh frum Toogoodoo, 'cep' him fuh tie 'spon-

subble to de man, en' him haffuh hab preachuh,
eeduhso Trial Jestuss, fuh tie'um.

"Jedge, dis gal schemy! 'E dunkyuh nutt'n'
'bout de law en' de chu'ch, 'cause him know suh
w'en de time come fuh man fuh lef' de 'ooman,
him fuh t'row'um'way en' gone, Uh dunkyuh ef
de chu'ch en' de co'thouse dey 'puntop 'e back!
De gal jis' talk so fuh mek de man b'leebe him ent
hol' 'eself too cheap. So de po' Pon-Pon Nigguh
t'row'way two dolluh fuh git da' stuhstiffikit, en'
de stuhstiffikit ent wu't' fuh hol' da' Nigguh no
mo'nuh leely grapewine kin speci*fy* fuh hol' range
bull w'en him git ready fuh buss' loose! De bull
en' de Nigguh alltwo fuh gone!"

"But what has that got to do with you and
Daphne; are you regularly married?"

"Yaas, suh, da' wuh Uh jis' bin tell you. Him
hab me, en' me hab him, same lukkuh mos' all we
Nigguh een dis neighbuhhood. Him iz de only
reg'luh wife wuh Uh got, en' me duh de only man
wuh him got; en', Jedge, suh, attuh Uh git loose
frum'um, him nebbuh fuh hab no mo' husbun'
en' t'ing een him house, 'cause all deseyuh man
know'um now, en' none fuh git ketch een de lion'
jaw lukkuh me bin ketch. Da' 'ooman' meat stan'
stylish, but 'e h'aa't too dainjus!"

"How did you happen to 'hab'um,' " Laguerre
asked.

"Well, suh, dishyuh Daphne come frum obuh to

212

"CAESAR....TURNED TO CLAY"

W'aley place, t'odduh side Doctor Paul Jinkin'
place, en' him bin hab man befo' him bin hab me.
Dat weh him hab de exwantidge obuh me, 'cause
Uh nebbuh bin hab no wife befo' Uh bin hab him,
en' Uh nebbuh *yiz* fuh hab none 'gen, no mo'! Uh
dunno wuh happ'n to de man Daphne bin hab obuh
to W'aley. Uh dunno ef 'e gone New Yawk uh
jump een de crick, but Uh know 'e gone, en' w'edduh him dey een dis life, uh gone to 'e Jedus, Uh
know him nebbuh fuh come back Toogoodoo long
ez Daphne dey yuh!

"Well, suh, one Sunday Uh gone chu'ch obuh
to W'aley, en' Uh see dishyuh Daphne comin'
'long, en' 'e stan' so stylish 'e ketch me yeye. Dat
mekso de man iz fool. 'E look 'puntop de 'ooman'
meat, en' 'e nebbuh see de 'ooman' h'aa't—en'
sometime de po' creetuh nebbuh look 'puntop de
'ooman' meat. Him t'ink 'e shum, but nutt'n'
dey dey.

"Well, suh, all dem 'ooman to W'aley dress'up
berry stylish w'en dem duh gwine chu'ch, en'
ebb'ry Gawd' one bin hab one dem high brustle
'puntop 'e back. You know wuh 'e yiz, suh. Uh
dunno wuh Buckruh' own mek out'uh, but Nigguh
haffuh do de bes' 'e kin, so de 'ooman git dishyuh
black moss off de libe-oak tree, en' dem roll'um
up en' twis'um 'tel 'e stan' sukkuh ottuh skin attuh
'e done stuff. Den de 'ooman wrop'um up een
papuh en' tie 'tring 'roun'um, en' pitt'um 'puntop

213

'e back, en' tie'um 'roun' 'e wais' obuh 'e sku't
befo' 'e pit on 'e frock. Den, attuh 'e t'row 'e
frock obuhr'um da' brustle fuh hice da' frock' tail
up high, 'tel 'e stan' sukkuh tuckrey gobbluh' tail
w'en him duh strut! De 'ooman do'um fuh fool
de man, but nutt'n' dey dey. De man know suh
nutt'n' dey dey, stillyet 'e lub fuh look 'puntop'um
en' 'e know de 'ooman duh fool'um, en' 'stead'uh
him git bex wid de 'ceitful 'ooman, him lub'um
'cause 'e fool'um! Dem iz man!"

"What the devil have the bustles on the women
on the Whaley place got to do with your sticking
your head in the lion's mouth? In this year of
grace, is a buck Nigger fool enough to run after a
woman because she wears a bigger bustle than
anybody else? Couldn't you see, to begin with—
and to end with—" he laughed—"that Daphne
didn't need any other bustle than that Nature had
so lavishly bestowed upon her! Eh?"

"Yaas, suh, Uh bin fool fuh true, en' all dis time
Uh binnuh suffuh 'cause Uh yiz bin fool.

"So, suh, Uh look 'puntop Daphne ez 'e comin'
to de chu'ch en', same time Uh ketch'um een me
yeye, him ketch me een him'own, 'cause same time
me binnuh pick 'ooman, him binnuh pick man,
en' w'ile me binnuh say to meself, 'Eh, eh! dishyuh 'ooman stan' stylish, 'e meat look good, en' 'e
step fas'. 'E look lukkuh smaa't 'ooman. Uh
'speck' ef man hab'um een 'e house him fuh tu'n

214

'roun' swif'. W'en chu'ch done out, Uh fuh quiz-zit'um, en ax'um ef 'e hab man. Ef 'e yent, Uh fuh tek'um fuh wife.'

"Jedge, all de time me binnuh study 'bout de 'ooman, him binnuh study 'bout me. 'Uh wunduh weh dis Nigguh come frum,' 'e say; 'Uh nebbuh shum befo'. 'E seem kind'uh chupit, but 'e look easy, en' 'e look lukkuh him kin wu'k. Ef 'e yent got no 'ooman, Uh fuh tek'um fuh meself; en' ef 'e yiz got 'ooman, Uh fuh tek'um'way frum de t'odduh 'ooman, 'cause Uh know, whoebbuh 'e yiz, 'e yent stan' stylish lukkuh me, en' 'ooman lukkuh me haffuh git wuh 'e want, enty?'

"Duh so da' Daphne talk to 'eself, en' soon ez 'e come out de do' Uh jine'um, en' me nuh him talk. Uh nebbuh loss no time. Uh ax'um ef 'e bin hab man. Him say no, 'e yent hab none, 'cause him lub fuh pick en' choose, en' 'e say dem man wuh lib to W'aley so no'count, 'tel de pick stan' sukkuh de choose. Dem all ent wu't'. 'E say all de man on de plantesshun wuh yent got wife binnuh quizzit'um fuh hab'um, en' dem bod-duhr'um summuch, dem nebbuh g'em no res', but him haa'd fuh sattify, en' him nebbuh fuh hab none 'tel 'e git one fuh suit. 'E *yiz* bin t'ink 'bout hab uh berry stylish man frum Wadmuhlaw, wuh come to W'aley fuh shum, en' him say 'e look fuhr'um fuh come Monday fuh git 'e ansuh. 'E nebbuh come duh Sunday, 'cause Daphne say all

LAGUERRE

dem W'aley man wuh him done 'jeck', stan' so
jallus, him 'f'aid dem fuh waylay da' Wadmuhlaw
man duh paat', en' cut 'e t'roat wid oshtuh shell.

"Jedge, w'en Daphne tell me 'bout hummuch
cow en' fowl en' t'ing him sweeth'aa't hab, en'
all 'bout 'e house en' 'e groun' en' 'e creetuh, en'
Uh yeddy 'bout how strong de man duh co't'um,
Uh git jallus meself, en' Uh tell'um no use fuh
bodduh wid Wadmuhlaw man, 'cause da' place
stan' fudduh, en' ef him ready fuh hab man,
him jis' ez well hab me, 'cause Toogoodoo stan'
close mo'nuh Wadmuhlaw, en' me dey yuh, en' da'
t'odduh man, him dey dey. En' Uh tell'um man
iz man, en' ef me pocket ent strong lukkuh da'
Wadmuhlaw Nigguh' pocket, me h'aa't strong fuh
lub'um, en' me han' strong fuh wu'k fuhr'um.

"Den, Jedge, de 'ooman tu'n'way 'e 'ceitful face,
'e heng 'e head, 'e yeyelash drap obuh 'e yeye, en'
'e mek'out lukkuh 'e shame fuh talk 'long man
'cep' him maamy dey dey fuh puhtek'um! You
shum, enty, suh? Den 'e tu'n 'roun' kind'uh slow,
fuh face me, 'e grin, en' 'e say berrywell, attuh Uh
push'um so strong, him willin' fuh t'row'way da'
rich man, en' tek me, 'cause me bin fetch'um to de
p'int fus'; but 'e say ef Uh hadduh wait 'tel tomorruh come Uh woulduh loss'um, sho', 'cause him
foot woulduh lean Wadmuhlaw. Den, Jedge, me
Jedus tek 'E yeye off me, en' Uh drap een de
'ooman' trap!"

216

"The spider and the fly, eh?"

"Yaas, suh—me bin de fly! En' Uh binnuh buzz me wing long time, but Uh jis' git'way!

"Jedge, come fuh fin' out, none dem man wuh lib to W'aley ebbuh bin quizzit da' 'ooman fuh hab'um fuh wife. Dem know'um too good! En' no Wadmuhlaw man nebbuh bin come fuhr'um needuh—no Wadmuhlaw Nigguh bin mek track 'pun W'aley fuh t'ree munt' befo' da' day Uh git ketch. All dem man bin een de 'ooman' min', en' de man stan' sukkuh bu'd een de tree. De 'ooman call'um him'own befo' him borruh de hatchitch fuh split de shingle fuh mek trap fuh ketch'um!

"En', Jedge, duh so dem 'ooman do we! Dem fuhrebbuh got man duh hide out een de bush. Ef de man ent dey dey, dem gott'um 'puntop Wadmuhlaw, eeduhso een New Yawk! But dem gott'um, Jedge, dem *gott'um!* En' all de man iz rich, en' all stan' stylish. No po' man dey dey, needuhso no oagly man. W'en 'ooman duh talk, po' man en' oagly man ent wu't', en' ef you only got da' man een you min', en' you nebbuh haffuh show'um to nobody, 'e jis' ez cheap fuh mek de man fuh suit, enty, suh? Berrywell.

"So w'enebbuh true-true man peruse 'roun' de 'ooman fuh co't'um, eeduhso fuh projick wid'um, de 'ooman reach een 'e min', 'e fetch out one de man, 'e pitt'um 'puntop 'e knee, en' 'e play wid da' man. 'E play wid'um sukkuh dem leely gal chillun een Nigguh-house-yaa'd play wid dem rag baby wuh dem got. Da' rag doll ent got hair no mo-'nuh punkin, but de leely Nigguh gal mek b'leebe 'e gott'um, en' 'e seddown een' de du't, 'e tek da' raggity t'ing 'pun 'e lap, 'e git piece'uh pine baa'k, en' 'e comb de hair 'pun da' smood head, 'e 'ile'um, 'e twis'um, en' 'e plait'um, jis' ez sattify ez dat!

"Duh so dem 'ooman do. Ebb'ry time man wuh hab on britchiz come fuh wisit'um, dem fuh trot out da' sperrit man wuh yent got on nutt'n'! Sometime de 'ooman fuh fetch'out two-t'ree man. Yuh dem come! You nebbuh see shishuh rich, stylish man lukkuh deseyuh sence you bawn! De 'ooman walk'um, 'e trot'um, 'e pace'um, 'e cantuhr'um. Dem all fuh wu'k haa'd, en' pull plow en' waa'gin en' cyaa't, fait'ful ez mule, en' w'en you hitch'um een da' light buggy, eeduhso t'row saddle 'pun 'e back, you nebbuh see nutt'n' lukkuh him, 'cause 'e bow 'e neck, 'e hice 'e tail, en' 'e jis' ez skittish ez ef him nebbuh bin look 'puntop no plow!

"En', Jedge, suh, da' man 'ooman got een 'e min'—da' man him tell you him got een de bush w'en him duh try fuh mek you jallus—him iz *two man*, eeduhso t'ree, 'cause Gawd nebbuh wrop'up all dem t'ing de 'ooman want een no one man' skin. No, suh! Him mek da' slim-foot race-hawss fuh run race, en' 'e mek da' stubbunt mule fuh pull plow t'ru da' tough j'int-grass—one ent fuh do all-two, en' needuh one ent wu't' fuh t'odduh man'

218

wu'k. Duh so Gawd mek'um. Him mek some de man fuh dance, en' some fuh hol' hoe. Ef you pit da' hoe man 'pun de flo', him foot fuh tangle'up en' t'row'um. Ef you pit hoe een da' dance man' han' en' t'row'um een de sunhot, him fuh cry fus', en' den him fuh creep off fuh leddown een de shade fuh sleep.

"Duh so de man stan' wuh Gawd mek, but de 'ooman t'ink him know how fuh mek'um bettuh mo'nuh Gawd, so *him* man—da' one wuh 'e mek een 'e min'—fuh run race, en' pull bulltongue t'ru da' j'int-grass, onetime! Him fuh play wid de 'ooman, en' wu'k fuhr'um. Him ent fuh talk 'cep' de 'ooman quizzit'um, but wuhebbuh de 'ooman ax'um, him fuh hab de ansuh ready, en' attuh 'e tell de 'ooman wuh 'e wantuh know, him fuh shet 'e mout' tight, 'tel de 'ooman quizzit'um 'gen. Him fuh look good 'nuf fuh mek all dem t'odduh 'ooman jallus 'nuf fuh please 'e wife, but ef outside 'ooman ebbuh cut 'e yeye att'um, him fuh run een 'e wife' house fuh hide. Dat fuh *him*, but, Jedge, w'en him wu'k haa'd fuh buy stylish frock fuh pit 'pun 'e wife, en' de outside Nigguh buzz 'roun' 'e wife, en' projick wid'um, en' praise'um, de man fuh be glad, enty, suh? Berrywell.

"So de 'ooman hab uh good time, long ez dem duh roll all dem man obuh en' obuh een dem min', but all dem man dem duh study 'bout, dey een de cloud, en' bumbye, w'en time come fuh pick man

219

wuh walk 'pun de du't, de 'ooman haffuh do de bes'
'e kin. Some de 'ooman pick man fuh dance, but
him duh buttuhfly, him fuh dance all 'e life, en'
bumbye, 'e dance 'pun de po' 'ooman' grabe. All
de 'ooman lub stylish man, but some hab tummuch
sense fuh bodduh wid no buttuhfly, so 'e say, 'Oh,
me Jedus, dishyuh man oagly, but 'e fait'ful, en'
'e lub fuh wu'k, en' 'ooman haffuh lib. Uh fuh
tek him, enty, suh? T'engkgawd!' En' de 'ooman
drap uh cutchy to 'e Jedus, 'e tek de man en'
gone!—en' him do berry well, 'cause 'e yent haffuh
look 'puntop de man *all* de time!

"But, Jedge, howebbuh de 'ooman' chance fall,
'e nebbuh git all 'e want. One de man always
git'way out 'e min', en' one de t'odduh 'ooman
gott'um, en' w'en de 'ooman wuh hab de fait'ful
man look 'puntop de stylish man wuh de t'odduh
'ooman got, him fuh say, 'Uh wish Uh bin hab
race-hawss lukkuh dat'; en' w'en de hongry
'ooman wuh got de no'count man look 'puntop de
nyuseful man wuh him tittuh got, 'e say to 'eself,
'Uh wish Uh bin hab mule lukkuh dat fuh plow
fuh me.' So, Jedge, none de 'ooman nebbuh sattify,
'cause, alldo' Gawd mix'up de good en' de ent
wu't' een *some* de man *sometime*, Him nebbuh
mix'um up 'nuf fuh suit."

Then came old Scipio, respectfully: "Maussuh,
not cutt'n' yo' disco'se, but dinnuh ready, suh."

"Discourse! *My* discourse! Why, this confounded Caesar who ran away from his wife because she talked too much, has been talking all the morning telling me about it!"

"Jedge, Uh yent done tell you."

"Tell me another day. Go around to the kitchen, and Scipio will give you something to eat."

"Yaas, suh, t'engkgawd!"

" 'Imperious Caesar, dead and turned to clay,' " quoted Laguerre, as he rose.

"Jedge, Uh bin tu'n to clay befo' Uh dead! Da' 'ooman tell me Uh bin nutt'n' but de du't, en' him done tromple me!"

"THE LAW AND THE LADY"

Mid-November. The first ice of the season had come with a brilliant white frost whose crystals glistened in the sunlight from every spear of grass in the fields and open spaces. Earlier and lighter frosts had touched the tender leaves that tipped the long limbs of the Sea-Island cotton-stalks, and nipped the sweet-potato vines, but, under the icy hand of the "black frost," these were now shriveled and dead.

Before the skirmish line of the early frosts the beautiful morning-glories, spread over grassy fields and fence corners, or clambering up tall cornstalks to fall in graceful festoons to earth again, though burned and wounded, bloomed riotously on, and glorified the autumn mornings, as, through suffering and tears, brave women smile to cheer a world in pain. But in the blackened vines that long had nourished them, the sap of life, now stilled, would flow no more. So, as weary hands are folded for the waiting grave, each tender chalice folded in the frost, and drew within itself, as all must do at last. But earlier blooms had left their seeds behind, and these, to lie long dormant on the chilled and unresponsive bosom of the earth, another summer's suns would warm to life, and other vines would run and climb and bloom again!

In the forests the early fallen leaves of the less hardy trees were slowly turning to mold. The painted oaks and hickories yet held in greater part the leafage they would later yield to wintry winds that would not be denied. Among their fruitful boughs, now dressed in soberer hues, gray squirrels played, or busied themselves with winter stores.

The wine-like tonic of the frosty air had set wild things astir, and under its urge, afoot, or on the wing, life seemed more restless, as winter, the iconoclast, drew near. For winter—intolerant of illusions, strips tree and shrub, and sees them as they are—as truth strips men.

And as the trees were bared, the wild creatures, that all through the summer had been sheltered by their protective foliage, became more wary and alert. So men, long sheltered, thrown upon their own resources, develop self-reliance, and become keener in life's struggle.

Deer, when jumped, made longer runs, for far-off coverts; flushed partridges whirred away for distant bays; and turkeys, put to flight, beat noisily on strenuous wings to far sanctuaries in lonely swamps.

Scared rabbits sprang more quickly from their forms, ran fast and far, nor stopped to look and listen, short of the sheltering arms of the briars, for the leaves of the scrub had fallen, and weak creatures take no chances when lynx and gray fox are afoot, and marsh-hawks on the wing.

Squirrels, that in early autumn had played among the heavy leafage of oaks, whose early ripening acorns gave promise of the heavier harvest to come, now watched more warily for boys, and men, and red-tailed hawks, and flattened out on leafless limb, or spiraled cautiously on unsheltered trunks.

But "Jedge" was little moved by the stir of wild life in the woods, by the vast panorama of field and forest. He knew the sun was warm, and the keen air tingled in his nostrils, and that, for the moment, was enough to put him at ease with the world, as he lounged in a comfortable rocking chair on his front piazza to hear the completion of Caesar's story, interrupted on the preceding day.

"Jedge, me wife cyan' mek me tek'um back, enty, suh?"

"Why, has she intimated a desire to return to your bosom, or, rather, bring you back to hers, as you were the runaway?"

"Jedge, Uh yent got no buzzum, een de fus' place, but, ef Uh yiz bin hab'um, Uh nebbuh fuh tek him back, not long ez Gawd pit staar fuh shine een Him sky! Long ez dem dey dey, Uh know suh Him dey dey too, fuh watch obuh we po' creetuh, wuh got 'ooman 'puntop we! Jedge, befo'

Uh fuh gone back een da' spiduh' nes', en' git tanglety'up wid'um, Uh mo' redduh graff de debble
by 'e tail, eeduhso ketch mule by 'e behine foot,
en' dead one time! 'Cause man jis' ez well dead at
de fus', ez de las', enty, suh?"

"Have you heard anything from your wife
since you took leg bail?"

"Jedge, me nebbuh tek da' t'ing you duh talk
'bout! Me nebbuh tek nutt'n' out me house 'cep'
de shu't en' de britchiz en' t'ing wuh Uh bin hab
on w'en Uh sneak out me do' en' git'way, en' dem
same t'ing, uh gott'um on now. Me Sunday jacket
en' me Sunday britchiz, en' all de t'odduh shu't
en' t'ing wuh Uh got, dey een me house. Dem all
dey dey, en', Jedge, dem fuh *dey dey*, 'cause
Daphne, him dey dey too, en' w'en him dey dey
trouble dey dey, sho' ez wawss got sting!"

"Well, what have you heard from the wasp? Is
she still buzzing?"

"Jedge, him duh buzz. Ebbuh sence Uh git-
'way, Uh binnuh stay to me cousin' house, en'
las' night me cousin gone to Daphne' house fuh
see wuh 'e kin yeddy. Me cousin mek b'leebe suh
him gone dey fuh borruh de 'ooman' washboa'd,
but de 'ooman know berry well him nebbuh come
fuh no washboa'd, 'e come fuh pick 'e mout'; so
Daphne mek up 'e min' suh ef him mout' fuh pick,
nobody fuh git nutt'n' out'um 'cep' lie—en' him
smaa't 'nuf fuh do'um, too. So befo' me cousin

kin crack 'e bre't', Daphne jump een, en' 'e woice
berry saaf', en' 'ceitful: 'Uh wunduh weh my
juntlemun gone?' 'e tell de 'ooman.   T'odduh
night, him pit on 'e hat en' gone out fuh tek uh
leetle walk, en' Uh yent shum sence. Ebb'ry day
Uh cook 'e bittle fuhr'um en' leff'um by de fiah
fuh keep hot, so ef him come een 'e house w'en me
yent dey dey, him wouldn' haffuh nyam col' bittle;
but 'e nebbuh yiz come, en' now Uh biggin fuh
git kind'uh oneasy 'bout'um, 'cause Uh 'f'aid 'e
mus'be bin hab acksi*dent*.'

"Jedge, you shum, enty, suh? You see how 'e
stan'? Daphne know berry well suh Uh bin to me
cousin' house, 'cause him binnuh peep t'ru de
bush fuh look 'puntop me ebb'ry day ez Uh gwine
een en' comin' out, en' him know 'sponsubble suh
me dey dey duh hide frum'um, en' de 'ceitful t'ing
nebbuh bin oneasy 'bout no acksi*dent*, 'cause him
know ef Uh *yiz* fuh hab acksi*dent*, Uh fuh hab'um
frum da' hoe handle een him han', 'cause, Jedge,
wehebbuh Daphne dey, acksi*dent* fuh dey dey
too! En' da' oneasy wuh 'e hab, iz 'cause, sence
me run'way en' gone, 'e yent got nobody cunweenyunt fuh 'buze, en', Jedge, you know, suh,
some 'ooman stan' lukkuh dat.   Dem too lazy,
en' too 'f'aid fuh gone out dem house fuh 'buze
nobody wuh stan' fudduh, en' ef dem ent got man
'pun dem own do' step fuh mek do'mat out'uh,

dem t'ink de Lawd ent treat'um right, en' dem bex wid de Lawd."

"True enough, Caesar, but some men are like that, too, you know."

"Jedge, Uh dunno nutt'n' 'bout man. Uh yent got no time fuh study 'bout man, but Uh know how 'ooman stan', 'cause 'ooman binnuh ride me min' long time, en', 'tel him git off'um, Uh cyan' t'ink 'bout nutt'n' else. En' seem ez ef him nebbuh yiz fuh git off, 'cause Jedge, ef you pit bridle een de man' mout', en' saddle 'pun 'e back, en' girt'um up tight, en' fetch'um to de 'ooman' do' step, him sho' lub fuh ride! But Daphne nebbuh fuh 'crape 'e foot 'puntop me no mo', 'cause Uh done!

"Jedge, you know suh, Uh keep study 'bout how fool some 'ooman stan'. W'en Gawd mek 'ooman, Him know suh 'e han' ent strong 'nuf fuh rule de man wid knock, so 'E mek de 'ooman smaa't 'nuf fuh git 'roun' de man, en' 'suade'um fuh gone him way. Gawd do dat fuh puhtec' de 'ooman, en' sabe'um, 'cause man' han' strong mo'nuh him'-own. Long ez de 'ooman sattify fuh nyuze de ecknowledge wuh Gawd g'em, 'e git'long berry well, 'cause ef 'e hab uh good h'aa't, him kin mos' all de time lead de man de right way en'—"

"If there's any good in a man, Caesar, a woman can get it out of him, if she wants to, but some

228

men are hell-bent and no woman, however good, can save them."

"Dat so, suh, en', Jedge, you talk de Gawd' trute w'en you say ef anyt'ing dey een de man, 'ooman kin gitt'um out! 'E stan' so, Uh dunkyuh w'edduh 'e dey een de man' han', uh een 'e h'aa't, uh een 'e pocket, him kin *gitt'um*. Ef Gawd dey een de man' h'aa't, en' de 'ooman want'um, him fuh tek'um, en' ef de debble dey dey, de 'ooman fuh tek'um same fashi'n, enty, suh? Berrywell."

"A shrewd observation," said Laguerre.

"Yaas, suh, dat w'at Uh bin say. En', Jedge, same lukkuh you say, some de man stan' so bad 'tel de 'ooman cyan' sabe'um, en' dem duh gwine to da' place weh de debble lib, en' all shishuh man lukkuh dat, w'enebbuh Uh shum, Uh wish Daphne bin hab'um fuh husbun', en' him bin hab Daphne fuh wife! Den dem alltwo kin fin' de debble w'en dem want'um, en' nebbuh haffuh bodduh fuh gone out de house, 'cause de debble him fuhrebbuh duh wisit een dem h'aa't.

"En', Jedge, Uh dunno how chance happ'n fuh mix'up man en' 'ooman lukkuh 'e yiz. Ebb'ry day Gawd sen', you look 'puntop oxin en' mule, race-hawss en' jackass, hitch'up togedduh, en' none de creetuh seem fuh sattify. De oxin t'ink de mule too stubbunt, en' de mule t'ink de oxin too slow; en' ez fuh de race-hawss en' him paa'dnuh, da' jackass, dem ent fuh git 'long none'tall, 'cause one de head look 'pun de sky en' t'odduh one look 'pun de du't!

"En' 'nuf man en' 'ooman haa'ness up togedduh sukkuh dem t'ing. You see de haa'd, mean man wid da' easy, fait'ful leely wife, en' de man 'buze'um en' run obuhr'um 'tel 'e dead. Den you see de good man wid de saaf' h'aa't, him fuh hitch to da' hebby bex 'ooman wid de debble duh bile een'um all de time, en' him mout' fuh pizen da' good man' life. En' w'en you shum stan' so, you wish Gawd coulduh reach down Him han' en' tek'way da' good man en' da' fait'ful 'ooman, en' hitch'um, en' de debble coulduh ketch dem t'odduh two—da' mean man en' da' bex 'ooman—en' fas-'n'um togedduh sukkuh cat tie by 'e tail, so needuh one kin git loose frum t'orruh one, en' t'row'um obuh tree limb, en' leff'um fuh fight 'tel dem dead! Den Gawd' sun coulduh shine een de sky, en' man en' 'ooman wuh sattify fuh be peace-ubble, coulduh lib peaceubble!"

"'A consummation devoutly to be wished,'" quoted Laguerre.

"Yaas, suh. But mos' all de t'odduh man, 'ooman kin manage'um ef him sattify fuh 'suade-'um, lukkuh de Lawd show'um how fuh do, but, Jedge, alldo' Gawd mek de 'ooman, seem ez ef de debble haffuh exwise'um, en' some de 'ooman done fuh lub fuh folluh de debble' exwice!

"Now, 'cawd'n' to Him plan, Gawd mek man

en' 'ooman two diff'unt way. De man' han' strong, en' ef him cyan' rule de 'ooman no odduh way, him haffuh knock'um, fuh fetch'um to 'e han'. En' de 'ooman, him mout' saaf', en' w'enebbuh 'e wan' de man fuh gone him way, him haffuh sweetmout'um; 'e yent fuh knock'um, en' 'e yent fuh dribe'um, 'cause Gawd mek 'ooman' mout' fuh coax, 'E yent mek'um fuh cuss, enty, suh?"

"That is both the poetical and the popular conception."

"You shum, enty, suh? So, sometime, w'en de debble git een de 'ooman, lukkuh 'e yiz een da' 'ooman Uh bin hab, him exwise de 'ooman fuh t'row'way de plan wuh Gawd mek, en' tek him-'own! De debble say 'Wuh use fuh bodduh fuh coax da' man, en' lead'um? De man blonx to you, enty? Ride'um! Dribe'um! Show you'self fuh be man!'

"Jedge, dat weh de 'ooman loss 'e chance, en' obuht'row de plan Gawd bin mek fuhr'um! W'en de debble tell'um fuh show 'eself fuh be man, 'stead'uh dat, 'e show 'eself fuh be 'ooman, 'cause attuh 'e done drap 'e shimmy, no britchiz dey dey, en' ebb'rybody fuh see how 'e stan'!

"Jedge, suh, w'en you got chillun 'puntop you knee duh play wid'um, en' de chillun box you en' obuhrun you, you ent fuh bex, long ez de chillun know dem iz chillun, en' know suh you hab pashunt wid'um jis' 'cause dem iz chillun, but ef de

231

chillun staa't fuh sassy you en' 'cratch you eye, den, play done obuh, en' you fuh pitt'um down en' switch'um.

"En' duh so man en' 'ooman stan'. Sometime w'en de 'ooman lead de man him way, de man nebbuh know weh 'e duh gwine, but ef de road ent boggy, nuh nutt'n', en' 'e yent got no deep rut een'um, de man nebbuh 'spute 'bout'um, en' 'e folluh de 'ooman fait'ful.

"En', sometime de man see t'ru de 'ooman' plan, en' see de 'ooman duh coax'um en' 'suade'um, en' know puhzac'ly weh de 'ooman' toe duh p'int, en' weh him duh try fuh lead'um; stillyet, ef de road ent look too dainjus, en' ef de man strong 'nuf fuh 'pen' 'pun 'eself, him fuh say, 'Eh, eh! da' po' creetuh duh try fuh fool me, enty? Him t'ink 'e got 'e finguh een me two eye, but Uh see weh 'e duh gwine. Ef Uh hadduh bin weak man, Uh woulduh bex, but Uh strong, en' de 'ooman weak, so no use fuh bodduh 'bout'um. Ef de 'ooman t'ink him duh rule me, Uh yent min', so long ez de 'ooman sattify fuh coax me en' 'suade me, but ef him hadduh try fuh ride me, Uh woulduh knock'um sho' ez Gawd! De road look good 'nuf, anyhow, en' ef Uh fin' 'e yent suit, attuh Uh trabble'um leetle w'ile, Uh kin leff'um, enty? 'Cause man oughtuh strong 'nuf fuh trabble een de 'ooman' road *sometime*.' So de man laugh to 'eself, en' 'e nebbuh tell de 'ooman 'e bin see

232

t'ru'um, en' de 'ooman t'ink him bin fool de man, en' him laugh to 'eself, en' de man en' de 'ooman alltwo gone 'long de same road jis' ez sattify ez dat!

"Jedge, dat de way Gawd mek man en' 'ooman fuh do, enty, suh? 'Cause dem alltwo ent stan' same fashi'n, but w'en de debble git een dat 'ooman' h'aa't en' tell'um fuh ride de man 'stead-'uh 'suade'um, den trouble fuh staa't! Ef de man stan' rough, him fuh lick de 'ooman; ef 'e easy, uh ef 'e yent strong 'nuf fuh lick de 'ooman, him fuh lock 'e mout', en' watch 'e chance, but him gwine fool da' 'ooman, Jedge, him gwine *fool'um!*

"W'en de debble gone een da' 'ooman, him fuh spile de man en' de 'ooman alltwo. Needuh one fuh peaceubble no mo', 'cause w'en de 'ooman tek 'way de 't'oruhty frum de man, en' shame'um een 'e own house, de man fuh 'spize 'eself 'cause 'e shame, en' 'e fuh 'spize de 'ooman 'cause him t'row da' shame 'puntop'um; so de man dunkyuh wuh 'e do, 'cause 'e yent 'speck' 'eself, needuhso 'e wife, en' soon ez Gawd t'row da' Nigguh-night 'puntop-'um fuh kibbuhr'um, him en' de owl fuh gone 'bout dem bidness, en' de man peruse 'roun' dem t'odduh 'ooman' house en' projick wid'um same ez ef him nebbuh bin hab no wife; en' attuh 'e gone home, 'e lie to de 'ooman jis' ez easy ez dat, 'cause, at-tuh de 'ooman tek'way 'e shame frum'um, de man dunkyuh wuh 'e tell'um. So, Jedge, dat de way some deseyuh fool 'ooman try fuh ride de man wuh Gawd bin g'em, 'tel, bumbye, de bridle twis' out de jackass' mout', de saddle slip off 'e back, de 'ooman seddown een de du't, en' de creetuh git'way—en' *yuh me yiz!*" he ended with a laugh.

"What did your cousin say to Daphne?"

"Jedge, me cousin, him iz 'ooman, en' him know how fuh lie berry well, but him know 'e yent no use fuh t'row'way no lie 'pun Daphne, 'cause him done bin look 'puntop me en' know Uh dey een me cousin' house, so him tell'um no use fuh be oneasy, 'cause Uh dey dey. Daphne mek'out luk-kuh 'e done fuh glad, en' 'e sen' uh ansuh by me cousin fuh tell me him hab uh berry 'pawtun' bidness fuh talk 'bout soon ez Uh come back to me house. So da' wawss duh buzz, Jedge, da' spiduh duh spin 'e nes', en' Uh yent gwine een-'um no mo', suh, ef you en' me Gawd stan' by me. You en' Him iz all Uh got fuh 'pen' 'pun, 'cause Gawd, Him rule de sky, en', Jedge, suh, same fashi'n you fuh rule obuh dishyuh Toogoo-doo, 'cause all dese Nigguh en' t'ing dey een you han'.'"

"Jedge" accepted the apotheosis graciously, and took thought upon the unhappy Caesar's plight. The situation was complex, for the master of the house had forsaken his own roof, stealthily, like a thief in the night, leaving behind him his house-hold gods, and a wrathful goddess, to him, if not to Greece, "the direful spring of woes unnumbered!" The fugitive was willing—passionately willing—to abandon his home and all his belongings, animate and inanimate, if only, in the same gesture of renunciation, he could divest himself of his wife! For Caesar was not on all fours with Coleridge in his jab at Job in respect to the first "Restoration" in history—"... shortsighted Satan, *not* to take his spouse!" Caesar believed that Satan had already entered into *his* spouse and would remain with her always.

Laguerre was familiar with the formal notice —published by the husbands of wives who had left the "bed and board" of their lords and made a break for liberty—warning the public that the forsaken husbands would not be responsible for debts incurred by the forsaking wives, and he resolved, in Caesar's name, to warn the public against crediting Daphne. Not that he thought the public would hold Caesar responsible, for his masterful wife had long held the purse-strings, and had managed the family finances efficiently, as is sometimes the way with masterful women. This Laguerre knew, for Caesar cheerfully conceded the termagant industry, efficiency, and thrift—qualities be held to be far outweighed, however, by lethal tongue and temper—but "Jedge" thought a warning posted on the door of Caesar's castle would draw its chatelaine, as badgers are drawn, wrathfully and precipitately, and, once in the open, Laguerre could test her mind in respect to Caesar, whom he was determined to take from her; even if a legal Caesarian operation should be necessary.

Drawing his chair to the writing table, Laguerre wrote in ink upon foolscap a proclamation which he read impressively to Caesar: "Notice: My wife, Daphne Wineglass, having left my bed and board, all persons are notified that I will not be responsible for any debts incurred by the said Daphne Wineglass in my name. Caesar Wineglass."

"Great Gawd, Jedge! Da' papuh fuh mek da' 'ooman bex ez wil'cat, 'cause w'en him yeddy suh me abbuhtize 'bout bed en' boa'd en' t'ing wuh blonx to me, him gwine suck 'e teet' at da' papuh, 'cause him claim all dem bed en' boa'd en t'ing blonx to him. Duh me mek de money fuh pay fuhr'um, but him buy'um wid da' money, en' attuh dat, dem duh him'own, enty, suh?"

"Whether hers or yours, doesn't matter. I only want to smoke her out and find out what is in her mind."

"Jedge, suh, ef you smoke da' 'ooman out, fiah fuh come 'long de smoke, en' no use fuh s'aa'ch 'e min' fuh see wuh dey een'um, 'cause me kin tell you dat befo' you quizzit'um. De debble dey dey, Jedge, de debble dey dey!"

"Then Caesar, we'll smoke him out. You've been talking about that devil a long time, and now I want to see what he looks like."

"Jedge, suh, Buckruh ent fuh shum. Nigguh fuh shum! W'en Daphne come yuh befo' you en' de law, him fuh kibbuhr'um up so close 'tel you nebbuh 'spishun da' t'ing dey dey. Him smaa't to dat, en' befo' 'e gitt'ru wid 'e sweetmout' talk, him fuh mek you b'leebe suh him duh de man wuh run'way, please Gawd, 'cause me bloody'um up wid da' hoe handle! You bettuh watch'um, Jedge, 'cause him will fool you, sho' ez Gawd! Him iz 'ooman, you know, suh!"

Laguerre having made up his mind to discipline the jade severely, or, at least, to frighten her, was undisturbed by Caesar's fear that she would wheedle him out of his purpose, so, sending for Cudjo, the constable, he gave him the notice and commanded him to proceed immediately to Caesar's house, presently Daphne's lair, and nail it securely on the door, directing him, further, that if questioned by the cockatrice, he should give no explanation, save to warn her not to tear it down on pain of whatever dreadful penalties his imagination and his disregard for the truth suggested. Cudjo, full of mystery and of importance, and with hatchet and nails in his pocket, departed, while Caesar, drowsing like a setter in the sun, lounged on the bottom step of Laguerre's piazza

237

to await the return of the dark minion of the law, with news from the front.

Cudjo swung along rapidly, his mind full of pleasant anticipation of the effect his proclamation would have upon Daphne. He had no idea of its portent, for he couldn't read. Neither could she, but he knew it spelled trouble for the masterful one, between whom and himself there was little love lost, for Cudjo was a hoe-handle man—a wife-beater—who often wished his legal right as an official of Laguerre's court could be accorded the latitude exercised by the black bucks of Slann's Island in respect to marital rights, so that he might, within the law, explore the Amazon with a hoe handle. Given the latitude—Mis' Wineglass was long on latitude—Cudjo thought he would lay on the hoe handle just south of the equator, where he was sure it would do the most good!

On the other hand, Daphne, deep-bosomed, tall and muscular, conceived herself quite competent to hold her own with the brutal and uncouth Cudjo, and she had often looked with interest at his ears, his big nose, and his prominent eyes and —like melancholy—marked them for her own tooth and claw—the *lex talionis* by which the dusky ladies of the plantations are wont to rule their lords! "Ef me Jedus ebbuh gimme uh chance fuh clabbuhclaw da' oagly 'ranguhtang, Cudjo, en' 'cratch 'e nose en' 'e yeye wid me nail,

238

en' bite off 'e yez 'long me teet'; w'en Uh gitt'ru wid'um, him fuh look lukkuh da' snag-toot' harruh bin 'cross 'e face, en' him nebbuh fuh beat 'ooman 'gen, no mo'!"

It was yet early afternoon when Cudjo came to Caesar's cabin, sometime the house of strife, but now given over to the solitary tenancy of Mis' Wineglass, alone with her smouldering temper and her now useless tongue. Often, during the self-imposed loneliness of the last few days, Daphne had thought bitterly upon the unkind fate that had deprived her of a listener, but "the spoken word" is of the things that come not back, and masterful ladies—critics on the hearth—who must have their say, though hearts break, come at last to empty hearths, and must, if they talk at all, talk up the chimney!

"Sence da' no'count Caesar run'way en' gone, me mout' duh dry'up, 'cause Uh yent got chance fuh nyuze'um. Ef Uh bin hab eeb'n da' black Quakoo frum Wadmuhlaw, Uh coulduh talk to him, lukkuh Uh bin do t'odduh day. 'E oagly ez mongkey, en' 'e deef ez de debble, but 'e woulduh bettuh mo'nuh nobody. Eeb'n ef 'e couldn' yeddy me, Uh coulduh limbuh up me mout' 'pun'um, but now Uh yent got nutt'n'! Uh 'f'aid fuh gone 'mong dem t'odduh 'ooman fuh talk, 'cause dem sho' fuh quizzit me, en' ax me weh my juntlemun gone. Dem ebb'ry one know weh 'e yiz, jis' ez good ez

239

me, but dem drat 'ooman gwine 'tarrygate me, jis' fuh mek me shame, so Uh yent gwine 'bout de 'ooman, none'tall. But Uh wish Uh bin hab Caesar back. Shuh! Dishyuh t'ing *ent wu't'!*"

Caesar came not, but Cudjo did, and announced his presence as boisterously as a medieval knight, hungry and athirst, battering on the outer door of tavern or castle with the basket hilt of his great sword! But Cudjo did not demand admittance. No welcome of knightly host or avaricious boniface awaited him within. No visions flitted through his mind of groaning boards set forth with boars' heads, barons of beef and Brobdignagian pies; of servitors in leathern blouse and buskin, bearing, high-handed over rush-strewn floors, great flagons filled with amber-hued and ruby-tinted wines; of toast, and quip and laughter! Nor any dream of oaken tavern table; of wide, deep-throated chimney, roaring flames, and glowing coals; of slowly turning spits, of roasting capons, lordly rounds of beef; great loaves of wheaten and of barley bread, and foaming pewter tankards filled with hot spiced ale! The fellowship of jovial friendly men—merchant, monk, adventurer—friendly, traveled men upon the hearth!

But Cudjo thought of none of these. The cabin door was closed, nor did he take thought whether the black panther lurked within; but, hammering lustily, each hatchet stroke drove a nail more firmly in the stout panels of the door, and fastened more securely the written warning of the law.

The panther was abroad, so, finishing his task, unchallenged save by the echoes of his hatchet from the pine forest nearby, he went his way to report to his magisterial master.

BED AND BOARD

After posting Caesar's warning on Daphne's door, Cudjo "took his foot in his hand" and hurried back to report to Laguerre that his commission had been executed.

"Jedge," he said, "Uh done do wuh you tell me fuh do. Uh tek me hatchitch en' Uh nail da' papuh 'pun de do', en' Uh hammuhr'um een tight. Uh pit two nail to de top, en' two to de bottom, en' t'ree to alltwo de side. Uh nail'um *'sponsubble!* En' Uh nebbuh see de 'ooman; nobody bin dey, 'cep' de house."

"Yaas," said Caesar, with a scornful laugh. "No use fuh tell we dat. Uh know berry well nobody bin dey, 'cep' de house."

"Hukkuh you happ'n fuh know summuch? Ef you so smaa't, tell me how you know'um," the constable demanded.

"Uh know'um, budduh, 'cause you got you eye een you head, en' you got you nose, en' you got alltwo you yez. Soon ez Uh look 'puntop you en' see how you stan', Uh know suh nobody bin dey, 'cep' de house. No use fuh 'spute 'bout'um, Buh Cudjo, 'cause Uh *know!*"

"You t'ink me 'f'aid 'ooman—man lukkuh me?"

"Uh dunno w'edduh you 'f'aid 'ooman, en' Uh dunkyuh w'edduh you iz uh you ent, but Uh know Daphne ent 'f'aid no man, en' ef him hadduh

243

ketch you w'en you binnuh nail da' t'ing 'pun 'e
do', da' 'ooman' ten finguh woulduh frizzle you
face 'tel 'e stan' sukkuh frizzle fowl!"

"Who, me? Me fuh 'tan'up en' 'low 'ooman fuh
clabbuhclaw me same lukkuh me bin de 'ooman'
own husbun'! Wuh you s'pose me fuh do w'en de
'ooman t'row 'e han' een me face; en' me got
hatchitch een me han?"

"Uh dunno wuh you fuh do, but Uh know him
claw swif' mo'nuh yo' hatchitch, en' ef you en' him
ebbuh hitch, him fuh tayre'off yo' britchiz befo'
you tayre'off him sku't!"

With a gesture of contempt, Cudjo went about
his business, leaving the question of Daphne's
combative prowess in the air, where, in a manner
of speaking, Daphne herself was at the moment,
for Cudjo's hurrying feet had hardly brought him
to Laguerre's when the chatelaine returned to
her castle, to find the dreadful warning some
impious hand had nailed upon the door! Dreadful,
she knew it was—more dreadful still, charged
with the mystery of the unknown, for the superstitious Negro would always rather suffer the ills
he has, than fly to those he knows not of!

To Daphne—so facile with the spoken word—
the written tongue of Toogoodoo was as a Cunei-
form inscription, and meant no more than Bas-
com's word to a Lily-white in Georgia! But at the
indignity some unknown hand had put upon her,

she flared up as angrily as the three bears after the invasion of Goldilocks, and, about the time Goldilocks was reporting to Laguerre, she set out hot-foot for Pa Tumbo; neither a scholar in politics, nor in the church, but the least illiterate among the unlettered black folk of the community.

Tumbo could read after a fashion—a lame and impotent fashion—that preferred print to penmanship, and, importuned by Daphne he set out at once for the maison Wineglass, gathering along the way half a score of his church sisters and an idle brother or two to season the stew now simmering over the fires of Daphne's wrath.

Almost silently, the little procession moved toward the house of mystery, for Mis' Wineglass had only been able to tell her beloved pastor that during her brief absence from home some jinnee or unfamiliar devil had placed upon her door a writing whose meaning she besought Pa Tumbo to reveal, and they were all too full of curiosity to waste breath in speculating upon a puzzle whose solution they hoped through Tumbo to come at so speedily. To Daphne's curiosity was added an intense anxiety that quickened her pace, as, stepping out like a drum-major, she hurried her companions toward the isolated cabin she called home.

Arrived at last, Pa Tumbo walked boldly up

to the door and faced his arduous task, for he always found difficulty in deciphering the written word. Before venturing to read it aloud, he went over the proclamation several times to himself, the silent sisters clustered about him watching with intense interest the movement of his lips as they mumbled unintelligibly. Tumbo read the signature first. "Caesar" presented no difficulties for, while he thought the spelling rather a high-brow affectation of "de Buckruh," his Bible had made him somewhat familiar with the word, and on several occasions he had heard the peripatetic "preachuh on de Sukkus," while visiting Slann's Island, render sonorously "unto Caesar the things that are Caesar's," but Daphne he found as elusive as did the nimble Apollo—and he could by no means come at the name by word of mouth. After several silent readings, however, he absorbed the meaning of the proclamation and, clearing his throat, proceeded to enlighten the anxious Daphne and her eager companions.

"Sistuh," he said, "dishyuh papuh iz uh berry cu'yus t'ing. 'E seem lukkuh de papuh call Sistuh Wineglass' name, but 'e hab uh funny way fuh write'um. 'E yent call'um lukkuh we call'um. 'E call'um 'Dap-ne!' 'E look cu'yus—Dap-ne, Dap-ne!"

"Nemmin' how 'e call'um," interrupted Daphne,

"tell me wuh 'e say 'bout me. Wuh 'e say? Wuh 'e say?"

"My sistuh," said Tumbo, impressively, "de papuh hab yo' name to de top, en' 'e hab Bredduh Wineglass' name to de bottom, en' 'e say dat attuh you done lef' yo' juntlemun' bed en' boa'd—"

"Bed en' *boa'd!*" she shrieked, "bed en' *boa'd!* *Him* bed! *Him* boa'd! Weh 'e gitt'um? Weh 'e yiz? *Man* fuh hab bed? Enty duh me buy de bed frum de Buckruh? Enty duh me pick'up de black moss onduh de libe-oak tree en' stuff'um een de tickin' fuh mek mattruss? Enty duh me buy de tickin' frum de sto'? Enty ebb'ry Cryce fedduh een dem two pilluh wuh Uh got come out my fowl? En' ez fuh de boa'd! Enty duh me buy boa'd frum de sawmill, en' pay Nigguh fuh fetch'um frum de mill een 'e oxin cyaa't fuh mek fowlhouse een me yaa'd? Enty duh me buy nail frum de sto' fuh nail'um up? Enty duh me stan' obuh Caesar en' mek'um nail'um up? Enty duh my eye haffuh watch'um, en' enty duh my mout' haffuh scol'um fuh mek'um do'um right?"

"Don't bex, my sistuh, don't bex," said Tumbo, soothingly. "You dey een de Lawd' han', enty?"

"Uh dey een de *debble'* han'!" she retorted, passionately. "Uh dey een de debble' han', en' Uh dunkyuh ef Uh nebbuh git out'um no mo'!"

"Oh, Jedus! De debble got ti' Daphne! De debble gott'um!" shouted a church sister.

Daphne turned on her furiously: "Shet you
mout', 'ooman! Shet you mout'! Ef 'e yiz, wuh
you got fuh do wid'um?"

"Be pashunt, my sistuh, be pashunt," Tumbo
pleaded. "You iz de daughtuh ub de Lawd, you
know, en' ef de debble dey dey, lukkuh you say,
yo' pastuh will haffuh pray'um out, enty, so dat
dy sperrit shill be cleanse w'ite ez snow."

"Don' bodduh me, Reb'ren', don' bodduh me!
Uh too bex fuh pray. Da' snow en' t'ing haffuh
wait 'tel Uh git cool, en' Uh nebbuh yiz fuh git
cool 'tel Uh ketch de Nigguh wuh bin to me house
en' nail dis t'ing 'puntop me do' w'en me back bin
tu'n. Read'um now, Reb'ren'. Read de odduhres',
en' see wuh 'e say;" and Tumbo, thus appealed to,
essayed another "spell."

" 'E say, my sistuh," said the scholar, stumb-
lingly, "de papuh say, 'e say, 'Notus: My wife
Dap-ne,' 'e say, 'My wife Dap-ne Wineglass hab
lef' my bed en' boa'd—"

"Oh, Jedus! Him duh talk 'bout da' bed en'
boa'd 'gen, attuh all wuh Uh done tell oonuh
'bout'um!"

"Hab pashunt, sistuh, hab pashunt. Da' papuh
cyan' yeddy, you know. De mout' kin change,
but de papuh, him ent fuh change. Ef mout' tell
lie 'puntop you, en' you fau't da' mout', en' 'cuze-
'um, him kin 'splain 'e wu'd, eeduhso tek'um
back, but han'write ent stan' so. Wuhebbuh him

say, haffuh dey dey. En' no use fuh 'spute de papuh, en' 'taguhnize'um, 'cause him ent do nutt'n'
to you. 'E yent do uh t'ing. 'E jis' fetch you de ansuh wuh Buh Caesar sen'. En', fudduhmo', dis papuh say, 'cawd'n' to you done lef' all dem t'ing
wuh you say him nebbuh bin hab, Buh Caesar ent
fuh pay none you debt. En' ef anybody credik
you, de somebody haffuh tek 'e chance, 'cause Buh
Caesar, him ent fuh be 'sponsubble, none'tall."

"Oh, me Kingdom come! Dishyuh t'ing too
hebby! De drat man run'way en' gone, jis' 'cause
'e too lazy fuh yeddy wuh Uh bin hab fuh say, en'
'e lef' me bed en' me boa'd, en' ebb'ryt'ing wuh
blonx to me, en' 'e eeb'n lef' 'e own Sunday britchiz, en' 'e shu't, en' 'e jacket—all duh heng up een
de room. En' all da' bed en' boa'd; hukkuh me kin
run'way en' leff'um! Enty Uh gott'um? Enty de
bed dey dey een de house? Enty de boa'd dey dey
een de yaa'd? Me fuh run'way en' lef' me own
t'ing? No, me Jedus! Man kin do shish t'ing
lukkuh dat, but 'ooman nebbuh do'um! 'E too
haa'd fuh git.

"En' ez fuh de credik! Hummuch me ebbuh git
'pun da' po' creetuh' name! Uh nebbuh git none!
Uh got credik fuh meself een de Buckruh' sto'
en' de Buckruh' compuhserry, alltwo, en' duh
Daphne Wineglass gitt'um, en' him name stan'
'sponsubble fuhr'um; 'e yent duh no Caesar!

"En' now Uh know wuh de papuh say, all Uh

249

want iz de Nigguh wuh fetch'um yuh! W'enebbuh Uh ketch'um, Uh dunkyuh who 'e yiz, him duh my'own!"

Suddenly a sleek and stoutish sister, coming up belated, joined the group just as Daphne confessed to an appetite for the dark meat of whomsoever had violated her front door, and Judy Chizzum, Tredjuruh-Lady of the I will Arise,—she of the uncovered mouth—opened it a little wider and poured a can of kerosene upon the incandescent temper of Sister Wineglass!

"*Me* know de man wuh do'um," she cried excitedly, full of joy at being able to add fuel to the flames, "Uh know puhzac'ly who 'e yiz, 'cause Uh shum w'en 'e bin comin', en' Uh shum w'en 'e binnuh gwine—"

"Who 'e yiz," demanded Daphne, "Who 'e yiz?"

"Uh know '*sponsubble* who 'e yiz, 'cause 'e bin jis' 'bout hour en' uh half attuh middleday, w'en Uh shum fus'. Uh know 'e mus' be bin close da' time; Uh know 'e yent bin fudduh frum da' time, 'cause Chizzum come home fuh 'e bittle teday. 'E yent come home fuh eat ebb'ry day, 'cause w'en him does go fudduh fuh wu'k, him nebbuh come home middleday, none'tall, 'cause 'e alltime cook 'e bittle soon duh mawnin'—"

"'Ooman! Drat de 'ooman! Wuh de debble me care wuh time Chizzum cook 'e bittle? Uh dunkyuh ef 'e nebbuh cook'um! Uh dunkyuh ef 'e nyam'um raw lukkuh dem canni*bel* him bin hab fuh gran'daddy een Aff'iky befo' de Nyankee ketch'um en' fetch'um yuh! Wuh de debble—! Uh bex tummuch! Tell me de Nigguh' name!"

"—En' w'en Chizzum cook duh mawnin', soon, 'e tote 'e bittle een 'e bucket, en' w'en middleday come, him en' all de t'odduh Nigguh wuh wu'k to da' place seddown fuh eat. Ef 'e dey een de summuhtime, all de Nigguh fuh seddown onduhneet' de tree een de shade, but een de wintuhtime, w'en de we'dduh col', Nigguh nebbuh hab no nyuse fuh shade, en' tree ent wu't' fuh Nigguh duh wintuhtime, 'cep' de leaf done drap off, so een de wintuhtime, w'en Nigguh seddown middleday fuh nyam dem bittle, dem fuh seddown een de sunhot—"

" 'Sunhot! Sunhot!' " Daphne screamed. "Me h'aa't duh bu'n'up wid fiah out da' place weh de debble lib, en' you tell me 'bout *sunhot!* Gimme de Nigguh' name, 'ooman, gimme'um!"

Pa Tumbo again sought to still the tempest of Daphne's troubled heart but, "on information and belief" he was ready to swear that no "Nigger squat on her safety valve" could hold in her steam until her passion had spent itself! "Now, sistuh," he essayed, "you iz berry bex dis mawnin', en' de Lawd tell we: 'let not dy angry passhun rise', en' 'e say, fudduhmo', to dem dat iz fait'ful unto him, 'de Lawd will relibbuh dy enemy eento dy han'.' "

"Reb'ren', ef Gawd ebbuh 'libbuhr'um een me two han', lukkuh you say Him fuh do, da' Nigguh fuh fin'out Uh got ten finguh 'puntop'um! Ef dis slowmout' ebbuh gimme 'e name, Uh nebbuh stop 'tel Uh ketch'um!"

But Judy's "slow mout'" could in no wise be hurried. Big with her news, she was determined to withhold it as long as possible, and then "break" it when she had led up to a dramatic climax. So, going over the back trail, like a careful old hound, she made another start.

"But Chizzum nebbuh bin gone fadduh fuh wu'k dis mawnin'; 'e gone close, so 'e nebbuh bin tek no bittle een 'e bucket, 'cause 'e come home fuh eat, en' attuh 'e done eat, 'e seddown 'pun 'e chair een de sunhot, jis' outside de do'. 'E nebbuh hurry fuh eat, 'e tek 'e time, 'cause de Buckruh tell'um nemmin' fuh gone back teday attuh 'e done eat, 'cause de wu'k wuh dem bin hab fuhr'um kin wait 'tel tomorruh, so Chizzum nebbuh bin gone back to de Buckruh, attuh 'e done eat; 'e jis' seddown een 'e chair outside de do', en' 'e 'tretch'out 'e foot befor'um, en' 'e tek 'e pipe out 'e pocket, en'—"

"Oh, Jedus!" said Daphne with a moan of martyred resignation, "Him duh git 'e pipe! En' den him haffuh 'cratch match, enty; eeduhso gone

een 'e house fuh git fiah fuh light'um! En' all dis
time de nail 'pun me ten finguh duh eetch fuh da'
Nigguh' two eye! Uh haffuh wait, me Jedus, 'tel
da' pipe done light, but all de time Uh duh wait,
me finguh nail duh grow mo' longuh, t'engkgawd!
Dem duh git mo' longuh!"

Judy lit the pipe. "Attuh Chizzum bruk up 'e
tubackuh een 'e han' en' ram'um een 'e pipe, den
'e biggin fuh s'aa'ch 'e pocket fuh match! 'E
nebbuh fin' none. 'E s'aa'ch alltwo 'e jacket
pocket, en' 'e s'aa'ch alltwo 'e britchiz pocket.
None dey dey. 'E ax me ef Uh got any match.
Uh tell'um no, Uh yent got none. Den 'e say
ef dat de case, Uh bettuh watch out puhtic-
'luh, en' don' 'low de fiah fuh gone out 'tel we kin
hab chance fuh buy match to de sto' w'en tomorruh come, 'cause tomorruh duh Sattyday en'
'ooman haffuh gone to de sto'. Uh tell'um Uh know
dat, en' Uh duh watch me fiah close, 'cause Uh
know him duh all we hab fuh 'pen' 'pun 'tel de
match git. Den Chizzum ax me please fuh fetch-
'um piece'uh fiah out de house, en' 'e ax me so
mannussubble, Uh tell'um yaas, Uh willin' fuh
'blige'um, en' Uh gone een de house, en' fetch'um
uh coals out de chimbly.

"Attuh 'e git de coals—"

"You nebbuh bin tell we," commented Daphne,
sarcastically, "w'edduh da' coals bin oak, eeduhso
hick'ry."

" 'E come off'uh oak log, 'cause Chizzum nebbuh hab no hick'ry."

"Uh glad fuh yeddy dat, 'cause hick'ry log fuh
hol' fiah summuch longuh mo'nuh oak. Uh 'f'aid
ef da' coals you bin fetch fuh Chizzum hadduh
come off hick'ry log, 'stead'uh oak, you woulduh
talk 'bout'um mo' longuh."

Daphne's grim humor amused the others, but
Judy, untouched, proceeded.

"Jis' ez Chizzum light 'e pipe en' 'tretch'out 'e
foot befor'um, Uh see somebody duh comin' t'ru
de pinelan', en' him duh swing 'e aa'm berry
swonguh ez 'e gwine, en' him duh walk fas'."

"Wuh time dat bin, my sistuh?" asked Tumbo.

" 'E bin 'bout hour en' uh half attuh middleday; dat de reaz'n Uh bin tell you so puhtic'luh
'bout Chizzum en' 'e bittle, en' 'e pipe, 'cause him
lef' de Buckruh middleday, w'en 'e knock'off, en'
him haffuh walk home en' nyam 'e bittle en' light
'e pipe, so, by de time 'e do dat, hour en' uh half
attuh middleday done pass, en' me en' Chizzum
see de Nigguh comin' 'long, en' alltwo uh we shum
good."

" 'Ooman," said Daphne, pleadingly. "You got
de Nigguh een you eye, tell me who 'e yiz."

"Chizzum en' me, alltwo, see de Nigguh at de
same time, but Chizzum talk fus': 'Uh wunduh
weh da' Nigguh gwine,' 'e say, 'seem ez ef him
mus'be hab some berry 'pawtun' bidness fuh 'ten'

to, 'cause him duh step fas'.' Uh tell'um de Nigguh step fas', fuh true, but Uh dunno, no mo'nuh him, weh de Nigguh duh gwine, Uh only know suh de Nigguh ent lib to we plantesshun, 'e yent blonx to we, en' 'e yent hab no bidness 'mong we, none'tall, 'cause none uh we people obuh yuh ent got no nyuse fuhr'um, en' us dunkyuh ef we nebbuh shum! En' w'en you see Nigguh' foot trabble swif' lukkuh dat, him eeduh duh gwine fuh wisit 'ooman, elseso 'e dey at some odduh debble*ment,* en' 'e 'f'aid man gwine ketch'um, 'cause deseyuh he-Nigguh stan' too drat lazy fuh walk fas', 'cep' dem *haffuh* do'um. W'en Uh tell'um dat, Chizzum say, yaas, 'e stan' so, fuh true, jis' lukkuh Uh bin say; 'cause Chizzum iz uh berry mannussubble man, en' w'enebbuh me en' him talk, him all de time 'gree to wuhebbuh Uh say, en' 'e nebbuh 'spute me, 'cause Chizzum hab sense."

"*Yaas,* 'e hab sense. Him *haffuh* hab sense," said a knowing sister, while the others, to whom the man's uxoriousness was as an oft-told tale, smiled approvingly.

Realizing the futility of attempting to stem the flowing tide of Judy's speech, she was allowed to proceed, without further interruption, to a "logical conclusion," or wherever else her insistent tongue might take her.

"So me en' Chizzum nebbuh say no mo', but we

alltwo watch de Nigguh long ez we kin shum, 'tel, bumbye, de tree en' de bush swalluhr'um'up en' 'e gone.

"Leetle w'ile done pass. Den, een 'bout ten minnit attuh we yeye done loss de Nigguh, we yeddy 'bram, bram, bram, bram, bram, bram, bram!' out yuh een de 'ood, en' we alltwo bin 'stonish. Dis time, me duh de man fuh talk fus'. Uh say, 'Wudduh dat, Chizzum? 'E soun' sukkuh dem big black Kate woodpeckuh duh knock pine tree.' 'Yaas,' Chizzum say, ' 'e soun' lukkuh dem Kate, fuh true, but 'e soun' mo' holluh, 'cause w'en woodpeckuh knock pine tree, de tree dead, eeduhso 'e staa't fuh dead, en' you ent fuh git holluh soun' lukkuh dat out'uh no pine tree, 'cause long ez 'e duh stan'up, pine tree nebbuh lub fuh hab no holluh een'um. Seem to me,' Chizzum say, 'seem to me da' t'ing soun' mo' lukkuh man duh dribe nail een boa'd wid hatchitch.'

"Den, attuh two-t'ree minnit we yeddy'um 'gen, 'bram, bram, bram, bram, bram, bram!' 'Yaas,' Chizzum say, 'da' duh man duh hammuh nail. 'E yent no Kate duh knock. De reaz'n 'e bin stop so long iz 'cause him haffuh tek dem nail out 'e pocket. Ef him bin hab'um een 'e mout' him coulduh git de nail mo' cunweenyunt, en' hammuhr'um mo' rappit.'

"Da' bin jis' wuh Chizzum say, en', please me Jedus, de man bin right! Uh nebbuh 'spute'um,

nuh nutt'n', 'cause Uh bin s'pishun all de time
him bin right, but Uh nebbuh tell'um so, 'cause
man iz uh t'ing, ef you 'gree wid'um, en' praise-
'um, him berry aps fuh swell'up en' git swonguh.
Him swell'up too easy! So Uh nebbuh tell'um
nutt'n', en' attuh leely w'ile we yeddy da' t'ing
knock 'bram, bram,' some mo', den 'e stop.

"Attuh 'e stop, me en' Chizzum keep on tu'n'um
obuh een we min' en' study obuh how de t'ing
stan', but we cyan' onrabble'um. Ef 'e *yiz* man,
wuh 'e duh do? Ef him binnuh mek house, eb'nso
ef him binnuh mek fowl-house, him woulduh hammuh mo' longuh. Him wouldn' bin knock shishuh
shawt time fuh nutt'n', 'cep' him binnuh fix 'e
fench, en' man nebbuh knock fench hebby lukkuh dat; de soun' too strong. Jis' ez we gitt'ru
tu'n'um obuh en' mek'up we min' we cyan' do
nutt'n' wid'um, please de Mastuh, Uh see da' same
debble'ub'uh Nigguh comin' back obuh de same
track him binnuh trabble w'en we bin shum at de
fus', only, dis time, him duh gwine 'pun 'e back-
track, sukkuh beagle trabble 'pun de back-track
fuh ketch de trail 'gen, w'en fox en' wil'cat t'row-
'um off.

"Dis time, duh *me* yeye wuh ketch de Nigguh
fus'. Uh shum 'way off een de bush duh trabble
one dem crookety paat' wuh Nigguh en' cow does
trabble, en' soon ez Uh shum, Uh tell Chizzum
fuh look 'puntop'um. Chizzum look 'puntop'um.

'Eh, eh!' 'e say, 'seem ez ef da' same Nigguh duh gwine back by de same road wuh 'e bin come by. En' seem ez ef 'e foot moobe mo' swif' ez 'e gwine, den 'e bin do w'en him binnuh come.'

"Uh tell'um yaas, en' w'en Nigguh' foot hasty lukkuh dat een de daytime, Uh haffuh s'pishun de Nigguh. You look fuh 'e foot fuh hasty duh night-time, w'en him duh ramify, en' t'ing, but w'en him do'um een de daytime, you haffuh s'pishus, 'speshly shishuh Nigguh lukkuh dis, 'cause Nigguh lukkuh dis, you haffuh s'pishun'um all de time. 'E so mean! En' w'ile we duh talk 'bout'um, de Nigguh come mo' closuh. De paat' him duh folluh tek'um pas' we house 'bout uh acre en' uh half. 'E cut 'e yeye at we, en' him see we good fashi'n, but 'e nebbuh crack 'e teet', en' 'e nebbuh mek no mannus, nuh nutt'n'.

"Uh didn' 'speck'um fuh mek none, 'cause him iz de wuss' no'mannus Nigguh 'pun dishyuh whole Toogoodoo. W'en Uh shum stan' so, Uh tell Chizzum, Uh say, 'Chizzum, you see da' heng-dog look da' Nigguh got 'pun 'e face, enty? Da' Nigguh binnuh do some mischeebus t'ing, sho's you bawn. 'Membuh wuh Uh tell you! You fuh see. You shum how 'e duh swing 'long, wid da' hebby hatchitch een 'e han'? Him duh de man wuh bin hammuh dem nail so strong! Him duh de berry man, en' Uh know him bin some place weh 'e hab no bidness fuh gone. Him bin attuh some

BED AND BOARD

debble*ment* 'pun dis plantesshun, sho' ez Gawd!
Him mean to dat. You kin s'aa'ch dishyuh whole
Toogoodoo nation, en' you yent fuh fin' no Nigguh mean mo'nuh him! Uh dunno w'ymekso Jedge
hab'um een place, 'cause Uh tell ebb'rybody suh
da' oagly 'ranguhtang, Cudjo—"

"*Cudjo!*" screamed the frantic Mis' Wineglass
as the name she had been waiting for slipped in-
advertently from the lips of the lady whose me-
ticulous and circumstantial narrative had been
designed to retard the revelation as long as possible—"Cudjo! Me Gawd nebbuh fuhgit me! Me
Jedus gimme de Nigguh! Him pitt'um een me
two han'! En' Uh got ten finguh, enty? T'engk-
gawd!"

Judy's balloon of self-importance collapsed suddenly and disastrously with the premature birth
of her portentous secret, and she was heard no
more, but her spirit still glowed with pride for
the labial continence that had held her hound of
mystery so long in leash.

Now Daphne took the stage, and she yearned
ardently to adventure with tooth and claw against
those parts of Cudjo's cranial and facial anatomy
whose mutilation constitutes mayhem under old
English law. Uh wan' da' Nigguh' yeye en' 'e
oagly nose en' 'e two yez. All dem t'ing duh my-
'own soon ez Uh shum," but she was advised by
her friends to be patient, for Cudjo, an officer of

259

the law, would come under "Jedge's" protection if she assailed him during the sittings of Laguerre's court, or while otherwise about his business as constable.

Few of the Negroes had any use for Cudjo, a rough, ill-mannered fellow—despised by the women as a wife-beater—so when Daphne, the only one among them physically competent to engage him in single combat, outlined her plan for bringing the black boar to bay, the feminine Board of Strategy promptly agreed.

"Uh know wuh Uh gwine do," said the fearless feminist. "Uh gwine bex da' baboon, en' mek-'um knock me fus'. Den Jedge dunkyuh wuh Uh do wid'um, 'cause Jedge, him ent 'low man fuh knock 'ooman een him country, en' all dishyuh Toogoodoo neighbuhhood blonx to Jedge, en' dey onduh him 't'oruhty. Eb'nso ef de 'ooman duh de man' wife, him ent hab no prib'lidge fuh knock-'um, 'cep' de 'ooman 'buze de man, en' jump 'pun-top'um fus'. Tomorruh duh Sattyday, en' de we'dduh stan' good, so Uh know Jedge fuh hol' co't to him reg'luh summuhtime co'thouse een de pinelan' close Toogoodoo bridge, en' Cudjo, him all de time gone to da' place long time befo' Jedge git dey, 'cause him lub fuh strut 'roun' de 'ooman en' t'ing fuh show'off, sukkuh him bin Jedge, 'eself. But da' 't'oruhty wuh Cudjo t'ink him got, 'e yent wu't', 'cep' Jedge dey een place. Bedout

BED AND BOARD

him dey dey, Cudjo ent nutt'n'! So tomorruh
mawnin' Uh gwine watch fuhr'um ez 'e comin'
'long, en' ketch'um duh paat', 'cause w'en him
dey dey, him iz nutt'n' but de pyo' *Nigguh*. No
't'oruhty dey 'puntop'um, 'cep' 'e black skin en' 'e
britchiz, en' ef me Jedus stan' by me, deseyuh ten
finguh wuh Uh got, fuh tayre off alltwo!"

"My sistuh," said Tumbo, impressively "my
sistuh, 'membuh de Wu'd say:

'Let dog delight to baa'k en' bite,
Let bear en' lion growl en' fight,
Yo' leetle han' wuz nebbuh mek
Fuh 'cratch one'nurruh eye.' "

"Don' bodduh me, Reb'ren', don' bodduh me!
En' don' tell me nutt'n' 'bout no Wu'd! Uh got
wu'd een me mout', enty? Uh gwine baa'k en'
bite, alltwo, en' 'cratch 'puntop'uh him! Uh gwine
cuss Cudjo fus', fuh mek'um bex, en' Uh gwine
cuss'um strong, sukkuh man. Den Uh fuh ride-
'um! Uh got de debble een me now. Uh gwine gi'
Cudjo de debble tomorruh mawnin', en' den, attuh
Uh done t'row'um een da' Nigguh, lukkuh him
bin gone een dem wil' hog een de Scriptuh, Uh
will ready fuh pray, Sunday. Uh yeddy suh dem
Scriptuh hog bin jump een de sea. Cudjo ent
got no sea fuh jump een, 'cause de sea stan' fudduh—'e dey t'odduh side Keewaw—but ef him
jump een Toogoodoo Crik, Uh dunkyuh. Now,
Reb'ren', lemme'lone!"

261

THE TAMING OF THE SHREW

On Saturday morning Cudjo was swinging along a neighborhood road on his way to Laguerre's court. An hour or two in advance of its convening, he was taking his time and looking about him as he walked, at the forest that was now changing under the frosts to its somber wintry garb.

As he came within a mile of the "Court" his interest was engaged by the flutter of a petticoat, as a woman rose from a log by the roadside, and came into the road a hundred yards ahead of him. In a moment a second stepped out. "One too many," thought Cudjo. Another joined the other two, and Cudjo was disappointed, for then there were two too many! "Uh wunduh wuh summuch 'ooman duh do yuh?" he grunted. He soon found out, for when he neared them and faced Sister Wineglass as a lion in the path, flanked by Sisters Chizzum and Fields, "summuch" became split'um, 'enty?"

"You iz de black Guinea-Nigguh, de oagly redeye' 'ranguhtang, wuh tek 't'oruhty 'puntop yo'self fuh come to me house w'en me bin tu'n me back, en' dribe ten-penny nail een me do' fuh split'um, 'enty?"

"Hukkuh you know Uh bin to you house?"

263

"Uh know 'cause you oagly twis'-foot track dey dey een de du't, enty?"

"Ef Uh yiz bin dey, Jedge sen' me. Him tell me fuh pit da' papuh 'pun de do', en' Uh do'um. Now, shet yo' debble'ub'uh mout' befo' Uh knock you!"

"Nigguh! Knock *me?* Uh know you lub fuh knock 'ooman—da' duh all you iz fuh knock, 'cause you nebbuh fuh knock no man—but befo' you knock me, lemme gi' you sump'n' fuh knock me 'bout. Lemme tell you wuh you iz. Ef you hadduh bin deestunt w'en Jedge tell you fuh fast'n da' papuh to me do', you coulduh tek light'ood splintuh en' jam'um een de crack, en' da' splintuh coulduh speci*fy* fuh Jedge' wu'd, jis' ez good ez nail; but no, you too mean fuh do dat, 'cause de house blonx to 'ooman, en' de po' 'ooman ent dey dey. En' you knock dem hebby nail een de do' wid you hatchitch en' spile de do', en' you do'um 'cause you mean to dat. En' you know w'ymekso you mean to dat? Lemme tell you. You mean to dat 'cause you iz buzzut, en' crow, en' Nigguh, en' 'ranguhtang, all one time! You gran'daddy bin mongkey. At de fus', Gawd mek'um wid tail, but attuh 'e bin too lazy fuh nyuze de tail de Lawd bin g'em fuh swing frum de cokynot tree, Gawd dry'um up; en' sence you gran'daddy loss 'e tail, all you fambly een Aff'iky, you budduh, en you tittuh, en t'ing, all stan' same fashi'n lukkuh

264

you. No tail dey dey, so dem haffuh lib een hole een de du't, sukkuh cootuh en' alligettuh, 'cause dem cyan' climb no tree! Now, lemme see ef you man 'nuf fuh climb 'ooman! You bin talk 'bout knock, now knock me, knock!"

Cudjo, a surly brute, was restrained by no chivalrous impulse from raising his hand to woman. Daphne, arms akimbo, tense as a coiled steel spring, stood invitingly before him, and the invitation was pressing for she was determined to goad him into hitting "de fus' lick" so as to save her the reproach of an unprovoked assault upon an officer of "Jedge's" court. As she laughed in his face and spat at him contemptuously, Cudjo drew back his right arm in the threatening gesture with which a plantation boxer is wont to apprise his adversary of a purpose to project a round-arm swing for the jaw—or anywhere else—a considerate warning to the adversary to get out of the way! As his arm was poised in this awkward posture, Daphne tauntingly made play upon the constable's name.

"Hawlback !" she shouted. "Cudjo Hawlback! Him is Hawlback fuh true. De name jis' suit. 'E han' ent wu't, 'e han' ent wu't'. 'E haul'um back, but 'e cyan' t'row'um out; 'e haul'um back, but 'e cyan' t'row'um out, 'cause 'e 'f'aid fuh knock, 'cause 'e 'f'aid fuh knock!"

Cudjo, now red-eyed with wrath, shifted his

long hickory staff from his left hand to his right, stepped back a pace and launched an awkward swing that, if it had landed, would have caught Daphne just abaft the beam. But it didn't land, for Daphne had anticipated the sweeping gesture and saw it coming, and, as it started, she sprang quickly within the unguarded gates, for Cudjo, depending upon his right hand alone, had not taken the trouble to put up his left, which hung idly by his side, until the sting of Daphne's talons furrowing his face impelled him to bring it into action; but 'twas then too late, for the Trojan horse was already within the walls, and he could only grasp his assailant in a gorilla-like grip and draw her nearer to him; which was precisely what his assailant wanted, for Mis' Wineglass was expert at in-fighting and the closer Cudjo clasped her to his bosom, the more poignantly was impressed upon him the perilous propinquity of her finger-nails. And she used them valiantly!

If the constable had had the wit to drop the hickory staff from his right hand, he could have hugged, and thrown, and mastered her, but he held it fast, and belabored the lady ineffectively over the back, whereon she was well protected; but, outraged by the indignity of the antipodal assault, Daphne, having achieved her first objective and sacrificed her victim's face, locked her arms about his neck, drew his head down suddenly and fastened her teeth in his ear.

With a hoarse scream of rage, Cudjo dropped his staff and threw the terror off, but before he could strike her, Sister Chizzum, who had picked up the long hickory, came to the rescue with a threatening gesture, while Sister Fields, feeling that "they also serve who only stand and wait," stood by loyally.

Cudjo knew he was no match for the three petticoated musketeers, standing as one, but his fury might have impelled him to take a chance, had not the quick-witted Judy shouted, "Jedge duh comin'! Jedge duh comin'!" and pointed down the road to a buggy slowly approaching.

It was not Laguerre and Judy knew it, for the burly figure of Pa Tumbo filled her eye at the first glance, but she knew no other name would so chill Cudjo's combative ardor as that of the testy magistrate; and her psychology was sound, for the constable cooled instantly, and when Tumbo jogged slowly up a few minutes later it was too late to get mad again.

Pa Tumbo, having left his entirely superfluous lawfully-lady behind him, was on his way alone to attend Laguerre's court. Upon reaching the group in the road, he stopped to express a surprise he did not feel, for one look at Cudjo's harrowed face and lacerated ear, told him that Sis-

LAGUERRE

ter Wineglass had kept yesterday's promise to her
Maker that, with His gracious help, she would
mar the countenance of the " 'ranguhtang." The
promise lacked somewhat of fulfilment, for he
had held his eyes inviolate, but nose and cheeks
were cruelly clawed, and his bitten ear dripped
blood, so Daphne felt the Lord would not hold the
eyes against her. She had done her best.

"Bredduh Hawlback," said the Reverend hypo-
crite, "you seems to bin hab uh bad acksi*dent*.
You mus'be bin trip you foot en' fall down, enty?
'Cause you face en' you yez look lukkuh you bin
stumble een uh harricane tree en' snag you'self.
You bettuh git one dese good sistuh fuh tayre uh
piece'uh clawt' off his shimmy en' tie up you yez
fuh you."

"Harricane! Uh *yiz* bin snag' wid harricane,
but 'e yent no tree do'um! 'Tis dem t'ree dyam
she-cat bin gang me w'en Uh yent bin look, en'
dem claw me face en' chaw me yez, lukkuh you
shum, en' dem ebb'ry one blonx to yo' chu'ch, en'
duh you spile'um en' pit notion een'um 'bout
'Syety, en' all shishuh t'ing, en' den, 'puntop'uh
dat, you dey dey wid you 'ceitful mout' duh tell
de drat wil'-cat fuh tayre 'e shimmy fuh tie up
me yez! Ef you didn' bin come so soon, Uh
woulduh tayre'um off all t'ree fuh meself, en'
tu'n'um loose een dis pinelan' nakit ez nyung
crow! Now, Uh gwine tek'um to Jedge!"

268

THE TAMING OF THE SHREW

"Oh, me Jedus!" cried Judy, "Yeddy'um duh lie! W'en you shum sputtuh lukkuh dat, en' all da' w'ite frawt' come out 'e mout', you *know* 'e duh lie. All dem blue-gum Nigguh stan' same fashi'n. En', Reb'ren', him say we all t'ree bin gang'um. Please me Jedus, nobody nebbuh tetch-'um 'cep' Sistuh Wineglass. Him lick'um by 'eself, him, one! En' Cudjo call 'eself *man!*—Him en' 'e *britchiz!*

"En' w'en him talk 'bout tek we to Jedge—Ki! Him duh t'row rabbit een briah-patch, enty? Only de 'ranguhtang haffuh tu'n eento taar-baby fuh tek we! Come 'long, wunnuh gal, leh we go!" And with a laugh at her conceit, Judy threw the hickory staff contemptuously at the constable's feet, and victors and vanquished moved off, with Pa Tumbo in the middle, spreading himself as far as possible over the buggy seat that he was too wise to offer to share with any one of the three sisters.

"My sistuh, Uh berry sorry Uh yent got room fuh ax wunnuh all t'ree fuh ride, 'cause dishyuh buggy seat too narruh."

"Dat so, suh. 'E stan' so fuh true," for the ladies knew that Judgments of Paris were not for Slann's Island parsons, who, in respect to the gentler sex, do not commit themselves in public! Cudjo didn't travel long in company, but walked ahead rapidly and, coming to the meeting place well in advance of Tumbo and his feminine escort, was the center of sympathetic interest until his assailants arrived and gave their side of the story. Among those present was Caesar, who was frankly delighted that his estimate of his wife's prowess had been justified.

"Enty Uh tell you?" he asked Cudjo tauntingly. "Enty Uh tell you Daphne' claw swif' mo'nuh yo' hatchitch? Enty Uh tell you him would frizzle you face? You bin too swonguh fuh yeddy wuh Uh bin tell you. Now, attuh you done clabbuh-claw 'tel you nose en' you yez en' t'ing done spile, you sattify, enty? Berrywell."

At noon came Laguerre. One glance at Cudjo's dour countenance told him the constable had run into a buzz-saw, and he more than suspected that Caesar's buzzing wasp had both buzzed and stung.

"What have you been up to Cudjo?" he asked. "Your face looks as if you had been on the devil's gridiron!"

"Jedge, Uh yiz bin dey. Deseyuh t'ree Satan-'ub'uh wil'-cat bin double-team me en' tayre me up lukkuh you see."

"If 'there was lack of woman's nursing,' there was no 'dearth of woman's tears,' eh, Cudjo?"

"No, suh. Da' Wineglass 'ooman hab claw luk-kuh de debble' gran'maamy, en' him duh de one wuh tayre me face lukkuh you shum, en' dem

270

t'odduh two stan' by'um so close, Uh didn' hab chance fuh 'fen' fuh meself."

"Judy, you seem to have been an innocent by-stander, tell me about it," said Laguerre to Sister Chizzum, who caught his eye as she bustled up to the front, with words almost jumping out of her mouth. "How did it happen?"

"Jedge, suh," said Judy dropping a brisk curtsy, " 'e happen dis way. Me en' Sistuh Fields en' Sistuh Wineglass binnuh walk een de big road, en' bumbye, w'en we foot git w'ary we all t'ree seddown 'pun uh log 'longside de road fuh res'."

"Lying in wait for Cudjo, I suppose."

"Jedge, suh," said Judy with a quizzical smile, "we iz 'ooman, you know, en' w'en 'ooman see stylish man lukkuh Buh Cudjo comin' down de road, de man full we yeye 'tel we haffuh gone een de road fuh look 'puntop'um, close. So w'en Buh Cudjo nigh we, all t'ree uh we dey dey duh wait fuhr'um, en' soon ez we shum we staa't fuh quawl obuhr'um, 'cause 'ooman is uh jallus t'ing, en' w'en shishuh stylish man lukkuh Buh Cudjo come'long, ebb'ry one de 'ooman say him haffuh be de one fuh pass de time uh day, 'cause all uh we lub'um tummuch!"

"Yaas, you 'ceitful debble," said Cudjo with an evil scowl. "Wunnuh lub me sukkuh hawn-owl lub rat! Wunnuh lub me wid you claw!"

"So, Jedge, attuh we 'spute obuhr'um leetle w'ile

271

me en' Sistuh Fields tell Sistuh Wineglass him kin hab de fus' chance, 'cause him kin talk stylish mo'nuh we."

"En' 'e drat fang en' 'e claw mo' shaa'p," interjected the clawed one. "Dat w'ymekso 'e cyan' keep no husbun' en' t'ing een 'e house! En', Jedge, de Satan cuss me sukkuh man, jis' 'cause Uh nail da' papuh 'pun 'e do' lukkuh you tell me fuh do, en' den 'e call me out me name fuh ebb'ry debble'ub'uh t'ing him kin lay 'e mout' to."

"How was that, Judy?" demanded Laguerre. "She abused an officer of the law for doing his duty?"

"No, suh, Jedge, him nebbuh 'buze'um fuh dat, 'cause him ax Cudjo 'sponsubble, w'ymekso 'e nebbuh nail'um up deestunt lukkuh you bin tell-'um fuh do, 'stead'uh split de po' 'ooman do' wid dem hebby ten-penny nail. En' Jedge, suh, Sistuh Wineglass nebbuh bin call Cudjo out 'e name! Him nebbuh call'um nutt'n' 'cep' Guinea-Nigguh, en' buzzut, en' 'ranguhtang! Him nebbuh call'um out 'e name none'tall, 'cause, Jedge, suh, enty duh you tell we suh Nigguh' gran'daddy en' t'ing een Aff'iky iz mongkey? Yaas, suh, you iz de berry man, en' you tell we *'sponsubble!* En' we b'leebe you, Jedge; attuh you tell we so, we *b'leebe'um,* 'cause you stan' nex' to Gawd 'puntop dishyuh Toogoodoo, Jedge, en' we *haffuh* b'leebe you.

"En', Jedge, enty 'ranguhtang iz mongkey wuh

done drap 'e tail? Hukkuh ti' Daphne call Cudjo
out 'e name w'en 'e call'um so? Enty you tell
we suh one time all de Nigguh bin mongkey?
Enty you know? W'en da' eegnunt Nigguh 'taguhnize ti' Daphne 'bout call'um 'ranguhtang, him
ent hab sense 'nuf fuh know suh him duh 'taguhnize him Maussuh, him ent duh 'taguhnize de
'ooman, him duh 'taguhnize *you*, 'cause all de
'ooman do iz fuh tek de wu'd out yo' mout' en'
t'row'um 'puntop de Nigguh. So, w'en you call
de Nigguh mongkey en' de 'ooman call'um 'ranguhtang, him nebbuh call'um out 'e name, Jedge,
him only tek off de tail you bin g'em, en' ef de
'ooman hadduh know suh Cudjo woulduh agguhnize en' 'spute summuch 'bout da' tail you g'em
en' de 'ooman tek off'um, de 'ooman woulduh gi'
de Nigguh de tail at de fus', en' call'um mongkey,
'stead'uh 'ranguhtang. You shum, enty, suh?"

"The point or the tail?" asked Laguerre,
amusedly.

"Great Gawd, Jedge, de p'int. No tail dey dey!"
said Judy, with a laugh.

"I see the point," said Laguerre, "and the point
is well taken. Now, who hit the first lick?"

"Jedge, suh, nobody nebbuh hit none, no fus'
lick, needuhso no las' lick. Nobody nebbuh hab
nutt'n' fuh knock no lick wid, 'cep' Buh Cudjo.
Him bin hab da' long hick'ry stick een 'e han',
but 'e yent hab sense 'nuf fuh nyuze'um. Him

t'reat'n de 'ooman wid'um, but w'en time come
fuh knock, no knock dey dey. De Nigguh too
slow. 'E name Hawlback, en' 'e haul back 'e han'
fuh true, but 'e nebbuh knock no knock, 'cause
de 'ooman too swif' fuhr'um. 'E run een en'
fluttuh een de Nigguh face sukkuh roostuh! Den
Cudjo tek de t'odduh han' wuh 'e hab—'e lef' han'
—en' ketch'um 'roun' de 'ooman en' hug'um up
close to 'e breas' lukkuh 'e binnuh kiss'um, but
Cudjo nebbuh hab no appetite fuh kiss no wil'-cat,
en' de closuh 'e hol' de 'ooman, de mo' sabbidge
de 'ooman clabbuhclaw'um; en' all de time de Nigguh try fuh lam'um obuh 'e back wid da' long
hick'ry stick, but de 'ooman' hanch tough, en'
Cudjo cyan' do nutt'n' wid'um, so all de lam 'e
lam only mek de 'ooman mo' bex, 'tel, bumbye, de
'ooman bite 'e yez sukkuh him bin tarrier, en' de
Nigguh bin hog!

"Den, de 'ooman teet' sting de Nigguh' yez
so keen, 'e drap 'e hick'ry en' t'row'off de 'ooman,
en' attuh 'e drap de stick, Uh pick'um up; but
nobody hit de fus' lick, 'cause nobody bin hit no
lick, none'tall. Cudjo duh de only man wuh hab
stick fuh knock wid, en' him bin tu'n 'roun' so
slow, 'e loss 'e chance. En', Jedge, Cudjo iz big
man, en' 'e bin hab big stick een 'e han', en' de po'
'ooman ent bin hab uh Gawd' t'ing but 'e finguh-
nail en' 'e teet'. Enty you t'ink de po' 'ooman bin

do berry well wid wuh de Lawd g'em? Enty, suh?"

"Jedge," amused by the plaintive note of Judy's plea for her militant sister, thought she had done very well indeed, and his admission brought smiles to the dark faces of the three feminists, who, at the moment, were banded together against man! The smiles broadened into grins as Laguerre turned upon his constable:

"Cudjo," he said, "confound you, you got what you deserved for hugging a wildcat in the open road. Next time, be more circumspect."

"Jedge, you gimme good exwice. Uh nebbuh bin s'peck' de 'ooman 'tel 'e jump me! Attuh dis Uh gwine s'pishun all de 'ooman! Soon ez Uh see 'e shimmy fluttuh, Uh gwine s'peck'um. Den none nebbuh fuh run up on me too close, no mo'."

"Daphne," said Laguerre fiercely, "Judy has been saying a great deal for you this morning, and saying it well. Now, what the devil have you got to say for yourself about Caesar?—Don't say it! If you had lived in New England in the old days you would have been ducked in the village horse pond for a common scold!

"Don't you confounded women know that a man is entitled to peace in his own house? Don't you know that if he can't get it there, he'll try to find it somewhere else? Don't you know that the marriage ceremony—'me hab him, en' him

275

hab me'—in which most of you Niggers are held in 'the holy bonds of matrimony' is a slip-knot that wouldn't hold a buck rabbit—much less a buck Nigger? Don't you know that Caesar can turn you out of his house whenever he wants to, or he can take his hat and his britches and quit you without a 'by your leave'? When you know these things, why are you such an infernal fool as to tongue-lash him all the time? He has left his house, now. Do you want to run him off for good?"

"Jedge," whimpered the Amazon, now strangely subdued. "Uh wan' Caesar fuh come back. Uh nebbuh bin want'um fuh gone 'way. Uh binnuh talk up da' chimbly too long."

"What saith the noble Caesar?" demanded Laguerre.

"No, suh, Jedge, Uh free now. Uh nebbuh bin free befo' sence Uh bin hab Daphne. Me en' dem crow duh git 'long berry well. Dem talk, fuh true, but dem nebbuh 'spute me, nuh nutt'n'. Uh yent want no home, suh. Uh yent want no wife, 'cause peaceubble h'aa't bettuh mo'nuh 'ooman en' house. Man wuh wan' dem t'ing kin hab'um, but 'e yent fuh me. Uh yeddy de Buckruh say 'one man bittle iz 'nodduh man' pizen.' 'E so, fuh true, en' Uh yent got appetite fuh pizen no mo'."

"You see where you stand, Daphne," said Laguerre.

THE TAMING OF THE SHREW

"Jedge, suh, Uh yent duh stan' no place," said the penitent. "Uh duh seddown flat 'puntop de du't, 'cause me sperrit berry hebby, en' please, suh, tell Caesar Uh sorry Uh bex'um. Uh do'um so jis' 'cause Uh bin mean, en' 'ooman t'ink ef him 'buze man, en' de man nebbuh knock'um, nuh nutt'n', en' nebbuh ansuhr'um back, de 'ooman hab prib'lidge fuh 'buze de man mo' hebby, 'cause 'ooman iz uh t'ing 'e lub fuh 'buze dem wuh tek'um."

"A privilege also exercised sometimes by weak men," commented the court.

"En' tell Caesar Uh bin mean 'cause de debble bin een me. Uh all de time t'reat'n Caesar, but Uh nebbuh knock'um one time. En' da' debble binnuh bile een me en' Uh couldn' loss'um 'tel Uh git chance fuh knock somebody. Uh nebbuh knock Caesar 'cause Uh lub'um tummuch, but dis mawnin,' soon ez Uh meet da' oagly 'ranguhtang een de road en' ride'um, da' debble wuh bin mek me so mean en' mischeebus, gone out me h'aa't en' gone een Buh Cudjo, 'cause Uh g'em de debble, en' de debble dey een'um now, en' ebbuh sence da' debble done t'row'way out me h'aa't, Uh nebbuh *yiz* fuh bex no mo'; en' now me sperrit stan' w'ite ez da' snow Pa Tumbo binnuh talk 'bout!"

"Amen, my sistuh!" said old Tumbo.

"Oh, Jedus! We fuh hab snow!" said a doubting sister.

"Sut duh fall!" said Cudjo, laconically, as he spat on the ground.

"Daphne," said Laguerre, with a laugh, "you've found a new way of taming a shrew."

"Jedge, Uh tame fuh true, lukkuh you say. Ef Caesar come back een 'e house, 'e fuh be him house, him fuh rule'um, en' wuhebbuh him tell me fuh do, Uh gwine do'um!"

"Well, Caesar?" asked Laguerre.

Caesar scratched his head.

"Uh dunno, Jedge. Uh mo' redduh watch'um fus'. 'Bu'n chile 'f'aid fiah,' you know, suh, en' 'cut finguh 'f'aid axe,' en' w'en mule' yez full'up wid sheep buhr him berry skittish 'bout bridle! But Uh kin wisit de 'ooman sometime. Uh kin gone to 'e house fuh shum."

"You kin wisit me now, Caesar," said Daphne, appealingly. "En' fus' t'ing you kin stop up dem crack Cudjo bin mek een de do' wid 'e hatchitch en' 'e ten-penny nail, so de we'dduh fuh keep out."

"Yaas," said Caesar, with an amused grin, as he joined her. "T'odduh day you bin tell me Uh bin nutt'n' but de du't, now you tek me fuh mek clay fuh stop crack!"

"'Imperious Caesar, dead and turned to clay,
  Might stop a hole to keep the wind away',"
quoted Laguerre, as with a whack of the red hatchet he adjourned the court.

A JUDGMENT OF SOLOMON

To those who care for nomenclature the old slave records of the Low-country plantations would offer an interesting study. The larger slaveholders, hard pressed to find names for the steadily increasing black populations of their estates, must have searched the pages of sacred and profane history to help them out. Adam and Eve, Cain and Abel, and Gabriel, the trumpeter. Abraham and Isaac, Moses and Jacob. Prophets and the sons of prophets. David and Solomon and Daniel. Joseph and his brethren—but neither Potiphar nor his wife—Sarah and Esther and Rachel. Mary and Martha, and John and Peter, and Paul and Barnabas. Jupiter and Juno, and Venus and Diana. Hercules—but not Antæus. Apollo and Daphne. Cæsar and Pompey and Brutus. Cato and Cassius and Cicero. Paris and Helen, Achilles and Hector. Antony and Cleopatra. Romeo and Juliet. Hamlet, Ophelia and Yorick. Rose and Violet and Lily. Phyllis and Chloe and Amarinthia. January, February, March, April, May, June, July and August. Sunday, Monday, Thursday, Friday. Cudjo, Cuffy, Mingo, Quakoo, Quash. London and Boston.

And how they were mixed up on the plantation books! With entire disregard of the morals, or the racial strains of history or mythology, a little black boy would carry the name of a Roman senator, though born to an Olympian goddess and sired by an Old Testament prophet of the House of Israel!—And the Old Testament prophets sired with facility!

So much for their Christian names—the names they commonly used and were known by. Surnames, or "titles", some of them had, but these they chose for themselves, independently of their masters. Of course certain fine old family servants bore respected patronymics through successive generations, but these were exceptional, and often the field-hands—the peasantry of the plantations—were known only by their first names, qualified, if there were several of the same name on the place, by the relationship of the individual to some landmark of the plantation, whom everybody knew. Thus, Ben Summers might have had a title of his own, while Ben Dimes was only Ben, the son of old Dimes, as Quash George was George, the son of old Quash, and George Cephas, George, the son of Cephas.

But with Freedom, all the freedmen who had come out of slavery without them made a wild rush for "titles," and they helped themselves to whatever struck their fancy, wherever they found them. A few were chromatically content with White, and Gray, and Green, and Brown, and

Black; others were satisfied with the simple and easily remembered names of the sturdy English Yeomanry who came with the early colonists, but the more ambitious of those who sought to find— if not to make—names for themselves, chose those of the great landholders—sometimes their former masters, but more often those of other large slaveholders.

So it came that in a very short time the names of Pinckney, Rutledge, Barnwell, Heyward, Middleton, Fraser, Allston, Ladson, Gadsden, Manigault, Moultrie, Ravenel, Gibbes and many others, became household words in ten thousand lowly cabins on the sea-islands or along the lower reaches of the great coastal plain; and the black folk traveling broad highway or lonely path, by day or night, exchanging salutations as they passed, would proudly mouth the sonorous syllables of "Middletun," "Mannigo" and "Rab'nel."

"Dat you, Mis' Wineglass?"

"No, ma'am. Uh *yiz* bin name Wineglass, one time, but dat bin munt' befo' las'. Me en' Wineglass bin hab uh fallin' out, en' me nuh him paa't. Uh coulduh mek up wid Wineglass, 'cause Uh nebbuh fau't'um much, en' him do berry well fuh husbun', de way dem stan', but 'e name ent wu't'. 'E hab uh cu'yus soun' sukkuh po'-buckruh' name, en' Uh shame fuh hab some de 'ooman wuh bin pick dem title out'uh 'ristycrat Buckruh' fambly, fuh call me Mis' Wineglass w'en Uh meet'um duh paat' en' stop fuh pass de time uh day. So, attuh me nuh Wineglass suffuhrate, Uh nebbuh bodduh fuh gone back, 'cause Hacklus Rab'nel him lady leff'um, en' Uh git chance fuh hab him, so w'en de Nigguh ax me, Uh tell'um yaas, 'cause 'e name stan' so stylish. Soon ez de Nigguh git loose, Uh t'row me yeye 'puntop'um; 'cause 'e name stan' so stylish Uh bin want'um fuh meself. Yaas, ma'am, duh dem eye Uh bin t'row 'puntop'um mek de Nigguh ax me fuh hab-'um. Him nebbuh know, 'cause 'e t'ink him bin ax me fuh 'eself.

"Him iz man, en' you know how 'e stan', yaas, ma'am. —No, ma'am, Rab'nel ent no 'count; 'e lazy en' 'e lub rum, 'cause 'e t'ink 'cause him hab 'ristycrat name him kin do sukkuh dem quality Buckruh. But 'e yent wu't' fuh feed no 'ooman, needuh fuh pit no frock 'pun 'e back; 'ooman haf-fuh feed *him!* Uh wouldn' bodduh wid de Nig-guh none'tall, 'cep' fuh 'e name, en' da' Rab'nel soun' so rich, de t'ing duh sing een me yez all de time. 'E soun' sukkuh cow bell w'en de cow duh comin' home late een de ebenin' duh summuh-time, w'en dem duh walk berry slow, en' stop now en' den fuh bite grass. De name sweet'n me yez 'tel 'e mek me h'aa't fuh peaceubble.

A JUDGMENT OF SOLOMON

"Yaas, ma'am, you, 'self, hab uh berry stylish
name; 'Mannigo' done fuh stylish! Ef Uh did'n'
bin hab Rab'nel, Uh woulduh hab him, but seem
to me Rab'nel soun' mo' richuh, so Uh nebbuh
fuh t'row'um'way, eeb'n ef Uh haffuh t'row'way
Hacklus. Ef 'e git too triflin' en' Uh haffuh lef'
de Nigguh, Uh fuh hol' 'e name, en' Uh yent fuh
hab no reg'luh husbun' 'gen, 'tel Uh fin' anodduh
Nigguh name' Rab'nel. Ef Uh cyan' fin' none een
dishyuh Toogoodoo country, Uh gwine Pon-Pon,
but Uh yent fuh cross Caw-Caw swamp, 'cause no
stylish Buckruh dey dey, en' ef *him* ent dey dey,
Uh know suh no Rab'nel Nigguh fuh dey dey!

"Ef Uh cyan' fin' de man' to Pon-Pon, Uh gwine
spang to Stono ribbuh fuh s'aa'ch fuhr'um, but
da' Nigguh haffuh *git!* Soon ez Uh shum, en'
yeddy 'e name, Uh fuh t'row me yeye 'puntop-
'um en' mek'um ax me. Ef de Nigguh hab wife,
Uh dunkyuh, 'cause Uh got uh good ecknowledge
how fuh toll man off frum 'e wife en' t'ing, en'
tek'um'way. Ef Uh ebbuh see de man, en' want-
'um, him duh my'own! En' ef de man name Rab-
'nel, Uh want'um! Eeb'n ef Uh yent lub de Nigguh, Uh fuh lub 'e name, en' Uh fuh hol' da' name
long ez Uh lib. Uh nebbuh fuh tu'n'um loose,
en' w'en Uh dead Uh fuh wrop'up een'um sukkuh shroud, en' attuh me sperrit gone to me Jedus,

283

Uh fuh leddown een Mis' Rab'nel grabe, enty?
Berrywell."

_____

On a bright Saturday in early December, Laguerre drove to his open air court for the last
session of the season before going into winter
quarters at home, for, during the colder months,
"Jedge" heard causes only "in Chambers."

Killing frosts had come earlier than usual and,
save for the tops of the tall long-leaf pines, there
was little green left in "God's Green Inn."

Here and there on oak or hickory, a red or yellow leaf, slow to die, held stoutly on, a spot of
light in the somber forest, where the brown
leaves clung tremblingly to the half-bare limbs
from which the winds and rains would presently
bring them to earth. So brave men—torch-
bearers—hold their lamps aloft unto the end,
though shadows fall and winter whelms the
world!

Around the court half a dozen little fires blazed,
and about them clustered half a hundred happy
Negroes, full of themselves and their own little
affairs—"the short and simple annals of the poor."
As "Jedge" drove up, the talk and laughter subsided, but many a woolly forelock was pulled,
many a foot scraped, and many a jumpy "cutchy"
"drapped" in friendly salutation, for, in the fellowship of understanding, these lowly folk be-

A JUDGMENT OF SOLOMON

longed to "Jedge," as "Jedge" belonged to them.

Laguerre took his seat and thwacked the box. In an hour all the minor causes had been disposed of and the calendar cleared for the consideration of a case whose complexities involved not only two aristocratic patronymics, but the respective marital rights of two dark ladies in the same husband! Husbands, upon occasion, on Slann's Island, as elsewhere, have been known, in such circumstances, to rise to the occasion and accommodate themselves to such embarrassment of riches as the gods provide; and by such riches Rambo Rab'nel found himself presently embarrassed, for he had loved not wisely but too well!

Rambo was a rover. No pent-up Utica contracted his powers. The boundless continent was his—at least as far as the boundless continent was traversed by the old King's highway between the Stono and the Edisto—for he worked intermittently at the Bradley phosphate mines at Rantowles, and the Baring mines at Pon-Pon. And Rambo, a peripatetic—a sort of traveling man—sometimes paused to gather black-eyed Susans along the way!

The gathering offered no embarrassment— "findings" were not necessarily "keepings"—for "Man ent haffuh hol' ebb'ryt'ing wuh 'e ketch een 'e han', *too* long. W'en you han' git full, you fuh

t'row'way some, enty?" Sound philosophy for
traveling men, or those who tread the primrose
path of dalliance, but Rambo had thoughtlessly
put two of the wayside flowers in his buttonhole
—and there they stuck. True, the buttonholes
belonged to different coats, for one flower had
been plucked beside the limpid Edisto; the other
where the salty tides of Stono ebb and flow with
the throbbing pulses of the sea. And both had
been gathered by the way, for neither was in-
digenous, the ladies having come to "wisit" from
Toogoodoo, where, having been born and reared
to bursting womanhood—they had come at last to
years of indiscretion, and so it was that Rambo,
the latest indiscretion of both ladies, was embarrassed!

———

Whenever a bride falls into the hands of the
bright young women who "conduct" Society
columns for newspapers, the bright young women
forthwith begin to flutter feathers and crow, and
the types begin to "née", and there's no word
for a wedding announcement like your "née"!
"The bride hath paced into the hall, Red as a rose
is she," but no sooner hath she paced out again
with husband "on the side," that the linotypes announce Red as a Rose as having been "née Jones"
—or Brown or Robinson. So far, so good, but often
the bright young women, flowering into speech as

profusely as a dogwood bursting into bloom, pin
or buckle on as a sort of verbal garter, just behind the née, a superserviceable "Matilda", or
"Mehitabel," or something. Of course the poor little soul was not "née Matilda Jones" or anything
of the sort. She just came into the world as Jones
—plain Jones, or beautiful Jones—and was
doubtless glad enough to get in, at that, and no
questions asked!

But, despite its frequent misuse, née is a very
good word—the better, because not one man in a
thousand can pronounce it—and, as there could
hardly be a marriage in fashionable circles without it, the moral standing of the word is unim-
peachable, and could no more be challenged than
could the nuptial music of Wagner or of Mendels-
sohn! So the bright young women responsible for
its inclusion in newspaper English, are quite as
bright as they are painted!

———

Rambo, a rolling stone, rather prided himself
on gathering no matrimonial moss, as he rolled
along. Moss was well enough for men who settled down, or stationary stones, but not for him,
thought Rambo, for moss caused friction, and re-
tarded speed, and cruisers must keep their copper
free from barnacles. As Jones, or Brown, or
Robinson, he might have jogged on "the foot-path

way" smoothly and irresponsibly enough, for, as
poverty has its compensations for those who would
keep out of the eye of the world, the names heard
every day on highway or on bridlepath do not ex-
act attention, but Rambo's rollicking name rang
like an alarum along the countryside—a Muezzin's
sunset call!

"The evil that men do lives after them"—sometimes—and when, with the coming of Freedom,
Rambo's sire, naked and very much ashamed for
want of a name, stepped up to the nomenclatural
clothes line of "de Buckruh" and wrapped him in
Ravenel, he chose for himself and bequeathed to
his son a singing patronymic whose music could
not be stilled. So, as Rambo lingered by the way,
the lichens grew upon the rolling stone almost
as he slept. And as they had grown upon both
sides, rolling stone and lichens were before Laguerre for a Judgment of Solomon!

The younger of the Mesdames Rab'nel was
Rena, née Rivers—though perhaps no more than
a spring-branch when she came bubbling up into
the dusty world. Rivers was a good enough name
—an excellent name—as Rena knew, and Rena
held it above riches; so much above worldly con-
siderations, that she had scorned the advances of
more than one plantation suitor, whose possession of mule or ox could not, in her critical mind,

make up for the possession of a simple uninspiring Brown, or an unæsthetic Limehouse, or Wineglass.

"Uh ready fuh hab man, en' deseyuh boy wuh duh quizzit me, do berry well—all 'cep' de name wuh de Nigguh got, but de name ent wu't'! Me fuh t'row'way de good name wuh Uh got en' swap'um off fuh dem Brown, en' Limehouse en' t'ing? No, suh! Ef dem t'odduh 'ooman call me name lukkuh dat w'en dem duh peruse 'long wid all dem stylish name lukkuh Middletun en' Mannigo, en' Rab'nel, 'e fuh mek me shame, same ez ef Uh bin gone chu'ch een homespun frock, 'mong all dem t'odduh 'ooman dress'up een calicro. Befo' Uh do dat, Uh redduh do bedout de man, en' keep de name wuh Uh got 'tel Uh kin ketch uh Nigguh wuh got name stylish mo'nuh my'own. 'Cause Ribbers stan' too good fuh t'row'way!"

The slim black girl curtsied to the Court and told a straightforward story. Going to Pon-Pon to "wisit," she had encountered Rambo and, falling under the spell of the two R's, she forthwith made such ocular demonstration of the receptivity of her mind in respect to Rambo, that her quarry was moved to propose to her what she had already determined to do. She graciously consented, "and so they were married," in the "hop-skip-

and-a-jump" fashion of the community—a long
jump from either the Law or the Gospel!

"Jedge, suh," she said ingenuously, "soon ez
Uh look 'puntop da' Rambo, en' yeddy de Rab-
'nel, Uh know Uh haffuh hab alltwo, 'cause Uh lub
de Nigguh, en' Uh lub 'e name. So Uh t'row me
yeye 'puntop'um, en', Jedge, Uh look at Rambo
berry keen."

"Yes," said Laguerre. "I know, I know!"

"En' den de Nigguh quizzit me."

"And you, though taken entirely by surprise,
graciously consented."

"No, suh, Uh tell de Nigguh yaas."

"What then?"

"Den, suh, me hab him, en' him hab me, en'
w'en dem Pon-Pon Nigguh say 'Ebenin' Mis'
Rab'nel,' de t'ing roll so rich, 'e mek me h'aa't
fuh swell. We bin git 'long berry well, 'tel, attuh two-t'ree week done pass, Rambo gone Rantowle fuh wu'k, en' 'e tell me fuh gone back Toogoodoo 'tel him come, so Uh do lukkuh him tell
me, but Rambo nebbuh come; en' attuh two munt'
done gone, Uh yeddy suh Rambo bin git ketch en'
tanglety'up wid 'ooman down to Bradley, dat
w'ymekso 'e nebbuh come Toogoodoo, en' jis' t'odduh day, come fuh fin'out, de 'ooman wuh bin
tanglety'up wid'um, iz dishyuh same Daisy Mannigo wuh lib to W'aley place; en', Jedge, please,

A JUDGMENT OF SOLOMON

suh, mek de 'ooman ontangle 'eself frum Rambo
en' tu'n'um loose, 'cause Daisy got stylish name
fuh 'eself, en' him bin hab heap'uh husbun' en'
t'ing, en' him gone en' tek my Rambo, en' my
Rab'nel, alltwo, en' dem blonx to me, Jedge,
'cause duh me shum fus'. Uh nebbuh bin hab
no husbun' befo', en' Rambo duh all wuh Uh got,"
and she whimpered pathetically as she withdrew.

Then the crowd opened and Daisy Mannigo
"busted" through, and Daisy boasted "a perfect
forty-six!"

Daisy was built like the continent of South
America. Above and about the equator,
in a manner of speaking, nature had endowed Daisy exceedingly, but, like the esteemed
southern continent, she tapered to tenuousness
toward the southern extremity, until, below the
Tropic of Capricorn, she became what the plantation Negroes call "dry-bone"—a form of physical
construction not infrequently met with—Nature
sometimes distributing her favors unequally!

And Daisy wore a corset! Corsets were corsets
in those days! None of your long, "straight-
front," slab-sided affairs, fitted with straps and
buckles and breeching, like a trotting harness!
Spineless things, with no more backbone than a
politician! Nothing of the sort; for in Laguerre's
day the corset was at once "the glass of fashion

291

and the mould of form!" The glass of fashion
was the hour-glass, and the mould—rigid and
uncompromising—was one into which all fashionable feminine forms—by expansion or contrac-
tion—were forced to fit themselves as best they
could, for there was little variation in the models
—at least those that came to the plantations—and
the manufacturers thought that if a 22-inch
waist called for a 36-inch bust, why, mathemat-
ically speaking, a 54-inch bust should go with
a 33-inch waist, and this, by sine and cosine, they
were ready to demonstrate, though the Lord,
working in His mysterious way, His wonders to
perform, doesn't always form them after this
fashion. But fashions are imperative, and will
not be denied, so the women—the work of His
hands—were poured into the moulds that man
had made! Some were poured hot, for contrac-
tion here or there, is sometimes cruel and trying
to the temper; and some were poured cold, for
expansion—the simple stuffing in of corn-shucks,
moss or cotton, could be done dispassionately!

But whether squeezed or stuffed, the women
had to fit the cuirass, whose steels and whale-
bones clasped them as closely as the armor-of-
proof enclosing the burly form of old Henry the
Eighth, astride his equine effigy in the Tower of
London!

A JUDGMENT OF SOLOMON

And these armored corsets—like the hour-glass —looked reversible—perhaps they were, for the fullness of the front, at the top, seemed to the unenlightened masculine eye, to match the fullness of the back, at the bottom, so they might just as well have been worn upside down!

As a further concession to fashion—perhaps farther would be the better word—Daisy had built herself a bustle—tall, and long, and wide, for Daisy, resting upon the Scriptural assurance that "to him that hath shall be given," had rested upon the liberal endowment of her own proper person, a comic supplement, a vast territorial hinterland, that brought laughing comments from the Negroes, and a contemptuous damn or two from "Jedge," who held shams of all sorts in utter contempt!

Daisy, sometime Mannigo, recently Rab'nel, had been born Brown, née Brown in Society. "She knew it for her mother told her so," but, as Brown, *mère*, prominent in the Smart Set of the Whaley plantation, had not been chromatically circumspect, Daisy might just as well have been née Gray or Green or Black; but her mother said she wasn't, so that's that!

"Well," demanded Laguerre, as he glared at Daisy's far-flung hinterland and longed for the paddle of a "trus'-me-gawd," "What the devil do

you mean by coming to my court dressed up like
an organ-grinder's monkey? Tell your story!"

"Jedge, suh," the witness simpered, "Uh berry
lub dress, fuh true. En' me story stan' berry
straight. Uh lib to W'aley place. Uh bin hab
husbun' las' yeah, name' Mannigo, but 'e yent
wu't', en' befo' de yeah done out, de Nigguh run-
'way. Him say me run'um off. Uh dunno 'bout
dat. Uh only know 'e gone, en' Uh dunno weh
'e yiz, en' Uh dunkyuh weh 'e yiz, 'cause dishyuh
Nigguh, Rambo Rab'nel, wuh Uh got now, mo'
nyuseful fuh wu'k, en' 'e name stan' mo' stylish,
so Uh dunkyuh ef Uh nebbuh look 'puntop Mannigo no mo'!"

" 'Off with the old love, on with the new,' eh?"

"Yaas, suh, Jedge. 'Ooman ent fuh keep on de
same frock, en' de same shimmy *all* de time. Him
haffuh tek'um off now en' den. En' man stan'
sukkuh dem sku't. Him haffuh shif' *sometime*,
enty, suh?

"So, attuh de summuh mos' gone, Uh bin wisit
me cousin wuh lib to Rantowle, en' Uh gone one
day to de Bradley rock mine, en' heap'uh Nigguh
dey dey duh wu'k, en' de Nigguh ax me fuh stay
to de rock, fuh cook fuhr'um, so Uh mek baa'gin
wid de Nigguh, en' Uh stay to de rock, en' dishyuh same Rambo bin one de gang, en' soon ez
Uh shum, Uh mek'up me min' fuh hab'um, 'cause

294

da' Rab'nel name roll rich mo'nuh my'own. W'en Uh fus' yeddy'um, 'e roll sukkuh dem railroad strain duh roll obuh Rantowle trussle duh night-time. Da' Rab'nel done fuh full'up me yez!

So, den, ebb'ry day Uh cut me yeye attuh Rambo, en' ebb'ry ebenin' 'e come to me fiah fuh talk, en' w'enebbuh 'e come Uh feed'um high. En', bumbye, Rambo ax me."

"Did he 'ax' you, or you 'ax' him?"

"Well, suh, Jedge, Uh yent puhzac'ly *ax* de Nigguh, 'cause Uh yeddy suh 'ooman ent fuh ax man. Uh jis' tell'um man haffuh hab 'ooman, en' 'ooman haffuh hab man, en' Uh tell'um 'e seem lukkuh man wid shishuh stylish name lukkuh him hab oughtuh hab wife fuh tote 'e name to chu'ch, en' show'um off, en' w'en Rambo tell me him yiz bin hab uh gal fuh wife, but 'e lef' de gal Pon-Pon, Uh tell'um me, 'self, bin hab husbun', but him dey off some place een de bush, so Uh nebbuh count-'um, en' Uh tell'um no use fuh bodduh 'bout de gal to Pon-Pon, en' de run'way Nigguh een de bush, 'cause dem stan' fudduh, en' me en' him stan' close, so me en' him jis' ez well fuh hab one'nurruh, 'cause we alltwo dey right yuh.

"Dat de way de Nigguh ax me, Jedge, en' den me hab him, en' him hab me. En' t'odduh day da' po'buckruh Trial Jestuss to Rantowle yeddy 'bout'um, en' 'e say him fuh swayre out warrant

LAGUERRE

fuh Rambo, en' t'row'um een Walterburruh jail,
eeduhso een Town, 'cause 'e hab two wife, but,
Jedge, him only hab one, 'cause Uh yent fuh 'low
da' t'odduh 'ooman fuh come close'um none'tall."

"Rambo Rab'nel", called Cudjo, and the rolling-
stone—presently apple of discord—stepped up
and pulled his wool. A pleasant faced young
Negro, his simple story revealed a nature too
guileless to protect him from the nomenclatural
fortune-hunters of the gentler sex.

"Rambo," said Laguerre, "How do you happen
to be such a devil among the women?"

"Jedge, suh, de debble ent dey een me, 'e dey
een me name, en' 'e yent dey een me fus' name, 'e
yent dey een Rambo none'tall, 'e dey een da' debble'ub'uh Rab'nel! Soon ez de 'ooman yeddy'um,
dem tu'n fool, en' dem hankuh attuhr'um 'cause
dem t'ink 'e stan' so stylish. De Rambo nebbuh
bodduhr'um. Ef one de 'ooman look 'puntop me
fuh de fus' time, 'e ax de t'odduh 'ooman 'Who dat
new Nigguh? Uh nebbuh shum befo'. Wuh 'e
name?' Ef de t'odduh 'ooman tell'um uh name
Rambo, de 'ooman nebbuh bodduh 'bout me no
mo', but ef 'e tie de Rab'nel 'puntop de Rambo!
Ki! 'Oh, me Jedus,' de 'ooman say. 'Uh haffuh
look 'pun da' Nigguh close! Da' name soun' too
rich. Lemme shum.' "

A JUDGMENT OF SOLOMON

"Well, then, knowing the danger you were in, how did you get caught in this double trap?"

"Uh dunno, Jedge. Uh jis' bin fool, lukkuh man haffuh yiz w'en 'e tanglety'up wid 'ooman. Da' fus' gal, Rena, him nebbuh bodduh me none. 'E jis' t'row 'e yeye 'puntop me, en' de yeye talk so straight, en' tell me so 'sponsubble, 'ax me, ax me!' 'tel Uh haffuh ax'um, enty, suh?

"En' me en' Rena git'long berry well, 'tel Uh gone Rantowle fuh wu'k, en' den dishyuh hebby Mannigo 'ooman t'row 'e yeye 'puntop me, en' *him* ax me 'long 'e yeye en' 'e mout', alltwo, 'causē him ent fuh tek no chance!

"En' now, suh, alltwo de 'ooman got me, en' likewise, also, dem got me name, en' Uh yeddy suh ef man hab two wife—'cep' him iz preachuh —him haffuh sen' Walterburruh jail, en' eeb'n de preachuh haffuh hide de t'odduh 'ooman een de bush! En', Jedge, suh, Uh dunno wuffuh do!" he ended plaintively.

"Daisy," said Laguerre, to the bustled one, "Rena had this man first, you know. Would you rather give him up, or let him go to jail for bigamy?"

"Jedge, him hab de Nigguh fus', but me hab-'um las', enty, suh? De Nigguh blonx to me, en' 'e name, alltwo, en' befo' Uh 'low da' t'odduh

'ooman fuh hab'um, Rambo en' 'e Rab'nel alltwo
kin leddown een Walterburruh jail."

"Jedge," said Rena, tearfully, "please, suh,
don' sen' Rambo Walterburruh! Him duh my-
'own, en' de hawk ketch me chicken out me han',
but him kin hab'um, Jedge, 'cause Uh lub'um, en'
Uh yent wan' Rambo fuh gone to no jail!"

"Rambo," demanded Laguerre. "How were
you married to these women? Were you chained,
or only roped?"

Rambo chuckled.

"Jedge, suh, needuh one de 'ooman nebbuh look
'puntop no preachuh, needuhso no Trial Jestuss,"
he said, "en' 'e yent bin tie wid rope, needuh wid
chain—nutt'n' but grapewine!" he added, with a
laugh.

"Well," said the Court, "one of your women is
going to 'look 'puntop a Trial Jestuss' this minute.
Step here, Rena," he commanded. "Catch hold of
this philanderer's hand. Now, Rena 'Ribbers',
do you take Rambo 'Rab'nel' for your lawful
husband together with the euphonious and aristocratic patronymic thereunto appertaining to
have and to hold talk fast damn it talk fast or
forever after hold your peace?"

"Yaas, suh! Yaas, suh, t'engk-gawd!" she cried,
excitedly.

A JUDGMENT OF SOLOMON

"Now both of you say 'me hab him, en' him hab me,' three times."

They repeated the formula in unison, and "Jedge" thwacked his hatchet thrice, and pronounced them man and wife, by authority of the State of South Carolina and the local usage of Slann's Island, and the beaming couple slunk away.

"Oh, Jedus!" cried Daisy, passionately. "Jedge tek'way me Rab'nel frum me en' t'row'um 'puntop da' blacksnake gal! Now, Uh haffuh fall back 'pun me Mannigo, en' do de bes' Uh kin. W'en Uh binnuh trabble 'pun da' Brown name Uh bin hab at de fus', Uh binnuh walk 'pun me foot een de du't; w'en Uh trabble 'pun de Mannigo, Uh binnuh dribe oxin cyaa't; but w'en Uh binnuh trabble 'pun da' Rab'nel, me Jedus, Uh binnuh dribe hawss een stylish buggy! Now, attuh Jedge tek'way me Rab'nel buggy, Uh haffuh gone home een me Mannigo oxin cyaa't, en' Uh 'speck' Uh haffuh greese de w'eel, 'cause Uh yeddy me sperrit duh groan!"

Laguerre turned upon her savagely: "How dare you hold Manigault so cheaply?" he demanded. "You dusky Darwinians toss about Huguenot names as lightly as your anthropoidal ancestors played with coconuts in Africa! It's got to stop! Those of you who got names from your daddies, may keep them, but if I ever hear of a new Nigger on Toogoodoo helping himself to a Huguenot name again, I'll fine him for contempt! And, damn it, if any one of you ever dares to call himself 'Laguerre', I'll send him to Walterboro jail for thirty days! Now, go! 'Man-ni-go!' 'Rab'-nel!' *Damn!*"

THE TRAGEDY OF THE MARSH

A bitter day in mid-December. Winter had come in earnest, and the ground was iron hard. A north wind on the night before had brought a heavy sleet, changing toward morning to a fine sleety snow that frosted each ice-sheathed trunk and bough and turned the forest into a wintry fairyland. Loveliest of all were the great pines, their tall purple boles in shining armor, each emerald needle of their lofty crowns glistening in its icy covering, while to windward, whence the boreal blasts had blown, the driven snow had powdered trunk and top with feathery crystals.

The myrtle thickets, at the forest's rim, shone like polished jade, and in the open fields that lay beyond, the tall broom-sedge and all the lesser grasses bent low, or stood erect, as is the way with grass and men—"if winter comes!"

And the wide marshes, sown with the dragon's teeth of the frost, upreared a million spears, sharper and more brilliant than ever Cadmus saw!

Now, although the snow had ceased, a keen wind blew steadily out of the north, swept through the woods and set the sleeted boughs a-tinkling with the music of far-off sleighbells. Then, stooping to the open spaces it touched more tenderly the strings of frozen marsh and grass until they sang in muted whisperings.

LAGUERRE

Far aloft the ducks came down the wind—
long lines of mallard and of widgeon—strung like
beads, or looped in necklaces against the leaden
sky, while hurtling flocks of green-wing teal swept
by their slower congeners like charging cavalry,
and rushed far in the van. Now and then a
wearied flock swung over the marshes to find
shelter in the little creeks that wound among
them, another stooped to the broad bosom of the
Dawhoo, while others—far-flung adventurers—
passed on unwearied wing toward the far horizon.

The little runs and branches, frozen hard, shone
along the roads like mirrors of dark steel, for the
fallen leaves that clogged their shallow channels
had stained their waters and tinted them like
wine.

No voice of any furred or feathered thing broke
the silence of the lonely forest, now wrapped in
its icy mantle; only the tinkle of the distant sleighbells as the branches swayed in the wind, and now
and then a crash, as a harder gust shattered their
crystal coverings and sent the broken fragments
shivering to earth. Nothing more, for squirrels
curled deep in their nests, rabbits snuggled down
in their sheltered forms in the briar-thickets, and
in the thick broom-sedges at the edge of the myrtles the partridges huddled closer together and
told their troubles in low and plaintive notes.

Such wintry storms rarely reach the coast

country, but when they do, the added rawness of the sea, makes their sting more poignant than in higher, drier, regions.

The sting of the penetrating cold bore heavily upon the scattered whites of the plantations, unprepared as they were to withstand its severity, but heavier still upon the poor black folk, poorly housed and poorly clad; for many an "Imperious Caesar, dead and turned to clay," would have been required to chink the log walls of their lowly habitations tightly enough "to keep the wind away" that now blew so fiercely from Hudson's Bay at the rim of the Arctic ocean!

And their clothing, particularly that of the older Negroes, was pathetically inadequate; the flimsy cotton fabrics and the gaping "Yankee shoes" of Freedom were a far cry from the stout plantation brogans, the knitted woolen caps and the warm "blanket" great-coats of slavery, when, as chattels—property—they had to be taken care of! And the poor old women—how they shivered! Happy the old Mauma who could boast a red flannel petticoat or a worsted scarf, as a gift from the "Big-house"—now, often small enough! The scarf she would wind around neck and face until only her eyes were uncovered, and whenever she walked abroad, however cold the weather, the overhanging skirt would be proudly "hiced" and reveal the ruddy petticoat in all its glory!

So, to the old black folk, men and women, Freedom meant very little, for, in their days of waning usefulness, under slavery, their tasks, if any there were, were light, and their old masters kept them warm. Now, God was their only Master, and God did not always keep them warm, save in summer, when they were warm enough! But whenever they were tempted to question His decrees and the weight of the hand He had laid upon them, if they but thought of fire, their hearts were stilled, for fire—God's greatest gift to the Negro—they had always, and He had taught them how to make it, while "de Buckruh" had made them free of their pinelands and hardwood forests. Woodpiles in the front yard of every humble cabin showed logs of oak or ash or hickory, and piles of lightwood knots, or "junks," and from the first streak of dawn, those who passed plantation quarters or isolated cabin, seeing a wisp of blue smoke rising from short clay chimneys, would know that the home fires had been lighted at the rising of the morning star, to be kept burning throughout the day until raked out at bedtime in the early hours of the night. And whenever black folk gathered out of doors in cold weather, whether clustered, palms outspread, around a roaring bonfire, or crouched over a pitiful pile of embers which they were feeding with fagots of green wood and trying to fan into flame, their hearts burned incense as the smoke floated away and the sparks flew upward!

During such storms in the Low-country few Negroes are abroad. Those whose lawful occasions impel them to leave the family hearthstone and brave the weather, swathe their throats up to the jaws with whatever wrappings they can command, leaving only their ashen cheeks exposed. Novelists often turn the cheeks of their villains or their heroes—never their heroines, however fearful, in these synthetic days—"ashen with fear," but if the novelist could "hold the mirror up to Nature" at Slann's Island on a winter's day he would see more ashes on a dozen black faces than his imagination could sprinkle on the cheeks of a thousand affrighted Aryans.

So on this bitter mid-December morning, white folk and black along the Toogoodoo slept late, then rose and hugged their hearths, nor dreamed of tragedy at hand; yet in the heavy hours of the night, in the dog-watch, just before the dawn, Death had stalked through the frozen marshes and touched and stilled a human heart!

———

Mingo Polite belied his name, for he was the meanest Negro on Edisto Island, a distinction that made him stand out among his fellows, for the Island Negro population was unusually well-behaved, as is usual in isolated communities remote from railroads, where the land was still held by the old families. Here the Negro was always happiest and at his best, for, along with his freedom, he still had the communal life of the big plantations, which he loved, and service under employers who understood him and whom he liked and respected.

Mingo was wily enough to keep straight with the whites, but among his own color he was surly and domineering. A gambler—both with cards and dice—he was so successful at crap-shooting, "rolling the bones," that when the Saturday night bouts were over his pockets usually jingled with small silver and, sometimes, when fortune's smile was broad and generous, a few greasy greenbacks were added to the coin.

And Mingo was a menace in marital as well as in financial affairs. A bold, if not a gay, Lothario, he held the other men so lightly that he seldom took the trouble to conceal his exploits, holding the heavy revolver he sometimes carried as more than a match for the razors and oyster-knives of those whose homes he invaded upon occasion.

But many a head shook knowingly, and many a beard wagged wisely, over the fate they knew would one day overtake the man who would!

"Wunnuh boy! 'Membuh wuh Uh tell you, en' don' 'low'um fuh leak out you head! Ef da' Mingo Puhlite ebbuh gone off dishyuh Edisto

THE TRAGEDY OF THE MARSH

I'lun' fuh cut 'e 'ranguhtang shine, lukkuh 'e do yuh 'mong we 'ooman en' t'ing, da' Nigguh gwine *dead!* 'E know suh all you man 'f'aid'um, en' da' hebby pistul wuh 'e got', dat de reaz'n 'e so mischeebus, but ef 'e ebbuh gone Pon-Pon, en' mix'up wid dem rockfiel' Nigguh 'roun' de Cross-road, Sattyday night, en' roll 'e bone crookety, lukkuh him roll'um 'pun dis I'lun', dem he-Nigguh gwine roll ball een'um, eeduhso cyaa'be'um up; 'speshly ef him binnuh 'dultri*fy* 'roun' 'mong de freemale wuh blonx to de Nigguh, 'cause man iz uh t'ing, ef you tek'way 'e money en' 'e 'ooman, alltwo, one time, you gwine bex'um, sho' ez cootuh got snout!"

"You talk trute, budduh, 'cause 'dultri*fy* duh da' Nigguh' name! Mingo *done* fuh 'dultri*fy!* En' 'e so wickity!"

" 'E wickity, fuh true, en' 'e keep on wid 'e wickity, 'cause nobody obuh yuh nebbuh 'taguhnize'um, en' da' jail to Mt. Pleasant stan' fudduh; but ef him ebbuh cross da' ferry fuh ramify 'roun' Slann' I'lun', een da' Toogoodoo nation, Jedge gwine ketch'um, sho' ez Gawd! En' w'en 'e *yiz* ketch'um, Walterburruh jail stan' berry cunweenyunt fuh t'row'um een, 'cause da' Too-goodoo nation ent dey een we county, en' Jedge nebbuh haffuh t'row Nigguh een no boat fuh sen-'um to *him* jail, none'tall! So, 'membuh wuh Uh tell you. Jedge gwine git da' Nigguh yit!"

307

LAGUERRE

But Laguerre was a long time getting him, for Mingo was circumspect and, watching his step wherever he traversed Slann's Island, he left no incriminating tracks behind him. And it was well that he did not, for, through his own Negroes, "Jedge" knew Mingo's bad reputation, and was all cocked and primed to give him the limit of the law if he ever fell into his hands. Edisto, like Wadmalaw, belonged to Berkeley County, and whenever visitors from these outlying Island communities violated within his jurisdiction any laws "made and provided" "against the peace and dignity of the State," "Jedge", for the honor and dignity of the State aforesaid, and for the exaltation of Colleton county and the enlargement of its magisterial revenues, always fined them heavily to remind them that Toogoodoo *did*, whatever others didn't!

The storm had come suddenly. Two days earlier, on Friday morning, Mingo, having business on Pon-Pon, started under bright skies for Parker's Ferry cross-roads, driving a mule to his buggy. By nightfall, his daylight affairs finished, he was able to devote the long winter hours of darkness to the more profitable business of fleecing the sporting element among the workers of the Baring Phosphate mines of the little that remained of the last week's wages. This, Mingo's loaded dice enabled him to do with surprising ease, many Negro sports, perhaps like other gamblers, being strangely willing to "take a chance" against odds they knew to be heavily against them.

More than suspicious of Mingo's "bones," and cognizant of the manual efficiency with which he "rolled" them, they watched—with the fascinated eyes of a bird under the spell of a snake—the deft twist of Mingo's wrist under which his weighted cubes would fall, on rough pine floor or smooth, packed earth, to Mingo's profit! But he was seldom challenged, for his truculence and his heavy armament—more impressive than any lethal tools carried by the Pon-Pon sports—gave them pause, though they grumbled exceedingly behind his back:

"Da' drat Mingo cheat we ebb'ry time him come yuh 'pun Pon-Pon fuh roll bone! 'E bone crookety, en' 'e han' crookety. Ebb'ry time 'e twis' 'e han' fuh roll'um, dem debble'ub'uh bone gwine drap fuh suit'um!"

"You talk trute, en' 'e mek me bex fuh hab dem oagly, black, pluff-mud Nigguh frum down on de salt come yuh 'mong we Pon-Pon man en' cheat we out'uh all we money. En' alldo' we know him duh cheat we, nobody kin ketch'um, 'cause 'e too schemy, en' ef you yiz ketch'um, nobody nebbuh bodduh fuh 'spute'um, 'cause 'e too

mean, en' da' hebby pistul 'e tote stan' too dainjus.''

"Dat so. No use fuh 'taguhnize'um, 'cause 'e
mean, en' 'e mischeebus, alltwo. Le'm'lone!''

"All de same, Mingo lub fuh drink rum, en'
ef him keep on wid 'e mean, lukkuh him duh
gwine now, some night een de daa'k uh de moon,
w'en him duh gwine back to de salt full'up wid
rum, Mingo gwine hab acksi*dent*, en', bumbye,
buzzut fuh fin'um een de bush wid 'e t'roat cut!''

So, both at home on the Island and on the distant marches of Pon- Pon, the wise men predicted
that, because of his sins, Mingo would die with
his boots on.

By dawn on Saturday, when Mingo's pockets
were heavy with silver, he forsook his sportive
companions of the night, in whom, having taken
all they had, he had now no further interest, and
going to a friendly house nearby, he "bedded-
down" for the day, intending, when the evening
shadows fell, to make play for the easy and un-
wary money of Saturday—money never able to
protect itself in the hands of the irresponsible,
black, or white. But when Mingo rose in the
late afternoon the sky was overcast, the north
wind shrieked through the forest, and "it grew
wondrous cold," so Mingo's thoughts turned toward the hearthstones of Edisto, where tolerance,
at least, awaited him.

LAGUERRE

He knew he could not reach the ferry before night, but, warned by the members of the household where he had slept through the day that it would be unsafe to risk a Saturday night among the gamblers of the cross-roads, who, having long scores to settle, might knock the winning man in the head and rob him at the close of the night's sport, he resolved to start for home while it was yet day, hoping to spend the night at some house on Toogoodoo, where his bulging pockets would make him a welcome guest. So, hitching up his mule he drove off, just as the sun must have been setting behind the dark clouds. ——

Mingo habitually drank, and seldom started on a journey without a comforting flask in his pocket, and now, if ever, he needed comfort, as the cold wind whipped about him. But, afraid to drive by the cross-roads, and apprise the Saturday evening crowd that he was leaving—for he was always apprehensive of being waylaid— he took the Landing-road where it crossed the Willtown road, drove through the Mitchell settlement, and came out into the King's Highway at the corner of the Oak Lawn plantation. Driving east, he passed the avenue and made for Jupiter Hill, a mile beyond. Here, "at one stride came the dark," and he took the right hand road for Adams Run with a lighter heart, for the wind, sweeping out of the unknown, mysterious north, beyond Caw-

THE TRAGEDY OF THE MARSH

Caw swamp—the border-land of culture and of civilization to the darkies of the Sea-coast—was now at his back, and the village store, with its whisky and its big sheet-iron stove, was only two miles away. These were soon covered, for the mule, urged by the cold, and headed for home, moved briskly.

As Mingo entered the store and came within the radius of the glowing stove, the comforting contrast with the cold without was almost intoxicating, and the dour Negro began to grin. He would have stayed and warmed him through and through, but the questioning eyes of the Negroes around the stove made him apprehensive, so, buying a quart of whisky, which he was careful to pay for without rattling the silver in his heavy pockets, he slipped out quietly and drove off through the night.

A mile beyond the village he passed the old church and, turning obliquely to the left, dipped, at a lower level, into the darkest stretch of the Toogoodoo road—dark by day, with its overarching forest trees—magnolias, beeches, gums and maples, and great vines that swung like pythons across the way—but of stygian blackness now in the starless, lowering night.

And, just as Mingo dipped into the dark, the sleet began to fall. A whisper first, like the faint strumming of violin strings or zithers, swept by

BEYOND TOOGOODOO BRIDGE.

fairy fingers, far away. Then, louder and nearer, the soft pattering of frozen drops on the topmost leaves of the great magnolias, and their musical tinkle as they slipped and tumbled over all the glossy leaves along the way, until they came to rest on the silent earth.

The wind bit more keenly. Mingo tipped his flask and drank deep. The whisper of the sleet now swelled into a song that blended with and softened the harsh drumming of the wind. And all around, the dark!

The mule knew the road as Mingo knew his dice, but, troubled by the tumult of the wind among the trees, and chilled by the driving sleet, he came down to a walk. Mingo drank again. The spirits warmed him, but the weird voices of the storm seemed mysterious and menacing; a thousand tongues were telling of his sins, and Mingo's rosary of remembrance told him they were many! The mule walked slowly on. Nearing Toogoodoo bridge, a great liana hung across the road. Swinging in the wind, it almost touched the mule's ears. He gave a frightened snort and started suddenly, and Mingo's spirit jumped with him. Just beyond, among some live-oak scrub, the road traversed a thicket of saw-palmetto, and, as the sleet fell whisperingly on a hundred pleated fronds, a strange new note of terror came to Mingo's ears—the distant flap-

ping, flapping, flapping, as of the storm-torn sails
of phantom ships, beating the shrouds, as grieving
women beat their breasts, crying for dead hands
to furl the restless sails of the spirit and quiet
them! And Mingo shuddered! Then, from the
cloistered darkness of the woodland road to the
outer darkness of a narrow sandy flat, flanked by
marsh—and Mingo knew the high unlovely bridge,
spanning Toogoodoo Creek in a rainbow-arch,
was but two hundred yards away. The mule
slowly climbed the steep incline and almost slid
to earth again on the farther side, the planks fast
taking on a coating of ice.

Once safely over, Mingo drained his flask, and
by the time he came to a road crossing a mile beyond was too muddled to know where he was
going. He tried to select a road leading to the
house of a Negro whom he knew, but the mule
chose the well-remembered road for home, and
thither, at a slow walk, the faithful creature held
his way, and came at last to the Slann's Island
causeway, a high road across the marshes. Half
way over, the mule reached an impasse, for three
bars forbade the way, and these, the work of
human hands, only human hands could displace.
Had Mingo been awake and sober, he could have
removed the cattle-guard in a moment, and passed
on, but as he was now slumped down in a drunken

314

stupor, the poor mule could only rest his head upon the topmost bar and wait.

The night wore on. The cold grew more intense. The slanting sleet flew faster. Mingo slept heavily. The nepenthe of the village whiskey had laid all his ghosts and calmed his superstitious fears with the blessed balm of forgetfulness. The sleet that now sang over the shivering marshes had not slighted Mingo, and his clothes were frozen stiff, but while the potent spirits kept up his steam he was oblivious to everything.

The night slipped away. At last, in the heavy hours before the dawn, when old men die, and the world bears more hardly upon the lonely and the heavy-laden, Mingo's steam ran low. The cold bit him to the marrow. He shuddered and awoke. And his Negro spirit yearned for fire. He had no idea where he was, and he didn't care. Tumbling out of the buggy, he searched his pockets for matches. Finding a box, he struck a light to look around for wood, but in the steady wind the match but flickered and went out, and not until a dozen little fitful beams had feebly shone like good deeds "in a naughty world" did Mingo make out, at the foot of the embankment, a pile of dry brush, thick marshmallows that had been cut away in the late summer while clearing the causeway.

Mingo's heart leaped, for he know there was

no better fuel for a quick fire. The brush lay almost at the water's edge and the tide was up. The bank was steep, and slippery with the sleet, but Mingo took no thought for danger, and, groggy and uncertain, blundered down the bank through the darkness toward the spot where the last flash of light had shown him the brush pile. He found it, and stooped to lift the precious load, but as he tried to rise, his feet slipped from under him on the frozen mud, and Mingo, with the marshmallows clasped to his breast, slid into the tide. The water was shallow, but the mud was deep, and poor Mingo was too cold and too sodden to help himself, and his feeble struggles but sank him deeper in the mud. A choking sob, a gasp, a gurgle, and the freezing mule was alone!

Then the sibilant whistling of the sleet was stilled, and the pitying snow came sifting down, softly, silently, and before it ceased with the coming of the day the glittering spears of the wide marshes were sprinkled with silvery dust, and over the poor black body in the frozen mud a silvery shroud was spread.

"Oh, Gawd! Dead Nigguh een de maa'sh! Dead Nigguh een de maa'sh!"

The excited cry reached Laguerre just as he rose from breakfast. Zouave was quickly hitched up, and, driven by Scipio and followed by half the plantation, he was soon at the scene of the tragedy. Mingo was quickly identified, and some of those who had more than suspected his attentions to their women-folk, now cried out upon him gleefully and unfeelingly:

"Aye, yaye! Dishyuh duh da' 'dultri*fy* man, enty? Uh bin tell wunnuh ef da' Nigguh keep on ramify 'roun' yuh, 'e gwine git ketch. Now, de maa'sh ketch'um!"

"Shut up!" ordered Laguerre. "When the poor devil was alive you were all afraid of him, and now 'there's none so poor to do him reverence!' The way of the world, damn it, the way of the world!"

The inquest didn't take long. The empty quart flask, the matches struck and blown out, half-burned, by the cutting wind, the stumbling footprints in the slippery mud of the steep embankment, the marshmallow fagots still clasped in the frozen arms—traced the tragic story, step by step.

The verdict rendered, Laguerre directed that Mingo's body, decently clad, be sent to Edisto in a farm wagon. Then the frozen semblance of a man was turned over, and "Jedge's" eyes flashed, for sticking out of an ample hip pocket was the handle of a heavy navy revolver! It was old and rusted, but it had been a concealed weapon,

317

and as concealed weapons were of the sins Laguerre had "no mind to," he exploded. —

"Damn scoundrel! Carrying concealed weapons on Slann's Island! What have you got to say for yourself? Talk fast, talk fast, or forever after hold your peace!"

"Maussuh," remonstrated old Scipio, "him cyan' talk. No use fuh quizzit'um. Da' Nigguh dead!"

"Shut up!" cried Laguerre, "shall I deny the accused the right to defend himself, just because he's dead? Not on Slann's Island! Not by a damned sight!"

"Jedge" turned again to the silent Mingo.

"Damn scoundrel doesn't answer," he said. "I fine him fifty dollars for carrying concealed weapons, and twenty dollars for contempt of court! Sell the mule to pay fine and costs!"

And it was so ordered.